At Plains University, they are graduate students.
But when they enter Wascana Park after midnight, they become something much more.

ANDREW is ROLDAN,
an auditor who specializes in combat magic.

SHELBY is MORGAN,
a sagittarius, expert with bow and arrow.

INGRID is FEL,
a miles—a sword-wielding gladiator.

CARL is BABIECA,
a trovador, skilled at music—and theft.

At the university, their lives are dull and predictable. In the city of Anfractus, they use their wits, their skills, and their imaginations to live other exciting and sometimes dangerous lives.

And now that danger has followed them home. . . .

PILE OF
BONES

BAILEY
CUNNINGHAM

ACE BOOKS, NEW YORK

THE BERKLEY PUBLISHING GROUP
Published by the Penguin Group
Penguin Group (USA) Inc.
375 Hudson Street, New York, New York 10014, USA

USA I Canada I UK I Ireland I Australia I New Zealand I India I South Africa I China

Penguin Books Ltd., Registered Offices: 80 Strand, London WC2R 0RL, England
For more information about the Penguin Group, visit penguin.com.

PILE OF BONES

An Ace Book / published by arrangement with the author

Copyright © 2013 by Jes Battis.
Ace Books are published by The Berkley Publishing Group.
ACE and the "A" design are trademarks of Penguin Group (USA) Inc.

For information, address: The Berkley Publishing Group,
a division of Penguin Group (USA) Inc.,
375 Hudson Street, New York, New York 10014.

ISBN: 978-0-425-26106-4

PUBLISHING HISTORY
Ace mass-market edition / August 2013

PRINTED IN THE UNITED STATES OF AMERICA

10 9 8 7 6 5 4 3 2 1

Cover art by Gene Mollica.
Cover design by Lesley Worrell.
Interior text design by Kelly Lipovich.

For my students

ACKNOWLEDGMENTS

If not for the support of many people, this book would have been impossible. My agent, Lauren Abramo, was enthusiastic about this idea from the beginning and encouraged me to pursue it. My editor, Ginjer Buchanan, has been wonderfully perceptive and kind since we first talked. She even led a starry-eyed first-time author through the Ace office, allowing him to gawk and make inarticulate noises. The University of Regina, where I teach, has provided me with the flexibility and security to spend my summers writing, and the Department of English in particular has allowed me to teach a range of eclectic courses. My colleague Garry Sherbert introduced me to the writings of Petronius, which has likely set the mood for this novel more than anything else. Latin came into my life at just the right time, and for that I will always be grateful to Garry. John Elder Robison's memoir, *Look Me in the Eye*, lent me some valuable insight into my own personality while I was writing this. My friend Rowan, with whom I share a voice, has been gracious enough to acknowledge me as "the person in your family who does not live at your house," which may be an indication of how frequently I visit. Mark, thank you for being a consummate teacher and for keeping me alive with your food. Medrie, thank you for the car conversations. Your poetry moves me. Bea, thank you for everything I can't describe, including a plot point that you gamely helped to resolve. Keith, thank you for sending me a Le Petit Prince day planner when I needed it most. Mom, thanks for the magnifying glass. Alfonso X, thanks for writing so engagingly about thirteenth-century games like acedrex and alquerque. Finally, I must thank Wascana Park—traditional Plains Cree territory and still Oscana.

PRONUNCIATION

Most of the terminology in the book comes from ancient Latin. We have scant knowledge about how people in first-century Rome may have actually sounded, but classical linguists have done their best to reconstruct this. I base my own pronunciation on the recordings of Wakefield Foster and Stephen G. Daitz, which can be streamed here: www .rhapsodes.fll.vt.edu/Latin.htm.

The vowels *a* and *o* are generally long, while the short vowel *i* sounds like *EE*. The consonants *c* and *g* are always hard, as in *cat* or *gold*. The modern-day term *Sagittarius* would sound more like *sag-ee-TARR-ee-us*. The consonant *r* is rolled slightly when singular, and more strongly when doubled, like the Spanish or French *r*. The word *Anfractus* has a slight growl to it: *an-FRRAC-tus*. The *um* ending is nasal, resembling the French *u*. French would elide the final syllable, but in Latin, it's voiced. The consonant *j* more closely resembles *y*, so *Julia* becomes *Yulia*. The consonant *v* is never pronounced as a hard *v*, but rather as *w* or *iu*, which means that *impluvium* would sound like *im-PLOO-wee-um*. The only exception is *trovador*, which comes from Occitan rather than Latin.

I've tried to obey rules of grammatical gender and plurality, except in the case of *nemones*, an invented plural form of *nemo*.

PART ONE

AUDITOR

1

ROLDAN TOUCHED THE WALLS OF HIS ALLEY. Islands of yellow moss broke through the stones, rippling slightly as his fingers came near. When he'd first arrived, he was naked and in some pain. He hadn't noticed the blond hairs moving in response to him. Where he came from, the moss was green and didn't have a mind of its own. How did he survive that day? The details were already decaying. He remembered stealing a sheet and a samosa. He had to run a lot in those days. Now he understood why so many people tolerated the furs. It was because everyone started that way. Everyone was a thief when they first came to Anfractus, trailing the shame of their sheets behind them like dirty and displaced children.

He wasn't quite anything yet. He had a few tricks, but that didn't make him an auditor. They saw him as a runt that might not survive, and so tended to ignore him. They had to keep their distance. Tricks were easy to steal. He had no hoard to protect, so burglary wasn't one of his fears. They didn't keep him around for his creativity. "Light it up," was all they ever said. "Is this candle magic, or is it nothing?" They didn't care about the small lives of the objects, the drama of the lapidary, what the knife remembered. "Will it light up?" That meant it was worth more. One of these days, he suspected, they would tell him to light himself up, and the colors he produced would determine his fate.

He stepped out of the alley and onto Via Rumor. His eyes stung from the smoke of the Exchange, and a shadow of grime settled on his robe as he walked through the cloud of cries and hammers. Colored screens hung from balconies, lapping up some of the heat, but his neck still felt like a roof tile. Everything was for sale: falchions with weighted stone handles, reversible cloaks, automata in the shape of pomegranates with concealed blades. The vendors declaimed each other in song while packs of hungry furs moved through the crowd. Roldan saw a fat spado eating lemon sharbah, his tall green cap wilting in the sun.

He wondered what it felt like to be a eunuch. Did desire flee, or was it simply mollified and dispersed along unexpected pathways? Many of the spadones were known to be insatiable lovers. It depended on how they'd been made. Roldan could remember a bit of a song that he'd heard once, about a eunuch lover. *By all my actions thou may'st see, my heart can spare no room for thee, thou art not made like other boys.* They weren't all powdered and soft. Narses, the high chamberlain, carried a sword.

He walked down Aditus Papallona, then turned onto Via Dolores, where people gathered beneath the shadows of the aqueduct. They threw dice, struck bargains, and embraced between the high granite bows. In the distance, he could make out the lights of the basia. Even he could afford an iron token, which would get him into the less exclusive houses, but thinking about the pictures stamped on the coins made him blush. A few positions strained the mind. From here, Roldan could see the Tower of Auditores. A crowd had gathered around its entrance, mostly to gossip and steal from each other. A few carried bacula with pommels of jade and sardonyx that flared in the sun.

Roldan heard his name. He turned and saw Babieca standing at the dusty curb, smiling. His lute case was strung over one shoulder, and he'd acquired a cape with rampant tigers. He crossed the street and they embraced.

"Where did you steal that?" Roldan asked.

"I'm no fur. I won it."

"With a loaded die?"

"Lower your voice. I have a reputation to maintain."

"Right. I wouldn't want to besmirch the honor of a trovador. I'm sure you always toss your dice straight, even in the dark."

"I can be good, when I want to. How about you? Working on any new tricks?"

"Nothing too exciting."

"Salamanders must love this weather. Isn't fire their chaos?"

"They'll curl up next to an old kettle if they sense the promise of warmth."

"Can you hear them?"

"Not right now. They're probably asleep near the hypocaust."

"That must be strange. I can't imagine what it would be like to hear the elder things whispering to each other."

"It's more distracting than anything else. Some of them don't like having to share the world with us. Some are tolerant, so long as we feed them from time to time."

For a moment, he let his mind wander. They might both be cats, coming alive at odd times, singing from opposite walls. He could move closer. Maybe they'd make a device, something with grooves and tongues. Still drowsy from the heat, he felt more like a wall-lizard, insensate, hanging from a patch of moss.

They walked up Aditus Festa. Rows of cauponae stood with their ale-posts raised high. Babieca led him through the doorway of the Seven Sages. The main room was full of smoke, and casks lined the corners. Roldan kept his eyes on the rush-covered floor, trying to avoid surprises. Every table had a candle, and most of the patrons were already deep in their cups. He heard oaths, polyphony, wild bragging. Sausages and dried peppers hung from the stained rafters, like edible finery, and the top floor had a hole in the middle to permit rising smoke. People crowded the dangerous balconies.

Everyone was gaming. Summer was winning at Four Seasons, while a rowdier group of seven drank their way through Planets. Two women faced each other in alquerque, gliding their stone pieces across the wood board. One played the part of sense, while the other was daring. The ale-wife liked to keep the main floor looking civilized, which meant that the higher-stakes games of Hazard were in the undercroft. The spadones deplored dicing, but he still noticed a few of them in the mix. Their green hats gave them away. There was an old saying about dicers: *Come in a cloak and leave bare-assed.* It was probably a good thing that he didn't have enough money to gamble.

The smoke in the room was like cobwebs. There were all sorts gathered on the long benches. An artifex was showing off something made of brass cogs that looked dangerous. An auditor in a striped cloak was talking to a miles. They were probably part of a company. He'd heard that some were even led by auditores.

Auditores with bacula who know how to fight. All he had was a weathered knife, which he kept only to flash at furs. In truth, he'd drawn it only a few times. Babieca had a short sword with a crooked cruciform hilt, which he was forever trying to lose. If not for Morgan's bow, they would have been sad conies with barely a lick of training between them.

Being in a company wasn't everything, but it could load the die in your favor. Companies ranged beyond the walls of the city. The greatest wouldn't show up until sundown. Roldan had never seen the city at night. Even Morgan, the most experienced among them, confined her visits mostly to the daytime. She'd told them stories about how the towers changed. Everything real seemed to happen at night. The stakes were so much higher.

Babieca got them a pitcher of sweet malmsey, along with a stew platter. Roldan was never sure where he found his money, but at the moment, he was hungry and didn't feel like prying. They ate their root vegetables in convivial silence. Babieca surrendered his parsnips in exchange for extra bread. Roldan could feel the drink going to his head, but that wasn't entirely bad. It would make talking easier and dull his senses, which were currently twitching. Babieca looked like he wasn't paying attention, but Roldan knew that his friend was also studying the room. He had the instincts of a fur, though he abhorred them.

Morgan appeared through the haze. She wasn't patrolling today, but she'd still worn a boiled-leather hauberk with a rust-colored cloak. Her short bow was strapped to her back, along with a painted quiver. Some looked at her, but most stayed focused on gaming and drinking. A sagittarius wasn't so captivating during the day. This crowd didn't care that she'd walked the battlements of the Arx of Violets, or that she'd once killed a silenus. They only saw a short woman with brown hair and a weapon that was next to useless in a caupona. She wasn't interesting enough to make them stop gambling.

She sat down and poured herself a drink.

"What is this?"

"Malmsey," Babieca said. "It was cheap."

"It tastes like sap."

"You're welcome to buy the next round."

"We shouldn't overindulge. You said you'd found us a piece of business, and I'd rather we all kept a clear head. Especially if you have to swing that sword."

"Mock me, and you'll never hear the particulars."

Roldan felt annoyed. Babieca might have told him about the job earlier. Once again, they both assumed that he would follow them anywhere. He would. That wasn't the point. He hated simply being told things, like a child.

"I suppose," he said, "you need something to glow."

"Don't be like that." Babieca smiled at him. "This could be fun. We're supposed to pick up something for the basilissa."

Only Morgan had ever seen the basilissa. *I just saw the back of her head*, she admitted, *but her hair was sharp and beautiful, like a flowering thorn.* She lived in the Arx of Violets with her foxes, who guarded her chamber and accompanied her to court. Morgan had never seen the foxes. Mostly, she just saw the backs of heads and the battlements, where she sometimes caught men staring at her through murder-holes. Roldan thought that, in spite of her complaints, the life of a sagittarius was far more interesting than his own.

"Will we visit the arx?"

"No," Babieca replied. "We're just delivering the item to someone."

Roldan stared at the table. Visiting the arx would have been nice, even if they'd simply stopped at the gates. He enjoyed walking through Vici Arces, where the walls were made of sweet porphyry that had weathered a thousand years, and he could hear the river below, full of murmuring undinae. The orange trees cast just enough shade over the marble benches, where courtiers paid too much for stale rumors.

"Who are we meeting?" Morgan asked.

Babieca shrugged. "Someone known to the basilissa. I didn't ask."

"Your plan sounds flawless. You know nothing about this item or the person that we're supposed to give it to."

"The plan is sterling. The artifex who hired us is some young thing. Just talking to me annoyed her, which means that she's distracted and wants the job done quickly. We can probably convince her to overpay, just so she'll be rid of us."

"Where did you find this artifex?"

"She found me. She was skulking around the Seven Sages, looking for someone who did odd jobs. I told her that ours were the oddest."

"Charming." Morgan closed her eyes briefly. "We know nothing about the girl. We could be delivering a murder talisman to a miles."

"It's not a murder talisman."

"Show me proof."

"How about coin? The job pays thirty maravedies."

Her expression brightened. "I could get some better

fletching for my arrows. Roldan could buy himself . . . whatever auditores need."

"Fortuna willing, he'll buy a better knife," Babieca replied. "I'm going to restring my cithara and maybe get a helmet. Something with acid etching."

"Absolutely not."

"I'd be dashing."

"You'd be a target in a metal hat. Trovadores don't wear armor."

He's not a trovador, Roldan thought, *and I'm not an auditor. We have no patroni.* He kept silent, though. Nobody likes being reminded of their bastardy.

He stared into the bottom of his glass, trying to augur the dregs of ale left behind. He saw nothing. Maybe he wouldn't light up anything this time. Would they still keep him around if his light fizzled? Another malmsey could answer this question, but Morgan was probably right. He should keep a clear head. The colloquy was simple, but if he said the wrong thing, it could still go badly. He wasn't skilled enough to improvise.

Because they weren't yet a company, they had pieces of business, not quests. A quest could earn you far more than money. People would talk about you. Doors that remained closed to most would gradually open for you, once you'd proven yourself. A group of three wasn't a company. If they ever planned to get anywhere, they'd need a fourth. But who would join them? He wasn't even sure why Morgan remained. She'd certainly had offers, even if she never spoke of them. Babieca would be fine on his own. Trovadores weren't exactly known for being the type to join a company. Roldan wasn't sure what kept them together. It obviously wasn't him. A miles or a medicus would be far more useful. Auditores could become powerful, but in the beginning, they were stubby candles that burned out quickly.

Babieca put down his ale. "We should go. First, I have to visit the murals."

Roldan had to as well, so he followed Babieca down the dim, rush-strewn passage that led to the toilets. They waited in line for their turn on the wooden seats with key-shaped holes. The fumes were inescapable, as were the various gut songs, but people still talked to pass the time. There were paintings on the walls, meant to encourage laughter and distract everyone from the situation. In one, two sages exchanged advice. *Fortuna says if your shit is tough, don't give up.* He'd never seen the women's murals, but they were probably nicer. He looked around the room, at all the men laughing and straining and the few that had fallen asleep, so delicate with their bare knees and nethers fit into keyholes.

They paid the ale-wife and left the tavern. Outside, the paving stones baked like spangled pie crust. Babieca cast a look toward the basia but said nothing. He often visited that part of the city. He had streams of revenue that he didn't like to talk about, and Morgan let it slide because he was usually more focused after he'd spent some time in love's undercroft. Roldan was never quite sure how to bring up these visits. Were men supposed to talk about what they did underground, the bodies they glided over in the dark? Roldan couldn't brag about bruised pillows or mumbling mattresses. He had very little experience, and some uncertain part of him thought that it might be rude to talk about such things in front of Morgan. In reality, he was simply scared that Babieca would ask him to supply his own stories. *No narratives, as yet. Only a few awkward stanzas, quick and ill-rhymed.*

Anfractus shone beneath the heat, a maze of sand-colored stone filled with oblique alleys like the one he'd emerged from. People wandered above them, peering down from the stone skyways that joined the buildings. They walked past a fountain made of green, cloud-veined marble. A meretrix in a silver mask rested on the rim. She wore a cream-colored silk tunica that exposed her arms. Her hair was tall, in the style of the basilissa, and her slim belt was studded with carnelians. She'd taken off her cork-heeled shoes and was letting water from a grotesque's mouth cool her feet.

Morgan looked dubiously at Roldan's tunica. "You'll have to re-dye that soon. It's also fraying along the sleeves."

"I'm not sure it can survive another repair."

"It barely looks convincing as it is. The scarlet dye is patchy, and you're practically tripping over the ragged hem. Eventually, it's going to unravel."

"I'll steal another one," Babieca said. "It's easy to steal from auditores. Most wouldn't notice if you set fire to their sandals."

He'd first met Roldan in the house of Domina Pendelia. After a few days in the city, Roldan had realized that he wouldn't be able to survive by gambling, as some did. Fortuna didn't favor him. Like most new visitors, he became a pedes. They had no gens to protect them, although their unseen labor was what allowed the city to function. He found himself working in the cramped kitchen of Domina Pendelia, which always smelled of baking boar. He dropped more vessels than he managed to deliver, but the domina had a tender spot for him. A flurry of shards would explode at his feet, and she'd simply laugh. Babieca worked in the undercroft, stoking the hypocaust that warmed her bath. Neither of them was good at his job. One night, after cursing the cold water, Domina Pendelia sent Roldan to the undercroft. Normally, she would have sent one of the more experienced pedes, but they were occupied.

The undercroft was lit by a few hanging lamps. The earth floor beneath him was damp and poxy with stones that might cleave his sandals. He found Babieca in the hypocaust chamber, filthy and stripped to the waist. He'd forgotten the fire and was playing his pipe. Roldan tended to distrust people, but there was something about Babieca that drew him in. Maybe it was the song, or the flash of teeth against his ashy face when he grinned. Maybe the smoke and the smell of packed earth was making him dizzy. Either way, he'd found himself agreeing when Babieca talked of escape. It wasn't hard. Pedes came and went every hour. He was still surprised that he'd had the courage to ask Domina Pendelia for eight maravedies. *For dyes and tablets.* He'd looked her in the eyes without blinking. She'd hesitated, then reached into a drawer and counted out the coins. That was nearly six months ago. It was hard to believe that his false tunica, made cheaply for a pedes, had lasted this long.

They passed by a crossroads shrine with a winking lamp. Rinds and bread crusts filled the stone embrasure. Roldan tried to listen past the sounds of the crowd. Softly, below the hum of the flame, he could hear the salamanders scratching. There must have been at least three of them, feeding on bread and lamplight. If he were an oculus instead of an auditor, he could actually see them. Most oculi went crazy, though. Hearing was safer than seeing. Morgan tossed some seeds into the bowl, and they kept going.

The road widened as they neared the Hippodrome. People were gathered near the entrances, forming clouds of colored tunicae. Most of them were gaming. The food stalls were packed, and he smelled fish sauce, roasted almonds, and sesame balls. The building was massive and fronted in pale yellow marble. People streamed in and out of the entrances, jostling each other, spilling their drinks, cursing. Fights erupted often, since they were all half-drunk and carrying daggers, but miles broke them up before they grew too serious. The miles circled the Hippodrome, baking in their mail loricae. Roldan was entranced by their leather boots, which were soft and woven into curious patterns. A young boy, probably a fur, drew close to the nearest entrance. He looked hungry. One of the miles made a warning gesture, halfway drawing his falchion, and the boy hurried away.

They paid the admission fee and entered the Hippodrome. A race was in progress. The charioteers kicked up dust as they pursued each other, and everyone stood, screaming bets and epithets. One of the drivers had night-black horses, while those who pulled his rival were the color of thrice-bleached linen. Roldan was hypnotized by the chariot wheels, bronze spokes flashing as they scattered sand. The whips were loud enough that he could hear them over the inebriated rumble of the spectators. Just as they managed to find a spot, the driver with the black horses pulled ahead. Those who'd bet on him cheered ecstatically. For a moment, they were two comets, dark and light, trailing debris as they circled the Hippodrome. Then the driver with the black horses won. The fortunate cheered louder, and the losers cursed.

"This could get ugly," he said. "Why would anyone want to conduct business in the middle of a race?"

"It's public," Morgan replied. "Less chance of a violent mishap in front of so many witnesses, no matter how drunk they are."

Once the race was over, a few attendants ventured onto the sands. They cleared away debris, then vanished. Moments later, doors opened on opposite sides of the Hippodrome, and two miles stepped out. There was a new wave of cheering. They made their way slowly to the heart of the circle, pausing at the shrines to give oil and crumbs. One of them wore a lorica of segmented leather, reinforced with metal plates. She had a single greave and a painted oak shield. A tarnished helmet covered most of her face. The other had on a lorica of bronze scales that rippled, like the sand. His helmet boasted graven neck guards. His shield was heavier, and scalloped mail protected the area below his studded belt. His vanbraces were silver-striped and had hungry edges.

Everyone looked to the high balcony, with its purple drapes. The basilissa wasn't there. In her place, Narses, the spado, presided over the spectacle. He wore the moss-colored tunica of his gens, along with a hoard of jewels. His red hair was beginning to thin, but it was still his own. Being high chamberlain, he knew every secret that danced through the Arx of Violets, or so it was said. Next to him sat a younger spado, and Roldan realized that it was the one he'd seen earlier on the street, licking lemon sharbah.

The high chamberlain raised his hand in a ceremonial gesture.

The miles drew their swords.

Both blades were short. One had a chipped stone pommel, its hilt wrapped in leather, while the other was gilded with onyx and jasper. Roldan had never understood the impulse to encrust things with gems, especially weapons.

Everything was about status. The color of a tunica, the flash of stones, the well-placed kiss, all were devices. Luckily, his status was so low that he didn't have to worry about reading signs.

Gilded sword was getting impatient. He swung high, but the other leapt back. She'd been waiting for something like that. Chipped sword feinted a blow to the chest, then ducked and slashed low. Her blade glanced off the other's greave, hissing, and then she spun away before her opponent could retaliate.

"She's playing with him," Morgan said.

"That's not smart," Babieca replied. "The other miles has better arms. The fool with one greave should be worrying about her lack of protection."

"Her shield is solid."

"It's practically tableware."

"The wood may be soft, but that can be an advantage."

"Because exploding wood is a distraction?"

"Because swords get stuck."

Gilded sword pressed another attack, thrusting low this time. As Babieca had predicted, he aimed at his opponent's right leg. Chipped sword brought down her shield. Roldan saw for the first time that it had an iron strip across its middle, enough to deflect the blow with a satisfying *crack*. Everyone cheered. Then chipped sword danced away. Her opponent gave pursuit. Chipped sword extended her arm, as if to swing, then ducked and lashed out with her shield instead. The shield caught gilded sword in the midsection, at the soft articulation between his belt and his scale lorica. He grunted, startled, and stepped back. Now chipped sword pressed her own attack. She cut high, and the glint of his weapon was sunlight moving over the face of the waters, one chaos mingling with another. Gilded sword managed to parry, but his movements weren't as swift as before. He was getting tired.

Chipped sword made a quick motion, switching sword and shield. Now she fought left-handed, with renewed strength. Her opponent struggled. He started to retreat, and the crowd turned ugly. *Craven! Cinna!* Narses was there, so none dared cry *Spado!* He watched the battle without expression. He was probably late for a significant dinner. For a moment, it looked as if gilded sword would rally. Then chipped sword struck him just below the shoulder, finding another gap in his lorica. Blood hit the sand. He staggered, clutching at the slick ties that held his armor together.

The crowd erupted.

"Primus sanguis!"

Even Roldan murmured it beneath his breath. Those were the day rules. First blood meant that the battle was over. At night, the rules were different, but he'd never seen the Hippodrome after sunset. He'd only heard stories.

The victorious miles helped her opponent to stand. It was customary for both of them to doff their helmets, but neither did. The loser was embarrassed, and wounded, but why wouldn't the victor reveal herself? Before, she'd been playful, like a cat who knew precisely the reach of her claws. Now she was suddenly modest. Roldan knew that there had to be another reason. Everything was a sign.

Chipped sword tried to help gilded sword, but the other pushed her away. He needed to save some face, at least. They made their way to the exits, one swiftly, the other limping and leaving a blood trail. After they'd both vanished, the attendants raked the sand. There would be a pause, then further entertainments. Roldan was about to suggest buying some lemon sharbah when an artifex in a checkered tunic sat down next to him. She had orange curls, limpid from the heat, and there were lines under her eyes. Maybe she'd been up all night working on something. *Artifices don't sleep. Their machinae sleep for them.* Who had told him that? Babieca, most likely.

"Are you the auditor?"

Babieca cut him off before he could reply. "Yes. He's quite skilled. If you had the gift of the vigili, you'd see a nest of salamanders hissing at his feet."

"Right." She reached into a leather case slung over her shoulder and withdrew a silk-wrapped bundle. She placed it in Roldan's palm. "Take this to Vici Secreta, fourth door, second insula. Keep it covered until you're safely inside. A friend of the basilissa will meet you there, in order to appraise the item."

"I could appraise it here," Roldan said. "It's not an ideal spot, but there are still a few lares around. Taking it across the city doesn't seem necessary."

"I have my orders, and you have yours." The artifex stood. "My part is done. You can improvise if you like, but if the basilissa discovers that you've disobeyed her, it won't go well for you. Her carcer is deep, and littered with the bones of people who thought they knew better."

She turned and disappeared into the crowd. Now he really wanted a sharbah, especially if they were walking all the way to Vici Secreta. He thought better of mentioning it, though. Instead, he looked at the sand, where spots of blood were still visible. If he listened closely, he could hear the unseen tongues, lapping it up like milk.

He followed them out of the Hippodrome. It was unfair. They'd paid for the whole afternoon.

They followed the aqueduct back to the center of town. People were gathered around the great clepsydra, whose wheel made a thunderous sound as it turned. Water from a series of tanks powered the clock, and every hour it would chime. Various aspects of Fortuna decorated the spokes of the wheel, each divided into day and night, since the goddess of fortune had very different faces after sunset. The two-toned heads turned with the wheel's progress, now in the sun, now in shadow, as machinae chirped and hissed from their ingenious niches. Water from the aqueduct powered the device, flowing from the high nexus of the two rivers, Clamores and Iacto, that surrounded the city.

Arces was the wealthiest vici, due to its proximity to the Arx of Violets. The ground sloped upward, and the shops and cauponae were replaced by villas with grand patios. The city was divided into blocks, called insulae, where various streets converged to form natural islands of recreation and commerce. Most of these blocks were owned by the wealthy elite, and in times past, the city in its entirety had been the property of the basilissa. She had been queen, landowner, and executioner. Now she rarely left the arx. Roldan tried to imagine her, ensconced in her secretum of porphyry and purple tapestries, or idly playing with her mechanical throne, which she could supposedly raise until it touched the vaulted ceiling. Her mother, Driope, had been cruel. If you displeased her, she fed you to her lampreys. But her daughter, in spite of what the artifex had suggested, was not known for such sadistic displays. She was barely known at all.

"This is it," Morgan said, coming to a halt. "The fourth door of the second insula."

The door of the house was painted blue. Roldan looked up and saw a second-floor clerestory, with what could have been an attic above. The wide stone patio was empty but clean, suggesting that it had recently been used. There was no door attendant, so Babieca knocked. He waited a moment, and after there was no response, he knocked again.

Morgan shouldered past him and opened the door, which was unlocked.

"This isn't a good sign," Babieca said.

"Really? And you were so confident about this plan earlier."

"You're loving this, aren't you?"

"Let's just get our money."

They walked through the narrow passageway, which led to a grand atrium. Light poured in from an opening in the ceiling, under which had been placed an impluvium to catch rainwater. Couches were arranged around the room, covered in rich fabric and enameled with ivory or tortoiseshell. The floor was a geometric mosaic, incorporating several shades of marble. To the right was a study, also well lit. Roldan would have loved to browse through the scroll cases and books, all painted and pumiced, but this wasn't the right time. A staircase nearby led to the second floor.

"Hello?" Morgan walked slowly around the atrium. "Is anybody here?"

There was no answer.

Roldan turned to examine a mosaic on one of the walls and nearly screamed. An enormous dog stared down at him, wearing a spiked collar. Its eyes were coals, and it had one paw raised, about to strike. He stumbled backward. Then Babieca began to laugh.

"Look," he said, pointing down.

Near the base of the wall, the words *guard dog* were scrawled. Roldan stared at the dog again. He couldn't believe it was only a painting. His heart was still racing.

"Clever," Morgan said. "Let's go."

They left the atrium and walked through the dining room, which had its own set of gilded couches and carved bronze side tables. The walls were painted in a dizzying style that made their images appear lifelike, as the dog had been. Flowers and strange creatures met at curious angles, straining to escape their borders, while vibrant red and yellow squares depicted scenes from the city's history. There was a horn bowl filled with fruit on one of the tables, and for a moment, Roldan couldn't tell if it was real. Babieca stole a grape, settling the matter. The room led to a columned peristyle, which opened onto the garden. Violets flamed next to marble statuary, whose eyes seemed to follow him. There was a deep pool with chairs and tables beside it. A masked man was sitting in one of the chairs, reading.

He got up as they approached. His silvered mask identified him as a meretrix. They always wore masks, to preserve the illusions that their gens sold. His pale yellow tunica was clasped by a carnelian brooch in the shape of a rose. The garment was sleeveless, and his bare arms were decorated with bracelets of silver and copper. He wasn't muscular, but his body still suggested a kind of strength. A dagger was cinched to his belt. He looked at Roldan. His eyes smiled, but that may have just been part of his training. Unable to meet the gaze of the meretrix, he looked down instead, at his sandals, which reminded him of tree bark.

"Salve." He raised his hand in a friendly gesture. "I'm Felix."

Morgan's eyes went slightly wide, but she said nothing.

She must have recognized his name. If he were truly a "friend" of the basilissa, he would be known throughout the city, if not by his name, then by his mask.

Roldan withdrew the silk-wrapped bundle from his tunica. He handed it to Felix. Their fingers brushed, and he drew away quickly. Touching a meretrix, even a high-placed one, was never a good idea. Their clients could get violently jealous. For them, the illusion needed to be complete, even if it was just perfume and mirrors.

Felix unwrapped the bundle. The item was a silver fibula—the kind used to pin cloaks. It was wrought in the shape of a bee alighting on a bunch of grapes. The craftsmanship was undeniably skilled, but it was unadorned. Even the silver, melted down, wouldn't have brought much money. He wouldn't have called it finery. It was like the second-tier jewelry that you brought out when unfavorable relatives were visiting.

Roldan's eyes narrowed.

"The basilissa really wants this appraised?"

"It's more than it seems, I imagine," Felix replied. "Everything here is."

Everyone was looking at him now. It was time to perform.

"All right. Give it to me."

Felix handed over the brooch. He looked at it critically. It was so simple. The basilissa knew what she wanted, though. There was no use questioning. He walked away from the pool. It wouldn't do to be near water. The others followed him slowly, making him feel like a piper leading sheep or curious children. He walked back to the dining room, where one brass lamp remained lit. Gently, he removed the lamp from its chain and placed it on the table. He set the brooch next to the lamp. Its flame trembled. He passed his fingers through the flame's white core. The twinge of heat focused him.

"Babieca," he said. "Get me an apple from that bowl in the atrium."

Wordlessly, Babieca left. He returned seconds later with a green apple.

"May I use your dagger?" Roldan asked Felix. "It's sharper than mine."

"Of course." The meretrix drew his blade and handed it to Roldan. It was made of tempered steel, with a gem-incrusted hilt. Gems again. It was, he supposed, all part of the city's intention to dazzle everyone, so they wouldn't feel the cut.

He peeled the apple, then diced it into small pieces. He laid the spiral of green skin next to the white bits. You could never tell what they were hungry for. Then he waited, listening. Babieca started to say something, but Morgan shushed him.

Eventually, he heard the sound of claws on the table. Delicate sniffing.

"Salve," he said. "This offering is for you."

The clawing stopped. He could tell that the salamander was looking at him, sizing up his level of power. Sometimes, the lares were only interested in mischief, but most of them would listen if you appealed to their appetite. The apple skin almost seemed to move slightly. Then he heard what was unmistakably the sound of contented chewing. As everyone watched, the skin began to disappear, spiral by spiral, until it was completely gone. He heard the salamander belch. Then he heard its claws, softly clicking against the surface of the table. He felt its heat as it drew closer to his hand. Then something unexpected happened. The heat grew more intense, and he felt, for the first time, the tip of a claw against his knuckle. He'd never been touched by a lar before. He was sweating. Its fire singed the hair on his knuckles, but he kept himself perfectly still.

"What's happening?" Babieca whispered.

"Quiet," Morgan replied, between clenched teeth.

Felix was watching him in fascination. Could he also feel the heat? It was amazing that everyone else wasn't sweating. When he breathed in, he could taste soot. The air burned his lungs, but he held it, like smoke from a pipe. He couldn't waver.

Good offering. The whisper sounded in his ear, as if the

salamander were perched on his shoulder rather than touching his hand. Its voice was crackling papyrus, green wood giving way to fire, settling ashes. The claw maintained its pressure.

Roldan exhaled. "I'm glad you liked it."

Was hungry. Bare shrines. No delicacies. We like apple.

"Yes. I know it's one of your favorite things."

It must have looked like he was talking to the table, or the diced apple, or simply to himself. Babieca and Morgan were used to it, but Felix couldn't conceal his interest. He had the expression of one who was watching a mad miracle unfold and couldn't quite tell if it was real. This was his painted dog.

"So." Roldan cleared his throat. "In the name of the twelve aspects of Fortuna, and the Gens of Auditores, I request a boon."

Boon?

They always pretended that they didn't know what you were talking about. Lares could be annoying in that regard. Their voices were tough to distinguish, and he couldn't see them, which meant that Roldan never knew if he really was meeting one for the first time. In any case, one caught more salamanders with honey than with vinegar, and it helped to stay polite.

"I would like to know if this brooch has any power," he said. "It's for the basilissa, which makes it valuable, by our standards. If you could convince the flame to kiss it, only for a moment, we'd be most grateful. I promise to leave some more food for you at the shrines in the forge district, where I know that your people like to congregate."

Yes. So warm there.

The salamander was quiet for a moment, considering his request. Then its claw dug into his knuckle. A drop of blood appeared against his skin. The pain was surprising, but Roldan willed himself not to move. Smoke rose from the invisible wound. He heard Felix draw in his breath sharply, but nobody said anything.

Give to the fire.

"Thank you," Roldan murmured, trying to ignore his watering eyes. He tilted his hand over the lamp. The drop of blood hesitated, then fell. When it struck the flame, the light turned a brilliant green. As they watched with widened eyes, tongues of the green flame curled lazily into the air, moving toward the brooch. Sparks fell onto the table, raising no smoke, making no blemish. The green fire surrounded the gift of the basilissa and suddenly flared up, flickering in variegated colors like light pouring through a crystal.

Your answer.

The flame guttered, then shrank back into the lamp, until it was nothing more than the usual tongue of orange. The salamander lifted its claw. He felt its heat recede as it began to move away, climbing down the table and back to the floor.

"Thank you," Roldan said weakly.

Go now. Although it was already halfway to the atrium, its voice rang in his ear. *They are coming.*

"Who's coming?"

But it was no longer listening.

"Roldan?" Babieca looked at him oddly. "What did you mean? Is someone—"

They heard the front door open, then footsteps in the hallway.

"We have to go," Felix said. "Follow me. There's an exit through the garden."

"I don't understand," Roldan said. "Who's here?"

"The aedile. You don't want to meet him. Come on."

They hurried after Felix as he led them through the garden. Behind a cluster of lemon trees was a narrow passage that led back to the street. They made their way outside. Roldan could hear shouting coming from inside the villa.

Felix rewrapped the brooch and placed it in his tunica.

"Your dagger," Roldan said. "Here—"

"Keep it. I doubt they could trace it to me, anyway."

He looked at them all for a moment, and there was a glimmer of approval in his expression, as if he were looking at a real company. Then he reached into a niche in the wall of the alley, which Roldan hadn't noticed before, and withdrew a ragged cloak. He drew it over his shoulders, covering his rich tunica. The cowl obscured most of his face.

"Go back to where you came from," he said. "Speak to no one of this."

"But—" Roldan wasn't sure why he spoke. Maybe it was the touch of the salamander that emboldened him. "What if we need to find you?"

The cowl hid his eyes, but Roldan saw him smile.

"That's easy," he said.

Then he turned and disappeared down the alley.

"We'd best go as well," Morgan said. "He's right. We don't want to run into the aedile, even during the day. Let's not push our luck."

Babieca glared at her. "We haven't been paid!"

"We'll be paid with a sword to the gut if we linger here. A meretrix keeps his word, and he said it would be easy to find him. We'll return tomorrow and pay a visit to the lupanaria."

"Boar shit." Babieca was fuming. "We paid for tickets to the Hippodrome. My tab at the Seven Sages has run out. Roldan's tunica is falling apart—"

"*Move.* I'm not getting thrown in the bloody carcer for this."

They hurried back the way they'd come, past the grand clepsydra, past the buzzing Exchange, working their way through the brightly colored crowd. Nightfall came quickly, and it wasn't safe to be here when the rules changed. Roldan stared at the Tower of Auditores. What night games did they play there? What gossip were the spadones privy to? He'd probably never know.

His hand still burned where the salamander had touched him. Why did it feel so familiar? A part of him seemed to remember the touch of another claw, ages ago, but the sweet pain was too distant to recall.

"See you on the other side," Morgan said.

They parted, heading back to their alleys. When Roldan arrived, he could already feel the pull. Everything was beginning to change. He undressed, replacing his belongings inside the wall. Once they were covered, he laid his hand against the warm stones. Now was the moment. He closed his eyes. Something moved through him, unraveling. He surrendered to the current, letting it pull him under.

When he opened his eyes, it was all different. Or the same, depending on the way you looked at it. They were back in Wascana Park. The power was still heavy on them, but the crossing had worked. Anfractus and its wilds were no longer visible. They were back in Plains Cree territory. The ground used to be littered with buffalo bones, which was what *Oscana* meant in Cree: "pile of bones." But the white settlers messed up the morpheme and called it Wascana instead. If they'd known Oscana's secret, they might have taken the time to get the name right.

It was dawn. The park was empty, so their nudity wasn't an issue. They pulled their duffel bags from the trees, dressing in silence. For some reason, synthetic fabric wouldn't make the journey from park to wild. He pulled on his jacket. He could hear the ducks, and faint strains of music from Party Island, where dawn was clearly no impediment to undergraduate drinking. They all had to be at work in a few hours. Now it was the university that seemed like a shadow, not Anfractus, but they'd made their choice.

Living between worlds meant paying rent.

2

Shelby was yelling from the bedroom.

He couldn't make out what she was saying, but there was profanity involved. He'd left her under a pillow again. The coffeemaker was confusing him. It was a gift from his father, and had a complex panel on it with a lot of choices, like a replicator from *Star Trek*. He selected "ordinary cup," whatever that meant, and returned to the bedroom. Shelby's voice was muffled by the pillow, but the cursing had stopped. He liberated her from the bed and placed her on the nightstand.

"—*huge*, I've never seen one like this before, it's like a queen, or some kind of monarch, what sort of government would centipedes have?"

"A republic? I don't know. Where did it come from?"

"The hole under the baseboard. I've trapped it, but I'm not really sure what my next step should be."

"What's it doing now?"

"Going apeshit in a mason jar. I'm about to slide some cardboard underneath it."

"Be careful. Do apartment centipedes bite?"

"No, they're very ethical. How should I know?"

He heard some rummaging. Then Shelby let out a whoop of triumph.

"Mission accomplished?"

"Absolutely. I'm going to put him outside. I'll be right back."

"Him? Did you two bond?"

"Shut up."

"If you don't kill it, we'll be having this conversation again tomorrow."

"I'm not starting my day with bloodshed."

He heard her footsteps recede. It was strange to think that houses and apartments had their own genre of centipedes. Were they evil geniuses, or a failed branch of the family tree that couldn't make it in the wild? He went back to the kitchen, hoping that he'd made the right choice. The travel mug was filling slowly. A yellow light was flashing, but it didn't seem to indicate danger, so he ignored it. He grabbed Shelby from the bedroom and attached her to the ear-piece.

"—*so* much marking left, I want to set it on fire."

"That might improve the arguments."

"One of mine referred to the nineteenth century as 'olden times.'"

"One of mine quoted Bryan Adams for their epigraph."

"Ouch."

He sat down to tie his shoes. Although he'd never admit this to anyone, he still had to visualize a rabbit leaping through a hole whenever he did this. The only solution was to wait until hipsters colonized Velcro, and then he could buy fashionable shoes that didn't require animal metaphors. He looked out the window, trying to gauge the weather.

"Muggy and windy with a chance of rain," he said. "Thanks, Regina."

"Bring layers," Shelby replied. "It's the only way. My hair is well and truly cursed, but I'm going to try something with a lot of clips."

"Sounds reasonable."

"I'm bringing a hat, just in case."

He grabbed his backpack, which felt like a rock on his

shoulders. A real academic would carry a delicate leather folio, or possibly one of those rolling bags, but the backpack was an extension of his body. It seemed to get heavier each day. He fiddled uselessly with the straps for a second, then stepped out of the house, locking the door behind him. Bugs were swarming around the light on his front porch. He shared the duplex with a retiree named Bob, and both of them had an attitude toward home upkeep that could only be called mellow. The lawn was overgrown, the shed full of dismembered furniture and unused garden equipment.

"My next-door neighbors just renovated," he said into the ear-piece. "Their crisp new siding is making me self-conscious."

"Just ignore them."

"I could scatter a few toys across the lawn. Then I could blame kids for the state of the property. Would a bubble machine and a Diego three-wheeler be too much?"

"Wow. You've put some thought into this."

"Maybe."

"I think that in the long run, a bit of weeding could be less trouble than inventing children. We could get it fixed up, get some painted rocks, trellises, *pinwheels*, oh man, can we go to Rona and make this happen?"

"I'll think about it. I'm not sure it's the summer project that I was hoping for."

"Carl and I both live in apartments. You're the only one with an actual lawn. Plus, he'll do most of the work if we give him beer."

Andrew stared at the lumpy yard. "It looks as if gnomoi have been digging up my front lawn. I can't imagine what they'd be looking for. The soil must be pretty bland."

"That's parking."

"It's not a violation of park rules if nobody's around to hear me." He paused. "I had the dream again—the one with the salamanders. I could hear the crunching of their paws. When I woke up, I swore I felt one in my bed, like that scene from *Amityville Horror* when the ghost leaves footprints on their sheets."

"Lares don't exist outside the park. Your brain is just overheated."

He walked down to Thirteenth Street. The taco stand wasn't open yet, but the cafés were already humming with undergrad activity. Cathedral Village, so named for the church a few blocks down, was Regina's urban community. It was only a few blocks in radius, but all of the city's boutique shops and trending restaurants were located there. It was impossible to grab a coffee without running into someone from school, which was why he'd started using a travel mug. He didn't want to make awkward conversation with his supervisor while waiting in line at Roca Jack's or Atlantis.

Shelby lived downtown, in a crumbling apartment above the Deli Llama. Her hallway smelled like yam fries. It was one of the few surviving apartments in the downtown core, which had been taken over by bank towers and tapas bars. He crossed Victoria Park, empty save for a group of stoned kids who'd set up camp in front of the war monument. Regina was a city of monuments and plaques dedicated to various atrocities. Louis Riel was tried on this spot, with a hungry crowd looking on. Both the park and the city were named after Queen Victoria. Later, Queen Elizabeth II had included this spot in her progress. She must have said something optimistic while the mud sucked at her gown. *What sharp rocks they have. The bugs are certainly robust.*

Regina was in the process of trying to rejuvenate its downtown, which seemed to involve a lot of freestanding sculptures and lights that changed color. Shelby's place was on Scarth Street, in the middle of a pedestrian mall. A metal buffalo stood at the entrance, with the word *Oscana* carved into it. He inclined his head. Reading a lot of E. Nesbit as a kid had taught him that statues often came to life at night, and it didn't hurt to be respectful. A few people were gathered around the hot dog cart, but otherwise, the square was deserted. It was flanked by the Globe Theatre on the right, advertising a production of Ovid's *Metamorphoses*, and a comic store on the left that played nothing but speed metal. He'd had his eye on a *Dark Crystal* action figure in the window but wasn't willing to face the music, even if the chamberlain's ceremonial garb was reversible.

"I'll be down in a second," Shelby said. "I'm just doing the dishes."

"Do you want a coffee?"

"No, I'm on a tea kick."

"Uh-huh."

"It's been going pretty well."

"Do you want a coffee?"

"I want your unqualified support."

"You always have that."

"Thank you. Shit! I hate this detachable spigot. It's a trap. I always manage to spray myself in the face."

He leaned against the concrete façade of the Globe, listening to the sound of water on the other end of the line. It was like a New Age CD with intermittent cursing.

"I'm pretty stoked about the lecture this morning," he said. "*Wulf and Eadwacer* is one of my favorite Anglo-Saxon poems."

"It's cryptic. The students are going to hate it."

"At first. But then they'll be intrigued."

"They won't."

"A few might be."

"Andrew, it's a service class. None of them want to be there, and we're forcing them to read a thousand years' worth of literature. We'll be lucky if anyone in our sections remembered to bring a textbook."

"I've got handouts."

Shelby hung up.

A moment later, she emerged from a door next to the restaurant. She'd decided to go with the hat, along with a scarf and skirt with a raven print. He was already sweating in his jeans, but teaching in shorts was one of the few rules that he refused to break. The entire Department of Psychology taught in khaki shorts, and it made them resemble a cult. Plains University had once been a hotspot for psychedelic experiments. They'd done work on LSD in the sixties, and there was still a room on the third floor with carpeted walls.

The Department of Literature and Cultural Studies, where he and Shelby both worked as teaching assistants, was more sedate. Aside from a mural featuring winged books, there wasn't a lot of consciousness-expanding going on.

"The weather's shifty," Shelby said. "I've brought plenty of layers, and if need be, I'm prepared to enter full Blossom mode."

"I guess that makes me Six."

"You both share certain qualities."

He was drawn back to the buffalo statue. They were plentiful in Saskatchewan before contact. Oscana was the buffalo ossuary of the Plains Cree, and now it was a park, surrounded by a manufactured lake. It was one of the first things he noticed when he arrived here. The park reminded him of playing Myst. He kept trying to press rusty buttons, hoping they'd yield up the Book of Atrus, or at least a mechanical puzzle.

"Did you hear about that guy who was mauled?"

He tore his attention away from the buffalo. "Mauled by what?"

"Coyotes, they think. It was on the morning news. They found his body on the southern edge of the park."

He frowned. "I thought the last coyote sighting was southeast of Regina. Closer to Richardson. That's nowhere near the city limits. What would they be doing in the park?"

"I have no idea. Maybe they're really into ducks."

"Coyotes hunt pets—not humans."

"I guess there was a pack of them."

"There's a pack of wild coyotes roaming the park, and nobody noticed until today?"

"Maybe the guy was drunk. I don't know. I was half-listening to the radio while I did the dishes. I only thought about it because animal control is going to be sweeping the area. We'll have to be careful to avoid them."

"We don't usually go that far south." Andrew shook his head. "Coyotes? I can imagine them killing a child, but a full-grown man?"

"Nature has to be respected. Otherwise, it hunts you where you live."

They walked to Broad Street. Carl lived above the red awning of Love Selection, which was one of the few spots open past ten in the downtown core. His thoughts returned to the chamberlain. He'd lose his mint status once Andrew sawed through the plastic, but the thought of posing him in the window, next to Willow and Tara, was fairly intoxicating. A fallen Skeksi should make them a triumvirate.

"So—I'm sort of e-mailing someone," Shelby said. "She responded to my OkCupid profile."

"What did she say?"

"That I had great taste in movies. But her profile is really sparse. I know that she's a grad student and she listens to Fleetwood Mac. That's about it."

"Have you figured out what department she works in?"

"I've narrowed it down to the humanities."

"Well done. What's her name?"

"Ingrid."

"I feel a website search coming on."

"Don't you think I tried that? She's not listed on any of the departmental sites."

"You could just ask her."

"It seems forward."

"Do you see a date on the horizon?"

"I was thinking of asking her to see a movie."

"Good call. *Prometheus* is playing."

"I'm not taking her to an *Alien* prequel. It should be something fluffy. Something without the possibility of incubation."

Carl was standing outside when they got there.

"Just a second," he said. "I'm texting my mom to figure out what time we're going to Skype tonight. If we stick to audio, I can still play Mass Effect with the sound off."

"You're a paragon," Shelby replied.

"She's distracted too. I feel like we communicate best in that state."

They decided to take the university bus, which vibrated with anxiety. Two students across from them were doing something with flash cards. He spotted a few professors reading.

"I hid the knife," Andrew said quietly.

"Parking." Shelby gave him a look. "That's two times in the space of an hour."

"It isn't parking if I avoid specifics. I could be talking about any kind of knife."

"We'll revisit this at lunch."

He must work in the Subura. That's where the basia do business, flanked by street popinae who sell mushrooms and chickpea soup. He could be on this bus right now, any one of these people. They all looked so different outside the park. When he first met Shelby, he thought: *She can't be Morgan.* They didn't trust their reflections. Babieca played the cithara, but Carl didn't know anything about music. Roldan talked to lares. Andrew could barely talk to Conexus Credit Union when they called.

They arrived at Plains University. Carl went to the Department of History, while Shelby and Andrew made their way to Literature and Cultural Studies. In order to complement the flying books, they'd recently put up images of theorists, magnified to frightening proportions. Michel Foucault regarded them sternly as they passed. Dr. Laclos had already left his office, which meant that they had about five minutes to make it to the lecture hall. He'd begun his PowerPoint presentation by the time they got there, but they were able to slip in beneath the cover of semidarkness. He talked about the opacity of medieval literature, the strange but familiar edges of Anglo-Saxon words that demanded more spit than modern English.

"The poem," he said, "is about two people separated from each other. A small life comes between them, carried to the darkest part of the woods. What does Wulf deliver that night? It could be a child, a pup, or a *giedd*. A shared riddle. The vocabulary frustrates us at every turn, refusing to decide even on a species. We're given only a thicket, rainy weather, the coming of a distant lord. 'Ungelic is us,' says Eadwacer. 'It's different with us.' We'll never know precisely what this means, or why they are."

"'Ungelic is us,'" Andrew whispered. It seemed suitable for multiple occasions.

After class, they delivered tutorials. He tried to keep his students distracted with images. In the end, he got sucked into describing a medieval shoe for twenty minutes, and discussion of the poem was rushed. They practiced alliteration, and then he let them go. Afterward, he reunited with Shelby, who confessed that she let her students talk about dire wolves.

"We were sort of on track. At least they were thinking medieval." She checked her phone. "Carl is stuck at some kind of wine-and-cheese thing for the History job candidate, and he needs us to rescue him."

They made their way into the multipurpose room of the History Department. Everyone was gathered in a semihostile circle around the candidate, who was eating Swedish meatballs and looking nervous. Carl hid next to the cucumber slices. He smiled when he saw them. Shelby grabbed him by the arm, and they squeezed through the circle of masticating academics.

The cafeteria had turnstiles, which made them feel like they were walking into a Zellers department store. He and Shelby made for the salad bar, while Carl got a burger from the counter known as the "fixin's station." Once they'd paid, they took their customary table near the back.

Andrew stared at his plate. For years, he'd had the same lunch at the cafeteria: potato salad, watercress, sweet pickles, coleslaw (his substitute for fiber), pickled beets, and croutons. He liked orderly things with pleasing textures. Ever since he was a first-year undergrad, he'd come to this cafeteria to talk about ideas. His friends also liked to discuss relationships, but he preferred to talk about words themselves rather than the ways that people misused them.

"Remember our first meal here?" he asked.

"I was sitting at this table, crying," Shelby replied.

"You'd overextended your credit card at the bookstore."

"I didn't have any money left. I couldn't pay my rent."

"You were a hot mess."

"I'd like to think I still am."

Carl turned to me. "Please eat some protein."

"There's protein here."

"I don't think you know what protein is, Andrew." He put half of his burger on my plate. "Here. It will make me feel better if you eat it, or at least part of it."

"You'll be hungry."

"I've still got fries coming. They just had to change the oil." He took a bite of the burger. "Will you sleep better now?"

"Yes."

"Okay. Can we talk about the knife?"

Shelby looked around the cafeteria. "Most of these people are distracted. I guess it's safe to park here for a bit."

"Okay—what about that fibula?" Carl asked. "It lit up like an unholy Christmas tree. What do you think it does?"

"There's no way of knowing," Andrew replied. "The lares aren't specific. If we want to find anything out, we'll have to ask the meretrix."

"The Subura is big," Carl said, "and full of dead-end streets that only go somewhere if you know the right people. We can't visit every basia. It'll take all day."

"We only have to visit the best ones. Did you see what he was wearing? He's obviously high up in the gens."

"All the more reason for him to avoid contact with us. Some of the houses won't let you past the front doors without a sizable donation."

"We could use part of our savings to get in."

"What savings?" He turned to Shelby. "There are meretrices at the arx. Could you talk to one of them?"

"They won't tell me anything. People who spend time with the basilissa aren't in the habit of giving away information."

"Maybe you'll run into him."

"We'd run into him in the Subura," Andrew said.

Carl shook his head, silent while a cafeteria employee

dropped off his fries. When they were alone once more, he said, "I don't think it's a good idea to wander around, looking for a meretrix that we know nothing about."

"Well." Shelby looked at both of them. "There is one person who might know. She's probably still angry about that whole desertion thing, though."

"I don't think so." Carl waved a fry, as if to emphasize his point. "We're not going back there. She'll murder us."

"Not if you pay her for lost wages."

"She's right," Andrew said. "Domina Pendelia used to brag about visiting the arx. She and the meretrix probably run in the same circles."

Carl looked miserable. "She's going to take every last coin. And she might not even tell us anything useful."

"She likes you," Andrew reminded him. "Wear something that shows off your arms."

He returned to playing with his croutons. It was fun to soak them in pickled beet juice until they were purple. Then he could pretend that they were alien food cubes. A flash of something caught his eye. He looked over at the nearest table, just as an empty tray fell off the edge, clattering to the floor. As he watched, the tray seemed to move an inch forward. He squinted. The tray didn't move again. Not a soul had noticed. It must have been—

"Andrew?" Shelby frowned at him. "Were you listening? I asked what edition of *Beowulf* you were using."

"Chickering," he replied absently, still staring at the tray. "It has a bit less verve than Heaney's translation, but it's more accurate."

"I never thought of Anglo-Saxon verse as being particularly high in verve," Carl said. "Anything employing a case system is too rich for my blood."

"Spanish comes from Latin, which has a case system." Andrew stared at the tray, willing it to move again. "Once you get the hang of how nouns decline, it's very efficient."

"I prefer my nouns to stand still. What are you staring at?"

He looked up. "Nothing."

For a moment, he imagined what would happen if lares took over the cafeteria. The salamanders could certainly help keep the pizza warm. The gnomoi could handle any necessary renovations, and the undinae would enjoy all the excess runoff from the soda dispensers. Andrew was trying to puzzle out what union the creatures would fall under when he realized that everyone was getting ready to leave. He'd barely touched his meal. He speared a purple crouton. A cafeteria worker collected the errant tray, setting it by the garbage.

3

HIS ALLEY WAS THE SAME. THE DEBRIS HAD
shifted slightly, but he still recognized everything. He didn't
quite understand the utility of this moment, the crossing,
which always left him in the same place. Morgan and
Babieca had their own alleys, in different vici. It didn't make
sense that a city ruled by chance would allow this. He
guessed that it represented a neutral square, a place to start
from. The city held infinite alleys. They'd meet at the clepsydra soon, but this moment was his. The golden moss was
incandescent. He smelled fish and smoke. People were
shouting, wheels were smacking the cobblestones, but it all
seemed far away. The alley was what he'd always wanted.
His personal honeycomb, never changing.

Via Dolores was full of traffic. Wagons jammed the
curbs, and several litters were jostling for pride of place on
the street. This was the time for sending messages and visiting patrons. Chances were good that Domina Pendelia's
front door would be unlocked, in anticipation of morning
obeisance. If they could get into the atrium, they had a
chance of making her listen. Her minor infatuation with

Babieca might prove distracting, and Morgan's presence would lend a touch of respectability.

When he got to the clepsydra, Morgan was waiting for him. The heat was climbing, so everyone clustered around the fountains. As he stared at the water, he noticed a cracked die, floating. It couldn't mean anything good.

"He'll be late," Morgan said. "It's his special talent."

"He also makes us money. We can't really complain."

"He's going to argue. Maybe he won't come."

"He always comes."

"Roldan, why exactly are we doing this?"

He looked surprised. "You defended the idea."

"Returning the knife is honorable, but it leaves us broke."

"You still have your stipend."

"That covers food and bow repair."

"You can have my emergency boot coin."

"The money isn't my only concern. After what happened in that house, I'm not sure it's in our best interest—"

"Nothing here is in our best interest. Anfractus eats people. Why do you think there are so many furs? They're small-time hunters, looking for conies like us. That's all we are to them. If we want to change that, we have to play the game."

"Returning a knife won't get you into the Gens of Auditores."

Roldan bit off his reply when he saw Babieca coming. She was right, of course. Domina Pendelia wasn't going to be happy to see them. Even if she knew the meretrix, why should she help them? You didn't become a citizen by giving away secrets for free.

"So?" Morgan looked at Babieca. "What's your alternative plan?"

"I don't have one."

"You weren't going to suggest that we sell it and split the profits?"

"Nobody would buy such a fine weapon from the likes of us. After dark, maybe, but not while the sun's out." He shrugged. "If you and Roldan want to do this, fine. There will be other jobs, but this is the first thing that's seemed like—I don't know. A quest?"

Roldan looked at Morgan. He could tell that she'd been thinking the same thing.

"Maybe nothing will happen," he said. "But nothing is all that's been happening to us for months, and I wouldn't mind changing that."

"That's not—" She stopped herself from saying something. "I mean, if we're all in agreement, there's no sense arguing."

"You were about to say something."

"I really wasn't."

"I don't hate change."

"Roldan—"

Babieca raised his hands. "Let's just go. We can decide who was right after she chains us all to the hypocaust."

They made their way to the seventh insula of Saxum. Domina Pendelia's house was two stories, with a covered balcony. Morgan knocked on the blue door. After a moment, a member of the house staff opened it. Roldan didn't recognize him.

He could be my replacement. I'll bet he has steadier hands.

"Do you have an audience?" he asked.

"We've come to pay our respects to the domina," Morgan replied.

"Is she your patroness?"

"Not exactly. We have a gift for her."

He looked at Morgan's bow and quiver. "A sagittarius bearing gifts? I've never heard of such a thing."

"I think she'd be interested in seeing us."

"My lady is quite busy."

Babieca withdrew a coin from his sleeve. "Of course she is."

He examined the coin, then tucked it away. "You can wait in the atrium while I locate her. Don't be surprised if she doesn't come, though."

"Her whim is our pleasure."

They followed him through the entrance. Morgan gave him a look.

"What?"

"How many more coins do you have hidden away?"

"We're inside. You've got nothing to complain about. Plus, Roldan—"

"I already know about his boot bank. It's *your* personal treasury that I'm interested in. You complain about having to spend money while it falls out of your sleeves."

"This tunica has many pockets. That's all you need to know."

The atrium was a bit smaller than the last one they'd visited, but she'd painted new frescoes in their absence. One of them was nearly pornographic, if you tilted your head. Couches were arranged next to a small table, which bore a glass ewer of wine and a tray of sesame balls.

Babieca poured himself a cup of wine.

"Stop that," Morgan said. "Stop it. That spread is for guests."

"We are guests."

"No, you're both deserters. Why would she want to feed you?"

"That's a good question."

Domina Pendelia stood in the entrance. She wore a dark blue stola with red fringe. He wondered how many insects had perished to make those strips of crimson. Her sandals were intricately laced, with bright buckles. Her jade earrings had faces, one smiling, the other sinister. Nobody spoke for a moment. Roldan could hear water dropping in the cistern. Then Babieca put down his glass and took a step forward.

"We're back," he said. "Did you miss us?"

She walked over to them. Her wig made her the tallest person in the room.

"You left in the middle of my bath," she said.

"We're very sorry. An urgent matter came up."

"You stole from me. Everything you're wearing is mine."

"Easily remedied." He slipped out of his sandals, then began to unhook his belt. "It's only fair that you should have your property back."

He was about to pull off his tunica when she grabbed his arm.

"Are you mad? I don't need a scene in my atrium."

Babieca smiled and stepped back into his sandals. "Too bad."

"Domina." Morgan withdrew a small leather purse. "I can vouch for them. Here's what they owe you in lost wages."

She stared at Morgan. "These two are no company for a sagittarius. What purpose do you have in being here?"

"It may become clear in a moment. For now"—she extended the purse—"I imagine you'll find use for these coins."

Domina Pendelia took the purse and opened it. "This is barely a third. How do they plan to pay off the rest?"

Before he could lose his nerve, Roldan stepped forward and spoke. "We're sorry, Domina, for the trouble we've caused you. But we need your help. And I think you'll find what we have to say more than compelling."

Her eyes narrowed. "I've forgotten your name."

"Roldan, Domina."

"Roldan." She smiled thinly. "Of course. You speak to the lares."

"Yes, Domina. When they're willing to listen."

"Did you ever speak to them on my behalf?"

"I had a few conversations with the salamander in your hypocaust chamber. She encouraged the fire, in exchange for milk and pumpkin seeds."

She blinked. "Isn't that something? Are there other lares in my house?"

"There's a gnomo in your garden. He doesn't do much, but if you gave him some marble, he could probably make you a nice frieze. Something to make your neighbors jealous."

Domina Pendelia gave him a long look. "You've become more interesting. And I did just order some rose marble from Egressus."

"If he's here, I can ask him about it. Then, perhaps, we could discuss the matter that brought us back to your doorstep."

She considered it for a moment. Then she took the coins and handed the purse back to Morgan. She opened an etched ivory drawer in the table and deposited the money.

"Let's go to the garden."

They followed her down the hallway, which opened to a columned peristyle. Light bathed the myrrh and olive branches. Just as she'd said, there was a square of blushing marble on the table next to the lemon tree. It was good bait for gnomoi, though some of them refused to breach ground for anything less than a carbuncle.

"The stone is exquisite," said Domina Pendelia. "I was going to a hire a mason, but—" She looked at him uncertainly. It was a change from her customary indifference. "How much do the lares charge for something like this?"

"It varies," he replied. "Stone is a gnomo's chaos. He may see the work itself as payment. They always take something, though."

Roldan sat down and tried to listen past the wind and the faint street noise that lingered beyond the house. Marble was like pastry to the gnomoi. He must be close. After a few seconds, he heard something, like a soft tapping. He looked at the marble again. The lemon tree cast shadows across its pink planes. The tapping grew louder as he listened. One of those shadows had a very odd shape. He could feel something there. It wasn't particularly interested in him, but it knew that he was listening.

"The stone is beautiful," he said. "Don't you think?"

The tapping stopped.

Delectable striae, a voice said.

"It came all the way from Egressus."

The gnomo said nothing.

"Their quarries are legendary," he continued. "Do you see how the stone is nearly translucent? Like a rose spun from glass. Whatever you made from it would last forever."

There was more silence. Then:

Why make something for you?

"Not for me. For the domina of this house." Roldan gestured to her. "She would be honored and delighted to display your work."

Her statuary offends me.

He sighed quietly, then turned to Domina Pendelia. "He has a problem with your statues. If you get rid of them—"

"Are you mad? They cost a fortune."

"They're very nice," Babieca interjected, "but they're not doing anything for your reputation. An original piece by a gnomo would be the talk of the insula."

She made a face. "Can I at least keep the Wheel of Fortuna? It has a water feature."

I hate that one most, the gnomo whispered.

Roldan shook his head. "They all have to go."

"Oh, very well."

He turned back to the slab of marble. "She agrees. Your creation will be the garden's new centerpiece, with no pretenders competing for attention."

It will take time.

"There's no hurry."

Touch the stone.

He blinked. "Why?"

"Why what?" Morgan whispered. "What is it asking?"

Touch the stone, the gnomo repeated, *and we are done.*

Slowly, he laid his palm on the marble. It was cool to the touch. Then he felt the pressure of a hand on top of his, smaller, but strangely heavy. The invisible hand pushed. There was a strange pinch in his fingertips. Then his hand sank into the marble, as if it were soft clay. His whole arm went numb. He bit his lip to keep from crying out. Dark spots gathered at the corners of his vision. He heard the voice again, much clearer than before:

The salamander spoke of you.

His teeth were chattering. "What—did she say?"

You have a dangerous talent.

"I don't understand."

Don't trust water.

Then the pressure disappeared. The stone rippled as he lifted his hand. The numbness was replaced by tingling, then vicious pins and needles. The gnomo was gone.

Domina Pendelia was staring at him. "What just happened?"

"We made a deal," he said. "The gnomo will make

something for you. Tonight, I think. They generally work at night."

Unexpectedly, she touched his hand. "You're cold."

"Yes."

"I thought—I mean, it looked as if—"

"That's never happened to me before."

Babieca placed a hand on his shoulder. "Are you all right?"

"I think so. It said something strange to me, though."

"What?"

"Don't trust water."

"Does he have something against the fountains?"

"I have no clue."

"Odd. Should we leave an offering of some kind? More apple skins?"

"No. I think it's happy with the stone."

Domina Pendelia looked at him with newfound interest. "I've met auditores before. I've heard them mumbling to themselves in corners, talking to spiderwebs. That was different, though. I felt something. I believed it was there."

"I'm no auditor, Domina. You said as much yourself. Only an eavesdropper."

She smiled. "Let's go back to the atrium. I hate to talk on an empty stomach."

Domina Pendelia sent for food, and it arrived in vast quantities: roast boar with a fruit glaze, hot chickpeas, wild cabbage, grilled sausages, and swan pastries, which Morgan avoided because they made her uncomfortable. They drank wine from goblets with suggestive carvings; Roldan's had a picture of two lovers being spied on through an open window. Although they'd eaten in this house before, it had always been downstairs, where the rats gathered in a hopeful circle at their lamp's edge. This was the first time they'd actually dined with the domina herself, and it was a very different experience. She told wry jokes, asked them about their lives, even flirted cautiously with Babieca, who was more than receptive. Maybe it was Morgan's presence, maybe she really had been impressed by his conversation with the gnomo, but for the first time, Roldan felt that they were seeing the real domina.

The man who'd met them at the door reappeared. He glanced at the three of them, and Roldan was surprised by the hostility in his look. Everyone knew that Anfractus ran by virtue of an insidious class engine. New arrivals had no gens to protect them, no money, no friends. They could steal to survive, but the Fur Queen was known to deal swiftly with those who encroached upon her territory. The most common solution was to labor for someone else, someone like Domina Pendelia, who needed people to stoke her hypocaust, peel her oranges, and deliver furtive tablets to her many lovers throughout the city. The jobs never paid well, but they certainly helped fend off starvation. They'd taken a chance when they left this house. If Morgan hadn't discovered them, who knows what they would have been reduced to?

We were in the same position, he wanted to say. *And it's not as if we're flush with coin at the moment. Now she's throwing delicacies at us, which you had to prepare, but once we leave we'll be back on the bottom of the wheel.*

Everything was cleared away. They reclined on couches, and Roldan was grateful to be even slightly horizontal, because the wine was reaching his brain. He was aware of the scant distance between himself and Babieca, who was still—incredibly—eating candied figs. The domina had a couch to herself, and Morgan had chosen to stand, unwilling to be within less than a few feet of her bow and painted quiver. She kept her eyes on the hallway that led to the atrium, silently following the movements of the house staff.

She's always on the battlements, Roldan thought. *She's good at her job—it's why the Gens of Sagittarii accepted her. She has focus. Unlike us.* He looked again at Babieca, who had three perfect droplets of wine on his tunica, like a bloody print. *Morgan watches. Babieca consumes. I wait. I just wish I knew what for.*

"Now that we're comfortable," the domina said, "I'd like to know what convinced you to come back here. I could still report your desertion to the aedile. Showing up at my doorstep wasn't without risk."

Her mention of the aedile reminded him of last night. Why would the commander of the watch appear at an empty house? It seemed improbable that someone as busy as the aedile would send a group of miles to recover jewelry. And if it was destined for the basilissa, what need would he have to intercept it?

It did light up. And the salamander knew that they were coming. Why would she tell the gnomo that I had a dangerous talent?

Morgan took this as her cue to rejoin the conversation. She walked over to their couch and stood in front of Babieca, as if to bodily prevent his words from reaching the domina.

"We were hired to test the veracity of an item—something on its way to the basilissa. Roldan, as you've seen, has a way with lares, so he provided the proof."

"What sort of item?"

"A fibula."

Her eyes narrowed. "Someone hired an auditor to test a brooch? That seems like a waste of a surreal conversation with invisible creatures."

I'm not an auditor—

He didn't say it this time. It was pleasing to be mistaken for one.

"Deadly things can come in small packages," Babieca said. "It practically caught on fire when Roldan touched it."

"We got it from an artifex," Morgan continued. "She told us to deliver it to a friend of the basilissa, who was waiting for us in an empty house. The friend turned out to be a meretrix."

"That stands to reason," Domina Pendelia replied. "Some of her most powerful allies happen to be members of that gens."

"The fibula burned with green light—it must have come from the salamander that Roldan was sweet-talking. Immediately after, we heard voices at the entrance to the house. The aedile himself was at the door. We hadn't been there long, so they must have left around the same time we did. They knew of our meeting with the meretrix."

"Where was this house?"

"Vici Secreta, fourth door of the second insula."

Her eyes glittered slightly. "Domina Niobe owns that entire block."

"Is she also a friend of the basilissa?"

"She wishes as much. She's a treacherous slut who enjoys playing games." Domina Pendelia frowned. "What role might she be playing? If the meretrix is truly a friend of the basilissa, perhaps she hopes to increase her reputation by acting as go-between."

"There are already plenty of those," Morgan said. "We've got an artifex, a meretrix, and an absentee householder."

"The artifex was nervous," Babieca added. "She met us at the Hippodrome, where the crowd might act as a shield. As soon as Roldan took the fibula, she was gone."

He'd been floating slightly, due to the wine, but he looked up at the mention of his name. He remembered the dueling miles at the Hippodrome, the smell of the throng and their wild cries, the steady gaze of the spado.

"Didn't her warning about the basilissa seem a bit hollow?" he asked. "From what little I know about the family's history, her mother was far more terrifying."

"She may know nothing of this gift," Domina Pendelia replied. "The basilissa receives trinkets all the time, from her suitors across the city and beyond. She probably spends most of her day unwrapping shiny things from desperate people. One more fibula on the gleaming pile wouldn't arouse suspicion."

"Could it be a weapon of some kind?" Morgan asked. "Or poisonous?"

"I touched it, and I'm fine." Roldan looked thoughtful. "It had some kind of power. Almost as if it were alive. I've never felt anything quite like it."

"Until today, you'd never stuck your hand into a piece of marble," Babieca replied. "Those listening skills are taking you in all kinds of mad directions."

"Was she truly an artifex?" Domina Pendelia asked. "The woman who gave you the fibula? Or was she simply a gem-smith?"

"She wore the tunica of the artifices," Roldan replied. "And she looked exhausted, like most builders do."

"Aside from fixing the machines in the Arx of Violets, and minding the fountains, there aren't many jobs for an artifex. She wouldn't be the first builder to supplement her income by dealing in gems."

"It didn't have any gems," Roldan said. "It was a plain silver fibula, with the likeness of a bee on a bunch of grapes. Does the basilissa even like bees?"

"I'm not exactly her confidant."

"But you've been to her parties. You spoke of them often."

She managed to look slightly awkward. "I've been in the same room as her, but she's never graced me with more than a few words. Her group is a tight engine, virtually impen-etrable. She only mingles with old citizens, and I haven't lived here for so long. She'd probably still consider me a new householder."

Roldan thought it must be strange to live in Anfractus day and night. Like them, Domina Pendelia had once lived beyond the city. She'd spent half of her time in another world. Did she have a family? A career? When someone became a citizen, they vanished from that other place, whose particulars he could barely focus on. It was strange to think that people might be searching for the domina, might be dreaming of her, praying for her return. Or maybe she'd left nothing behind at all. Disappearing would be easy, if that were the case. But to be a citizen, you needed to endure the night, full of venom, arrows, and crooked lares. How had she done it?

The domina turned to Morgan. "You still haven't explained to me how you managed to fall in with these two. If the Gens of Sagittarii knew that you were making money on the side, they'd punish you. Perhaps they'd even expel you."

"You know a lot about the gens for someone who isn't a

member." Morgan lowered her gaze slightly. "With all due respect, Domina."

"Perhaps I once was a member—of that gens, or another." She smiled. "That would be a story for another time, though. Stop dancing around my question. What is your part in this, sagittarius? Why are you helping these nemones, clever as they are?"

Babieca sat up. "We're not nemones. We may not belong to a gens, but that doesn't make us nobodies."

"*Nemo* means 'without a gens.' That makes you both nemones by definition. It's no grave insult. Anfractus runs on nemo labor. It's a temporary condition—for some, at any rate."

"We don't think of ourselves as nemones."

"Because you have a sagittarius with you? Because you're no longer shoveling coal or chasing rats out of my under-croft?" A flicker of the old domina had returned—perhaps this was the true version after all. "Meeting her was a lucky turn of the wheel, but that's all." She looked at Morgan again. "Now, my dear—you've eaten my boar, drunk my wine, and I've asked nothing in return. However, it is cus-tomary for strangers to repay their host with a story. Do you really want to violate the laws of hospitality?"

Morgan started to protest—then thought better of it and nodded. "Of course not, Domina. You've been very kind."

"She misplaced her quiver," Babieca supplied.

Morgan's eyes narrowed. "That wasn't quite the way of it."

"She was in her cups—"

"The domina asked for *my* story, not your inebriated version of it."

Babieca raised his hands. "Of course. I'm an unreliable narrator."

"I was with a companion," she continued. "We'd both spent our day on the battlements, and we wanted to share a few drinks. It was a festival day, though, and all of the respectable cauponae were full. So we tried the Seven Sages. While we were drinking, we set our quivers under the bench.

I had to use the necessary. When I returned, both quivers were gone, along with my companion."

Domina Pendelia looked confused. "Why would he take yours?"

"He was going to bet it in a game of Hazard," Babieca said. "Roldan and I were sitting at a nearby bench, and I saw him take it downstairs. He had a grin like a pig in shit. We followed him, and Roldan created a distraction—what did you do, again?"

"There was a salamander, asleep under the brazier," Roldan replied. "I convinced her to set fire to the dice. It's not easy, but stone will burn if the fire is hot enough."

"At any rate," Morgan said, "they helped me recover my arrows. It was peculiar. I realized that a member of my own gens had betrayed me, not even for money, but for the mere possibility of money. These two—" Roldan could see that she was about to call them nemones but then stopped herself. "They helped me without any promise of reward. They seemed like far worthier company than the jackass who'd tried to gamble away my arrows."

"The wheel often makes an odd turn." Domina Pendelia smiled. "Look at the three of you—practically a company. You only lack for one."

"*Nemones* can't be part of a company," Babieca said. "A blind spado would have more luck than us finding a quest."

"Oh? You seem to have found one already."

Morgan reached into her quiver and withdrew the knife, which she'd wrapped carefully in linen. She laid it on the table. Domina Pendelia examined it with interest. Her eyes fell to the gems encrusted in the hilt. If she knew where to properly fence such a piece, she could probably afford to redecorate the atrium from top to bottom. Roldan could almost feel her adding sums and managing possibilities. Finally, she looked up from the blade.

"Where did you get this?"

"It belonged to the meretrix," Morgan said. "He lent it to Roldan. In the middle of the chase, we all forgot about it."

"This is no courtesan's toy. Its owner must have enemies."

"We thought you might recognize it."

"Why? Because I spend my time at court studying weapons?"

"No," Babieca said. "Because the make of the weapon suggests wealth and power. This meretrix has to be part of—what did you call it?—the basilissa's *engine*. Her inner circle. Why else would he need such protection? Surely, you would have noticed a masked man who spoke with her, maybe even danced with her?"

"The court is full of people in masks. That's nothing new. Meretrices have always been a fixture in the Arx of Violets."

"The mask was—distinctive," Roldan heard himself say. "It was silver, with delicate filigree, and precious stones around the eyes. It reminded me of the moon."

"It sounds like the meretrix made an impression on you."

He looked down. "That's not important. We can't simply carry his knife around—if we're caught with it, we'll answer to the aedile. There's no point in trying to sell it. If we return it, he might tell us something more about the fibula."

"Wouldn't it be safer to remain ignorant?"

"Everyone here used to be ignorant—until we found ourselves alone and naked in a strange alley. Were things really better before Anfractus? Was that bliss?"

Domina Pendelia looked at the dagger again.

"I slept better," she said. "In that other life."

Roldan hoped she might say more. Instead, she opened the ivory drawer, withdrawing a wax tablet and stylus. Roldan stared at them both enviously. She wrote a quick message on the tablet, which she handed to Morgan.

"Take this to the black basia, in the Subura. There's a guard who watches the door—she used to work for me, ages ago. Show her this, and I believe she'll let you in. Her shift doesn't start until twilight, so as noncitizens, you'll be cutting it close. There won't be time to take in much of the scenery." She looked at Babieca when she said this. "If you throw the dice true, you may just find the one that you're looking for."

He could tell that she knew more than she was saying. Had she recognized the dagger? He thought that he'd seen something in her eyes when he was describing the mask. Desire? Fear? He didn't know her well enough to read her silences.

"Thank you," Morgan said. "We're in your debt."

"Yes." She reached for more wine. "You most certainly are."

The sky was beginning to darken by the time they left Domina Pendelia's. Had they really spent the whole day there, eating and comparing shadows? Time didn't always flow smoothly in Anfractus. It had the habit of escaping from you, like a cat, leaping swiftly through the open space of an unguarded door. Babieca had matched the domina cup for cup, but she had a surprisingly high tolerance for her own wine. Now he was a bit unsteady. He put his arm around Roldan, leaning on him for support. His breath smelled of cloves and raspberries.

"I'm at the Arx of Violets tomorrow," Morgan said. "I won't be able to meet you until it's time to visit the Subura. Will you be able to stay out of trouble in the meantime?"

"Roldan's going to keep me safe," Babieca said. "He's got a knife, remember? And if we run into trouble, I can either sing or get naked. Both have the element of surprise."

"Yes. Play to your strengths." She turned to Roldan. "You heard what the domina said—we won't have much time once we reach the basia. We can't just wave a knife around, asking if anyone's seen its owner."

"Maybe the guard will recognize it. Failing that—do you think there's some secret room full of labeled masks? That would be our best bet."

"This is going to go so well."

"You had faith in the idea when you were sober."

"I'm still sober. I mixed my wine with water, remember?"

"That's because you're sharp as a t—" Babieca's tongue

stumbled over the word. "—sharp as a sharp thing, with lovely barbs and hooks."

"I'm choosing to take that as a compliment."

"We should go," Roldan said. "It's nearly time."

They made their way back to the clepsydra, joining the crowd that was also leaving the city. Roldan studied his fellow noncitizens in the waning light, the people who, like him, divided their time between worlds. Domina Pendelia had slept easier when she was one of them. He barely slept at all. Sleep had always been his enemy, the monster prowling the edges of his thought, waiting for him to blink first. Sometimes he wanted to give in, but his wheels kept turning, powering the infernal machine that refused to gather rust. Staying awake was a talent that helped him in that other life, where reading seemed so dreadfully important. The closer they got to the alleys, the more he was able to think of his twin, the one on the opposite shore.

Words are his shield. He thinks he can read the whole world.

Once the sun dropped, the silenoi would appear. They used to hunt beyond the city walls, but now they roamed the streets in packs.

The hairs on the back of his neck stood on end. He smelled something, like a mixture of iron and rain-soaked ground. His alley was close. A part of him always resisted this moment. It wasn't that he hated change. It was that he feared it. He wanted the alley forever, the blind corners of Anfractus, the smoke, power, and din that made him Roldan. It would all unravel. He couldn't hold it together.

Just as they were about to part, Babieca squeezed his hand. "*Tack*," he said, grinning.

4

THE SALAMANDER WAS SITTING ON HIS CHEST.
He couldn't see it, but he could feel it. Also, its breath was
smoke, which meant that his bed appeared to be on fire. He
tried to meet its gaze but couldn't quite tell where to look.
He felt its claws kneading him.

"You don't exist on this side of the park."

This one thinks it knows everything.

The kneading grew more enthusiastic. Andrew grimaced.
Drops of blood appeared on his bare chest. He felt the lizard
shift position.

What do you desire?

"I'd need to make a list. Can I get up? My notepad is on
the dresser."

No. What is the one thing?

"It isn't just one thing."

It is.

He closed his eyes. "There is something."

We can give it to you.

"Really?"

Yes. Would you like to make a deal?

"What do I have to give in return?"

You know.

He swallowed. "Okay. I accept."

The salamander paused, one claw still on his chest. *You are certain?*

"Yes. Do it."

The claw sliced him open. He screamed. The salamander reached both paws into his chest, tugging on the sides of the incision. It grew, until it was large enough to accommodate the lizard's head. Andrew gasped as it pushed its way inside him.

Everything must go.

He woke up sweating. He couldn't catch his breath. There was a dull pain in his chest, which he tried not to think about. Surely it was indigestion. Nothing a little ginger ale couldn't fix. There wasn't actually a lizard setting up shop in his chest cavity. He swallowed around the dry lump in his throat. Coffee first, with a ginger ale chaser. That seemed like the healthiest option. He got out of bed and made his way to the living room.

Their drive back from the park had been curiously silent. Carl dozed in the backseat, and Shelby kept her eyes on the road. The white noise of the wipers put everyone in a trance. He remembered watching fat drops of rain strike the window, Albert Street a blur of trees in shadow. Then there was the silence of the house, a short fall into the empty bed. Sleep as heavy as hemlock, until the salamander dream.

He argued with the coffeemaker. Once the green light was on, and he was sure it wouldn't explode, he allowed himself to look at the pile of marking. Professor Laclos had asked his students to write about the problem of obscurity in Old English literature. Most of the short essays began with a *Webster's* definition of *obscurity*, followed by spliced Wikipedia articles pertaining to various topics. One student had written on *Hamlet*, firmly believing that Shakespeare was alive and well in the ninth century. He moved that essay to the bottom.

There comes a time—usually during the second semester of a master's degree—when all graduate students ask themselves the same question: *Why am I doing this?* It was a more neurotic version of the poet Rilke's question: *Must I write?* If you answered in the affirmative, it meant that you were a writer. But Rilke never asked: *Must I write a thesis?* The desire to be an academic was poorly understood. Andrew didn't fully know why he'd chosen to pursue graduate studies. Complicating things just seemed to be what he was good at.

Carl and Shelby had more obvious connections to academia. Carl was one of those kids who'd started watching the History Channel when he was six years old, entranced by animated reenactments of siege warfare. Shelby's mother was head of the Cree Languages Department, and she'd practically grown up in the translucent corridors of First Peoples University. Andrew had no such pedigree. For as long as he could remember, his father had managed a used furniture store. His mother lived in various places, none of them nearby. She was an avid reader, as evidenced by the funny, well-written postcards that she sent him. The rest of his family held reasonable jobs, which granted them things that he still regarded as magical: dental benefits, deductible prescriptions, vacation time. They smiled kindly when he described whatever paper he was working on, like you do when someone tells you they want to become a graphic designer.

He sat down at his kitchen table, separating the essays into piles of ten. They remained sinister, and so he divided them again into piles of five. *Mark five, and you can do something fun, like watch a commercial or go to the bathroom.*

When he was first applying to graduate school, he'd asked for reference letters from a number of surprised college professors. They were surprised because he'd barely spoken in class, and most of his essays, while competently written, had been late and off-topic. When he'd asked his favorite professor what the hardest part of her job was, she'd replied, without hesitation: "Marking. It's like yard work. It never gets easier, and you always have to do it."

Everyone had different strategies. Shelby wrote detailed

comments that were uniformly encouraging, while Carl liked to scrawl *What?* or simply *no* in the margins. Andrew had tried everything—a marking rubric with codes, a form of shorthand, typewritten comments, even colorful stamps (a jumping rabbit for *use the active voice*)—but in the end, none of these tactics cut down on the labor. His professor had been right. Of course, she'd also taught four classes per semester and still been available during office hours, while he could barely get through the work of forty-five students. College professors had guts.

He turned on the radio.

—found stripped to the waist in an overgrown area of the park. Drugs and alcohol were most likely a factor, although police are not releasing any more information at this time. The hiker may have already been disoriented and suffering from exposure when the wild animals discovered him.

Andrew shook his head. Wascana Park was in the middle of the city. How could a pack of coyotes get this close without being seen? It was like being attacked by wolves in the Cornwall Centre food court. They were supposed to be shy animals. He'd heard of them teaming up to take down a deer, but a full-grown man?

The phone rang while he was pouring the coffee. Andrew turned off the radio, then hit the speaker button. Shelby's voice filled the kitchen, singing: "Maaarking paaarty, we've got wine and highlighters!"

"I was just about to have a coffee."

"Perfect. Coffee lays the foundation, which you can then sprinkle wine on."

"When exactly did we plan this marking party?"

"It all came together about fifteen minutes ago, when I woke up Carl. Now we're on our way. He's not super-awake yet, so he could probably use some coffee as well."

"Wouldn't it be more efficient for you to just mark at a pub?"

"Your place has the best lighting. Be there in a sec."

He hung up and surveyed the piles again. Was five pushing it? Bundles of three seemed more humane. Three was a sacred number, after all. The doorbell buzzed. Andrew realized that he still wasn't wearing pants. He threw on a pair of shorts and went downstairs. Carl appeared first, holding a box of pilsner.

"She's got more in the trunk," he said.

Still barefoot, Andrew made his way across the unkempt lawn, avoiding the dandelions. Shelby handed him two bags.

"What's all this?"

"Comestibles. We have to feed our minds."

"Is there anything here that isn't a starch?"

"You're in no position to critique anyone's eating habits. Besides, I got you those dried mango slices that you like, even though they creep me out."

"Thank you."

Carl had already set up camp in the living room. The table was now covered in essays and exam booklets. He had both a beer and a coffee in front of him.

"That was mine," Andrew observed, pointing to the mug.

"Sorry." He gestured toward the kitchen. "There's still some left, I think."

Andrew bit off a caustic comment. He returned to the kitchen and poured himself what remained, which was about two thirds of a cup. He gathered his essays and walked back into the living room. Shelby had already deployed her marking, next to Carl's. There was no room left. Andrew exhaled. Then he piled his essays on the nearby chair. The living room was modest in size, and two extra people made it feel snug. He loved them both to death, but there was something about having people over—even great people—that never failed to make him anxious. It seemed like he should be cleaning, or handing out coasters, or something.

Carl opened up a bag of Funyuns. "Want some?"

"God, no."

"Suit yourself."

"I brought Malbec," Shelby said, "in case you want to feel like an adult."

"I'm older than both of you," Carl reminded her. "I'm

like the hoary-headed sage of this group. You should listen to what I say."

"You told me in the car that pilsner gives you unholy gas."

"And that was true."

"I'm going to open all of the windows," Andrew said.

"Good idea," Shelby replied. "While you're up, can you put the Brie in the oven?"

"You brought Brie?"

"It's amazing with Triscuits. Which I also brought. No thanks necessary."

I could start a fire in the oven, he thought idly, while unwrapping the soft cheese. *I can see the headline now: Promising grad students maimed by Brie.*

When he returned, Carl and Shelby were mired in their favorite debate: whose discipline was clearly better.

"History deals with things that exist," Carl was saying, "or at least things that used to exist: fortifications, weaponry, governments. English is totally subjective."

"You sound like these essays."

"Historians actually have to dig around in the dirt."

"When's the last time you were near dirt?"

"I'm more of an archivist."

"Literature has to be read within its historical context. I'm as much of an archivist as you—I just don't use an indecipherable method of notation."

"There's nothing wrong with Chicago style!"

"Are you kidding me?"

Carl looked up. "Andrew, what do you think?"

"I think that none of us are getting jobs, so it doesn't matter."

"I can't believe you just went there."

He sat down. "I've been thinking—"

"Don't become a librarian," Shelby interrupted him. "I know it seems like the greatest job in the world, but the competition is just as fierce."

"That's not it." Andrew blinked. Some of the fuzziness

had vanished, and he could remember more about the previous night. "I'm still thinking about the fibula."

Carl stared at him, still holding a Funyun. "Dude. No parking."

"We're not in public. This is my house."

"He has a point," Shelby said. "The rule of anachronism cuts both ways. Talking about work or school when you're in Anfractus weakens the power of the city. Parking, when you're not actually in the park, weakens the fabric of our lives here."

"Maybe it brings us closer to being citizens."

Shelby gave him a look. "Is that what you want?"

"I don't know. It seems more interesting than marking forty-five versions of the same essay. In Anfractus, things are different. We have a quest—not some job that barely lets us break even, but a real quest, for the first time ever."

"You don't just become a citizen," Carl said. "It's not like applying for a student loan. Once you cross that line, your life here is over. Anfractus claims you."

"A person could do it gradually, at first."

"What would you tell your dad? *I'm going to live in a made-up city?*"

"At least finish your thesis," Shelby said, only half-joking.

"I just—" Andrew stared at the carpet. "Sometimes I don't know why I'm doing this anymore. Going to class, spending hours in the library, trying to write something original when I know that my ideas aren't impressing anyone. When I'm in the park, I have a purpose. Lares talk to me. Things actually happen."

Carl touched his shoulder. "You're just in a funk, man. Besides—none of us has the resources to become a citizen. We wouldn't survive the night."

"Speak for yourself," Shelby replied. "I've spent nights in the city before."

"Right." Carl took a sip of beer. "In the arx, surrounded by sagittarii."

"There's no place that isn't dangerous at night."

"The Arx is impregnable."

"That's not historically—"

"The Brie's ready." Andrew rose. "I'll be right back."

He lingered in the kitchen, spreading warm cheese on Triscuits, listening to them debate who would die first once the sun went down. He poured himself a glass of wine. It would clash with the coffee, but he didn't care. He needed a distraction, something to keep him in this world, rather than endlessly wondering about the other.

Dad might even believe me if I said I was going to live in a made-up city. We used to build cities out of sofa cushions.

He remembered storming the love seats and leather sectionals, then fleeing to the bunk bed section, which provided the best cover. His father would chase him, brandishing a fluorescent light tube like a bastard sword. *I'll never yield the Papasan chairs! Not even under torture!* And they would run in ever-expanding circles, around the legion of recliners and glass-topped tables that formed the boundaries of their kingdom. Even now, when Andrew found himself in strangers' living rooms for the first time, he always wanted to arrange their furniture into a citadel. They were rarely amenable to it.

He brought the plate of Triscuits back to the living room. Shelby was viciously circling something on an exam. Carl saw his wineglass and nodded in approval. The next hour was a frenzy of eating and underlining. They managed to reduce their piles. Carl was only marking historical précis, which required fewer comments. After the third essay, Andrew stopped trying to explain what a caesura was. Gradually, marking-and-drinking became just drinking.

"I want to write a song for my exes," Carl said, half-reclining on the couch.

"To apologize?" Shelby asked.

"No. I'm a great boyfriend. The song would celebrate their best qualities. Like, my ex Trish worked at Cinnabon, so I'd sing about how she always brought home icing in little containers. You could stay up all night after huffing one of those."

"Access to icing was her best quality?"

"Definitely one of them."

"My exes don't need a paean. They need a curse—something I could plug all their names into at once, to save time."

"Really? There must have been a few good ones."

Shelby refilled her wineglass. "Brent cheated on me, and stole my Costco membership, for some weird reason. Simon gave me mono. Extreme Kim broke into my car just so she could reposition all of the mirrors. Who does that?"

"Did you dump her?"

"Sort of. I wasn't firm enough about it, though. She still thought we were dating when she saw me dancing with Stacey, who was just a friend. Things got ugly—hence, the breaking and entering that occurred later."

"You have to be firm about these things," Carl said. "I have a speech."

"That's cold."

"Not at all. It works. I cover all the essential points and, by the end, we both know that it's over. There's no ambiguity."

"I never really know when it's over." She sighed. "There's always that moment, where you look at the other person and think, 'Maybe we can turn this around.'"

"You never really turn it around, though. You just end up exposing an uglier angle." He shook his head. "Better to make a clean break."

"With footnotes."

"Endnotes." He looked at Andrew. "What about you, buddy? How do you end things?"

I don't begin them, he thought.

The truth was that most of his relationships had been short-term. He'd meet someone for coffee. They'd tell him what a good listener he was, not realizing that he was too nervous to talk. Coffee would devolve into quick sex, and then he'd find himself back on the bus, slightly disheveled and amazed that he'd been naked with another human only a few moments ago. He remembered their apartments, their bowls and teakettles, the hospitality of their animals, even as their names faded. He remembered their smiles and the shock of being in their hands, the odd trust that you could feel with a stranger.

But mostly, he remembered waiting for the bus afterward. For a moment, he'd expect to see the lot of them walking down the street. He'd give them a questioning look. *Did I forget something?* They'd all kiss him.

Come back. Let's watch Firefly. *Let's crawl into bed and read over each other's shoulders. Let's compare all of our favorite things, and then make a whole new list. We can start over completely. We can be who we want.*

"Andrew?" Carl asked. "What are you thinking about?"

"The bus always comes."

"What?"

"Never mind. It's not important."

Carl got up. "I have to piss. Then we should stop by campus. I have some interlibrary loans waiting patiently for me behind the library counter."

He disappeared into the small, turquoise-tiled bathroom. The fan rumbled to life once he'd closed the door. Shelby turned to Andrew.

"What was that all about?"

"I don't know what you mean."

"Your spacey comment about the bus always coming."

"I never know what to say when people ask me about relationships. I just wanted to change the subject."

"I don't believe you. I could tell you were thinking about something."

"I'm always thinking about something. Last night I was awake until three A.M. thinking about how humans probably learned their pack instincts from wolves. The night before, I couldn't get to sleep until I'd declined the noun *gladius* in all five of its cases. My brain is a hamster wheel plugged into an electric current. There's no use in trying to figure it out."

She shook her head. "No. Something's going on with you. All this talk about becoming a citizen, abandoning your life here—"

"It's just talk. I don't really do things, remember? My faucet's been broken for three months, and all I need to do is buy a tiny piece of rubber from Canadian Tire in order to fix it. Simple as replacing an elastic band. Instead, I jammed a screw into the place where the handle used to be, and I use a wrench to switch from hot to cold."

"That's more than a little odd."

"Don't you think I know that?"

"I can drive you to Canadian Tire."

"I know that too. I just—" He shrugged. "It's like, whenever I think about visiting the store, I can see all of those aisles full of bright, necessary things wrapped in plastic, and they start to spin, like some wheel of misfortune in my head. All the colors blur until I can't see straight. Then I have to turn out all the lights and watch an episode of *Big Bang Theory*, just to remind myself that people as socially dysfunctional as me actually exist."

Shelby smiled kindly. "Maybe we need to get you a pair of blinders, like they use for skittish horses."

"Could I decorate them with stickers?"

"I don't see why not."

He sighed. "I keep dreaming about lares."

"I dream about all sorts of park-related things. Our subconscious minds are still plugged into that world, even when we're on this side of the park."

"The dreams are becoming—vivid. And I saw something yesterday, when we were at the cafeteria. Nobody else noticed, but I saw—"

Carl emerged from the bathroom. "Were you talking about me?"

"What's it like to live in your world of delusion?" Shelby asked him. "Are there imaginary tabloids that discuss your every move?"

"Of course. There's even an academic journal: *Carl Studies*."

"Good luck getting council funding for that."

He shrugged off her sarcasm. "Right. Let's make some coffee and walk to campus. If we take our time, we might even sober up on the way. We'll hit the library and the computer lab—"

"I hope you're referring to your own department's lab."

"Come on. LCS has the best printer."

"The fact that History still embraces sketchy ink-jet technology doesn't mean that you can use our printer whenever you feel like it."

"Nobody's going to notice."

"They will if I tell them."

"Where's your grad student solidarity?"

"Pony up some cash for a new printer cartridge, and I'll think about answering that."

Andrew brewed another pot of coffee. He had only two travel cups, so he poured his into a Dodd's Used Furniture mug instead. He'd just have to walk carefully. They gathered up their marking, then left the house. They must have been an odd sight, passing around a box of Triscuits while they walked down Albert Street, one of them carrying a chipped porcelain cup. Shelby led the way. Andrew lagged behind, distracted by all the branches and debris that a recent storm had knocked to the ground. Carl talked about the paper that he was working on: a study of Byzantine buttons and their role in courtly culture. He was applying for a travel grant to visit the Royal Ontario Museum, which would result in endless blurry photos of silk scraps and stonework.

As they continued up Albert, the parliament building loomed in the distance. It was a grand Victorian edifice, which saw surprisingly little use throughout the year, except when it was being toured by schoolchildren. The sky was clear, which meant that people were gathering on the edges of Wascana Lake, sharing ice cream or riding rented bicycles. The bugs were starting to come out but hadn't yet formed an impenetrable curtain. Andrew sipped his coffee while Carl and Shelby forged ahead. The phone number of Dodd's Used Furniture, printed in Comic Sans beneath a picture of an easy chair, reminded him that he needed to call his father. Neither of them was especially skilled at carrying a conversation, but they did enjoy watching *Storage*

Wars together on speakerphone. They would talk during the muted commercials, then return to the narrative, laughing at the same parts.

They crossed over to Broad Street, which led them to campus. Most of Plains University had been built after 1966, in the brutalist architectural style: heavy on concrete, sharp corners, and balconies that resembled darkened honeycombs. The buildings huddled close together, in an effort to keep students from freezing when they had to go outside. In a province where the temperature routinely dropped below −30 degrees Celsius in the winter, it was essential to minimize your exposure to the elements. Nobody walked anywhere. If you were willing to put on a snowsuit and a balaclava, you'd always have the streets to yourself. Now that they were in the middle of summer, people wore as little clothing as possible. Students generally put on shorts at the first sign of thaw, in spite of the chill wind that persisted. They soaked up the sun desperately, knowing that it wouldn't last. Torontonians or Vancouverites would have regarded snow in May as a freakish portent of doom, but in Regina, it barely turned heads.

The campus reminded Andrew of a city-state, where boundaries and jurisdictions were often vague. Newer buildings encircled the older colleges, which were Lutheran and Jesuit, respectively. First Peoples University stood some distance away, still technically a part of campus, but separate enough to maintain its isolation. In contrast to the maze of concrete that was Plains, First Peoples University had no angles; it was smooth, a wave frozen in glass, gleaming as the light rushed through it. Andrew loved to visit their library—it was like being inside a silent quartz filament— but Shelby tended to avoid it, for fear of running into her mother. The two of them were engaged in a long-standing battle over her thesis.

They entered through the Innovation Centre, which contained both the university bookstore and the global food court. It was late enough that everything had closed, save for the soup place that had pioneered "chicken barley" as its most popular hybrid. Andrew liked the campus at this time of day. Most of the frenetic undergrad activity had died down, and the students who remained were attached to their laptops, mainlining coffee. Light flickered from the student gallery. He couldn't quite make out what was being projected, but it had something to do with tractors and face painting. They walked past the computer store, whose various tablets had all been locked up for the evening. Andrew smiled at the orange clock next to the stairwell, which had been frozen at half past six for years. He liked to fantasize that it was the clock from the movie *Labyrinth*, and that if he stared at it for long enough, David Bowie would materialize and give him directions to the goblin city.

As with most universities, you could gauge the operating budget of each department by what building materials they used. The science wing was new, a mixture of polished concrete and glass with elevators that announced each level. Formulae had been etched into the walls. As they neared the Faculty of Arts, the floor abruptly changed to linoleum. Missing ceiling tiles reminded him of the Mr. T sliding puzzle that he'd had as a child. He wanted to arrange the dimpled panels into something more interesting, but there wasn't a ladder in sight. He contented himself with studying posters. *Queer Student Alliance. Spanish Club. Weekend Bible Study.* Shadow students high-fived, held hands, or pumped their opaque fists in the air. Promotional materials for the university itself featured bright-bordered testimonials, with diverse youth frozen in the act of reading or picking up a baby.

They reached the Douglas Wilson library, which was virtually empty this late in the evening. Only the dedicated were stationed at computers, avoiding essays by repeatedly checking their social media profiles. The librarian at the information desk was reading a copy of Alan Moore's *Top 10*, oblivious to the student who'd just burst into tears because he couldn't get his flash drive to work. Andrew gazed up at the faux vaulted ceiling, which lent a devotional character to the study space. Whenever he entered a library, he became fiercely aware of his desire to vanish into the stacks of print, to be declared a missing title. Although most of his students favored electronic media, he could never escape the smell of mellowing adhesive, the moth-wing texture of aging leaves. Carrying a stack of hardcover books made him feel invincible.

Carl approached the circulation desk. He flashed the smile that routinely got him out of paying fines. Andrew had never mastered this particular strategy. He was about to say as much to Shelby, when he noticed her staring fixedly at the bank of computers.

"What is it?"

"She's here."

"Who?"

She grabbed his sleeve, pulling him behind a pillar. "*Her*. Ingrid."

"The girl from OkCupid?"

"She's right over there."

"The one with the Roch Voisine button on her knapsack?"

"Not her. The girl next to her—the cute one with short hair."

"Oh." He studied her for a moment. "I thought you were more into femme girls."

"I'm into people who might be into me. It's a philosophy that tends to get me laid once a year, so I stick with it."

Carl returned with a tower of books. "Why are we hiding in the shadows?"

"Shelby just spotted her online crush," Andrew explained. "She's sitting—"

"God, don't point!" She grabbed his arm. "Okay. Let's come at this logically. What are my options?"

Carl shook his head. "You're overthinking it. Just go over there and ask her out."

"That would never work."

"It works for me."

"You have an imaginary journal and a buttload of confidence. The rest of us are just tiny fish, totally at your mercy in the dating pool."

"Don't be a wimp. You're brilliant and sexy. All you have to do is walk over there, lean in close, and invite her to a poetry reading, or the animal shelter—wherever queer girls go when they're on a date."

"I think Erin Mouré's launching her new chapbook," Andrew said. "That could be your in. She has this routine with a suitcase and gloves that's always a hit."

"No. I'll freeze up. One of you has to do it."

Carl stared at her. "How will that work?"

"I don't know. One of you could start a conversation with her, and just kind of steer her into queer waters, to see what her type is. Then at least I'd know if I stood a chance. I swear, this girl has almost no information on her profile. Her messages are practically in cipher."

"If I do that," Carl replied, "she'll think I'm trying to hit on her."

"Then tone it down. Or—you know—tone it *up* instead. Act queer."

"If I knew how to do that, my dating pool would be a lot wider." He looked thoughtful. "Andrew could pull it off, though."

He glared at Carl. "What are you suggesting?"

"You've got—okay, how can I put this gently?" He smiled, which was distracting. "You've got a very academic vibe."

"So do you."

"That's not what I mean. When you talk to people, you seem genuinely interested in what they're saying. You listen. It doesn't feel like you're trying to pick them up."

"You're saying I'm *that* guy." He sighed. "The friend-zone guy. I've got all the sex appeal of a cuddly Lorax."

"Don't sell yourself short, buddy. You're at least as sexy as Yertle the Turtle."

"I'm not really liking either of you right now."

"Please, Andrew." Shelby hugged him. "You're funny, and creative, and if you do this for me, I'll buy you coffee for a month."

"Coffee and a cruller, Monday to Friday."

"Done."

He stepped back. "Fine. Don't blame me if I return empty-handed, though. You might as well send a code monkey into a cage match."

Andrew walked over to the bank of computers. He took a seat by the machine next to Ingrid, which made distressed noises as it booted up. Introductions were his Kryptonite. He never knew how to break the ice with someone. He lacked a group instinct; at parties, while everyone else was colliding with each other, he would stand silently with his back to the wall. Shelby and Carl were both patient with his silences. They knew that talking to him required a certain amount of fishing with brightly colored lures. Most people were in a hurry, though. He hated the pressure of being concise. If he was going to talk, he needed to editorialize a bit, to slide adjectives like tiles until he found the best configuration.

He also resisted looking people in the eye. If he knew someone well, trusted them, he could maintain eye contact. But it felt intimate—sensual, even—not something to be practiced casually with strangers. As a result, he'd developed highly effective peripheral vision. While appearing to stare at the progress bar on his monitor, he could also see that Ingrid was looking up articles on the ProQuest Education database. That didn't bode well for starting up a conversation. He studied Anglo-Saxon poetry—what did he know about K–12 education? Maybe she was a research assistant, though. Her field might be entirely different.

She clicked on an article titled "Teaching Young-Adult Fantasy Fiction."

Screwing his courage to the sticking place, he turned to her. "I'm sorry. I don't mean to eavesdrop, but I've read that article by Kearnes, and . . . it's not great."

She looked at him with interest. "Really? My supervisor recommended it."

"It's full of holes. The introduction's okay, but then she goes off on this tangent about wizardry schools and doesn't even mention Ursula Le Guin."

"Well—the *Earthsea* books aren't strictly considered young-adult literature."

"You don't think *Tombs of Atuan* is a girl's coming-of-age story?"

"She spends most of her time being chased through catacombs by a chubby eunuch. I'm not sure that most North American girls can relate to that."

"True, but isn't it also about finding her voice? Sure, there's the weird sexual tension between her and Sparrowhawk—who's seriously into the prince, anyway—but in the end, it's just Arha alone, a Kargish girl on the edge of the void. She refuses her fate and finds her true name, the one word in all the world that belongs to her. And she does it without a spellbook, or a sidekick, or archery expertise. She walks out of the dark and into a brand-new life."

"Do you study the genre?"

"No. I study old poetry. But I've been reading fantasy forever. I used to skip gym class and read *The Prydain Chronicles* in the parking lot of my middle school. I'd crouch behind the cars and wish that I had an oracular pig of my very own."

She smiled. "I can relate to that."

"I'm Andrew."

"Ingrid."

She extended her hand. He tried to shake it firmly, even though touching a stranger's hand made him slightly uncomfortable. He met her eyes, counted two beats silently in his head, then looked back at her monitor.

"You can also try CBCA Education," he said. "Depending on what you're researching."

"It's for my thesis. I'm writing on gender in YA texts."

"There's no shortage of cross-dressing knights."

"I know, right?"

He felt himself hitting a conversational wall. Carl would know what to do. He'd ask something mildly inappropriate, but his smile would soften the implication. He looked over at Shelby, who was still half-hidden behind the pillar. She gave him a thumbs-up. She had no idea that they'd been talking about Ursula Le Guin the whole time.

"So—" he began unsteadily. "Have you seen *Farscape*?"

"What's that?"

He resisted his desire to explain the history of the Sebacean Empire. "It's a science-fiction show about an astronaut who gets shot through a wormhole."

"I don't watch a lot of television. Except for *Dinosaur Train*."

Andrew had no idea how to respond to that. "Well, there's this character named Aeryn Sun, who's powerful, but fragile. And there's another character, named Zhaan, who's blue and bald, and she can have mind-sex."

She raised an eyebrow. "Okay."

"Anyways—they're both attractive in their own way, but Aeryn has some serious female masculinity going on, while Zhaan's more conventionally—"

"Why are you explaining this to me?"

He blinked. "I—have no idea. I should let you work on your thesis."

"Yeah. It was nice to meet you, though."

"You too. Good luck with those databases."

"Thanks."

He walked back over to the pillar.

"I'm impressed," Shelby said. "You talked to her for a while."

"That's true. And even if I don't have any useful information, that shouldn't stop you from buying me coffee on Mondays and Wednesdays. I'll forfeit the cruller."

"What did you guys talk about?"

"Databases. Then fantasy novels. Then *Farscape*." He stared at the carpet. "I may have tried to ascertain her sexual type by describing characters from the show."

"That's . . . *not* extremely weird."

"Did she have a thing for tiny emperors in floating chairs?" Carl asked. "That could be a difficult fetish to satisfy, outside of the Uncharted Territories."

"I found out that she's in the Department of Education," Andrew said. "That's something. If you want to stalk her, you at least know where to hide. Also, she studies young-adult fantasy fiction and watches something called *Dinosaur Train*. What is that?"

Shelby frowned. "It's a children's show."

"Maybe it's part of her thesis," Carl said. "You never know."

"You promised there'd be no blame," Andrew reminded her. "If you'd gone over there yourself, the results would have been very different."

"I would have either peed my pants or gone mute. Possibly both."

"I can teach you how to talk to girls," Carl offered.

"Right. I don't think inviting her to look at my Lego castles will work."

"I've never done that." He sighed. "Okay. Maybe once. But she seemed really into my description of the miniature trebuchet."

"Trust me—she wasn't." Shelby turned to Andrew. "Thank you. The outcome wasn't ideal, but we know a bit more about her. It's a start."

"A start would be asking her out," Carl said.

"We have very different rule books. Let's just go."

They walked to the Arts building, which housed their departments. Carl persuaded them to let him use the printer in the LCS computer lab. Andrew and Shelby checked their TA mailboxes, which were both empty. As they walked back to the south entrance, Shelby lingered outside the library. Carl and Andrew both took her by the hand, leading her forward.

The night was warm. They followed the path lights that led them through Wascana Park. Everyone was avoiding the south side, where police had set up caution tape and posted signs about the coyotes. The north end seemed empty, but when Andrew looked closely, he saw small groups milling together. They spoke in low voices, trying not to attract attention. He couldn't tell if they were companies planning their latest quest or just students getting high and complaining about their majors. From what he *could* tell, everyone had a separate entry point, a piece of the park that resonated for him or her. If you spent enough time in a group, you'd eventually find a single spot that worked for all of you. Their spot was in a copse of trees next to the gazebo, just within sight of the lamppost that always reminded him of Narnia. No Mr. Tumnus in the true park, though. Only the silenoi, whose cloven feet struck the rocks as they hunted you.

They waited until the shadows had thickened. Then they undressed, stowing their clothes in plastic bags, which they stuffed into trees. A wind came off the water, licking at them. Andrew shivered. Carl put one arm around him, the other around Shelby.

"Ready?"

They nodded. The air changed. The darkness attained a pitch that they could feel, that their blood remembered. They stepped forward. As he unraveled, Andrew's last thought was of a girl running through catacombs, in search of a broken ring.

Then the park closed its jaws.

5

Rain was rare in Anfractus, like an eclipse, or a winning streak. It sang against the stones, drenching the moss until it resembled a wet yellow pelt. Steam rose from the ground as febrile clouds spread across the sky, stuttering thunder. Roldan stood in his alley, naked and grinning. The rain covered him in a mixed blessing, which was his favorite kind. He felt the water streaming through his hair, down his chest, pooling warmly between his toes. It reminded him of a dream where he'd been floating through seaweed, eyes closed, trusting the lazy current. When he looked into the water, he could see anemones with familiar faces. He stood for a few moments more, then pulled the loose bricks out of the wall. His boots, tunica, and smallclothes were as he'd left them, along with his coin purse (mostly empty) and the knife, wrapped in musty silk.

He dressed and pulled the cowl over his head, which blocked out the rain's touch but not its sound. He liked the chorus of whispers. If he listened closely, he could hear the muffled calls of the undinae, carried by the raindrops. Their liquid messages were mostly unintelligible, but he could pick out a few words. *Pearl. Patience. Need.*

When he'd first arrived in Anfractus, the voices were all indistinct. Murmuring laughter, the occasional snort, empty morphemes that tickled him like bug bites. Finding himself naked in an alley, it was an easy leap to assume that he'd gone insane. As his fear increased, the voices grew louder, more insistent. He wandered the city wrapped in a stolen bedsheet while sinister plosives made a racket around his feet. They padded after him, shadowed him, until he found himself back in the alley. Pushed to the wall, shivering, he closed his eyes and listened. The words began to move along obscure chains, adhering to each other, forming liaisons. Then he heard the question, stinking of sulfur and sun-baked rust:

Lost?

Over time, he'd learned to both isolate and suppress the voices. He could numb his ears by concentrating on other senses—the tongues of the cobblestones that wanted to cut his boots, the reek of night soil and unwashed bodies, the taste of rain and iron. The lares always grew more strident when they could tell that he was ignoring them, but like a sore throat or dirty thought, he could push them away if he concentrated. Eventually, they'd grow bored and whisper to someone else. Why did they even talk to him? What could a nemo possibly have to offer? Maybe they just liked the sound of his voice.

You have a dangerous talent. The salamander had whispered it, flicking her tongue in the gnomo's ear. But what had she meant? If his talent was so dangerous, why was he wearing patched boots and a soiled tunica? Nobody saw him as dangerous. Yet the salamander had remembered him. Lares didn't usually do that.

He met them at the clepsydra. Morgan was not impressed by the rain. Her dark hair was wilting. Babieca stuck his tongue out to catch the drops.

"I can't carry a bow in this weather," she said miserably. "I had to leave it in the alley. I feel naked without it."

"You've got your hunting knife," Babieca replied. "I've got my short sword, and Roldan has the lupo's dagger. We'll be fine."

"He's not a lupo," Roldan said. "He's a meretrix."

"They both mean *whore*, don't they?"

Morgan gave him an odd look. "I hardly think you can take the moral high ground. You're a trovador without a gens. A meretrix commands respect."

"You can't fuck your way to respectability."

"You're no stranger to the basia. If you have no respect for the people who work there, why do you go?"

"It passes the time."

"You're being irrational," Roldan said.

Babieca turned to him. "Why?"

"You share a side. The meretrices belong to the night gens, and you belong to the day. Same side, different dice. If you ever decide to roll the night die—"

"I'd rather be a fur."

"Even so, it's more likely that you'll—"

"Don't bother," Morgan interjected. "He's getting sulky. Let's just go."

"Where? We've got hours to kill before we can visit the basia." Roldan could feel the weight of the knife. He wanted to be rid of it. "I suppose we could visit the Seven Sages and try to win back some of our lost money."

"I have a better idea," Babieca said. "Let's try a different caupona."

The Brass Gear was on the edge of the Subura, although still technically in Vici Secreta. It was one of the few cauponae in the scholars' quarter, save for the infamous undercroft of the lyceum, whose existence had never wholly been confirmed. The lyceum itself was a grand building, fronted in pale blue marble, whose cupola reflected the sun like a brass helmet. Roldan would have given anything to wander among the tabularia, sampling scrolls and books with freshly pumiced covers, but only spadones and artifices had access to the building, along with a few other high-ranking citizens.

The Gens of Spadones controlled the circulation of documents in Anfractus, while the artifices spent most of their time repairing old machinae. They also looked after the fountains, the aqueduct, and the great cloaca, which required constant maintenance. Although few liked to admit it, the city functioned only because of the work of eunuchs and builders. Without them, Anfractus would crumble into piles of rusty cogs and mildewed parchment.

They entered the caupona, whose doors were studded with spare parts. It was surprisingly bright on the inside—dozens of lamps hung next to polished brass discs, which scattered a warm glow over everything. There were also plenty of glass lenses connected to smaller lamps, which provided enough light to read by. Many of the customers barely paid attention to their drinks. Instead, they tinkered with machinae of every sort. There were cabinets on wheels, made of embossed ivory, with compartments that slid open and closed. Miniature fountains with preening doves attached to cylinders. Wheels of Fortuna that shrieked as they spun endlessly on golden pins. The artifices squinted through their lamp-lit lenses, consulting wax tablets covered in spidery formulae. Occasionally, they would take a bite of cold sausage, a sip of warm ale, then return to their calculations. Roldan had never seen so many silent souls in a caupona. It would have resembled a workshop entirely, if not for the smell of wine and smoke.

Roldan knew very little about the Gens of Artifices. Long ago, or so it was said, Anfractus had been full of wondrous machinae: speaking tablets, perpetual torches, iron mice that carried secret missives. Now only a few of the true machinae remained, kept safely within the Arx of Violets. The power that made them no longer existed. The machinae that now filled the caupona with their sparks and peculiar breathing were no more than toys, designed to mimic the shadow of life. They could dance in circles or rock back and forth, but that was it. The only true machina that Roldan had laid eyes on was the great clepsydra, nearly as old as the city itself. The artifices knew how to maintain it, but the secret of its construction eluded them. None of their toys, currently on display before him, would attract the green fire of a salamander. Not like the fibula. It had been different.

"Look," Babieca said. "At the corner table."

A woman with red hair was studying a tablet. Her table was covered in springs, cogs, and tiny brass wheels. Her food—cabbage and salted pork—remained untouched. It didn't look as if she'd changed her tunica, or slept, since they'd seen her at the Hippodrome.

Babieca started to make his way forward, but Morgan stopped him.

"Wait. What are you going to say to her?"

"Remember us? You gave us a crazy fibula that caught fire when our friend touched it. Care to explain why?"

"We're in a caupona full of artifices. All she has to do is say the word, and they'll be shoving our charred bodies into some oily undercroft."

"You have a wild imagination."

"This is their territory, Babieca. Furthermore, we have no idea what her place is within the gens. It might not be the best idea to annoy her."

"We could terrify her instead. You've still got your hunting knife. Roldan could threaten to burn the place down—there must be a salamander here."

"There is," Roldan confirmed, "but she's asleep on the grill. I doubt she'll be much help. Lares hate to be woken up."

Morgan put a hand on Babieca's shoulder. "I'll admit that you did a good job charming Domina Pendelia. Some people actually like you. In this case, however, I don't think your sparkle is going to have the desired effect. Let me talk to her."

"Your gens and hers aren't exactly bosom friends. The sagittarii look down their noses at virtually everyone."

"Don't pretend to know anything about us." Morgan looked at Roldan. "If this doesn't go well, be prepared to create a diversion."

"The salamander—"

"It doesn't have to be a fiery diversion. It just has to be something."

He wanted to say that it didn't work like that; lares wouldn't simply create a spectacle for you at a moment's notice. They needed to be convinced. Her look told him that he shouldn't argue further, though, and he simply nodded.

At least she wasn't asking him to light something up again. He hated feeling like a lamp.

Morgan approached the corner table. Babieca and Roldan stood discreetly behind her. Roldan tried to listen for any lares that might be hiding under tables or in shadows. The room was quiet enough to hear a cog drop, but aside from the snoring of the salamander, he couldn't make out any of the usual murmurings. It was strange. Gnomoi loved metal, and the miniature fountains were creating enough humidity to attract undinae, yet the caupona was almost entirely free of lares. Perhaps the machinae repulsed them on some level.

"Salve," Morgan said. "Do you remember us?"

The artifex didn't look up. "You're standing in my light."

Morgan shifted to the left. "Could we have a moment of your time?"

"I'm generally paid for my time. Do you need something built? If so, I charge eight maravedies for a consultation."

Babieca started to say something, but Morgan stepped on his foot. "Right. I'm sure you've very good at what you do. The truth is—"

"—that I'm very busy, and you're interrupting my dinner. The rate for people who interrupt my dinner is twelve maravedies."

"You've barely touched it," Roldan observed.

At this, she looked up. "An auditor with a sense of humor. How odd. Don't most of you go crazy from listening to invisible monsters?"

"You're thinking of vigils. Auditores just tend to develop ringing in their ears."

She looked at him more closely. "As I recall, you're not actually a member of the Gens of Auditores. You're a nemo."

Morgan sat down. "I promise this won't take long. We just have a few questions about the item you gave us."

"I have no reason to tell you anything."

"No. Of course you don't." Morgan was silent for a beat. Then, casually, she picked up a metal disc from the table. "What does this do? It looks important."

"Don't touch that."

"Why not?"

"It's delicate, and I need it."

"What are you making?"

The artifex reached out to snatch the component. Morgan drew her hand back. The woman stared at her in disbelief.

"Give it back."

"I don't think I will."

Her eyes narrowed. "You're surrounded by my people. You don't even have a bow. Did you forget it somewhere?"

"What does this piece do?" Morgan repeated. "It's a simple question."

She sighed. "It turns a mechanism."

"What kind of mechanism?"

"A bloody dove's beak, all right? It's part of a ridiculous machina that the basilissa wants for her throne room. Water enters through small pipes, and the dove sings. Half of the builders in here are working on similar toys—machinae designed to impress idiots."

"But you'd rather design something different."

"Of course I would. But this is what they pay for. Cooing birds, hooting owls, cute little frogs that hop about on mechanical lily pads. When rich people watch them, it makes them feel like they're living in the past, when machinae were real. But they're not. They're empty."

"That fibula wasn't."

"Fortuna. Keep your voice down."

"What—don't your people know all about it? Or was that a commission you'd prefer not to speak of in public?"

The artifex stared at Morgan, saying nothing. Roldan saw something more than annoyance cross her face. She was actually scared. She put down the lens. Morgan gently replaced the disc on the table. The woman looked at it, then chuckled.

"It's the smallest pieces that can be the most dangerous."

"What was it?" Morgan asked. "What did we deliver to the basilissa?"

"I—don't fully know. I didn't make it."

"Who did?"

She looked at the table. Roldan could feel her weighing something in her mind. He couldn't tell if she was crafting a lie or working out a sequence of events. Most likely, it was a bit of both. Finally, she swallowed, then spoke:

"I found it—a long time ago. I don't remember where. It never did anything. It just sat there, looking plain. I live with other apprentices. A few of them were curious about it, but mostly we keep to ourselves. There was nothing I could tell them. It was just a fibula. Then one day, I came back to my cell and found a note."

Morgan leaned forward. "What kind of note?"

"It was in the hand of Narses, the high chamberlain. I guess the basilissa was interested. She'd heard about the fibula—I don't know from where, but artifices like to gossip. She wanted it, but first, it needed to be appraised. I was supposed to find an auditor"—she looked up at Roldan—"but not from within the gens. That part was explicit. The transaction would be made at the Hippodrome, where Narses could watch."

"He was watching," Morgan said. "From his customary place. But why all of this evasion? Why couldn't the spado just deliver it himself?"

"I know little of arx intrigues. It seemed best not to ask questions."

Morgan gave her a level look. "A note appeared in your chamber, written by the high chamberlain, and you didn't once think to ask: *Why me?*"

"That can be a fatal question in this city. Besides"—she managed to look slightly uncomfortable—"I needed the money. What was I supposed to do? It was a large sum, and all I had to do was hand over an ugly brooch. I don't know why she wanted it. Maybe bees are in fashion now."

Morgan's eyes narrowed. "The basilissa could have any gem that she wished. Why would she send her most trusted advisor to buy your 'useless' fibula?"

The artifex stared at her pile of shining gears. "I thought—maybe—it had to do with me, not the bee. That it was because of my talent. I had the audacity to think that someone had noticed me. I was tired of making water features, and then this happened. What would you have had me do—ask the high chamberlain about his business, in front of the entire Hippodrome? I did what I was told and used the money to buy more parts. That's where my story ends."

"It lit up," Roldan said.

She looked at him. "What do you mean?"

"I showed it to a salamander. I've never seen a lar so interested in something made by human hands. She took my blood and gave me some of her fire. When it touched the fibula, the whole room filled with light."

She blinked. "The whole room?"

"We all saw it. I felt it."

"It's still possible to infuse machinae with a bit of power," she said. "Something to make them move on their own, to increase the life of their parts. An auditor would perceive it as a spark—nothing more. That's what I figured—" She shook her head. "Our ancestors could forge machinae that came alive. The process required a soul—or something—I don't really understand. But that art was lost."

"What about the basilissa's foxes?" Babieca asked. "Isn't she supposed to have two mechanical foxes who follow her about, like ladies in waiting? They breathe, and speak, and sometimes cast judgment on her enemies."

"I've never been to the Arx of Violets. I always assumed those machinae were just a story, like her movable throne."

Babieca turned to Morgan. "Have you seen the foxes?"

"Of course not. If the basilissa truly had machinae that walked and talked, do you think she'd let them wander around the battlements?"

"The point," Babieca continued, "is that some of them still exist. The clepsydra, the throne, maybe even the foxes. And this fibula. It didn't just make a spark—it practically burned the house down. Aren't you the tiniest bit curious about what it might do?"

"Of course I am," the artifex whispered. "But I could lose my head just for having this conversation with you."

"You must have examined it," Morgan pressed, "before

handing it over. You're a builder. Weren't you curious about how it was made?"

"I—" She stared at the table. "I only looked at it a few times. It seemed deceptively simple. But a tremendous amount of precision went into making it. And I think there was something inside. Perhaps a hidden mechanism."

"That hidden mechanism is on its way to the Arx of Violets right now," Morgan said. "It could be a weapon. It could be anything. All we know is that the high chamberlain wanted it appraised and delivered. Of course, everyone trusts a spado. Right?"

"What do you propose to do?" The artifex chuckled. "Knock on the basilissa's front door and ask if she has a moment to talk about her jewelry?"

Morgan managed to look uncomfortable. "We haven't quite smoothed out all the wrinkles in our plan."

"You don't have a bloody plan."

"At least we're not sitting in a caupona building water-powered birds," Babieca said.

The artifex started to say something sharp in response, then rubbed her eyes. "I'm so tired," she said, almost to herself. "Tired of making shit."

"Help us, then." Morgan touched her hand lightly. "Was there anything else in that note? A clue about who made the fibula, or what it might be for?"

"I don't know who made it," she snapped. "I received instructions about where and how to deliver it. That's all."

"Narses just left the note in your room?"

"I suppose. People are always coming and going. The caretaker has a set of keys to every cell. Someone could have slipped him something for the room key. Either way, it matters little. You don't cross Narses. He could have you thrown in the carcer with a snap of his fingers."

"Well—this is something. We know a bit more than we did earlier." Morgan rose. "Thank you. We won't take up any more of your time."

"You never told us your name," Babieca said.

"No. I didn't." She looked at Morgan. "Please don't come back here. I can't be involved in this."

"You already are," Morgan replied. "But I understand. We'll leave you in peace."

She picked up her lens and returned to studying one of the tablets. Roldan saw a slight tremor in her hand as she manipulated the glass. Then he heard a voice—it was the sleepy whisper of the salamander, rising like steam from the grill.

She knows more.

He started to say something in response, but then a faint snoring filled his ears. The salamander had drifted back to sleep. He followed Morgan and Babieca out of the tavern. The rain continued to blanket everything.

Babieca turned to him. "You had a look back there—a listening look. I've seen it before."

"The salamander spoke to me."

"I thought she was asleep."

"She woke up for a second."

"What did she say?" Morgan asked.

"'She knows more.'"

"I didn't need a fire lizard to tell me that. Let's go."

They still had some time to kill, so Babieca decided to play at the Seven Sages. It was busy when they got there. The original entertainment—a bit of mummery involving masks and dirty pantomimes—had evaporated at the last minute, and the crowd was restless. Babieca spoke briefly with the ale-wife, smiling and lightly touching her arm.

What's it like, he wondered, *to have a perpetual charm fountain? To get everything you want just by winking and knowing where to put your hands?*

He played a few ballads, then a more somber piece, something Roldan hadn't heard before. He was all focus as he played, his fingers gliding across the strings. He stared at something that only he could see. The notes seemed frozen with melancholy, but the barest trace of a smile played across his face the whole time. When he finished, there was an unexpectedly still moment, a beat of confusion, during which nobody moved or breathed. Roldan heard the hearth chewing through tinder. He saw smoke hanging in wreaths made of untouchable blue petals. Even the salamander had crawled from the oven to listen, cocking her wrinkled red ear toward the music. Finally, as if waking from a dream, the crowd began to cheer.

That was Morgan's cue. She stood up and made her way around the common room, collecting money. Roldan knew that she hated dealing with soused and surly men, but the music had pacified them somewhat. They were always happier to part with coin when the collector was a pretty, dark-haired woman. If they got too fresh, she'd simply flash her hunting knife, reminding them that she knew how to gut large animals.

The sun was beginning to dip as they left the tavern. Roldan was nervous about visiting the basia. He wanted to see the meretrix again but didn't know what he should say. Talking with lares was easier, because they always got to the point. Besides, nobody else could hear their side of the conversation. Talking with people was a game whose rules escaped him, full of false moves and pieces that leapt when he wasn't looking.

"I liked that last song," he said to Babieca, as they walked toward the Subura. "Was it one of your own compositions?"

He chuckled. "My compositions are shit. That was 'The Amber Tunica.' It's a bit obscure, and there's a lot of complex string work, so I was worried that I'd ruin it."

"You didn't. Everyone loved it."

He shrugged. "I made some mistakes. I always do."

"Your compositions aren't shit."

"How would you know? I've never played them in public."

"I just know."

The Subura was noisy and full. Vendors sold ale and sausages from popinae whose bars crowded the street. The rough music of fucking sounded from open casements, while streams of people made their way down blind alleys in search of indefinable pleasures. After nightfall, the streets became a dangerous labyrinth, but now they rang out with laughter,

obscenities, and the clamor of people in motion. "Fur!" The
cry was distinct. "Fur in the water!" Moments later, a boy in
rags burst from the entrance to the nearest balneum, running
as fast as he could. Two wet and naked men pursued him,
cursing as the cobblestones bit their tender feet. Nobody
reacted to the spectacle. Passing by the open door of the balneum, Roldan heard water, singing, and the faint, open-
handed slaps of the masseuse working over some tense body.

The road sloped as they neared the basiourm district,
which some called the wolf's den. *Lupa*, or she-wolf, was
slang for a female prostitute who belonged to no gens, working instead from a windowless cell barely large enough to
hold a stone cot. *Lupo*, the name for men who worked in the
same manner, had a sense more ironic than predatory: a
wolf who rolled over, once a few base coins had been
exchanged. Meretrices had a certain measure of status, but
lupae were seen as a class of fur, thieving through sex rather
than skullduggery. A well-known phrase had emerged to
describe their unsanctioned business. *Fucks unmasked.*

The largest basia was fronted in black marble. The main
building was two stories tall, and connected to nearby ten-
ements via a series of covered walkways. All in all, it must
have encompassed at least four separate structures. Women
and men lounged in various states of undress on patios,
drinking, fanning themselves, occasionally waving at passersby. Although the marble-fronted building was pristine,
its satellite structures were covered with graffiti. *Here I
focked Felicia. Viktor—fok well, fare well. Pharsia eats
women's middles.*

They approached the door to the basia. A miles was leaning against the wall, looking extremely bored. Light from
the setting sun flashed against her single bronze greave.
Roldan glanced at the chipped hilt of her sword and was
struck by recognition. She was the victor from the Hippodrome, the one who'd bested her opponent without hardly
trying. Now that she wasn't wearing a helm, he saw that she
had close-cropped hair and gray eyes.

Morgan cleared her throat. The miles looked up. She

didn't smile, but something like bare amusement played across her face. Morgan stared at her for a beat. She didn't say anything. It was as if she'd lost the ability to form words. Babieca stepped in front of her.

"Salve," he said. "We were hoping to visit this fine establishment."

She looked him up and down. "You're a nemo."

His smile wavered for a second. "Yes. We have coin to spend, though."

"Let's see it."

He handed her the pouch full of tavern booty. She opened it, counted the coins, then handed it back to him.

"This isn't enough to purchase a look from the worst meretrix in the basia. Get out of here. Come back once you've made something of yourselves."

"Ah—" Morgan had finally found her voice. "Domina Pendelia sent us. She mentioned that, as a personal favor to her, you might be able to let us in. We have an important matter to discuss with the mother and father of this house."

"Pendelia? What's that crafty bitch up to?"

"She said that you used to work for her—and that you still owe her something."

"I don't owe that woman a fur's turd."

"She seems to think differently."

The miles gave her a long look. Then she sighed. "I suppose she did help me when no one else would. She said that if I let you pass, we're square?"

"Exactly."

"Well—the house mother isn't here. She's at the arx, drinking nectar with the fucking basilissa herself. I can take you to speak with the father, although I can't promise that he'll give you more than a minute. The house is practically full tonight, and with Drauca gone, he's got twice the amount of work to do."

"We won't take long."

She shrugged. "All right. Come with me."

The miles led them through a narrow passage, which opened into a bright atrium with vaulted ceilings. The black marble floor was decorated in mosaics, some tasteful, others that made Roldan blush. Lush murals decorated the walls, depicting various pairs and threesomes engaged in passionate play. Musicians sat on recessed benches, playing citharae and cymbals, while a woman in a violet tunica sang something lovely and indecipherable. The syllables were liquid and reminded him of low, languorous purring. Her golden armbands clinked as she swayed in place, and the high ceilings gave her voice a wild echo.

They followed the miles down another chamber, which led to a smaller, more densely packed room. He saw two men whose tunicae were halfway undone, kissing against a pillar. One had a smooth chest, white and slightly flushed, while the other's body was dark-skinned and dusted with hair. Various others reclined on couches or sat on stone benches, drinking, touching, murmuring things to each other. A large woman was playing a drum, and beads of sweat gleamed on her cheeks as she pounded out the sinuous rhythm. People danced around her, barefoot and shining, wreaths in their hair and mead on their lips. The cadence thrummed across the ground, teasing Roldan's feet until he wanted to join in the dance. He was overdressed, though, and half-afraid of knocking someone over with his clumsy gyrations.

The miles pointed to an opening in the southern wall. "The father's office is through there. I can't promise he'll be in, though. He might be somewhere else entirely."

"That's fine," Morgan replied. "We don't mind waiting."

"I'll stay here," Babieca said, eyeing the drummer. "I think I can do some serious investigating in this room. You and Roldan go on ahead."

"You're unbelievable."

"I'll let you know if anything turns up," he said with a grin.

Roldan and Morgan passed through the entrance. They walked down a hallway lit by multicolored lamps. Roldan could still hear the drum, and more faintly, moaning. He wondered where the actual cells were. They were probably grand, with carved wooden beds and braziers to keep the clients warm. He saw a few glittering coins, discarded in the corner. They were tokens stamped with lurid images, rendering words unnecessary. Language didn't matter when your coins possessed an extensive vocabulary.

The hallway terminated in a door, which was slightly ajar. Cautiously, Morgan pushed it open, revealing a modest room with a stone desk in one corner and a small tabularium in the other. Unable to stop himself, Roldan walked over to examine the books and scrolls. They were various: poetry, legal texts, a few scientific treatises, and heavy tomes that were probably meant for recording accounts. A mural on the far wall depicted a group of naked undinae, locked in suggestive embraces beneath aquamarine waves.

"So this is the office of a house father," Morgan said. "Not nearly as tacky as I thought it would be. I was expecting phalloi everywhere, perhaps a chandelier of crystal nipples."

"We used to have one of those," a voice said from the doorway, "until it decapitated one of our clients. Then we had to settle for less dangerous lighting."

He stood in the entrance, wearing a black tunica and a silver mask. The garment was sleeveless, and Roldan tried not to stare at his arms. He looked down instead, at the house father's bare legs, which proved to be equally distracting. Finally, he settled for staring at an invisible point directly above the man's shoulder, which seemed safe, if a bit odd.

"I'm Felix," he said, walking over to the desk. "The father of this house."

"We know who you are." The words came out before Roldan could stop them.

Felix smiled. Then he sat down and poured himself a cup of wine. "Of course. Everyone knows who I am."

Morgan gave him an expectant look. Although she normally would have taken charge, she was clearly leaving this up to him. Roldan wasn't sure if the trust was well placed. Carefully, he withdrew the knife and placed it on the desk. "I believe this is yours."

Felix looked at the knife. In the lamplight, Roldan could see that a faint scar crossed his eyebrow, like silver thread, exposing the flesh beneath. The meretrix pursed his lips, as if considering something. His brown eyes flicked from the knife back to Roldan.

"You're mistaken," he said. "This isn't mine."

Roldan frowned. "You left it."

"No. The knife isn't mine. It's yours."

"I don't understand."

Felix picked up the knife. "It's beautiful. That's what makes it so deadly. People see it and think it's merely decorative. But the hilt is perfectly weighted, and the blade is tempered steel, folded dozens of times by a master smith. With just a few pounds of pressure, you could shear off a finger."

"I doubt it." His voice trembled slightly. "I'm awful at shearing, cutting, anything related to disarticulation. I'm a listener, not a fighter."

"Everyone has to fight eventually. Here. Give me your hand."

Roldan extended his hand, willing it not to shake. Felix touched his palm lightly. The tips of his fingers were cool.

"Soft," he said. "But soft doesn't necessarily mean weak."

He placed the knife in Roldan's palm. Gently, he curled his fingers around Roldan's own until they were both holding the knife. He smiled.

"See? It was practically made for you."

"But—it's yours."

"No. I've never seen this blade in my life."

"Oh? What about us? Not even a hint of recognition?"

He looked at Roldan, still smiling. Then he took his hand away. Roldan nearly dropped the knife—which was heavier than he'd expected—but managed to hold on to it.

"Perhaps a hint," Felix said. "I see a lot of people in my line of work, though. You'll have to forgive me if I don't remember every face."

"This is a fun game and all," Morgan replied, "but we didn't just come here so that you could give him a knife. We were hoping you had some answers."

"In this house, an answer is like a kiss. Both have their price."

"We need to know more about the fibula," Roldan said.

"I have no idea what you're talking about."

"I'm sorry if your memory fails you," Morgan interjected, "but have you considered the possibility that this thing could be dangerous? Brooches don't normally catch fire when an auditor touches them."

"Sounds like your bauble put on quite a show."

Morgan approached the desk. "This isn't a game. There's something very odd about that thing. It may have some kind of hidden mechanism."

"Are you an expert in machinae? A rare skill for a sagittarius."

"You saw how it lit up," Roldan said. "Maybe you can't admit it, but I remember the look in your eyes. Nobody could forget something like that."

Felix looked slightly uncomfortable. "I'm not sure what your intentions are, but let me give you some advice. Don't meddle in the affairs of the basilissa."

"Or we'll end up a foot shorter. Right, we've heard that before." Morgan put both her hands on the desk and leaned forward. "Only I don't quite believe it. I may not know much about the woman who controls Anfractus, but I do know that she isn't her mother. She's not going to feed us to lions for being insolent."

"You're right about one thing—you don't know much about her."

"I don't know much about you, either, but I can still tell that you're spinning lies like spider-silk right now. And someone of your status would only do that if he were afraid of something. Or someone."

He stared at her coldly but said nothing.

"Felix," Roldan said. "If the fibula truly is dangerous, we need to warn her."

"Why would the basilissa order something that might harm her?"

"She didn't order it. Narses did."

His eyes widened.

"Didn't know that, did you?" Morgan stepped back. "It looks like we aren't the only ones in the dark."

"You're certain that the chamberlain is involved?"

"Absolutely."

"Can you prove it?"

"Absolutely not. But trust us—he hired the artifex to deliver it. He arranged for us to meet in the Hippodrome. His hands are all over this."

Felix stared at the desk for a moment, lost in thought. Then he folded his hands and looked at them. His expression was, if anything, wary.

"All I know," he said, "is that it has something to do with a celebration that she's having, two nights from now. She has an important guest coming, and everyone who craves her favor will be there. I don't fully understand how this item relates to the festival, but she told me to ensure that it was safely delivered."

"Did you mention to her that it was glowing like an unholy candle?" Morgan asked. "That seems like something she'd be interested in knowing."

"I didn't give it to her directly." He looked slightly cross. "We were supposed to meet, but then it turned out that she was indisposed. A young spado met with me instead, and I gave him the item in question."

"I wouldn't call Narses young."

"It wasn't him. It was one of his servants—a youth. I didn't catch his name."

Morgan gave him an incredulous look. "You handed it over to some freshly gelded boy, without any questions?"

"He bore the seal of Narses. And he seemed very efficient." A note of defensiveness crept into his voice. "I had to return to this house, to ensure that all was in order. The basilissa wasn't going to see me, and I didn't have time to interrogate an unknown spado."

"Impressive. You clearly have a mind for espionage."

"Careful, sagittarius."

"This is all going in a crazy direction," Roldan said.

"Let's pause for a moment and think about how we might proceed."

"Can you get us into the banquet?" Morgan asked.

Felix laughed. "Don't be absurd. Even the greenest spado—a freshly gelded boy, as you so poetically put it—would recognize that you didn't belong there."

"Not if we were dressed for the part."

Roldan looked at her in surprise. "I thought you didn't really want to pursue this. Babieca and I don't have much to lose, but the arx is where you work."

"I think I'm done with the battlements. This seems far more satisfying. If Felix could just procure us some fancy tunicae—"

"I'm not about to dress you so that you can infiltrate the basilissa's banquet. Even with the right clothes and the proper ciphers, you'd never get close to her. And what would your presence even accomplish?"

"Nobody else is prepared for the possibility of chaos or carnage," Morgan replied. "Except for maybe Narses. If something terrible does happen, we'd be the only ones there with a chance of stopping it."

"You're not even a company."

"Yes we are," Roldan said. "We may not look it—we may be only three—but this is our quest. This is our time. And you know it. Why give me the knife, otherwise?"

Felix looked at him thoughtfully. He was about to say something when Babieca stumbled through the doorway, half-naked, mead dripping from his hair. The drummer appeared behind him, one of her breasts exposed, along with a man wearing nothing but a torque.

"Sorry to interrupt," Babieca said. "The sun's going down, and someone puked on my tunica. We'd better go."

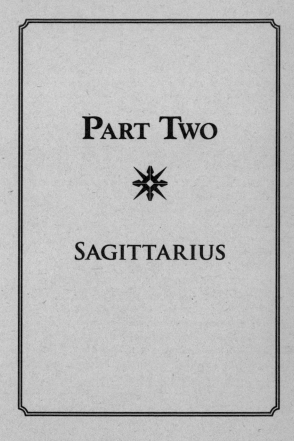

PART TWO

SAGITTARIUS

1

SHELBY WOKE UP DAMP AND ANGRY. SHE'D sweated through the comforter again. It was the old dream, the one where her mother pushed her out the window. *You have to be more independent,* she said, before shoving her into empty space. It took forever to fall. Like Alice, she passed all sorts of people in slow motion. Andrew sat on a cloud, reading intently. He still noticed her out of the corner of his eye, though, and waved as she fell. Carl had tied himself to a flock of birds and was heading west. He gave her a thumbs-up, then returned his attention to the foldout map he'd been studying. Finally, she saw Professor Laclos, addressing a cirrus cloud. *You're spread too thin,* he was saying. *You need to consolidate. Did you do the reading?*

She checked her pockets, looking for anything that might break her fall. But she only had a pack of Starburst, a rusted arrow, and her ATM card. As she was pondering what to do with these things, the ground rushed up. She laughed. Then she screamed. Then she opened her eyes. It was hard to move— she'd rolled herself up in the comforter, like a piece of sushi. For a moment, all she could do was lie there, breathing hard.

The phone rang. She managed to free one arm.

"Hello?"

"Morning." It was Andrew. "Were you falling again?"

"What else is new?"

"There's a coffee waiting for you. I said your name was Carlotta, because I thought it sounded empowering, so the barista wrote it on your cup."

"I can't believe you've already left the house."

"It's nine forty-five. I'm already downstairs."

Shelby looked at the clock. "Motherfuckit. My alarm failed."

"Did you set it?"

She peered at the clock's innocent display. There was no little bell icon. The alarm switch was in the off position.

"Why do you ask questions that you already know the answer to?"

"We've all done it. I once slept all day because I set my alarm to nine P.M."

"That sounds amazing."

"It was."

Shelby got out of bed slowly, as if pulling herself from quicksand. The comforter was still partially wrapped around her feet. Shaking it off, she looked in the hamper.

"Oh no."

"What?"

"These sweaters are bullshit."

"It's too hot for a sweater."

"You know it's my instinct to layer." She dug to the bottom. "What would you think about a black sweater over my Earl of Rochester shirt?"

"Do you mean the sweater with the safety pin—"

"That's in the back. You can barely see it."

"Well, the shirt is solid. Will you be wearing pants?"

"No. I'll be naked from the waist down."

"That should increase attendance in your tutorial."

She pulled on a pair of jeans. There was an ink stain on the knee, but she decided not to mention this. "I think I should wear the boots."

"They give you blisters."

"But the pain makes me stand up straight. That's good for something, right?"

"Just wear comfortable shoes."

"Sorry. You cut out there for a second, or maybe you were talking crazy and I didn't understand you. I'll be right back—I have to put on Band-Aids."

She eventually made it downstairs, still shoving papers into her bag. Andrew gave her the coffee, which she took with her free hand.

"Remember when you were drinking tea?"

"Nobody likes a smartass."

"I sincerely hope that isn't true."

The first time they'd spoken to each other was at a colloquium series called Liminal Encounters, which had attracted visiting speakers from several major schools. Shelby and Andrew had come for the food, along with a clutch of graduate students from various disciplines. They lingered on the edges of the room, waiting for the crowd to part so they could strike the buffet table. She'd seen Andrew before but had never talked to him. Unlike the other members of her cohort, he didn't cleave to a particular group. In fact, she'd only ever seen him alone, grading papers, reading, or frowning at a computer screen. Once, while walking past the shared TA office, she thought she heard him talking to someone. But when she looked in, he was alone, staring out the window.

They both reached the buffet at the same moment. He looked at the warming tray full of Swedish meatballs, then at her.

"Four left," he said. "Want to split them?"

"That's okay. You can have them."

"I only want two. Four will make me sluggish, and I have to get some writing done later tonight." He studied the buffet. "If we take four meatballs, two mini quiches, a Nanaimo bar, and a handful of carrot sticks, we'll basically have dinner for two."

She blinked. "Are you asking me out?"

"I'm asking you to share carrot sticks with me on a balcony."

"That—actually sounds pretty good."

"Okay. You grab the quiches and the roughage. I'll get the protein." He began parceling meatballs into a napkin. "On second thought—get the Nanaimo bar first. They go fast."

"I'm on it."

A few minutes later, they were ducking through the window of the TA office, which led to a concrete patio. Cigarette butts and spiderwebs decorated the corners. Andrew divided the food equally, and they ate in companionable silence.

"So—you do Restoration stuff."

Shelby wiped her mouth with the napkin. The mini quiche was sitting like a rock in her stomach, but at least the hunger pangs were gone. "Basically. I'm studying Margaret Cavendish, the Duchess of Newcastle."

"Wasn't she crazy?"

"Crazy like a seventeenth-century fox."

He laughed. "I liked *The Convent of Pleasure*. Especially the part where the women keep trying different sauces, and each one is better than the last."

"Yeah. It was a rock-and-roll convent." Shelby smiled. "She said that her plays were her children. Her paper bodies, she called them. And when she committed them to the flames, it was like burning her own flesh and blood."

"So—crazy."

"Any woman who wrote during that time was considered crazy."

"What drew you to her work?"

"She wrote these letters to an imaginary friend. They're so lively, and bitchy, and they feel—I don't know"—she stared at a spiderweb—"like they were written to me, or something. When she complains about annoying children, and bad makeup, and ignorant people who make her feel small—I understand where she's coming from. Plus, we both love boiled chicken and suffer from panic attacks."

"Fair enough."

"What are you studying?"

"These two Anglo-Saxon poems. *Wulf and Eadwacer* and *The Wife's Lament*."

"That's intense. Old English makes my mouth hurt."

"Sometimes I speak it in my sleep." He smiled. "So many fricatives."

"Who are you working with?"

"Natasha Black."

"She scares me. She's always wearing a pantsuit."

"I just pretend that she's Bea Arthur."

"That might actually work."

"It does. What about you?"

"I'm cross-appointed. Trish Marsden in Gender Studies, and Victor Laclos in English. I feel like they're always having brunch to complain about me."

"I doubt they think about us at all."

Andrew was looking at her strangely. "Where did you go?"

Shelby blinked. She realized that she was standing in the middle of Scarth Street Mall, holding her coffee. A few feet away from her, a guy was doing some sort of act with a crystal ball, letting it dance across his fingers. A boom box positioned behind him played "Orinoco Flow." She studied the crystal's progress for a second, then returned her gaze to Andrew. He was frowning slightly, as if she were a questionable footnote.

"Sorry. I was just remembering that time we shared meatballs on the patio. We had to use a letter opener to cut the Nanaimo bar."

"It was either that or go back for a knife, and that room was way too full of critical energy. I didn't want to get sucked into a conversation about being post-human."

She sipped her coffee. "When you asked me to dinner, I thought for a second that you might be into me."

"You were extremely interesting."

"Nobody knew anything about you."

"That's because nobody asked."

They walked down to Broad Street to pick up Carl. Their

conversation drifted, like a slightly intoxicated person wandering through a department store. After a while, Andrew began saying "Right" to everything, then simply nodding, which made her realize that he'd checked out. He was studying bright, misspelled signs, vague promises stenciled on windows, or anything else that caught his attention. He had a loose tether, but Shelby had grown accustomed to it. As they continued in silence, she thought about how odd their group was—their company, if you could call it that. Andrew was an introvert who studied poems that didn't rhyme, sawtoothed alliteration and white space that had slept on vellum for a thousand years. Carl was a material historian with the self confidence of a male pageant contestant, twirling his baton in any direction.

Who am I? A slightly damaged girl who likes to read old letters? A girl in serious debt, with a shelf full of Broadview editions but only three usable plates?

Why be a grad student? It was such a boring question, but they all asked it, every day—while drinking (why), while smoking (why), while fucking (why), while sleeping (zzz), the question followed them around on little cat feet. *Why am I doing this?* Andrew probably knew, and his answer had notations. Carl might not have known, but he went through the motions beautifully. In the end, he'd fall into something. He'd become a cute archivist or pilot some kind of project that involved ground-penetrating radar. He'd find a lost Byzantine button hoard and land a front-page feature in *National Geographic*, looking happily smudged in his sweat-stained vest and cargo pants.

Her research wasn't about to appear in the pages of *Restoration Culture*. Nobody gave a shit about how closely she was reading the letters of Margaret Cavendish. Academia was about finding something obscure, something lost at sea or misfiled in the British Library. In Restoration circles, the work of Cavendish had become feminist-mainstream. Unless she could unearth a lost play, a libretto, or a lock of Margaret's hair, chances were slim that she'd be able to parlay her research into a job. The seventeenth century was still the misfit kid, the period that scholars politely avoided on their way to the Victorian era. Not sexy enough to be Early Modern, not functional enough to be Medieval, it hung out behind the bleachers, watching girls while comparing expansion packs.

Maybe her mother had been right. She should have studied something that applied to her, something immediate and political. But Shelby couldn't help it. She loved reading about syphilis and dancing masters. Just the thought of Early English Books Online gave her a thrill, as if she were a country wife visiting the big city for the first time. Why couldn't she hang out with the vizards and the wise orange-girls? Why hadn't she received an urgent letter? Unopened collection notices from SaskTel were not the same thing.

Her mother had it all figured out. She had an office inside a translucent crystal cliff, with built-in bookshelves and art on the walls. She wrote action plans, returned calls, and attended meetings for something called "executive of council," which Shelby thought must be some kind of admiral in vermilion robes. When her mother used the word *community*, she wasn't referring to a sitcom or a gaming website.

"How big is a silenus?"

The question jolted her. "What's with you and parking lately?"

"Nobody's listening. How big are they—on average?"

She didn't want to think about silenoi. "I don't know. The size of a sasquatch, I guess. Taller than the average human, and about three times as strong."

"You're the only one of us who's actually seen one up close. You must still remember a few physical characteristics."

"I wasn't exactly paying attention to its height." For a moment, she could see the rain on the battlements and smell the creature's dank hair. "Why do you need to know?"

"I was just curious."

"Andrew. I think we're past cryptic."

"Okay. Just—humor me for a second."

"Our friendship is based on mutual humor."

"You know what I mean." He wasn't looking at her. That was a bad sign. It meant that his brain was working furiously. "A silenus could easily"—she felt him hesitate over the word *kill*—"incapacitate a human. They hunt with weapons, but they could probably take down a fully grown adult with bare hands. Correct?"

Fingers locked around her throat. Its eyes were a feverish green in the darkness. She'd expected its gaze to be purely animal. Inside, a terrifying intelligence regarded her, cold and patient, as the hands continued to squeeze.

"Yeah." It came out as a half whisper. "Easily."

"You were lucky to survive."

"Morgan was lucky. I—barely remember. Why are you making me talk about this?"

"I'm sorry. It's just—"

"Andrew."

His left hand was lightly drumming against his pant leg. He was anxious. Finally, he stared at a spot directly above her nose.

"What if silenoi were hunting on this side of the park?"

"That's impossible."

"Is it? We don't really know what they're capable of."

"Look. Your crazy salamander dreams aren't coming true. Things can't cross over to this side of the park."

"You don't know that."

Shelby looked around to make sure that they were actually alone. Then, lowering her voice, she turned back to Andrew. "The silenoi are a wild gens. They only exist on the other side of the park. They're *characters*—just like the ones that we play. Some of them choose to live in the wild, beyond Anfractus. But most of them are part-time players, like us. The moment they return to this side, they go back to being normal people."

"How do you know that we're just playing characters? It doesn't feel that way. I know that parts of Roldan are rattling around inside me."

"If silenoi were prowling the city of Regina, we'd hear about it."

Carl walked through the doors. "What are you guys talking about?"

"Andrew thinks that there's a pack of sasquatch on the loose."

"What?"

Andrew stared furiously at the ground. "Forget about it."

"Pack of sasquatch. That's a great name for a band." Carl reached into his pocket and withdrew a granola bar. "Here. Provisions for the journey."

Andrew blinked, then unwrapped it. They kept walking in silence, while Carl texted and Andrew chewed. Shelby took the opportunity to study Carl. His thumbs moved rapidly, spinning narrative, as he avoided potholes and weird things on the ground. He'd packed an extra granola bar, knowing that Andrew had probably forgotten to eat. Whenever his blood sugar bottomed out, he had a more difficult time concentrating than usual. Carl's gesture had a maternal trace to it, but without the pointedness of giving someone a juice box or a handful of vanilla wafers. It reminded her of the time she'd seen a ten-year-old boy flip over his handlebars in the park. His friends had gathered around him, gently probing his injuries while keeping their expressions neutral, like medical interns.

Carl was attractive, but not her type, as far as guys went. His beard did nothing for her, and she couldn't understand why he wore hiking boots everywhere. They lived in a flat province, and he rarely left his apartment unless he was renting a movie or visiting campus. He spoke Spanish, but she'd only ever heard him yelling at his sister or pleading—at least it sounded like pleading—with his mother, who would call randomly to ask him about his girlfriend. A year ago, he'd made up a girlfriend named Tammy, and they were always on the verge of getting serious.

Ingrid was her type. Ingrid, whose gray eyes made her ache slightly, as if she had a low-grade fever. Andrew had actually spoken to her. Shelby had tried to flirt via texting, but after rereading all of her texts for the eighth time, she realized that they were awkward and pretentious, not flirty.

She'd kept using the word *interrogate*, as if she were a police officer instead of a graduate student. She'd admitted that *The Fountain* was her favorite movie to watch while high—especially during the scene when Hugh Jackman was eating tree bark—yet Ingrid had merely typed *hehe* in response. She was probably a mature, straight-edge academic with her shit fully in order, someone who wouldn't drop everything to get stoned and watch a three-hour film about time travel and Mayan spirit possession.

They crossed over to Wascana Parkway. The sky was a painful blue, and without a scrap of shade to be found, they were all sweating. Andrew was the most sensibly dressed, in a House Stark T-shirt, broken-down jeans, and sneakers. He refused to wear a hat, though, on the grounds that he could never get it to sit perfectly on his head. Carl was sweating the most, but his clothes already looked dirty, so the overall effect was minimal. Shelby worried that her armpits now smelled like the opposite of sugar and spice.

The park bloomed on their right side, already full of couples jogging in tandem. Beyond the tree line, Wascana Lake boiled in light, its polluted striae hidden by patches of reflected sky. The sun made everything look natural. It was only by night that the contours of the true park grew visible, teased out by long-suffering lamps and the glowing eyes of ducks. All those blind corners and moonlit sutures that made you reach out your hand and push, even when you knew that it wasn't the best idea. That was how you found yourself naked in a strange alley, wondering where the grass had gone.

"My students have a quiz today," Carl said, breaking up her thoughts. "There's a bonus question on the English long-bow. If any of them get it, I'll be fucking elated."

Shelby turned to Andrew. "What's the lecture on again?"

He actually managed to look hurt. "*The Wanderer.* The first stanza."

"Ugh. Well, it's in the reader. I'll skim it before Laclos arrives."

"You're supposed to break it down line by line for the students in tutorial."

"That's why you're going to explain it."

"And if I refuse?"

"You'd never refuse the chance to describe that poem to me."

"This feels like scholarly blackmail."

"It's not blackmail when you love explaining things."

Carl laughed. "She's got you over an Old English barrel."

"I suppose she does."

They arrived at the Innovation Centre and refilled their coffee cups. As promised, Andrew recited the first stanza of *The Wanderer* to her while eating a strawberry-sensation muffin. By the time he reached *hrimcealde sæ*, his dire-wolf was covered in icing sugar. They parted with Carl at the entrance to the lecture hall. A fair number of students were present, clustered in texting clouds near the back or sleeping near the front. When Professor Laclos arrived, about half of them looked up, while the rest kept staring at their phones. He talked about the nameless wanderer, whose heart was full of rime-cold secrets. He drew connections between the ancient poem and present-day political exile. When all else failed, he showed a picture of the Sutton Hoo helm and talked about warfare. Several of the male students perked up at this.

Shelby looked over to see Andrew silently mouthing syllables to himself, as if he were part of an ecstatic rite. He grinned as he bit fricatives and tongued plosives. He was tasting English origins, mulling over words ripped from bronze-smelling hoards. Words that had slept beneath centuries of dust and small rain, sharp and bright as scale mail. Poetry had never moved her quite so much as drama. She loved the shock of a colloquy, the beat and treble of words doing what they had to on stage. Andrew preferred the echo of poems buried alive.

After the lecture was done, they met with Professor Laclos to discuss the midterm. He was still referred to as a "recent hire," which marked him as a newly minted PhD. He had the youthful energy to survive a thousand-year survey course, but Shelby couldn't help but notice the deep lines under his eyes or the fact that his collar was lopsided. His desk was covered in books, interoffice envelopes, and photocopied materials of every sort. Whenever he finished a sentence, he would take a sip of coffee, then begin in the middle of the next sentence. Andrew wrote down everything, while Shelby found herself nodding and smiling gently, as if she were listening to one of her younger cousins talk about Dora the Explorer.

When the meeting was over, they went to their respective tutorials. Shelby taught on the dreaded mezzanine floor, which had no coffee stand and could be accessed only via a hidden staircase in the academic quadrangle. Her classroom was next to something called the C.L.A.W. lab, which must have dealt with the study of robotics, or zoology. She liked her Monday tutorial group. They were lively and asked questions. Nearly half of them did the reading, and the rest were more than happy to offer random contributions that kept the discussion afloat. Shelby had become adept at linking every tangent back to the assigned reading—*Jersey Shore*, Ryan Gosling, farm narratives, tales of personal growth, and invectives against homework. She compared 3D technology to illuminated manuscripts, and *Fifty Shades of Grey* to filthy Old English riddles (*no, that's not a skullcap or a loaf of bread*).

She spent the last fifteen minutes of class fielding questions about the midterm, which resulted in a wildly entangled diagram on the board. They ran out of time just as she was drawing a weird arrow that led nowhere. The students filed out, while Shelby tried to minimize the chalk damage to her black T-shirt. Ultimately, chalk dust was better than marker fumes, which had once persuaded her to assign dioramas in a class that focused on the Marquis de Sade.

Andrew was waiting at their customary bench. He gave her a maple-dip doughnut, which she took greedily. Her pastry levels had already reached a dangerous low.

"How was it?"

She mainlined the doughnut. "Not bad. We took turns pronouncing the more difficult words. George—the guy who loves *Dragon Age*—went on this tangent about falchions, but I pulled him right back." She made a vague motion with her hands. "I'm miming the tractor beam of focus that I used on him."

"Impressive."

"What heroics did you resort to?"

"I spent about a half hour explaining what a thorn was, and why it's different from a yogh. That was pretty much all they could handle. Then we did a midterm flowchart. I had to assure one student that there'd be no questions about computer science. I guess she's been having nightmares about that particular test."

"When's Carl finished?"

"I believe his tutorial ends at twelve thirty."

"You don't believe. You have his schedule memorized."

"Yours as well."

"Right. I'm just saying—why equivocate?"

"I'm not."

"Yeah, you are."

He shrugged. "Most people are comforted by a bit of uncertainty. If you act like you know everything, they get suspicious."

"I'm not those people. Neither is Carl."

"Maybe I'd like to pretend that I don't have arrays of data in my head. That I'm a normal person who actually forgets things."

"You forget things all the time. That's why your power always goes out."

"I don't mean paying bills. I mean words, songs, routines, memories. Most days, I feel like a flash drive that's about to explode."

She kissed his cheek. "Don't worry. If you explode, we'll rebuild you. But only if you promise not to enslave us immediately after."

"I fail to see the humor in that."

"Sorry. Don't enslave us. Hashtag sarcasm."

Before he could reply, she stood up. "I'm going to see my mother."

"Will you need anything afterward? Drugs? Sour candies? *Archie* comics?"

"I should be fine."

"I'll bring all of them just in case."

"Thanks. Also, text me in twenty minutes, then again five minutes later. I want her to think that I have a raging social life."

"On it."

She walked past the residence towers and across campus, back to Wascana Parkway. There was a wrought-iron buffalo mural in the green patch across the street, which gradually gave way to the marshy lake edge. She skirted the lake, crossing what felt like an acre of flattened grass, until she found herself at the entrance to First Peoples University. Light gripped the edifice, making it burn in place. The walls were smooth and transparent. She walked in and took the stairs to the second floor, where her mother's office was. Mel Kingsley was the head of Cree Languages. Her office seemed to glow. A south-facing window captured the endless sky, while plants thrived in every corner. She sat at her desk, listening to a pair of noise-canceling headphones. Above the desk hung a clock in Cree that read fifteen minutes to *peyakosap*.

Shelby moved a pile of books and sat down across from her. Mel was oblivious, eyes still closed, mouthing something. Shelby was struck by how beautiful her mother was. Her hair, now patterned with gray, hung across her shoulder in a long braid. She wore turquoise earrings in the shape of parrots and a sleeveless blouse. Shelby's skin was light and freckled, but her mother's was olive. She smelled of aloe, with the slightest hint of nicotine. When Shelby was little, she'd deployed tactics of shame designed to force her mother to quit smoking. She would hide her cigarettes, complain about her breath, and cough whenever she entered the room. *I just want you to live, Mama,* she used to plead. Over the years, Mel had cut back, and now Shelby let it slide. Although she'd never admit it, the whisper of smoke that clung to her mother's skin had become familiar, even comforting.

She finally noticed Shelby. Smiling, she put down the headphones. "Hello, dear. Were you teaching today?"

"Yeah. I just finished a tutorial on Old English poetry."

"You know, we really need teaching assistants for Introduction to First Nations Studies. We're in the middle of a crisis."

"I know, Mom."

"What's your schedule like next semester?"

"My supervisor's teaching a course on Restoration playwrights. It's upper division, so I'd actually be able to give a lecture."

She made a face. "You know so much about that genre. Wouldn't it be interesting to learn something new? I can lend you—"

"I've already got stacks of reading."

"Just one book. I know it's here somewhere—the new Qwo-Li Driskill. I think it's going to be pretty controversial."

"That isn't on my reading list."

"It should be."

Shelby closed her eyes. "And we're back here already. I've barely sat down, so that's got to be some kind of record."

Mel gave her a long look. "You're an adult. I understand that. You can study whatever you want."

"I'd like to record you saying that."

"Sweetheart. I respect that you want to be different. I think that—what's her name—Margerie Cacklefish—"

"*Margaret Cavendish.* She was a freaking duchess, Mom."

"Whatever. Her work has a certain appeal—if you enjoy listening to an aristocrat complaining for hundreds of pages. I'm just saying that there's other literature out there, writing that's a bit closer to home."

"You mean native writing."

"Obviously."

"Mom, I love native writing. I read it all the time. But it's not what I study."

"I just don't understand—"

Shelby raised her hands. "You don't understand because you want me to be like you. I'm not like you. I can't learn six different dialects and give papers on Swampy Cree folk-lore. Maybe that makes me a traitor, but I don't know what else to say. I like reading about sex in carriages, notes at the opera, suitors who carry around their own ladders. None of it's close to me—none of it ever happened to me—but I wish it had. Do you get that?"

Mel folded her hands. "Not really. I love you, though."

"I'm sorry."

"Will you at least take this? It's a cutting-edge anthology—"

"Mom, for the love of—"

Mel placed the volume in Shelby's hand. "You don't have to read it. I'll feel better just knowing that it's in your possession. That you might accidentally open it up one day."

"Fine." She put the volume in her bag. "I'll add it to the tower. I've almost reached the point where I can turn my library books into functional furniture."

"That sounds dangerous."

"A guy on the Internet did it with FedEx boxes. Why can't I do it with hardcovers?"

"Boxes aren't liable to crush you. Maybe we should go shopping for some appropriate surfaces. I haven't seen your place in a while—are you still using the oven as a drawer?"

"No. You were right about that being a terrible idea."

"I'm glad you listen to me sometimes."

Shelby squeezed her mother's hand. "I always listen. I just reserve the right to make my own dumbass mistakes."

"At least let me buy you a new bookshelf. And silver-ware."

"I have silverware."

"I don't believe you. Come for dinner tomorrow, and you can raid my cupboards. I'll make spinach salad."

"You know I can't resist bacon bits." Shelby stood. "I'll text you later."

"You're so much faster than me when you text. I misspell things—it's embarrassing."

Shelby smiled. "Nah. You're better at it than you think."

She left her mother's office and walked into the fierce

sunlight. Halfway across the field, she took off her shoes and socks, letting the dry grass crunch beneath her toes. The sky devoured her from all sides. When she reached the shade, Andrew would be waiting for her, with sour candies and a double digest. Smiling, she broke into a run.

2

TODAY WOULD BELONG TO THE BATTLEMENTS.
Morgan pressed a palm against the familiar stones of her
alley. Currents of green moss tickled her lifeline. Naked,
she let the hot air settle over her shoulders. She could hear
the sounds of the city, breathing close, but here she remained
untouchable. She wondered what it must be like for Roldan,
who could hear the lares muttering at his feet, or for Babieca,
whose mind tipped with melodies. All she could hear was
the city settling, and above, the racket of gulls. They probably expected her to hear the sigh of arrows, the complaint
of the bow as it bent to her will. She heard none of these
things, though. Only the frayed edge of a voice that she
couldn't quite recognize, pronouncing the same word over
and over. She heard it among leaves and between notes,
over the white silence of worms decaying in street pools,
louder than the constant fizz of flies around drying meat. The
word was a drum sounding far away. It meant nothing and
everything, and she'd stopped trying to understand it. Like
a name, it was something she lived with.

The sagittarii were the eyes of Anfractus. They saw everything from their stone aviary, high atop the Arx of Violets.

Like gargoyles between the crenellations, they scanned the intramural space beyond the city that bled into forest. The silenoi were the only true threat in that direction, and they could never take the city. Night hunts kept them sated, for the most part. There was always the possibility of invaders from beyond the sea, but in her two years on the battlements, Morgan had only seen a handful of vessels willing to brave the fierce nexus where the rivers met. The city had never depended on sea trade. It had never depended on anything, really. It seemed to graze on some invisible substance, growing and perspiring without any obvious source of nourishment. There must have been other cities like it, but she'd only heard them spoken of quietly, like the dead.

Morgan pulled the bricks out of her wall. The bundle was untouched, like always. The city swarmed with furs, but none of them had ever wandered down this particular alley. No soul had discovered the hairline crack in the wall, the loose bricks that could be moved aside to reveal the humid cell of her belongings. The bundle smelled of moss and weathered stone, cradled in its knot of darkness. *We all have our cells and bundles,* she thought. *Our untouchable alleys, the only safe spaces on a dangerous board.* She looked up. Something must be watching from above, keeping track of all those blind corners. It stood to reason. Something must have arranged those stones, calculated those cracks where light and shade met like accidental animals. Morgan reached as far as she could into the darkness of the crack, but beyond the bundle, there was nothing. Just currents of warm air.

She dressed in a light leather lorica, knotting her rust-colored cloak over one shoulder. Her quarrel was light, but the flexible sinew case retained its shape and was crush-proof. Seen from the top down, it resembled a cut pomegranate, with holes for barbed, brass-toothed, and trilobe arrows. Her short bow, edged in horn, felt familiar in her hands. The core was made of polished bone, and her fingers knew every groove. She liked the idea that every part of the weapon had once been alive. The miles liked to brag about how they

kept the city safe, but it was the bow, not the sword, that
protected Anfractus. Whatever might come for them, she'd
be the first to see it. Not that she usually saw anything other
than smoke, gull fights, or the dance of rooftop cats. If there
was an enemy, it knew how to stay hidden. Perhaps it would
devour them from below rather than above. Arrows would
be useless in that case. The furs would have to protect them.
She couldn't imagine them emerging from their underground warrens, like perfectly blind moles, carrying broken
knives. But anything was possible.

Morgan walked toward the clepsydra. Even approaching
from a distance, she could hear the din of its gears and the
noise of people gathering around it. People lazed on the rims
of fountains, while link-boys hurried by with crucial wax
tablets. Wagons rolled along deep ruts cut into the road, and
the smell of animals was thick. Flies clustered everywhere,
glistening like layers of black fish eggs on hide and stone
alike. The street-level popinae had already begun to fill up,
and people lined the stone bars, drinking wine and spooning
hot chickpeas from wooden bowls. Morgan could hear the
owners cursing as they reached into the round stone ovens.
Many of the customers were well into their cups, in spite of
the early hour. An aging meretrix sat at one of the nearby
bars, eating spiced cabbage. Her mask was gilded in opals,
and between bites, she dabbed her lips with the corner of a
fine napkin.

Cold whores of the mind, someone had once called the
meretrices. Those who rose above the level of the cheap cell
were treated with an odd mixture of dignity and mistrust.
Polished and educated, they still weren't allowed to forget
the den of wolves from which they'd risen. Certainly they
had power and status, but they would always be lupae,
wolves who'd formerly prowled the stone circuits of the
necropolis. They'd stood beneath the night-flowering plants,
calling themselves glass-mongers, hairdressers, match-
sellers. Those upon whom Fortuna smiled were accepted
by the parents of a basia, given lessons in everything from
seduction to ancient languages. But Fortuna didn't smile

often. Most had to fight for their masks, and nobody would fail to point out the scars of that struggle.

The older meretrix caught Morgan looking at her. For a moment, she was frozen beneath the woman's green eyes. Her mask seemed to glow in the sun, until Morgan felt that she was looking at a face cut by sharp planes of light. Then she smiled, raising her cup slightly. Her lined hands were dark and beautiful. Morgan inclined her head politely, then hurried toward the great clock. Roldan and Babieca were waiting for her, beneath the water-driven wheel. As Roldan raised a hand in greeting, one of the carved spokes cast a shadow over him. Morgan looked up and saw that it was the aspect of constant change—the throw forever in motion.

"Are you sky-gazing today?" Roldan asked.

"It looks that way. I'll be alone mostly. It will give me the chance to ponder how absolutely terrible this plan is."

"There's a one-in-six chance that it will work," Babieca said. "Like all things here. I thought the"—he almost said *lupo*, but managed to stop himself—"the meretrix seemed to have faith in us."

"He has a name." Roldan spoke while studying the fountain. "Felix. There's no cause to keep reminding us of his profession."

"I met a lot of people that night. Some of their names escape me, so it's simpler to refer to them by their skill sets."

"What do you know about his skill set?"

"There's no time for this discussion," Morgan said. "We simply have to roll. And since I'm the only member of this company who actually has a die, that falls to me."

"Is this the part where you show it to us?"

"You should be so lucky." She turned back to Roldan. "We have a day until the basilissa's banquet. Felix can get you past the gates. I'll be somewhere close, but I need to remain hidden. If we run into each other, we've never met."

"I still think you should come in a dress," Babieca said. "Who's going to recognize you out of uniform?"

She gave him a long look. "Despite what you might think,

I am known to a few people in the Arx of Violets. Wearing something with layers of taffeta won't serve to disguise my face, and I'm certainly not qualified to go masked. I'll be more useful if I stay armed."

"You could fit a dagger in the right dress."

Morgan ignored this. "Roldan, how do you feel about your part?"

He was still staring at the fountain. "I understand what's expected."

"Babieca will pass for a courtier, if he doesn't drink too much. You, however, will not. Auditores make people nervous. The surest way to disappear into the scenery—"

"—is to become his cup-bearer. I grasp the plan."

"I think what Morgan may be alluding to," Babieca said, "is that cup-bearers must be silent and obedient. You're adept at the first part, but I wouldn't call you obedient by any stretch of the imagination."

"Am I so contrary?"

"Not necessarily. But you don't always listen, either. You get distracted by the lares whispering around you."

"I won't say anything to reveal us."

"That includes not exposing fallacies, drawing attention to lies, or pointing out that most of the people we'll meet are idiots. Your job is to be silent and keep the wine flowing. I won't be drinking much, although it will seem like I am."

"I've heard that before," Morgan said.

Roldan made no reply. He was lost in his own thoughts. There was no point in belaboring the issue. She'd have to trust him to play his part. Instinctively, her hand went to the collar of her lorica. Beneath the leather, she could feel the die around her neck. She'd won it after spending her first night on the battlements, alone, listening to the city below. At first, the noises had been indistinct. But after a few hours, they began to separate: love cries, imprecations, the song of coins, the pulse of lives moving down endless alleys. Near the end of her watch, she could distinguish between the sound of animals and the footsteps of the few silenoi who hunted along the darker streets. Even that high up, she felt vulnerable. They were, after all, her opposite on the dark die. They had arrows of their own.

There were several things that made her nervous about this plan. The first—which she didn't want to admit to Roldan—was that she didn't entirely trust Felix. Should the evening come crashing down around them, he was the one with the most to lose. It was a long and perilous plummet from the good graces of the basilissa. It was convenient to think that he cared for her, that he wanted to shield her from potential danger, but his part in this was still obscure. He knew more than he was willing to say, and Morgan didn't believe for an instant that he'd been a passive player thus far. He would turn on them if the situation worsened. Only a fool would do otherwise.

The second problem was knowing, unavoidably, that Narses was manipulating all of them in some way. The spadones ruled the arx, and he ruled them. What if he'd wanted them at the banquet from the very beginning? They could take the blame for whatever he had planned. Nobody positioned themselves against the Gens of Spadones, because it was like fighting an enemy who saw three moves ahead of you. They'd practically invented the board, and people were just stones that they nudged from square to square. They hunted their own way, different from the silenoi, but just as effective. They could destroy you with a tablet, a whisper, a poisoned ring, or a perpetual kiss dissolved in wine. Unlike the furs, who clung to certain standards of roguery, eunuchs dealt with everyone.

"Let's part," she said. "Earn some coins so that you'll have something to jingle at the banquet. Courtiers always jingle. While you're fleecing drunkards, I'll see what I can catch a glimpse of inside the arx. They'll be preparing like mad, and it shouldn't be hard to move relatively unseen through the halls. I may even catch a glimpse of the high chamberlain, or at least one of his shadows."

"I'm not an automaton, you know," Babieca replied. "My fingers are still raw from the last time I played."

"Trovadores are supposed to bleed for their art."

She walked away before he could respond. He'd play well—not because he wanted them to succeed, but because he was in love with music. His fingers had no choice. And if the crowd was too drunk to care, Roldan would persuade a salamander to make the lamps dance. That always loosened a bit of coin. She supposed that most people thought the lares were a kind of miracle, the only magic left. They made Morgan uneasy. She didn't like the hold that they had over Roldan, or the fact that they always did what they wanted. As queer little gods, they were powerful, but not to be trusted. She supposed that she'd be difficult as well if people tore down her lararium to reuse the pink marble, leaving her with nothing more than a scattering of crumb-dusted roadside shrines.

She walked along the edge of the market, which was no less crowded than the center. The tang of sulfur hit her nose, rising from the impluvium of the fullonica. She heard the clothes being beaten inside. There was a line of people waiting to drop off their laundry at the window. Underneath the sulfur, she smelled the urine that was used to fix colors. Morgan loved the idea that tunicae belonging to rich citizens were soaked in piss. Color required sacrifice. Hundreds of sea snails had perished for the red fringe on her gens-issued cloak. Thousands of madder berries were plucked for the cheaper scarlets, and a certain unoffending insect, when pulverized, yielded up the indigo currently in fashion.

As Morgan crossed the street, the smell changed to baking bread. She closed her eyes for a moment, standing before the pistrinum where she used to work. That was when she'd first arrived in the city and couldn't find a wage anywhere else. Now the rumble of the grinding stones made her feel oddly reassured. She'd enjoyed pouring grain into the neck of the hollow stone, although the smell of the mules that turned the mill was somewhat less appealing. Still, furs lingered nearby, hoping to steal a few rings of freshly baked bread. Her stomach did a flip, but she didn't want to brave the line. There was a free ration waiting for her at the arx—

not fresh by a long shot, but she couldn't argue with the price.

She needed a bath. Her tunica smelled fine, but the heat was making her sweat. It would be unseemly to visit the tower without bathing first. Fortuna didn't mind, but the sagittarii would wrinkle their noses and avoid her. Morgan headed to the Stabian baths, which were cheaper and less appointed than those in Vici Arces. You could still purchase food, receive a bracing massage, or visit the love cells in the next building. The entrance, floored in sea-green tesserae, offered a picture of sandals with the message *Bathing is a virtue*.

Morgan paid the attendant, then headed to the apodyterium to change. Men and women bathed during separate periods, which meant that there was a single room for changing. She undressed and placed her clothes in a stone cubicle, next to a picture of a leaping fish. Some women laughed at the dirty pictures on the opposite wall. Laughter deflected jealousy, and it was hard not to snicker at the painted man riding a double-ended dildo. Morgan glanced again at the fish, which would aid her in recalling where she'd left her clothes. Then she walked toward the tepidarium, beginning to relax as the damp air touched her skin.

Women sat on benches or stood beneath the window. Morgan recognized several dominae, laughing, trading stories, or merely watching each other from a calculated distance. The boiler in the next room warmed the walls, while a bronze chandelier cast heat from above. Morgan sat by herself for a while. She tried not to stare too openly at the women, even though scrutiny was never discouraged. A few gave her promising looks. *It's my gens that rouses them,* she thought. *Not me.*

After a while, she went to the caldarium. The hypocaust cooked everything from below, mystifying the mosaics with pliant air. The women nearby seemed hazy, as if she were looking at them through steamed glass. The hollow walls flickered and breathed in her ears. She crossed the platform in the center of the room, descending the worn steps that led to the pool. Swimming turned her into a radish. Outside, she could hear the din of weights coming from the palaestra. When she could no longer stand the heat, she rose and walked to the basin, pouring water from the round labrum over her head. A dark woman with pinned hair took the ladle from her, smiling. Morgan fled to the frigidarium to cool down. Then, returning to the change room, she dressed quickly and walked back outside.

As she approached the Arx of Violets, she noticed the growing presence of miles, perspiring beneath their scale loricae. They ignored her. The gens weren't exactly rivals, but each liked to cast aspersions at the other. The miles didn't respect the bow, seeing it as an auxiliary weapon at best, while the sagittarii considered themselves more versatile in combat. Miles were standing targets for the javelin, while sagittarii had freedom of movement and could bite at the edges of a phalanx indefinitely. One of the tasks of the miles was to cover the sagittarii, but when relations between them were especially strained, they might allow the enemy to pick off a few unlucky archers. It was best to stay polite.

She followed the road uphill until the crowded insulae gave way to boxwoods and flowering lemon trees. A steady stream of human and wagon traffic surrounded her. Ahead, she saw a gold-canopied litter being supported by four women. Courtiers liked to brag that litters came cheap, but the arabesques proved that this one wasn't. Morgan couldn't make out who was inside—only a gauze of light moving behind the curtains was visible. The line moved slowly, pressing against the stone walls on either side. Now that they were higher, she heard the hiss of the Iacto striking the rocks below. The harbor looked empty, but it was probably teeming with undinae that she couldn't see. Going down there was a wild throw. They might ignore you, tease you, or sing you to your death underwater.

The violets began as she neared the gates. At first they resembled fine purple napkins, then pennants, then curtains that flamed in the air. The first gate was entirely covered in them. The miles let her through with a bare nod, which was more than she usually got. The temperature dipped slightly as she walked beneath the first arch. The corridor narrowed, forcing the crowd to move slowly. Above them, sagittarii stood on platforms, their bows trained on the mass of visitors. They acknowledged her silently. The corridor took a sharp left turn, and Morgan found herself squeezed into a corner. She looked up and saw another group of sagittarii, crouched before murder-holes in the ceiling.

The corridor turned again, then opened into a reception area whose ceiling had been carved to resemble stalactites. It was supported on all sides by red horseshoe arches, engraved with delicate rhombuses. A group of meretrices were gathered around a reflecting pool, deep in conversation. A mock naval battle had been arranged with toy ships, bobbing like a spiral of painted apples. Morgan couldn't imagine a time when Anfractus would have had enough ships to form a navy. Now the porta was haunted. When the rare ship did arrive, it was ushered in and out as quickly as possible, like an unpopular relative. The water lares were unpredictable, and it was dangerous to wander about, even if you could see or hear them.

Morgan walked by an impluvium, feeling the heat of the sun from the open space above. The battlements would be cooking by now. The Tower of Sagittarii was busy when she got there. Sagittarii lingered on the stairs, comparing strings, eyeing one another. They were trained to be a pair of eyes, and for them, surveillance had grown habitual. She was breathing a bit quicker by the time she reached the top floor, awash in light from its bank of windows. Morgan knelt by the statue of Fortuna, lightly touching her wheel.

After paying her respects, Morgan descended the spiral staircase. The tower's undercroft was where they kept supplies. A sagittarius that she didn't recognize greeted her at the entrance to the chamber. She looked new. Morgan nodded to her, then stepped into the vaulted room full of weapons and missiles of every kind. Short recurved bows lay on shelves, while imported longbows were stacked carefully against the walls. Quivers plain and painted sat in recessed panels along the walls. Naked shafts were stacked, ominous little pyramids with their sharp heads piled above them. She saw all kinds of arrowheads: brass and iron, some slender as reeds, others like fat thorns. The half-moon heads, reserved for the arquites, were particularly devastating at close range.

Morgan exchanged her short bow for one of the flatter longbows, nicknamed the *battlements bastard*. It took everything she had just to string it, using her boot as a kind of fulcrum, and the effort reminded her that she should have visited the palaestra. She swapped out her arrows for a more piercing bouquet, then placed her own bow on a marked shelf, along with the others. It was just like visiting the baths, only there was no leaping fish painted on the wall. The longbow was heavy, and she tried to nod gracefully to the woman guarding the door as she left, but it came out as more of a grimace. She much preferred the short bow, especially on the rare occasions when she'd used it on horseback. When she turned to fire over one shoulder as the horse shot forward, she felt like death on the wind.

On her way to the battlements, Morgan reviewed the plan. It probably wouldn't work. They couldn't get close to the basilissa, not even if Felix drew her into conversation. There would be spadones behind every pillar, miles at every entrance, ready to seize upon anyone who didn't seem to belong. If Narses had singled them out, it meant that his loyal attendants were already their shadows. Morgan didn't sense that anyone was following her, but the arx was full of hidden places, and sagittarii weren't the only ones who'd been trained to move quietly. She looked up at the patterned stonework of the ceiling, expecting to see a pair of eyes. She saw only colored stalactites, which didn't mean that nobody was there. Living among lares had accustomed her to the presence of invisible things.

Lost in thought, Morgan nearly walked into a girl when she rounded the corner. They surprised each other. The girl, about ten years of age, wore a saffron-dyed tunic with a trapezoidal belt covered in stones. One of her earrings, a web of pearls, had gotten caught in her wild black hair, and she was trying to untangle it. When she saw Morgan, she froze for a second. Then her expression faded to a kind of disinterest.

"Oh. It's only one of you."

Morgan inclined her head. "Eminence. May I offer you assistance?"

Eumachia was the daughter of the basilissa. Technically, she shouldn't have been wandering the halls of the arx, but few had the nerve to stop her. The girl had never taken much of an interest in her mother's affairs.

"I doubt it," she replied. "Unless you're an excellent fox hunter. Propertius's hiding somewhere. Probably in the walls."

Like Babieca, Morgan had heard of the basilissa's foxes but had never seen them. As far as she understood, one of their tasks was to keep an eye on Eumachia. Once, she'd almost heard what might have been brass paws on the stone floor, but there'd been nothing there. It made her anxious to think of mechanical foxes hiding in the walls. That was just as disconcerting as the stalactites with eyes.

"I'm afraid that I've got the wrong bow for it. I'd only end up piercing one of your mother's tapestries."

"That's fine. I work better alone."

"Very good, Your Highness. May Fortuna bless your hunt."

"And your watch."

For a moment, Eumachia looked far wiser than her ten years should have allowed. Then she smiled and kept walking. Morgan watched her recede, a frail yellow flame in search of a clockwork animal. If his gears made any noise against the stones, Morgan was sure that the girl would detect it. Like her mother, she had excellent hearing.

Finally, she climbed up to the battlements. The sun was high, and the blasted stone shimmered uncertainly before her. Anfractus boiled over with sound and smoke. Morgan took a seat by her favorite crenellation. She placed the longbow beside her. This was where she'd been sitting that first night, when she heard the noise that didn't belong. The same spot where she'd almost died, blood streaming from her head as she groped for a weapon in the dark. She would always remember the hunter that had stepped out of thin air. Green eyes and cloven feet.

Morgan touched the die once more.

She'd never thought of using it until now.

3

Nôsisim.

Her grandmother was calling.

Nôsisim. Granddaughter.

Shelby opened her eyes. Light streamed in through the blinds, and she realized that it wasn't her grandmother's voice. Instead, it was a clash of ravens, which seemed to be happening on the roof of a nearby building. Shadows moved down the wall, flickering across her posters. The screaming of the ravens filled up every part of the room. Shelby tossed away the comforter and stood up. Her legs were sore. For a moment, she wasn't sure why. Then she remembered her watch last night. Even though nothing had climbed up the battlements, she'd remained tense, fingers itching to grab an arrow. Sometimes her bow felt like a missing limb. She didn't need it here, and probably couldn't even string it. Morgan was stronger than her. She had proper instincts, while Shelby got lost in the supermarket.

The bow didn't belong, but she missed it. For some reason, it was easier to remember Anfractus when she was back home. The other way around was much trickier, because the park took control of them. Sometimes, when she was there, a fragment would return. But it was hard to interpret, like scattered memories after a night of heavy drinking. Maybe citizens lost those memories completely. Shelby understood the appeal of starting over in a place whose rules you could comprehend. The park was logical. The prairies were not. A silenus might eat you, but he wouldn't force you to talk about building a stadium with a retractable roof.

Her phone was blinking. She had two missed texts from Andrew. The first was a screenshot from the episode of *The Borgias* that he'd been watching. It was a close-up of Jeremy Irons looking enraged. The second was a description of what he'd just had for breakfast: coffee, saltines with peanut butter, and a Kozy Shack tapioca pudding. She called him on speakerphone while searching the bedroom for something to wear. He answered while she was pulling on the same jeans that she'd worn for the last two days. They didn't smell yet, and most academics had poor pattern recognition, so she doubted that anyone would notice.

"Hey. What's that noise?"

"Raven fight. Sounds like it's happening on the roof of the comic store."

"Who's winning?"

She peered through the blinds. "I can't see anything. I can only hear them, and they're both pretty fired up."

"Did you get that screenshot?"

"Yeah. What was going on?"

"Jeremy Irons was just raging at everyone in that episode. His papal disapproval was crushing. Even Lucrezia got the stinkeye."

"How many episodes did you watch last night?"

"Three. Then I lost consciousness."

"My sleep was bullshit." She didn't mention the sound of her grandmother's voice. It wasn't the first time that she'd heard *nohkô* in her dreams. "Then I woke up to the raven smack-down. I wonder how long it's been going on for."

"Maybe they're fighting over a graphic novel."

"It's weird to see them in the city. In my head, there's this rivalry between them and the geese, which is why they don't hang out by Wascana Lake."

"They might also be wary of the lake's radioactivity."

"It's contaminated, not radioactive."

"Are you kidding? We've all heard about the three-eyed fish. That sort of thing has to be the product of gamma rays."

Wascana Creek was dammed in 1883, which made the false lake. In the 1930s, the city drained and then deepened the lake, as part of a make-work project. Now it was surrounded by nine kilometers of park, designed to complement the university. The idea of a false lake girdling a false park seemed odd. Maybe that was why she'd been drawn to it at first. That, and the fact that many of its features—including plaques, walkways, and a contained island—reminded her of playing Myst. Nothing about Wascana felt entirely natural. The trees were barely teenagers; the lake wasn't even supposed to be there, and the bridge that crossed it was ornamented with terra-cotta buffalo heads gazing at the profile of Queen Victoria. Before she arrived, this had all been *Oscana*, pile of bones, named for the buffalo skeletons that covered the ground.

"Where are you now?"

"Just passing the light sabers."

The light sabers were giant blinking sculptures that had been installed across from Victoria Park, along with a series of hollow rectangles that she'd originally thought were ineffective trash bins. The facing street had also been closed to traffic, but the city's answer to this was simply to create a detour using flowerpots, which only confused most drivers. They would slow down and stare at the path of pots, as if it were a group of will-o'-the-wisps attempting to lead them astray. The old traffic lights, rather than being removed, were simply taped up and left in their original position. Strange casualties of the renovation, they had no advice to offer.

"Oh, man. I need seven minutes. Maybe twelve."

"Sure. I'll be in Tramp's."

"You can finally buy that doll."

There was a pulse of cold silence on the phone. "He's not a doll. He's a chamberlain Skeksi action figure with movable parts."

"I'll see you in a bit."

Fifteen minutes later, she made it to the hallway, which smelled like baking tofu. The Deli Llama was preparing its lunch menu. She checked the mail: only a bill from Sask-Power telling her what a valued customer she was. They would have valued her more if she didn't carry a perpetual balance on her account. When she got to the comic store, Andrew was among the toys sealed in their plastic habitats. There were endless variations of Milla Jovovich from *Resident Evil*, along with superhero busts and obscure Japanese products that she couldn't identify. Andrew was examining his fantasy figurine of choice, as if he hadn't already memorized every inch of it.

"Just buy it," Shelby said.

"I should, right? I deserve him."

"Absolutely."

"Except that he's twenty-nine dollars."

"Really? Wow."

"He has a detachable outfit. Plus, he's limited edition."

"So buy it."

"I don't have twenty-nine dollars. I just used my student Visa to make a payment on my Canadian Tire card. I should be taking away some kind of lesson from this."

"Andrew, you've got years of relative poverty to come. That's not going to change. If this strange, demonic vulture-dude makes you happy, I think that you should buy him."

"Technically, he's from another planet. And he's not a vulture. The Skeksi and the Uru were once part of—"

"I'll kick in half if we don't have to talk about their origins."

He blinked. "Fair deal."

"I thought so."

They paid for the action figure, which Andrew placed

gently in his knapsack. Then they left the comic store, heading for Carl's place.

"If I had a real office," Andrew said, "instead of a shared TA space, I could put him on my desk to freak out students."

"Don't let go of that dream."

"Do you think we'll get jobs?"

"A grad student drops dead whenever you ask that question."

"I know it's a bleak market, but there's got to be something, right? We're smart. We've presented papers, and Carl has that book review."

"Not even my mother can help me find a job. I'm going to end up working at Chapters with an ironic name tag."

"It might be fun if we all worked there. We could trade off on reading books at the Storytime Pajama Party. Lately, their selection has been a bit too focused on the Rough Riders, and I'd like to throw some Dennis Lee into the mix."

"Let's make a pact," Shelby said. "If none of us have tenure-track jobs in the next four years, we'll invest in my library-slash-nightclub idea."

"I'm still not sure I get that."

"The club is on the first floor. The library is upstairs. Long-suffering partners can hang out there, along with the club kids who are tired and want to sober up. Obviously, there'd be no drinking among the stacks, and we'd have to pay the librarians more to work at night."

"How could they read with the racket downstairs?"

"We'd use thick floors and lots of insulation."

"I think you've been watching too much *Holmes on Homes*."

They stopped beneath the red awning directly below Carl's place. A steady stream of people went in and out of the adult video store. Shelby had gone in once or twice to look around, but their selection of lesbian erotica was designed for straight men: every video featured topless women kissing inexplicably on staircases, or in what appeared to be unfinished garages. They made strange kittenish sounds and didn't resemble any of the girls that she'd ever been with. Not that she'd been with a lot.

Carl emerged from the narrow door that led to the upstairs apartments. He was unshaven and looked tired.

"Bad sleep?" Shelby asked.

"My neighbor decided to break in his new karaoke machine around three A.M. I got to listen to a truly horrific version of 'Radar Love.'"

"Ouch. Well, let's get some coffee in you."

"It'll provide a good base for drinking later."

"I thought we were supposed to stay sharp," Andrew said. "Once the sun goes down here, we won't get much of a chance to rest."

"We're going to a fancy party, with more wine than any of us can possibly imagine. Drinking will help us fit in."

"Parking," Shelby murmured, although her heart wasn't in it.

"Not a single person is listening," Carl said. "They're glued to the screens."

"Whatever. Just don't sing. Promise me that."

"What if the spirit moves me?"

"You're there as an observer, not as a performer."

"What if a moment comes when—"

"I'll shoot you with an arrow."

"She really will," Andrew said. "I've seen her pretend-aim in your direction before, when you were being tedious."

Carl looked slightly uncertain. "But we're in the same company."

"A company requires four. We're in a sketchy threesome at best, and if you start crooning in front of the basilissa, I'll shoot you in the leg. Understood?"

"You're scary sometimes."

"Someone has to be."

They stopped at Sweet for a coffee. The old brick building was surrounded by a swath of construction. The proto-condos, their foundations exposed and scattered, reminded her of urban bones drying beneath the sun. All of this used to be *paskwâ*, and the buffalo were *paskwâwi-mostos*. Prai-

rie cows. That was one of her favorite Cree words. Because
she couldn't speak *nêhiyawéwin*, the words that she did
remember had the feel of bones to them, partially submerged
and out of context. Plains Cree was her grandmother's first
language, and her mother could also speak it with great
facility. The only complete phrase that Shelby knew was
Namôya nipakaski-nêhiyawân. Basically, it meant "My
Cree sucks."

Campus was fairly sedate when they arrived. Carl headed
toward History, while Andrew and Shelby made their customary circuit through the halls of Literature and Cultural
Studies. There was a line of students waiting outside the
graduate chair's office. Nobody was crying yet, but the day
had just begun. Everyone carried stacks of books with pho-
tocopies teetering on top. By Shelby's second year, she'd
learned to balance a tower of hardcovers, a travel mug, and
a purse, all without walking into anyone. Some students
employed luggage on wheels, making the narrow hallway
resemble an airport terminal. She preferred to carry her
things back to the library in old shopping bags, loading them
up until the plastic bit her palms.

Andrew had to print something out, so they stopped at
the computer lab. It was more of a small corridor than a *lab*,
which conveyed the sense of open space. This was a computer closet, with muttering fluorescent lights and a pile of
broken chairs in the corner. The warm space behind the
machines was covered in dead flies, and the air smelled of
cigarette smoke, pot, and academic desperation. Every
few months, a doctoral student would lose her shit and trash
the place. *Comps rage*, they called it, like a form of cabin
fever. Right now, the only other person there was an MA
student whose name Shelby had forgotten. Her thesis
had something to do with food and Fellini. She prepared
herself to say something friendly, but the woman's eyes were
glued to her computer screen. There was no sense in making
contact. She wouldn't have noticed if they set the place
on fire.

Andrew printed out an article, which he was clearly

excited about, since he could barely wait for it to appear. He touched each page as it came out of the printer, warm and inviting. She half-expected him to rub the pages against his cheek. Shelby couldn't remember a time when she'd had so much raw enthusiasm for research. She loved reading primary sources but also feared that her arguments were trite and unoriginal. Who was going to read her thesis? Did she even fucking have one? Andrew didn't seem to ask himself these questions—or, if he did, he asked them silently. It didn't bother him that scholars had been dissecting his poems for centuries, analyzing every glottal stop.

Someday, she would no longer feel like an imposter. She'd publish and buy conference scarves and get asked to review things. Like her mother, she'd have an office with sunlight, happy plants, a radio always tuned to CBC.

"You're pensive," Andrew said. "What's up?"

"I just never know if I belong here."

"You wear Restoration T-shirts. I think that should answer your question."

"Maybe I was supposed to become a travel agent."

"You're exactly where you should be." He glanced down at his phone. "Carl just texted us from the library."

"He's probably lost on the fifth floor again."

"It is pretty disorienting up there."

"He'll want a drink by now." She sighed. "I guess he's right. If we're going to"—she glanced once more at the other student, who still hadn't noticed them—"crash this party, so to speak, we might as well do some pre-drinking."

"Maybe we'll sober up when everything—you know—switches."

"I've tried that. It doesn't work."

"Too bad. It would be an amazing hangover cure."

Supposedly, the rules against "parking"—discussing the park during the day—had emerged to protect it from discovery. But most people weren't even listening. They were checking their e-mail, proofreading papers, and obsessing over arguments. If she suddenly began talking about lares and silenoi, they'd assume that she was referring to an RPG or some weird seminar on the ancient world. It was more likely that the nondisclosure rules had been invented to conceal those who actually visited the park, to ensure that companies didn't overhear each other. It was difficult to recognize people that you met in Anfractus and beyond. They looked and sounded different. She'd met Andrew and Carl by chance, but they were the only ones she had a relationship with on both sides. It was strange to think that anyone she met by day could be a completely different person by night, and she'd never know unless Fortuna decided to show her.

Nobody knew if it was the park that found you, or the other way around. Shelby had discovered it by accident, while walking along the paths of Wascana in the early hours of the morning. She'd been ruminating about an article, something to do with female stage presence in the Restoration. Now the critic's name escaped her, but at the time, she'd been thinking about the power of being looked at, the peculiar scrutiny exerted upon women who decided to appear publicly in the seventeenth century. Aphra Behn was called a prostitute for staging her plays and for daring to visit the theater at all. She was likened to the masked vizards and orange-girls who had sex behind the proscenium. She'd been thinking about fruits and offstage sex when, out of nowhere, a naked man stepped from the gazebo.

He couldn't see her, and she felt like the nymph Salmacis, getting an eyeful from her obscure vantage point. He was lightly muscled, with short hair and nice legs. His body steamed in spite of the cold, as if he'd just emerged from a tropical climate. His dick was matter-of-fact, a modifier dangling from dark curls. It didn't necessarily fill her with desire, but she wasn't looking away, either. As she watched in mute fascination, he walked over to a nearby tree and pulled a nylon drawstring bag from its depths. He untied the bag and withdrew a pile of clothes. In spite of his surroundings—a park in the middle of the night—he didn't seem to be in a hurry. He dressed casually, as if this were normal and he had nowhere else to be. Once his shoes were on, he swung the bag over his shoulder and walked toward the street.

Logic told her that he must have been crazy, but Shelby couldn't scrub his image from her mind. How had he stepped barefoot out of the darkness? Where had he come from, and why did she feel like this was something that he did all the time? She'd gone back to Wascana the next night in search of him. Although he didn't appear, she caught a glimpse of a woman running barefoot through the trees, clutching a pile of clothes to her chest. It took a few weeks of visiting and wandering, but eventually, she went down a certain path and ended up naked herself in an unfamiliar alley. That first time, there were no clothes tucked safely in the wall. She had to scale a low balcony to steal someone's tunica.

That had been nearly two years ago. Sometimes she lingered by the gazebo while Andrew and Carl were occupied, but he never reappeared. It wasn't until they walked into that empty house, years later, that she finally recognized him once more. The mask disguised his face, but she remembered the rest of his body. That must have been the last night that Felix returned to this world. After that, he became a citizen. She didn't trust him but couldn't really explain why. It felt now as if she'd gone too long without admitting that she knew him, or at least that she'd once seen his shadow getting dressed. It would only provoke Carl's own suspicions and possibly upset Andrew. It seemed better to say nothing.

They picked up Carl in the Department of History.

"We should toast Regina's Olympic rowing victory," he said. "Most of the history grads are already at Athena's."

"I've never known you to be patriotic," Shelby observed.

"I happen to think that both rowing and drinking are awesome. What's wrong with celebrating a prairie win? Maybe you're being antipatriotic, and it's my duty as a proper Canadian to keep your malaise from spreading."

"Just don't overdo it."

"I never really understood that phrase."

"Exactly what I'm talking about."

Athena's, located in the Student Union, was loud but not yet packed. Various televisions delivered instantaneous coverage of the games in London. Although it seemed perfectly functional, the upstairs of the pub had been closed for as long as she could remember. The hipster boys occupying leather couches reminded her of Sparkish from *The Country Wife*, who loved a fine spangle. Not much had changed since the Restoration. There were still sparks and bubbles, still fops, changelings, and manly women. But there were also student loans, and OkCupid, and thumb drives that contained their own gorgeous libraries.

They ordered a round and sat by the window. Shelby looked away for a moment, and when she returned her attention to the group, Carl had finished his first pint. She hadn't even seen him pick up the glass. He ordered another, and she gave him a look.

"Don't stinkeye me. I'll be good."

"I don't believe that."

"Let's take the emphasis off me for a second. Have you been making any progress with your online Sapphic flirtations?"

"Don't be a dick."

"I have a dick, therefore I am a dick."

"Lovely."

"Come on. Just tell us."

Andrew was staring out the window. She knew that he was partially listening, but he'd be no help in offering a distraction. His mind was chasing salamanders.

"I heard from her yesterday," she said carefully.

"Did you trade emoticons? They have ones that mean *hug* and *blush*. There must also be one for *scissor*—"

"You're disgusting. This conversation is over."

But Andrew chose that moment to come back into focus. "What did her message say?"

Carl grinned. "Good question. Let's get to the bottom of this."

"If you'd like," Andrew said, "you can focus him out. Just pretend that we're on the bus, and he's the crazy guy who carries around his own radio."

The waitress brought Carl's beer, which momentarily distracted him. Shelby turned to Andrew, trying to speak in a low voice. "She suggested that we have coffee."

"Holy shit." Carl ignored the beer. "Coffee is the entering wedge that leads to full-on social interaction. This sounds like real progress."

"It seems best to take things slow."

"Right. You should get to know each other, first. Then, once she's into you, find a tactful way to reveal how you stalked her in the library."

"It wasn't stalking."

"It most certainly was stalking, abetted by your own friend."

"I abetted nothing," Andrew said. "We barely spoke."

"Oh, there was a shitload of abetting. We both saw it happen." He turned to Shelby. "Now you've got a choice. You can hope that she never sees Andrew again, or come clean and tell her about your harmless sociopathy."

Shelby looked up at the bank of televisions, attempting to avoid him. One was tuned to the news and displayed a picture of a coyote. The sound was turned off, but she watched as they showed grainy footage of the park at night, followed by an interview with a stern police constable. Hadn't there been a death in Cape Breton a few years ago? Coyotes did kill people—it was rare, but it happened. Anything was more likely than Andrew's hypothesis. The idea of silenoi wandering around Wascana—as they wandered through the tangled alleys of Anfractus—made her blood run cold.

Before she could think of a reply, her phone started buzzing. Shelby clicked on the message, and saw that it was a text from her mother. *Bring dessert.*

"Fuck," she hissed. "I forgot about dinner."

"Dinner?" Carl looked interested. "I thought it was just coffee."

"No, not with her. With my mom and my grandma."

"Great. Count us in."

"You weren't invited."

"Your mom loves us. Andrew defrags her computer each time he visits, and I eliminate the need for leftovers by having thirds." He smiled with peculiar pride. "That's why she calls me her garburator."

"She calls you other things, too."

"Don't try to poison our relationship."

Shelby couldn't think of an excuse not to invite them both along. Her mother did enjoy Carl's endless stomach, and her grandmother loved the look of sharp focus on Andrew's face whenever she decided to tell stories. He would listen to her in captive wonder, like a child hearing *The Cat in the Hat* for the first time. They picked up a dessert from Safeway— something in the chocolate log family—and then walked over to the North Central neighborhood. Her mother and grandmother shared a house on the Piapot urban reserve. Her grandmother's garden was abuzz with sunflowers and prairie crocus.

"*Nôsisim.*" Her grandmother hugged her at the door. She was holding a cup of strong black tea, which she held at arm's length while they embraced. She drank tea all day long, which may have been why she slept so little. "*Tawâw.* Welcome home, sunshine."

"*Nohkô.* Good to see you."

She hugged Carl and Andrew in turn. Andrew didn't like most people touching him but made an exception for her grandmother.

"You made it." Her mom walked out of the kitchen, holding a yellow-checkered dish towel stained with meat sauce. "And you brought company. Hey, boys."

"Hello, Dr. Kingsley," they said politely, in unison.

"Mel is fine." She glanced at the plastic contained in Shelby's hand. "What is that?"

"A German chocolate log."

She looked skeptical. "Well, at least it's got icing."

They ate lasagna and garlic bread with fresh spinach

salad. Her mother threw the chocolate log in the oven, which made it change form slightly but wasn't a real improvement. Adding ice cream did the trick, though. After they'd cleared away the dishes, they drank mulled wine in the living room. Her grandmother told a story about her brother—known to Shelby as Uncle Pete—who sometimes washed his hair with toothpaste. "You could smell him coming a mile away," she said. "Not a single cavity in that man's hair."

Shelby didn't mean to glance at the clock, but she was wary about keeping track of the time. They had a long night ahead of them. Her mother led Andrew to the study, most likely to show him a conference paper that she was working on. Carl ran to the bathroom after his third cup of grog. Shelby was alone with her grandmother, which meant that she was being thoroughly and silently analyzed. She stared at her feet, in an attempt to hide her expression, but it was like trying to hide from the sun. Her grandmother, without looking up from a game of solitaire that she'd just begun with herself, asked:

"What is it?"

"What's what?"

"Don't what's what me. Something's bugging you."

"I'm fine, *nohkô*."

"You aren't."

She sighed. "I've just got stuff on my mind."

"School?"

"No. Other stuff."

She had no intention of saying anything about Ingrid. Her grandmother didn't pry into that part of her life, and although she probably wouldn't have cared that Shelby was interested in girls, that was no reason to volunteer the information.

"Did you hear me?"

Shelby blinked. "Sorry, did you say something, *nohkô*?"

"I meant in your dream. Did you hear me calling?"

She looked up sharply. Her grandmother was still paying attention to the cards, but a part of her also seemed to be looking directly at Shelby. Now she could hear the ravens fighting once more and, beneath their din, the bright wave of her grandmother's voice.

"Yes," she whispered.

"Good. I wasn't trying to be subtle."

"Why were you in my dreams?"

"Just checking on you. That's an old woman's prerogative."

"They make phones for that."

"The other way's always been easier for me. And for you."

"I'm not sure you're right about that."

"Heard me, didn't you?" She picked up a card. "All you need to remember is that I'm always with you."

"Mom does say that you're going to outlive all of us."

"*Okēýakiciskēsīsak!* That's not what I meant."

Shelby laughed. The word meant *little butt itcher*, and was something that her grandmother hadn't called her since she was little. It came from a Plains Cree story about Wīsahkēcâhk, who ate too many rose hips and suffered fiery consequences. Her grandmother only called her that when she was being a pain in the ass.

"I'm sorry," she said. "I know what you mean."

The older woman stared at the card that she'd drawn. Shelby couldn't see what suit it was, but her grandmother was studying it closely. Then she laid it facedown on the table and finally looked at Shelby.

"You're about to face a storm," she said. "You can't fight nature—it was here first, and it knows more than you. Best to be careful."

She didn't know what to say. Did her grandmother know something about where she went at night? Did she suspect what was really going on? Unlike her mother, who wrote essays on superstition and the spirit world, her grandmother actually seemed in tune with it. Maybe she really did understand. Shelby opened her mouth to say something, but just then, her mother and Andrew reappeared. He was holding a stack of books, no doubt thrust upon him. Carl returned with his mug refilled, which meant that he'd taken a detour through the kitchen. They all sat down and began talking.

But somehow, she was still alone with her grandmother. Both women listened to each other from across the room. They'd always shared a similar frequency. Her grandmother made no motion, but Shelby felt someone touch her hand, lightly.

Maykisikaw!

The ravens were yelling in her head.

Bad weather.

4

MORGAN DRESSED QUICKLY AND STEPPED OUT
of the alley. The banquet wouldn't start until midday, but
she needed to hit the ground running. There were too many
dice in the air for her liking: Narses, Felix, Domina Pendelia, and even the nameless artifex. She felt like a peon in
someone's game of acedrex, waiting for a glass elephant to
trample her. Those who spent their lives clinging like vines
to the arx had grown adept at playing games, while she was
still a neophyte. The problem was that Fortuna had invented
too many games, and citizens had added their own subtle
variations, trying to tip the wheel in their favor. Everything
depended on the lucky throw, the proper spin, the calculated
glide of one piece overtaking another. The die around her
neck felt like something that didn't belong to her, something
that she'd stolen, although she remembered exactly how
she'd earned it.

Maybe her parents had been better gamers. Like most
visitors who still crossed between worlds, she knew almost
nothing of her childhood. She supposed that once you
became a citizen, some of those memories returned, spilling
over the old ones. It was hard to think about that other world,

though, where she was weaponless. Her mind was sharp enough to perceive its outline, to recall that some part of her belonged there, but it was like peering through fogged glass. Much easier to think about the blind corners of Anfractus, the dangers large and small that waited for her beyond this protected corner. She returned to the dice. Narses, Felix, Domina Pendelia, the artifex. It was strange to think that the high chamberlain might be weighing them in a similar manner. Morgan, Roldan, Babieca. Not yet a company, but undeniably stronger and more resourceful as a group.

The basilissa wins all. That was an old saying. Fortuna had invented games to occupy those who stayed home from war. Acedrex was the noblest game, followed by latrinculi, alea, word strike, tables, and finally, dicing. The games made it possible to win your fortune through skill and deception rather than fighting. They threatened the power of the gens, yet everyone played them, because victory was intoxicating. The only rule, which had endured since the first acedrex figurines were carved, was *the basilissa wins all.* Nobody could play her and win, not even Narses. Perhaps not even Fortuna herself. But if that were the case, how had so many of the basilissa fallen by xamat, the fatal move? Why hadn't they seen it edging like a shadow toward their home space?

She walked to the forum. There were more wagons on the streets than usual, most of them carrying supplies for the banquet. The popinae were working overtime, and a huge crowd had already gathered around the pistrinum, hungry for bread. She met Babieca and Roldan by the clepsydra. Babieca seemed relaxed, but Roldan was pacing, wearing down a small circle of the cobblestones with his sandals. Before she could say anything, Babieca reached into his tunica, withdrawing a small tablet.

"What's that?"

"Read it. Domina Pendelia sends her sunniest greetings."

The tablet read simply: *Come at once.*

"We've no time for this."

"She did gain us access to the basia," Roldan said. "The least we can do is answer her summons and return the tablet."

"At any rate," Babieca added," we can start our libations at her place. She had some passable wine, if I remember."

"Isn't it a tad early for that?"

"Not in this city."

They both looked at her expectantly. Babieca could be defiant, but he still trusted her. Roldan listened to both of them, but ultimately, he considered her plans to be the most logical. If this scrawny near-company had a leader, it was her, regardless of whether she'd agreed to take up the position. As the only die-carrier among them, she had the power of the throw, the momentum to carry them forward, even if she'd never used it before.

Her bow fingers twitched. Arrows were easy—they had infinite forms, but she understood them. Bows were marvels of curvature and living tendon, breathing in her hands, ready to serve. But ultimately, they were still tools that she could manipulate and understand. Leadership was something else entirely. She felt blind and childish, as she had upon her arrival. Why did they trust her? Once, bleeding on the battlements, Morgan had narrowly danced away from the killing move. There was no guarantee that she'd ever be able to do it again.

"All right," she said. "But curb your drinking. We have to remain sharp."

"Like a dagger." Babieca grinned. "Or the stone in my sandal."

Morgan led them to Domina Pendelia's insula. The same man greeted them at the door and looked just as unimpressed to see them.

"Of course," he said thinly. "She's in the hortus."

"Is she angry?" Babieca asked.

For a second, the ghost of a smile crossed his lips. "You'll see."

They followed him through the atrium, which was in the process of being cleaned. Sunlight brushed their heads through the impluvium, bringing with it the tangle of burning city smells. The triclinium was set with trays of food, which Babieca looked at longingly. Morgan grabbed his elbow, steering him toward the row of peristyle columns that led outside. They found Domina Pendelia sitting impatiently in the hortus, wearing a pearl-studded tunica. Her hair was elevated by jeweled pins. When she saw them, she rose and gestured toward something on the small table in front of her.

"Can you explain this?"

It was a box, carved out of pale pink marble. The craftsmanship was otherworldly, and Morgan realized that it must have been carved by the gnomo. Various aspects of Fortuna decorated the wrought panels. On one side, she stood with her wheel, and on another, she crouched beneath a window, holding a dirk. That must have been how the furs saw her, as the architect of stealth.

Roldan stepped forward, examining the box without touching it. "Amazing," he said. "The gnomo has given you a peerless gift."

"The gift is locked," she said flatly. "I gave that creature a small fortune in marble, and this is what it produced: a box that I can't open. Is this a jest? Did the auditores plan this, so that they could snicker behind my back?"

Before Roldan could remind her that he wasn't yet an auditor, Morgan stepped forward. Domina Pendelia could make their lives unpleasant if she felt slighted.

"Domina," she said, "the ways of the lares are unfamiliar to us. Perhaps if you let Roldan take a look, he'll be able to open it for you."

Roldan gave her a wide-eyed look. "There's no guarantee that—"

"Just try," she whispered in his ear. "Otherwise, we might end up chained to the bitch's hypocaust and miss the banquet entirely."

Roldan blinked. "I'll see what I can do."

He sat at the table, placing his fingers over the box without touching it. Suddenly, he cocked his ear, as if listening to something. All that Morgan could hear was the wind in the flowers and the tapping of Domina Pendelia's nails against the stone.

"You're certain?" Roldan asked the air.

Domina Pendelia stared at him but said nothing.

Finally, he grasped one of the panels and turned it slowly, until it clicked. For a moment, Fortuna's wheel seemed to turn before her eyes. Then the lid of the box opened. Roldan reached in, withdrawing something.

"The gnomo says that the box is for you, Domina," he said. "But what's inside the box is for Morgan."

"What?" Both women pronounced the word at the same time.

Roldan opened his palm. Morgan saw that he was holding an obsidian arrowhead. It was shaped like a half-moon, which made her breath catch slightly. He handed her the arrowhead with exquisite care, as if it were alive. Morgan took it, surprised by how cold it was, and by how it barely weighed anything. She touched the tip of her finger to the half-moon's edge and drew it away sharply. A bead of blood appeared on her skin.

"You're telling me," Domina Pendelia said slowly, "that your crazy lar turned all of that marble into a pretty little box, just to hold *that*?"

"The box must be extremely valuable," Babieca volunteered. "Nobody else will have anything like it. As for the arrow—like you say, no one understands how lares think. You should just be happy that your insula has one. Gnomoi are good fortune."

She considered his words. "I suppose the box is unique."

Babieca smiled. "More than unique. Your neighbors will be screaming when they see what you have."

Domina Pendelia touched the box lightly, as if it might eat her hand or catch on fire at any moment. "You're right. The arrowhead was a strange gesture, but the vessel itself is beautiful. Gnomoi must have steady hands." She looked at Roldan. "They do have hands, don't they? I've never seen one."

"Nor have I," he admitted. "But yes, they do. I've felt them."

"That must be odd."

"To say the least."

Holding the box, she began to smile. "Yes. It will be a delight to show this off at the banquet. I'll need to change, though. Pearls and marble look cheap together."

"Wait." Morgan could feel this situation slipping wildly out of her control. "There's no need for you to accompany us."

"I've been planning for this night since I first received my invitation. Attendance is mandatory. And besides—I shan't be accompanying you. That would be ludicrous. You will accompany me."

"Aren't we already accompanying Felix?" Roldan murmured. "There must be some sort of social etiquette that dictates how many accompaniments can occur at the same time. Unless Felix decides to accompany—"

"The meretrix may vouch for you, but he'll forget you as soon as you pass the first gate," Domina Pendelia said. "That's their way. If you want to avoid suspicion, it makes far more sense for the two of you to accompany me." She pointed to Babieca. "You'll be my man-bracelet for the night. The baby auditor can be your cup-bearer."

Roldan sighed. "I see that some things never change."

"Man-bracelet?" Babieca looked mildly insulted. "I was to play the role of a petty dominus, not some lupo that you've bought for the night."

"Petty they will believe," she replied. "But dominus? No. If it makes you feel better, I can say that you're my cousin."

"That's somehow worse. And off-putting."

"Yet believable."

"She's right," Morgan admitted. "Felix's plan had some merits, but this is better."

"I'm glad that you've come around to my way of thinking, dear."

Morgan gave her a look. "I suppose you planned this from the start?"

"Don't put anything past me."

At this point, Morgan wasn't sure in whom she had less faith, the meretrix or the domina. You couldn't always choose your allies, though. Felix had something to lose, which made his treachery more likely, but Domina Pendelia had much to gain by arriving at the banquet in memorable style, with an entourage that would have the courtiers buzzing.

"Fine," she said. "Babieca, you're the cousin. Roldan—"

"Nothing has changed," he said, a trifle sullenly. "I understand."

Domina Pendelia touched his shoulder. "It's all right, sweetling. There's no shame in being an attendant. I'll even give you some new clothes—something with a nice fringe. And obviously those sandals will have to go. This is a party, not a necropolis."

"While you're sorting out the outfits," Babieca said, "I'll just pour myself a little something. I noticed a nice decanter in the triclinium."

"Stay away from my wine," the domina said. "First, both of you will need to bathe and get out of those filthy clothes. Follow me."

"What about Morgan?"

"She smells fine. And I assume that she won't be mingling with courtiers."

"That's okay. She hates fun." He turned to Roldan. "You're going to love her bath. There's a mosaic in the shape of undinae doing amazing things."

Domina Pendelia frowned. "When did you get a good look at my mosaic?"

"It's best that you don't let him answer that," Roldan said, following them both down the chamber that led to the bath. Morgan found herself alone in the atrium. She sat on one of the couches, trying to smooth out the wrinkles in her tunica. She'd never worn anything like Domina Pendelia's gem-studded gown before. The thought of dancing in layers of purple-dyed silk didn't totally repulse her, as she thought it might. Eventually, she got hungry and went to explore the spread of food in the triclinium. There were grapes and dried figs, to which she helped herself. There'd be no chance to eat at the banquet, so she might as well fortify herself now.

Eventually, Domina Pendelia emerged, followed by the

boys. Morgan was impressed by their transformation. Babieca wore a scarlet-dyed tunica with a black belt, and Roldan had on a green tunica, bordered in saffron. It looked slightly beyond the reach of a cup-bearer, and he was fiddling with the sleeves, which were a bit too long. Still, nobody would be paying attention to him, and he did look nice. The domina had changed into a dark blue stola with silver edgework along the bottom. Her hair was even higher, and she now wore a chalcedony brooch in the shape of a teardrop.

"Impressive," Morgan said. "New sandals, too. How much will we owe you for these fine things, Domina?"

She smiled archly. "That will depend on how the night ends. For now, you may consider them a gift. My contribution to your fledgling company."

Morgan had never heard the woman describe them as a company. Might she actually be investing in them? It seemed a bit premature, and nothing about Domina Pendelia's tone reassured her. Strange things happened every day, though. Brass foxes roamed the arx, while fountains whispered to the basilissa, or so they said. Why couldn't they trust this woman, who'd already given them several advantages? Sagittarii were taught to trust the natural world, which followed logical patterns. Animals could be ferocious, but they weren't irrational. People were the only animals who said one thing and meant another.

"We're ready," Domina Pendelia said. "I'm going by sedan, but the three of you should walk. I'll rejoin you at the gate."

Of course you will, Morgan thought.

They gave a head start to the domina—it took her a while to wrangle herself into the chair, and it would have been unseemly to arrive before her. Morgan hadn't heard of that particular piece of etiquette before. They made their way to the arx, joining the crowd of riders, wagons, and foot traffic already heading in that direction. There was a sharp division between those dressed in their finest and those who would actually be working tonight. Roldan kept tugging at his sleeves, until Babieca rolled them up. She had to admit that Babieca looked good in the tunica. He'd left his cithara in the alley, which decreased his chances of causing a spectacle. Maybe he would actually listen to her this time.

Felix waited for them near the gate. He stood on a curb, wearing his mask and a topaz tunica. Roldan wasn't looking at him, for some reason. He seemed to stare fixedly at a point just beyond Felix's right shoulder. Babieca looked him up and down but said nothing.

"Salve," Felix said. "Are you ready?"

"There's been a slight change of plans," a voice replied. They turned to see Domina Pendelia descending from her sedan. "The boys are with me. Wherever the sagittarius goes is her business, although I'd caution against hiding behind tapestries. They look pretty, but they won't protect you from a sword thrust."

"Domina Pendelia." Felix inclined his head. "I'd forgotten entirely that you were involved in this."

"I'm involved in everything. And weren't you planning to abandon these poor souls once you reached the atrium?"

"Not exactly." The fleeting expression of guilt on his face told Morgan that the domina had been right. "I would have kept them within reach."

"For shame. They're people, not pieces. It's rude to move someone from their home space without even asking them first."

"What side of this are you playing?"

"Every side." She took them both by the arm. "If these two can keep their heads, the night should pass amiably."

One of Roldan's sleeves had come down again. Felix fixed it. Roldan finally looked at him, but only for a second.

"Remember what we talked about," he said. "We're here to observe. If something goes wrong, the miles will take care of it."

"If you believed that," the domina said, "you'd never have invited these three. The miles don't know what's coming."

"And you do?"

She smiled. "I'm prepared for anything."

They approached the miles at the gate. Domina Pendelia announced them. The miles glanced at their tablets, then nodded, letting them through. Felix followed, and the miles didn't even consult their tablets. The presence of the meretrix was assumed. When they saw Morgan, they looked bored. Just another sagittarius. They waved her through without a second glance, and for once, she was happy to be invisible.

Felix fell into step beside her.

"You're the leader," he said, matter-of-factly.

"They tend to follow me, but I'm not sure I'd call myself that. You can't lead a non-company. I'm more of the head rabble-rouser."

"They listen to you, at any rate."

"What are you driving at?"

He gave her a look that she couldn't quite decipher. "Roldan has abilities that may be harmful to him. I think you should watch him carefully tonight. There will be a lot of competing powers present, invisible, but not inaudible—at least not to him."

"You think he's in danger?"

"I think he's vulnerable. That's all."

"Do you care for him?"

"I'm not sure I understand the question."

"I know that you do."

"I find him interesting. He has potential. I'm not boxing Fortuna, though. Running the basia with Drauca leaves me little time to pursue my own desires, whatever they might be."

"You gave him a present."

"A knife is utilitarian. It's no love token."

"Depends on the lover."

They passed under the first balcony. The number of sagittarii had doubled, and Morgan put up her hood to avoid being recognized. Although extra bows were always appreciated during events such as these, her presence wasn't technically required. If the arquites saw her, she might dispatch Morgan to the battlements. There was certainly no good reason for her to be skulking around the oecus, where most of the banquet would take place.

"We should part here," Felix said. "If you want a good vantage point—"

"I've got a nicely shadowed clerestory in mind," she said. "You aren't the only one familiar with the Arx of Violets."

"Of course." He gave her a small smile. "May Fortuna smile on you."

"And you."

She reached down to adjust her tunica. For a second, her finger grazed the outline of the obsidian arrowhead. Morgan looked up, and instead of Felix, she saw two blurry outlines standing before her. The first was recognizably the meretrix, but the second was a nude stranger without a mask. She peered at them both in confusion. Some part of her had seen the stranger before, but he was on the tip of her mind, like an annoying crumb. She blinked to clear her eyes, and Felix was a single image again.

They went in opposite directions. He was heading for the oecus, which would already be full of guests. Morgan's route was more circuitous. Keeping her hood up, she made use of the shadows, trying to avoid the glaring lamplight. The fewer people who recognized her, the better. Once, she heard a group of sagittarii approaching. She ducked behind a pillar, waiting for them to pass. They were all complaining about how they wouldn't see any of the banquet.

You could, she thought, *if you were willing to hide, like me.*

After they passed, she climbed to the second-story balcony. She followed it toward the oecus, until it began to widen. Morgan smelled smoke and delicious food. She found the corner that she'd been looking for. The stones held a whiff of piss. A broken lion's-head fountain was attached to the wall. Its dry basin was covered in dust, and one of the lion's ears had a crack in it. There were old rinds and mouse droppings on the floor. Nobody would think to watch the banquet from this spot.

She looked down, and for a moment, the dazzling scene

took her breath away. The oecus—where the basilissa normally held court on her pneumatic throne—had been converted into a space for dancing and pleasure. Courtiers, meretrices, and dominae circled each other, winking like small fires or bits of precious silk. Trestle tables had been set up, and they were covered with delicacies of every sort. There were silver trays with dormice rolled in honey, sausages grilling on braziers, and plates full of large spotted eggs with spiced yolk inside. Fish swam in hot sauce, next to rabbits decorated with caps and wings. There was a massive pig, roasted together with her babes still attached to her teats. Morgan assumed that some kind of birds had been sealed within the mother's body, and when the time was right, they would fly forth singing. Everyone loved that.

The basilissa sat on her throne, which was raised only a few feet high this time—a deferential gesture to the crowd. She was dressed in a tight-fitting chlamys, with gold-threaded shoes that turned up at the toes. Her diadem was encrusted with rubies and sardonyx. Two strands of pearls fell from it, dangling across both shoulders. In addition to that, she wore an emerald choker and belt of interlocking golden ovals. A ceremonial dagger hung from the belt, although Morgan couldn't imagine that she'd ever drawn it. She was surrounded by miles carrying swords and halberds.

Beyond them, spread out but still visible, was a ring of sagittarii. Their rust-colored cloaks made them resemble leaves that had only fallen haphazardly into a circle. The arquites wasn't there. Many of the bows were spread throughout the arx, to compensate for the dozens of miles who'd been diverted to this room. There was a slim chance that anything would get past the two rings of defense, but Morgan was still nervous. Her mind raced. Should she have brought a longbow instead? The short bow was faster and easier to string, but it wouldn't penetrate armor. The gnomo's arrowhead could do incredible damage, but even if her aim was true, she had only one of its kind. If she lost it, Roldan would go crazy. Surely it was bad fortune to misuse a gift from the lares.

Domina Pendelia and Babieca had found a space by one of the trestle tables. Roldan was dutifully holding a wine vessel. Babieca was caught up in conversation with a young spado, although she couldn't make out what they were saying. Behind them, a group of spadones were playing some game that involved green balls and a cup. Morgan scanned the room for Narses. He stood a short distance from the throne. Occasionally, he would lift a flagon to his mouth, but she could tell that he wasn't actually drinking from it.

If only Babieca were that clever.

She heard pipes. Then two giant silver platters were carried out, made in the likeness of Fortuna's wheels. The day wheel had six different types of food, corresponding to the six day gens. The spoke of the sagittarii held arrow-shaped pastries, while the spoke of the medica held wild cabbage, for encouraging digestion. The spoke of the spadones held raw bull testicles, which must have been the kitchen's idea of a joke. Narses did not appear amused. Morgan had to remind herself that not all spadones were completely gelded. Their desires often depended on how they'd been cut, and when. The night wheel had a stranger assortment of delicacies: blood-soaked grapes for assassins, swan necks for meretrices, and rinds for the furs who would sneak in after everyone was asleep.

Servants passed by with silver chafing dishes, plates full of olives and honeyed pastries, finger bowls with snow-chilled water. Bumpers of wine and mead cruised the oecus, as if the drinks themselves had grown wings. Morgan felt her stomach beginning to complain but ignored it. There'd be time to eat later, and she'd sampled enough of Domina Pendelia's food to at least keep herself awake. Still, it seemed unfair that she couldn't at least try one of the arrow-shaped pastries, which were dedicated to her gens.

"Are you enjoying the view?"

Morgan jumped. She hadn't heard anyone approach. She looked in both directions but saw nothing. Then she looked down. A mechanical fox sat at her feet. He was a marvel of gears and shining cogs. His eyes were two black orbs that swiveled in delicate cases. He raised one of his paws, and she watched in wonder as the hinges and gears articulated silently. His tail was an intricate chain that moved on its own. Those black eyes regarded her, and Morgan couldn't tell if she was looking at an automaton or something with a soul. It seemed wise to accept the latter possibility, so she inclined her head in a polite gesture. She wasn't sure exactly how to show deference to a fox.

"Hello. Are you Propertius?"

"How did you know? Most people can't tell me apart from Sulpicia, my sister."

"It was just a guess."

"You didn't answer my question."

She was suddenly aware of the fact that Propertius was, for all intents, a spy for his mistress. He would be analyzing whatever she said. As she looked at him now, it didn't seem as if he had any weapons or hidden abilities, but the fact that he could talk was sobering enough. Automatons could make noises and perform simple motions, but Propertius was a different thing entirely. His dark eyes watched her every move. His builder had given him the spark of life, and he was indisputably the oldest thing in this fortress. She needed to be careful.

"It all looks lovely from up here," she said.

"The rest of the sagittarii are below, or on the battlements."

"I'm—"

Morgan looked into his eyes. The lie that she'd been about to weave suddenly tangled in her mouth. Propertius had no expression, and that was somehow worse than a disapproving look. "I'm here to protect the basilissa," she admitted. "And my friends. I think something's going to happen tonight. I can't explain it, but I can feel it."

"You aren't supposed to be here."

"Not technically."

The fox seemed to consider this. He flicked an ear, and in the silence of the piss-stained clerestory, she heard his mechanism whisper. As she listened more closely, she could hear the various sounds of his articulations. His whole body sang.

"Propertius!"

It was Eumachia's voice. Morgan resisted the urge to swear. That was why she hadn't seen the basilissa's daughter below. She was fox hunting, as usual. The girl emerged from the shadows, wrinkling her nose as she got closer. "What is that—" Her eyes widened slightly when she saw Morgan. "Sagittarius, why are you here?"

"I've already asked her that," Propertius said. "Her reply was not particularly edifying, but I believe that we can trust her."

Eumachia drew closer to the edge of the balcony. She wore two smaller strands of pearls in her hair, to match those on her mother's diadem. Her stola, however, was dusty and even had holes in places. Fox hunting could be dirty work, it seemed.

"Look at them all," the girl said. "They don't even care that it's twilight. They'll stuff themselves until they burst all over each other, like rotten grapes."

"Why aren't you with them?" Morgan asked.

"Does it look like I belong there?"

"You're the daughter of the basilissa. You should be at her side."

"She has Narses for that." Eumachia's voice had a hint of anger. "She doesn't listen to me, anyhow. Not ever."

Morgan returned her attention to Roldan and Babieca. The former was filling the latter's cup, and looking fairly unimpressed about it. Domina Pendelia had maneuvered them into conversation with a courtier in a bright saffron tunica.

"Who are you looking at?" Eumachia asked. She leaned casually over the stone rim of the balcony, which made Morgan nervous. The last thing she needed was to explain how she'd let the daughter of the basilissa plummet onto Fortuna's wheels below.

"Nobody."

"Don't lie. You're looking at those three over there. I've seen that woman before, the one in the black dress."

"Have you?"

"She hangs around the atrium with the others. They never see me there. I listen to them talking about my mother."

"I'm sure they only say good things."

Eumachia fixed her with a look. "I'm nearly ten. Don't talk to me as if I were a baby."

Morgan suppressed a smile. "You're right. I'm sure you're old enough to understand that some people like to gossip and say foolish things."

"Not everything that they say is foolish." Suddenly she grinned. "Why don't we see what they're saying right now?"

"I have to stay here."

"That's fine. We can listen through the fountain."

"What?"

"Eumachia," the fox said sternly. "I showed you that trick in secret. You aren't supposed to share it with anyone."

"You said we could trust her."

His tail clinked against the ground. "I'm not right about everything."

"Come here," Eumachia said. "I'll show you. It takes practice, though."

She approached the dry fountain skeptically. It wasn't making any noise. How could it help them? She knew that some of the fountains in the arx had wondrous properties—they could pipe, or make mist, or display mechanical dramas—but the lion's head with the cracked ear didn't seem to have any obvious abilities.

"We have to wait until they get closer," Eumachia said. "There's a fountain below that connects to this one. Get ready to put your ear to the lion's mouth."

"I can't imagine that ever being good advice."

"They're getting closer—the loud one wants a pastry, and he's moving toward the fountain. Nearly there. All right, do it now. Do what I said."

Afraid that the fountain could bite her after all, Morgan carefully put her ear next to the lion's mouth. At first, she heard nothing. Then, faintly, as if from underground, Babieca's voice came floating up to her.

"—another honeyed dormouse."

"Stop drinking so much." That was Roldan.

"I'm fine."

"You're not. You're one cup away from obnoxious."

Another voice said something, but it was inaudible. Domina Pendelia must have been standing too far away from the fountain. They passed by, and the voices faded. Morgan stepped back and stared at Eumachia.

"Does every fountain in the arx do this?"

"No. Just the lion-headed ones."

"What an amazing device."

"Don't say that in front of Propertius. You'll hurt his feelings."

She turned to the fox. "I'm sorry. You're much more amazing."

"Obviously." He was paying attention to a brass paw.

"Oh, look," Eumachia breathed. "Here she comes."

Morgan felt herself snap to attention. It was the guest of the basilissa. Everyone in the room hushed as she entered, wearing a studded chlamys with a purple veil. She approached the throne. Morgan heard a rush of escaping steam, and the basilissa's pneumatic throne lowered until it was completely on the ground. She rose and stepped forward, her pearl strands casting shadows beneath the lamplight.

She reached out and gently lifted the woman's veil.

"Welcome, Pulcheria." Her voice rose in the sudden stillness of the oecus.

"Latona. You honor me with your invitation."

"Come closer. It has been ages."

Pulcheria stepped forward. The basilissa touched her cheek. Then she lightly grazed her lips with a kiss. Pulcheria had no diadem, but her chlamys and gem-encrusted lunate necklace were as fine as Latona's raiment.

"Is she a basilissa?" Morgan whispered.

"She rules in the south," Eumachia replied.

Morgan's eyes widened. She knew, of course, that there were different cities, ruled by different basilissa. Until tonight, though, she'd never seen one in the flesh. Pulcheria moved with the same grace as Latona. They shared an aura of power, an expression of iron certainty. She also had a dagger affixed to her belt. Her lack of a diadem was probably meant as a gesture of respect, and she had enough gemstones to make up for it.

"Sister, I have a gift for you." Latona smiled. "It's only a small thing, but I hope that you like it."

Narses chose that moment to step forward. He handed Latona the silk-wrapped gift, which she carefully opened. Morgan saw the fibula. Her stomach went cold. They'd been wrong. The fibula wasn't for Latona—it was a gift for Pulcheria. All this time, they'd been trying to protect the wrong basilissa. In the crowd below, she saw Roldan drawing closer to the throne. His eyes were on the fibula. Babieca had a hand on his shoulder, but he wasn't paying attention. Domina Pendelia was staring at Pulcheria with a look of great interest. Felix was gone. She couldn't see him anywhere.

It stands to bloody reason that the domina was right all along.

Latona reached out to pin the fibula. Pulcheria regarded it with a mixture of fascination and apprehension.

"You know how I feel about bees," she said.

"Of course, my sister. Think of this as an elegant way to conquer your fears. How could you be scared of something so beautiful?"

Pulcheria touched it gingerly. "It's warm!"

"It was made by a master artifex. Listen closely."

The room was still. Then, gradually, a noise began. At first it was a soft hum, then a kind of whisper. As everyone leaned forward, it became a buzz.

"Oh dear," Propertius said.

The buzzing grew louder. Suddenly, the bee leapt from its silver perch. It flew around Pulcheria's head, buzzing louder and louder, until it sounded as if a whole swarm had filled the oecus. The guests shifted nervously. Pulcheria looked confused, yet at the same time fascinated by the mechanical insect that was circling her head.

"That noise," Eumachia murmured. "It's going to attract—"

"Get away from the balcony!" It was Propertius's voice, suddenly sharp, like a hammer striking. Eumachia backed away, but Morgan didn't. Instead, she reached for her bow.

Another sound had become apparent over the buzzing. A low growl. The miles moved instantly, tightening around both women. The sagittarii leveled their bows. Then Morgan heard glass breaking. Three dark shapes poured through one of the broad windows. From the waist up, they resembled horned men, but their legs were covered in fur. Their cloven hooves sparked against the stones. They carried long spears. One of them screamed, and it was a terrifying sound. It filled the chamber, until it seemed like the walls themselves were screaming, high and thin.

She remembered those burning green eyes. The silenus on the battlements hadn't screamed. He'd approached her in silence, but his eyes made a kind of noise, sizzling like butter in a pan. The first blow knocked her flat. Claws raked against her head, leaving burning tracks that blinded her with pain. She was on her knees, bleeding in the dark. The silenus gloried in her fear. He opened his mouth, and the sound that emerged was far worse than a scream. It was braying laughter.

The crowd shifted from bemused to hysterical. They were running in all directions, pushing each other, fighting to escape. The silenoi moved forward. They were drawn to the screaming bee flying around Pulcheria's head. Two miles stepped in front of the woman, who was too shocked to move. A silenus hurled one into the nearby table, which shattered, sending food everywhere. The second miles tried to attack, but the silenoi were too quick. One grabbed him by the arm like a poppet and flung him into the wall. The archers began firing. The shafts found their mark, but the silenoi didn't seem to mind. They pressed forward.

The miles fell upon them, slashing wildly. Their swords drew blood, but the creatures kept tossing them aside. Armored figures crashed into tables, bounced off walls, skidded across the floor like howling turtles. Their spears whirled. Twilight was their time, and they had the advantage. One of them was inches away from Pulcheria. He was full of arrows and bleeding green ichor on the stones, but he kept moving.

Morgan grabbed a shaft and fixed the black arrowhead to it. She took aim. The angle was poor. She couldn't make the shot. Eumachia was staring at her, openmouthed, as if she'd just realized now that this wasn't a game.

The shot was nearly impossible.

Morgan closed her eyes for a second. Her heart was racing. She put down the bow and withdrew the die from around her neck. The fact that nobody else had dared this only confirmed her fears: This was an assassination. Pulcheria had been fated to die. Not stung by a mechanical insect, but torn apart by silenoi, night hunters who'd been attracted by the infernal buzzing that filled the chamber.

She raised her die in the air, and said in a clear voice: "I choose to roll."

Everything stopped. The crowd stood still. The noises below died, and even the silenoi were rooted to the spot. Propertius was frozen with one paw raised. Eumachia leaned over the balcony, silent and terrified.

"What is the task?"

Morgan turned. The voice seemed to come from the lion's-head fountain, but nobody in the crowd had spoken. It was a woman's voice.

She looked uneasily at the fountain. She'd never done this before, and still wasn't convinced that she'd done it correctly.

"I need to make this shot."

"Even with a lar-forged arrowhead, the angle is unfavorable."

"Tell me about it."

"You'll need a high roll. Five, at least."

"I was afraid of that." It felt strange, talking casually with a fountain, while time ceased to operate in the room below. Morgan understood now why people didn't roll often.

"What are the stakes?" The lion's head regarded her impassively.

"If I lose," she said, "I'll offer you my bow."

"That's nothing. You can easily get another bow."

"What do you want?"

There was a pause. Then: "If you win, the shot is yours. The silenus falls. If you lose, someone else will."

Morgan stared at the crowd. "Who?"

"So much depends on the angle. It might be anyone."

She looked at the half-moon arrowhead. It would kill whomever it struck. Perhaps Domina Pendelia. Perhaps Babieca, or Roldan, or Latona herself.

"You're running out of time," the fountain said.

"All right." Morgan exhaled. "I agree to the stakes."

"Then roll."

She kissed the die for good luck. Then she tossed it against the ground. It bounced off a few stones and came to rest by Propertius's paw. Shaking, Morgan approached the die.

Five pips.

"The roll is high." She almost detected a note of satisfaction in the disembodied voice. "Take your shot, sagittarius."

Time crashed forward. Morgan readied the arrow. She waited until the silenus was almost touching Pulcheria. Then she fired. The shot was a miracle. The shaft cut through the air, following a nearly inconceivable arc. The obsidian half-moon drove through the neck of the silenus. It staggered backward. Green blood sprayed from its mouth, covering Pulcheria, who screamed and tried to shield herself from the awful rain. The silenus fell. Morgan could see the spark leave his eyes. It was the second time that she'd seen such a thing, and it still made her feel hollow inside, as if a great pit had opened within her.

The remaining silenoi looked at the body of their fallen companion. They watched his emerald blood pooling at the base of the marvelous throne. Neither the miles nor the remaining sagittarii moved. Nobody knew what to do, and the only sound was Pulcheria's harsh breathing as she wiped at her face with the slick edges of the veil. Then, moving too quickly for anyone to react, the silenoi grabbed the body and crawled back through the window.

The crowd began to make insensate noises. A few of the miles who'd been dashed against the walls now stirred, although some didn't. Some people were crying, and many were cowering beneath the remains of the tables. The bee was gone. Perhaps it had flown out the broken window. Latona made a move to comfort Pulcheria, but the woman recoiled from her. The other basilissa's face was still spotted with green blood.

"Where in Fortuna's name did that shot come from?" Latona demanded.

Narses pointed to the balcony. "There."

Everyone in the oecus looked up. Latona, the ruler of Anfractus, was now staring at her, along with the terrified basilissa whom Latona had just tried to kill. Narses was also staring, and his eyes were like flint.

"You're in so much trouble," Eumachia whispered.

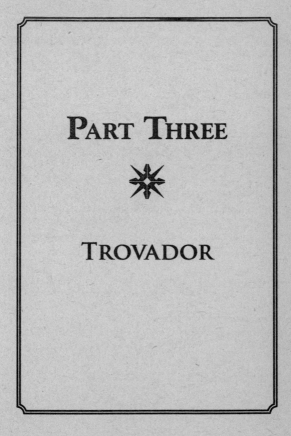

PART THREE

TROVADOR

1

WHEN HE SAW MORGAN PULL OUT THE DIE, Babieca knew that it was time to run. Most people had fled once the silenoi began climbing through the window. They frightened him, but this was the Arx of Violets. The oecus was padded with miles and sagittarii. The silenoi must have been some strange trick, a bit of spirited entertainment to impress the beautiful visitor. The thing with the bee was a bit random, but maybe there would be bracing heroics to follow. When the first miles bounced off the floor, he realized that this was no performance. He turned to warn Domina Pendelia, but she was already gone.

I knew she wasn't really going to visit the toilets.

He grabbed Roldan by the arm, steering him toward the nearest exit. The silenoi were only interested in Basilissa Pulcheria. If they moved in the opposite direction, they merely had to avoid being crushed by hysterical guests. Babieca noticed that Felix was gone as well. The meretrices had no honor. All they cared about was reputation. At least musicians would sometimes help you. They might even divide the takings from a successful night. Felix had left them to be trampled or riddled with arrows.

Then Morgan drew the die. Babieca's breath caught. He'd been caught in a roll only once before, when a bloodthirsty game of acedrex was about to go south. One of the players had cast his die, asking Fortuna not to let him win, but to grant him the speed necessary to stick a dagger in his opponent's eyeball. Fortuna gave him a high roll. Babieca had no die, so he didn't understand how it worked. It was an old power made by Fortuna, the very first game, or something like that. All he knew of Morgan's path to the die was that she'd won it after nearly getting killed by a silenus. It climbed the battlements and gave her a scar on the back of her head. Morgan told the story only when she was drunk, so the details remained imprecise.

"It's for the shot," Roldan said. "Look. She's using the arrowhead."

"We don't need to look. We need to run, before—"

I choose to roll. Morgan's voice rose from the dark clerestory.

Which of her offerings would please Fortuna? What would she promise? Dozens of possibilities crowded his head. *I'll go blind for two weeks. You can break my hands. I'll throw Eumachia over the edge.* Fortuna could ask for anything. Suddenly, he realized what the price would be.

"We have to run."

"We can't."

He stared at Roldan. "She's about to roll. If we're caught in the mix, anything could happen. Our presence could even be making her hesitate."

"She won't hesitate," Roldan said. "And we might be part of the offering. There's the chance that it won't work without us."

He grabbed Roldan by the hand. Then he felt a strange pressure. Darkness fluttered at the corners of his vision. Everything slowed down. The movements around him were thick and attenuated, like honey. The die was cast. His heart beat three times. Then there was screaming. The silenus had an arrow in his neck. The edge of the half-moon peered out from the other side, stained in emerald blood. Pulcheria was backing away, terrified, her veil dripping. He looked up and saw Morgan holding the bow. She hadn't hesitated.

"Where in Fortuna's name did that shot come from?" Basilissa Latona's question had a note of astonishment to it. Narses answered, pointing directly at Morgan. His beard was almost red in the lamplight. A lot of spadones didn't have any hair, but some, like Narses, were wiry and bearded. It was said that if the chamberlain fixed you in his gaze, a murder of rumors would go flying on the wind. Babieca knew that not all spadones were fully gelded, but even if he could still fuck after a fashion, he wouldn't have chosen that gens. He loved his cock too much.

A flash caught his eye. He turned and saw Felix standing by a column. The meretrix beckoned them over. Babieca was suspicious. When someone runs away, then comes back to help you a short time later, their act of compassion doesn't erase the fact that they just left you in the jaws of death. At the moment, however, Felix was their best chance for escape.

"Morgan—" Roldan started to say.

"—can take care of herself," Babieca finished. "And we can't rescue her if we're stuck in the carcer. Let's go."

"What will they do with her?"

"Her gens must question her first. She'll be brought to the tower."

"How do you know this?"

"I slept with a chatty sagittarius once. Now follow me."

They ran for the arches. Felix was waiting for them, next to a narrow door that Babieca hadn't noticed upon their arrival. It smelled like a hidden passage. Only fitting that a meretrix had discovered it, then.

"Are you unharmed?" Felix asked.

"There's no time for your false sentiment," Babieca said. "Sagittarii are swarming that balcony, and they're about to drag our friend to the top of the tower. We're of no good use to her sitting around like toadstools."

Felix ignored him. "I can put you somewhere safe, for a time." He unhooked a lamp from its chain. "We need to go now."

They followed the lamp of the meretrix as it led them down the corridor, which was otherwise dark. Babieca stumbled twice and skinned his knuckles on the wall. Roldan's eyes seemed to have adjusted more quickly than his own. Maybe some lar's voice guided him. Sometimes he found Roldan's dialogues with the lares to be unsettling, but he kept his mouth shut. People weren't overly fond of musicians, either. Best not to insult one of the two friends that he'd made since coming to Anfractus.

Felix opened a door that was nearly invisible, and they passed into a small chamber. It was a room for guests, and not the important kind. There was a stone pallet in one corner, and a dusty wall hanging that depicted Fortuna with a distaff, weaving fates. The margins of the room were littered with cloth scraps and small bones. Felix lit the room's lamp with his own.

"Darkness suits it better." He pointed to something small and white beneath the tapestry. "Is that a tooth?"

"It's far away from the oecus, and nobody will find you here."

"Rats might. This chamber is what they dream about."

"I have to speak with someone," Felix said. "I'll return as soon as I can."

"Be a good butterfly," Babieca said. "Don't get too close to the flame."

Felix sighed. "Just stay put."

"Be safe," Roldan said.

"You as well."

Then he left, closing the door behind them. It had no lock that Babieca could see. On a hunch, he walked over and pushed on it. The door didn't budge. He probed the surface of the wood for anything resembling a device, but there was nothing. It must have opened only from the outside. Felix had brought them to a different sort of carcer.

"We're shut in here," he said.

"The door won't open?"

"It can't open. It's even less useful than the tapestry. At least we could use that to wipe our asses."

"I believe that would be sacrilegious."

"Do you see anything else to the purpose?"

"Felix will return before it becomes an issue."

"Of course. He left us with a pack of silenoi, but we can certainly trust that he won't fuck us in this instance."

Roldan sat on the edge of the pallet. "What explanation do you have for this prejudice against meretrices? You visit the basia plenty."

"I've got no problem with the transaction. That's logical. I've learned, though, that when you wear a mask for a living, it tends to make you feel untouchable. You can distrust the spadones all you like, but they're still a day gens, and they obey certain rules. Meretrices are a night gens. They do whatever they want, and they don't care who's destroyed by it."

"They're your neighbors on Fortuna's wheel, you know. Meretrices and trovadores share a spoke. One side may be in shadow, but they're still connected."

"Day gens and night gens are completely different."

"So says the musician who gets paid at twilight."

"Careful of that bed. If stone had a mouth, it would probably scream."

"It's the only place to sit."

Bending to logic, Babieca sat beside him. The wine had made him a bit flushed, but it was currently being absorbed by the mountain of food that he'd eaten. There was no way to watch this moment hazily unfold, no sweet edge to make the cell they were in appear bright and comfortable. His pulse increased slightly. Being that close to emerald-stained death had made him remember how much he loved his cock. Roldan was probably listening to the mad ramblings of a salamander beneath the bed. Babieca took a moment to study him while he was distracted. He'd seen Roldan naked before, but only a few times. The details were clouded. He remembered hairs, a nipple, an arched foot. That was all. Then the light took over, and the city was torn away.

His pleasures at the basia remained varied. Although he'd never call himself a cinna, he'd lain with both men and women, often at the same time. He followed beauty, wherever it happened to lead. Being with a man wasn't too different, although it did sometimes require a knowledge of calculus. His first time was with an older man, bald and bearded. He'd liked the silky feel of the man's chest hair, the warmth of those bare feet pressed against his shoulders. They'd seemed fragile at the time, and Babieca wanted to shield them, to rub oil into the cracks of those precious soles. He died, forgetting the kindness.

"Is there a lar in the room?" He asked to break the silence, and to keep himself from touching the auditor's hand.

"No," Roldan said. "Although I am feeling something rather odd. It's like an itch, or a sneeze that I can't quite expel."

"There are things to help with that."

"What kind of things?"

Babieca blinked. He couldn't stop himself from making dirty jokes, but Roldan was generally oblivious. He trusted sentences. He gave words the benefit of the doubt, even when they sounded impossible. The more he thought about it, the more he could see a shadow of Roldan, a fragment that was part of him, yet distinct. They shared some things. Both Roldans were honest and direct, but only one could speak to lares. The other was surrounded by what looked like furniture—a stack of chairs, lamps, and nested glass tables—but they didn't resemble anything from Anfractus. They were made of something between wood and stone, no grain or veins, just smooth. It repulsed him. Then the image was gone.

He wanted to ask Roldan about the alien furniture, but his body had already started to pick a fight with itself. His mind was thinking of another question, while everything south of his mind was beginning to demand attention. He grabbed the edge of the stone bed. It was sharp against his fingertips, and the light pain focused him.

"Tell me about lares," he said.

Roldan looked at him. At the same time, he managed to look away slightly—it was something that he could do. His eyes demurred.

"Everything has a chaos," he said. "An element that holds

us. For us, it's air. Water would kill us, but air lets us pass, lets us breathe. The chaos of the undinae is water, although most of them are amphibious. The chaos of the gnomoi is earth. They breathe basalt like the undinae breathe water."

"And the salamanders breathe fire."

"Sometimes their breath is like flaming ale."

He laughed. "What's it like to hear them?"

"Some of them are louder than others. Undinae sound like water on rocks. Salamanders make your ears sweat. Gnomoi have a bit of a stony accent. Sometimes they don't speak at all; they just hum, or tap, or thump the ground. Conversations aren't guaranteed."

"How do they survive outside their chaoses?"

"They spend time in the gaps where chaoses meet. Light a lamp, and eventually some salamanders will come to investigate. Hang out at the water's edge, and you're bound to meet a curious undina. I mean, you're lucky if they're just curious. Sometimes they're starving."

"So"—Babieca smiled at the thought—"we're lares too. Our chaos is air."

"Some say that we destroyed the lares of the air. We took their chaos by force and replaced them."

"What were the original lares called?"

"Caela."

"And they're all dead?"

"We don't know. They hide in storms and smoke. I've never heard one, though. I don't think anyone has in a very long time."

Babieca looked closely at Roldan. At first, the auditor didn't quite look back. He studied him obliquely, as you would a grotesque in the margins, still secondary to the text. Gradually, though, he looked Babieca in the eyes. His face was uncertain, but at the same time curious. That was a window that didn't stay open for long, the most exciting of moments, when the letters might leap from the page. He couldn't be sure of the auditor's preference in this area, but he had caught Roldan staring at him, once or twice, in the apodyterium.

Babieca looked at everyone, but Roldan had only been looking at him. At his collarbone, not his cock. Staring fixedly at
his neck with an expression that Babieca recognized.

"They haunt us," Roldan continued unsteadily. "Someday, they'll probably want their chaos back. I doubt we'll be
able to fight them. Lares and love are Fortuna's perfect
inevitabilities. I heard that once. I don't remember when."

Babieca took his hand. It was soft, and the knucklebone
of his index finger jutted out slightly, a little unmoored
island. He kissed the spot.

Roldan raised an eyebrow. "What are you doing?"

"Saying hello."

"You usually do that with sharp words."

"I know more delicate salutations. Perhaps this is how
lares greet."

"Lares are territorial. They scream when they see each
other."

"Roldan."

"What?"

"Back at the oecus, when Morgan was about to cast her
die, all I could think of was how long your sleeves were.
How much I wanted to fix them."

"You were thinking about my tunica?"

"I was thinking about you."

He looked at Babieca's hand on top of his. "And now?"

"Still you."

"I didn't think—" His eyes demurred again. "I always
imagined that you saw me as a friend, and nothing more."

"Friends mean a lot to me. I have only two."

"That isn't an explanation."

Babieca smiled. "I've never tried this with Morgan, if
that's what you're getting at. She's more of an annoying older
sister."

"I—" He looked at Babieca again. Then his expression
changed slowly, as it had in the apodyterium. "—don't care
what the explanation is. I just realized that."

Babieca kissed him. Roldan was slightly taller, so he had
to stretch slightly to meet the auditor's lips. They were soft,

a bit worried around the edges, but in a way that reminded him of gently frayed cloth. He smelled of Domina Pendelia's raspberry soap. Babieca kissed deeper, and Roldan squeezed his hand. His tongue was a hot wire, a lock-pick, a string whose snap produced the unlikeliest note. Roldan's other hand grazed his neck, returning to the site of earlier fascination. Still kissing, Babieca wormed halfway out of his tunica, pulling away for a second to yank the fabric over his head. Roldan smiled. He didn't smile often—not in the way that he was smiling now—and seeing it made Babieca want to crow.

Roldan touched the fur on his chest, lightly and with a kind of disbelief, as if he were running his thumb along the edge of some weapon. He was shaking slightly. Babieca fought with the auditor's tunic, pulling it down to reveal the plane of Roldan's throat. He kissed his way south, tonguing the small nipple, which drew a shudder. Roldan had very little fur, just a few innocent curls that Babieca nuzzled, inhaling the smell beneath the soap. They were pressed against the wall now. Roldan, surprisingly, reached down Babieca's tunica. He touched the coarse hair between his legs, then farther down, teasing his cock. Babieca smiled as Roldan took hold of him. In the curve of his friend's hand, he felt strangely at ease.

They shed their tunicae, not gracefully, but with extraordinary clumsiness. Roldan nearly fell over with one leg still trapped, while Babieca's sandal got caught in reams of fabric. They laughed while it was happening. There was no shame in being odd to each other, in cavorting around with a single nude leg or a stuck sandal. There were no false notes, only quiet little surprises, like the rose-tinted mark on Roldan's thigh. A daub of extra color, which must have dropped from Fortuna's paintbrush when she wasn't looking.

Roldan lay on top of him. That was a surprise as well, but Babieca didn't mind. It was sweet to be pinned in this way, held in place by one of Fortuna's inevitabilities. Roldan's chest was warm and steady against his own. Babieca moved his hips. They rocked back and forth on the stone pallet. The heat of their bodies was startling. Sweat stood on his forehead, while his feet made dark prints on the bed. Roldan's hair was slick. Babieca grabbed some, pulling him into a kiss that was feather tongues, hot babble, cinders.

They were a crossroads. Roldan ground against him, until Babieca died suddenly and sharply. It was such a remarkable surprise that he bit Roldan's lip, harder than he'd intended. His muscles clenched as he held the auditor, dazed and swimming in fire. He buried his head in the curve of the man's neck, heart racing, feet trembling like strings on the verge of suicide. Roldan said something that he couldn't quite hear. Then Babieca felt him die. He slumped forward, breathing hard, trembling as if he might fly apart. Babieca held him close. Roldan laid his head on Babieca's chest, and they stayed like that for a while.

"That was"—Roldan was still trying to catch his breath—"quite friendly."

Babieca laughed. "I thought so."

"You said something."

"What?"

"As you were dying, you said something. A word."

"I didn't have much control over my tongue. I'm not sure what I said."

"'Carl.'"

The voice made them both jump. Babieca looked down. A mechanical fox had emerged from the bed and was staring at both of them. Her gears moved quietly in thought. She didn't have a proper expression, but he would have bet money that she was amused. He'd heard of the foxes, the basilissa's wondrous automata, but he'd never seen one.

"Are you—"

"Sulpicia," the fox supplied. "My brother and I attend the basilissa."

"What are you doing in this room?"

"I was searching for Eumachia, and someone locked me in. The door, as you've no doubt noticed, is tricky. I was investigating the bed, to see if there might be a hidden mechanism somewhere, and then you came in. I decided to conceal myself until I knew what your intentions were." The links of her tail clicked against the ground. "That became clear immediately."

"Did I really say 'Carl'?" Roldan stared at the fox distractedly. It didn't seem to bother him that she was a network of wires and bright bolts. He looked directly into her swiveling black eyes, as if their spark of life were obvious.

"That was what I heard," Sulpicia replied. "You said it clearly. 'Carl.' Then you spilled your seed."

He blushed and looked down. "What is Carl? Why would I say it?"

"This isn't the first bed that I've been trapped under. You people say all manner of nonsensical things before you spill."

"But—Carl?" He frowned. "Is it a place? A name?"

It sounded oddly familiar to Babieca. He could even hear himself saying the word, his mouth settling upon it with familiarity. For a second, the contours of the room shifted. The tapestry and the trash were gone. He saw high windows, and a ceiling with no impluvium. There was a balcony, though, overlooking a road paved in smooth black stone. He was sitting in a strange little chair, made from tight bands of cloth. On a small table next to him was a glass bowl filled with ashes. The image hovered before him, then disappeared. He blinked. Roldan and the fox hadn't even noticed. He was putting his tunica back on, while Sulpicia studied one of her paws. Babieca wiped himself on the tapestry, then dressed.

The door opened. Felix stepped in, holding a lamp in one hand, a sack in the other. He looked at Roldan and Babieca. Even beneath the mask, his expression was clear. Babieca was a little surprised by what he saw. He'd expected Felix to be annoyed, even angry. But his eyes held disappointment. The expression vanished as quickly as it appeared. As a meretrix, he'd probably been trained to keep his emotions in check, to perform when the need arose.

That was what made the flash of naked disappointment so unusual. Babieca recalled the way he'd looked at Roldan, the way he'd taken every opportunity to touch him. He'd assumed that the meretrix was just playing a role, trying to use Roldan's desire against him. But perhaps it was more than that.

"I see you two found a way to pass the time," he said. Then he looked down, and his eyes widened beneath the mask. "Sulpicia. Were you here the entire time?"

"Lamentably."

The meretrix sighed. "At least you both stayed put."

"What about Morgan?" Roldan asked. "Have they taken her to the tower?"

"Yes. She's to be questioned by the arquites." His jaw tightened. "The kind of questioning that normally involves sharp edges."

"Those games won't start for a while," Babieca said. "They'll wait until the fear sets in before beginning the interrogation."

"If you're talking about the sagittarius," the fox replied, "she'll be under heavy guard. How do you intend to free her?"

"I"—Babieca gave Sulpicia an apologetic look—"don't mean to offend you, but you're the basilissa's attendant. Logic dictates that we shouldn't trust you."

"Actually," Roldan said, "logic dictates that Sulpicia shouldn't trust us. We're uninvited guests in her home."

"You're not helping."

"Both of you are right." Sulpicia crossed her paws. "Neither of us should trust each other. But my brother saw what happened in the oecus, which means that I saw it as well. Your friend saved the life of Basilissa Pulcheria. She does not deserve to be tortured for that."

"You serve Latona," Babieca protested.

"No. We serve the sisterhood. All machinae do."

"Fine." He pointed at the meretrix. "I'm just going to come out and ask, then, since nobody else has mentioned it. What's in Felix's sack?"

"I suppose you've been waiting all night to make that joke."

"We're only a few hours past twilight, so it hasn't been that long. But if we keep debating this, the shadows will grow. Maybe your pretty mask will protect you against the night horrors, but I'd just as soon get out of here, before another pack of silenoi arrive."

Felix drew a cithara from the bag. It was slightly larger than Babieca's, and certainly not as dented. The wood had been brightly polished. He took the instrument, dragging his fingers across the strings. They were a bit unfamiliar, but they had a nice tone.

"You're a trovador," Felix said. "Or nearly one, at any rate. You must be able to do something with this."

"You want me to serenade the guards? Even if I appeal to their romantic side, I doubt they'll let us walk away with Morgan."

"Distract them. Hypnotize them. Obviously, we can't just walk up to them with weapons drawn. They'd take us apart. But a half-drunken musician isn't a threat to anyone. They'll let you get close. Just be sure to pick the right song."

"I'm practically sober."

"Of course. A trovador would never let wine cloud his judgment."

Roldan missed the edge in his voice, but Babieca caught it. For a moment, he thought of hitting the meretrix, but the effort didn't seem worth it. Roldan was oblivious to the awkward equation they now formed. Ignoring both of them now, he watched Sulpicia's mechanical ablutions with great interest.

"You're right about the lack of time," Felix said. "I'm safe because of my gens, but you and your friends are vulnerable. We'd best move quickly."

"I get why the fox wants to help us, but what's your game?"

"I'm just trying to keep the balance."

"What does that mean?"

"It means that you'd better sing for your life. Now let's go. I can take you as far as the tower, and then—"

"You'll run away. I remember from last time."

"We all have something to lose, Babieca."

Was he talking about his reputation? Or did it have more to do with that look of disappointment from earlier? There was no time to figure it out. Morgan would be facing pincers and sharp hooks if they didn't get to her before the arquites.

"All right," he said. "Take us to the tower."

Sulpicia followed them to the doorway.

"Are you coming with us?" Felix asked.

"Naturally. This promises to be interesting."

"You're somewhat conspicuous," Babieca said.

"You certainly didn't notice me under the bed while you were rutting."

"It's settled," Roldan replied quickly. "We'll go together. And that's the last time that anyone uses the word *rutting*."

They followed Felix's lamp through a warren of passages, which eventually led them toward the atrium. Their path widened, and after stepping through a gap in the wall, they found themselves at the entrance to the Tower of Sagittarii.

"This is where I leave you," Felix said. "If you make it out of the tower, a friend of mine will meet you at the entrance to the arx. She'll ensure that you have safe passage beyond the city. May Fortuna smile on you."

"And on you, Felix." Babieca returned the blessing ironically.

The meretrix turned and went back down the passage. For a moment, they could see his lamplight bobbing, like some peculiar spirit. Then he was gone.

"I have an idea," Sulpicia said. "Auditor, lift me."

"What?"

"You heard what I said. Lift me, and watch the tail."

Gently, Roldan lifted Sulpicia from the ground. The fox settled against his chest, reminding Babieca of a cat.

"I will pretend to be injured," she said. "Don't be alarmed if you see sparks. It should prove to be a fitting distraction."

"Sparks?"

"I just told you not to be alarmed."

"It's better than nothing," Babieca said. "Pull down your hoods. If anyone recognizes us from the banquet, we'll be pincushions."

They climbed the spiral stairs—Babieca holding the cithara, Roldan holding the machina to his chest with great care. Sagittarii lounged on the stairs, dicing, playing stones, or gazing out the small windows. A few fixed them with suspicious looks but relaxed when they saw Sulpicia in Roldan's arms. They'd learned to associate the foxes with the basilissa, which meant that anyone bold enough to pick up the machina was probably not someone to be questioned.

The top floor was guarded, but not excessively. After the silenoi attack, many of the sagittarii had been diverted to the battlements. Four archers were milling around the statue of Fortuna. The arquites was not among them. Morgan was chained to the wall. She saw them, and her eyes brightened, but she said nothing. Babieca saw that they'd already begun to work her over. Her right cheek was bruised, and she had a split lip. Nothing permanent, though. That was the job of her commander, the arquites, who would take great delight in extracting further details from her. Babieca had never met her, but she had a reputation for cruelty.

Suddenly, Sulpicia began to tremble in Roldan's grasp. She pawed at the air, her black eyes spinning faster and faster. Sparks flew from her mouth, and a few of her joints. The fox made a sound that chilled Babieca, like a screaming spring, going beyond its limits. Not knowing what else to do, Roldan dropped her on the floor. Her gears twitched and smoked. Then her brass carapace gave a great shudder and was still. Babieca stared at the fox's body in horror, not sure if this was truly a performance or some kind of awful malfunction. She'd been right about its potential as a distraction, though. All four sagittarii had gathered around the smoking fox, staring down at her with similar expressions of panic and confusion.

"Don't just stand there!" Babieca cried. "Find an artifex! If the basilissa's pet dies, we'll all be fucked. Run!"

Two of them ran down the stairs, cursing. The other two remained.

"Hey." One of them was looking at him strangely. "What are you, trovadores? Why would the fox—"

"I don't have time to answer pointless questions. Haven't you ever seen a case of mechanical apoplexy before?" Babieca knelt before the still-sparking Sulpicia. "She's out of tune, like a bad instrument. We need to calm her gears, and music is the only way." He had no idea what he was saying, but his tone seemed to work. They both drew closer. "If I can achieve the right pitch, I should be able to fix her."

He began to play. It was a simple melody at first, soft and unassuming. Then he began to layer in different notes. The cithara had been tuned beautifully, and it responded to his fingers, delivering a sound that was high and clear. The sagittarii were no longer staring at the fox. Now they were staring at him. So was Roldan. Each staff of notes was like a furrow in the air, drawing invisible lines that settled over them. It was a lullaby, the only one that he knew, but he poured all of his willpower into it.

He thought of heavy blankets, of familiar bodies lying like commas next to each other. He thought of incense burning faintly in the bowl, a lover's even breathing, the tender staccato of rain on the shutters. Most of all, he thought of Roldan's head on his chest, the slow descent of their heartbeats, the sweet lassitude after they'd spent themselves. The feeling of being held in place, of mattering beneath someone's limbs. For a moment, he heard what must have been his mother's voice, singing him to sleep. She was far away, but he still heard her, still felt her cool fingertips on his brow. His fingers danced across the strings. Everything was listening—the stones of the tower, the arrows stacked in corners, the dagger beneath his tunica. He looked at the statue of Fortuna, and saw that she, too, had leaned forward.

Good night, parapets. Good night, bows, long and short. Good night, silenoi, prowling beyond the walls. Be held. Be still. Dream.

He played the last note, then looked up. They were all asleep. Even Roldan was curled up on the floor, softly snoring. Morgan sagged against the chain holding her, eyes closed. Only Sulpicia was unaffected. She'd stopped sparking and was engaged in the type of composure grooming that made Babieca want to look away in embarrassment. Finally, she pulled her gears together and looked up at him.

"That seems to have worked."

"I didn't mean to put everyone to sleep."

"You clearly did." She sniffed the sagittarius next to her, who'd fallen asleep facedown against the floor. "This one has the key. I can smell it."

"You can smell keys?"

"It's not quite the same as smelling. We can talk about my mechanism later."

Babieca retrieved the key and unchained Morgan. She fell into his arms, heavy as a pile of logs. He eased her to the floor as gently as he could.

"I can't carry both of them downstairs."

"Allow me."

Sulpicia nipped Morgan on the ear. It was very light, but a spark still leapt from the point of contact. Morgan woke with a small cry. She looked around her in confusion.

"What happened? Did I pass out?"

"A little."

Her eyes widened. "You put me to sleep?"

"We'll discuss it later. Come on."

Sulpicia bit Roldan, who also woke with a start. He rubbed his swollen ear, looking around the room in mild shock.

"You really knocked them out."

"I don't know how long it will last. We should go."

"How do you expect to get out of the city?" Morgan asked. "When the arquites reaches the tower, and sees that I'm gone—"

"Felix has a plan. Now let's go."

"Did they hurt you?" Roldan asked, noticing her bruise.

"Barely," she said. But Babieca could tell that she was a bit shaken. He put an arm around her, guiding her down through the entrance. Hoods drawn, fox in tow, they hurried down the stairs. They kept to the shadows, making their way as quickly as they could back to the gate. When they got there, a miles was waiting for them. She looked familiar, and Babieca realized that she was the one who'd let them into the basia. The miles with one greave.

"You're just in time," she said. "Felix has managed to distract most of the city guard, but not indefinitely. We need to move."

"How exactly is he distracting them?" Babieca asked.

"The arx is full of meretrices. Use your imagination." She looked at Morgan, and her expression changed slightly. "Are you all right?"

"I'll be fine," she said.

The women exchanged a look. A magnificently dirty joke occurred to him, but he wisely kept his mouth shut. It was stupid to antagonize someone with a blade. She led them through the maze of the Subura, down countless interconnected alleys, until it felt as if they were wandering through a dangerous honeycomb. Morgan and Roldan were still yawning slightly. Babieca wondered if he'd be able to do something like that again. Maybe it was just the cithara, or the fact that they'd been in one of the towers, where Fortuna's influence was strongest. He tried to remember the fragment of his mother's voice, but it was already gone.

They stopped before a run-down house that was pressed against the city wall. The miles unlocked the door.

"Go straight to the back," she said. "If you climb out the window, you'll find yourself beyond the wall."

"That's all well and good," Morgan protested, "but it's the middle of the night. All manner of things could tear us to pieces out there."

"Trust me. I'm not a citizen, either, and I've made the trip at night before. Try to remember something from the other place. If you keep focused on it, the moment will come. You'll be able to smell it, just like twilight."

"What about our possessions?"

"You'll have to leave them in the house. Don't worry. I'll hide them."

"You're saying we have to climb naked through a window?" Babieca shook his head. "This had better not be Felix's idea of a joke."

"I've done it more than once. Now go."

The house was dark and empty, save for a bit of moonlight that passed through the southern window. Babieca looked at it dubiously.

"This seems ridiculous."

"More so than anything else you've seen tonight?" Sulpicia asked. They couldn't see her, but she sounded close by.

"Fortuna! I forgot that the fox was still with us."

"Trust the miles," she said. "Take off your skins and climb through."

They disrobed slowly and awkwardly in the dark. Then they helped each other through the window. On the other side, the moon was bright enough to see by. They were naked and shivering on the edge of the woods. Babieca heard a growl. He thought he could see the outline of a spear in the fog.

"What should we think of?" Morgan asked.

"Something, and quickly. I don't like what I'm hearing."

"This isn't like twilight. I can't feel the pull."

"Try to remember," he said. "Anything."

"Carl," Roldan murmured.

The word clicked. It was a name, Babieca realized. Carl was someone who lived in that hazy place, which they could barely remember.

"Carl," he repeated. "Think of . . . a room with high windows. There's a balcony that looks over the street, but the city is different. There's black stone everywhere, with yellow lines painted on it. Carl is on the balcony. His balcony. There's a glass bowl next to him, full of ashes."

"I remember," Roldan said.

"Think of Carl's balcony. Think of his funny chair."

"And his barbecue," Morgan said suddenly.

Now he could feel the pull. The moonlight wavered. Babieca saw the alien city before him, a chessboard of steel and glass. He looked at Roldan.

"My barbecue," he said. "My funny chair."

The light washed over them as they stepped forward.

2

HE WAS NAKED ON THE BALCONY, HIS ASS
pressed against the barbecue. The metal was hot, and he
took a step forward, treading on Andrew's bare foot. They
looked at each other in surprise. They'd often seen each other
in this way, opening their eyes to realize that they were
naked and shivering in the park. But this was the first time
they'd appeared naked and sweating on his balcony. Their
condition was familiar, but the new location was odd. Shelby
stepped over the lawn chair with as much grace as was
possible.

"If that sliding door is locked," she said to him, "you'll
be the one scaling the wall."

"In case you haven't noticed, I lack suction cups."

"You could use your—" She tried the door, which offered
some resistance, then slid irritably forward on its sun-
warped tracks. "Oh, thank Fortuna."

"Parking," Andrew said.

"We're standing naked above an adult video store with
all of Broad Street looking at us. The rule of secrecy is a
write-off. Let's just get inside."

"I left the door open," Carl said. "Not Fortuna."

Shelby stepped into the living room. "I don't care. Just find us some clothes."

"How did we get here?" Andrew asked. "I didn't even know it was possible to cross after twilight. And——" He looked at Carl, and his eyes suddenly widened. Normally, Andrew's range of expression was, for lack of a better term, laconic. But Carl saw something close to astonishment in his eyes. They'd both remembered at the same moment.

"And what?" Shelby asked.

"Nothing." Andrew stared at the linoleum as if it had suddenly become a Byzantine mosaic. "I agree with the clothes thing. Let's do that."

Carl went to his bedroom, which resembled a cave. The blinds were drawn, casting slatted shadows over the unmade bed. The yellow shag hadn't been vacuumed in a while and was a breeding ground for paper clips, pine needles, and spare change. The blue plastic tote that served as a hamper was overflowing, and dirty clothes were scattered across the carpet, floating like desultory islands. He threw on a shirt and boxers, then searched his dresser and returned to the living room with a bundle of clothes——the only clean specimens he could find. Shelby was grateful for the Plains U sweatpants, even though she had to double-tie the drawstring to keep them up. She was less enthusiastic about the promotional Moosehead T-shirt, which had come from a twelve-pack. Andrew's outfit consisted of cargo shorts and a collared shirt, which made him resemble a tourist visiting Bermuda.

"We'll just have to wait until dark to get our clothes back from the park," he said. "I do have a spare key, so technically we could visit the park now, but pulling a duffel bag out of a tree would look suspicious in broad daylight."

"People must do it all the time," Andrew said. "If it's theoretically possible to move between places at any time, then a person could become adept at hiding clothes. Maybe there's even an underground clothing network that we don't know about."

"If there is," Shelby replied, "we don't have access to it. Carl's right. Unless we're willing to hit up the Cornwall Centre and buy new clothes, we'll have to wait." She looked down at the sweatpants. "These are actually comfortable."

"There's a hole in the ass," Carl said.

"Yeah. I felt that. Not much I can do about it, though."

"We can trade," Andrew offered.

"No. Of us all, you're the only one with a clear ensemble." She glanced at Carl's understated outfit. "I assume this is what you normally wear around the house."

"Depends on the day. Sometimes I don't wear anything."

"Please tell me that you don't sun yourself on the balcony."

"I won't confirm or deny that."

Shelby sat at the kitchen table, which was covered in books, old receipts, and economy-sized boxes of granola bars. "I'm still getting my bearings. Okay. We were in that abandoned house—which people must use all the time, since it's pressed right against the gate—and then we crawled through the window and into the woods."

"We were both there," Carl said. "You don't need to reconstruct it."

"This sort of crossing has never happened to us before. Don't you think we should take a moment to figure things out?"

At the moment, he was trying to figure out what, exactly, Babieca had done with Roldan. He remembered bits and pieces, and they were all good, but there were gaps as well. He couldn't remember what the fox had to do with any of it. More important, he couldn't figure out why Andrew refused to look at him. Was he embarrassed? Did he regret it? The most confusing thing was that the memories felt secondhand. They belonged to Babieca and Roldan. It was like recalling a moment of intense pleasure from your childhood. The outlines of the experience were visible, but the distance created a profound separation. Andrew played with his zippers. He would not look up.

"Let's try to accentuate the positive," Carl said. "We're alive. Basilissa Pulcheria is alive. Nice fucking shot, by the way."

"Thank you."

"So what was the wager?"

"I'd rather not talk about it."

"I'm curious, though. A shot like that would have taken a very high roll, and from what I understand, those don't come cheaply."

"Can we drop this?"

"Why? I think we're entitled to know."

She looked at Andrew. "You're burning with curiosity as well?"

"Not so much," he replied, eyes still on the zippers. "But I'd be lying if I said that I hadn't considered the possibilities."

Shelby stared at her hands for a moment. "The shot had to kill someone," she said finally. "If not the silenus, then someone else in the crowd. The details weren't specific beyond that, but whatever the roll, someone had to die."

Carl remembered Roldan's comment from earlier. *She won't hesitate. And we might be part of the offering.*

"It could have been us," he said.

"I know."

"But you took the shot anyway."

"I had no choice."

"You could have dropped a lamp on its head, or created a diversion."

"Three seconds later, that silenus would have ripped her in half. A falling lamp wasn't going to stop him. Why do you think the gnomo gave me that arrowhead?"

"Because the lares enjoy fucking with us. We're interlopers who stole their precious chaos, or whatever, and now they love to pit us against one another."

Andrew finally looked up. "Did I tell you that?"

"You told Babieca. It's true, right? We pushed them out

of their chaos and moved in. If I were them, I'd want to make us suffer."

"I've never sensed hostility from them."

"You can't even see them. You just hear their voices."

"That was before. Now I can touch them—sort of."

"You shouldn't trust them. You shouldn't trust anyone."

Shelby gave him an exasperated look. "Why are you freaking out? You know how dangerous this all is. However the wheel turns, there's always risk."

"That's easy to say when you're the one holding the bow."

"Carl—" Andrew finally looked at him. "Shelby wasn't the one holding the bow. It was Morgan who cast the die, and her decision saved us."

He could feel an argument coming on, but then the anger began to dissipate. Andrew was right. What happened in the park would always remain slightly beyond their reach. Different actors populated that stage. Morgan was a part of Shelby, but she was also a separate person, with desires and fears of her own. Babieca felt so close to him sometimes, like a second skin, but they were not the same. Carl didn't sleep with friends. It was one of the only rules he had regarding sex. He'd slept with a friend back in high school, and things were never the same between them afterward. They were jumpy around each other. They could no longer settle onto the couch and watch television, or drive around listening to music, as they had before. Everything took on a peculiar and uncomfortable significance.

"You're right," he said. "Shelby, I'm sorry. I don't know what I'm saying."

"It's fine. We're all a bit ragged." Her stomach growled. "And hungry. What are the chances that you have something edible in your fridge?"

"There's—ah—some Balkan yogurt, I think. And a shrimp ring in the freezer."

"Balkan yogurt? Who are you?"

"It's spicy. I like it."

"We can have a barbecue," Andrew said. "If you give me

the spare key, I'll go pick up bratwurst and smokies. And buns, I'm assuming, unless you happen to have those."

He sounded slightly eager to leave. Carl didn't blame him. The apartment wasn't big enough to hold their collective neuroses.

"Buns too," he said. "The keys are in the junk drawer."

Andrew opened the drawer. "You've got about a hundred bucks in change here."

"I know. It's where I keep my bus fare."

"Can I take some? My wallet's still in that tree."

"Knock yourself out."

He grabbed a reusable bag and left, closing the door behind him.

"Want some tea?" Carl asked. "I've got a sampler."

Shelby didn't reply. She waited a moment, until they both heard the sound of the building's front door as it banged closed. Then she looked at Carl.

"What did you do?"

"Excuse me?"

"Something's happened between the two of you. Andrew's being weirder than usual, and you look guilty as shit."

"He's the one who just ran out of here. Doesn't that seem like guilty behavior?"

"Carl."

"It wasn't even me. It was Babieca."

"What did you do?"

"Nothing!"

"Bullshit."

"Look, I'm not taking the blame for this. He made a choice. You may think he's a wide-eyed innocent, but he knew what he was doing."

Her eyes widened. "Holy shit."

"I didn't mean for it to happen. We were alone in this room—well, not alone, there was actually a fox under the bed—"

"And it just sort of happened?" She shook her head. "You could have had anyone at that party, and you chose Roldan."

"*Babieca* chose him."

"You both did."

He wanted to leave the apartment, to escape from the realization that she was right, but Andrew had the keys. The thought almost made him laugh.

"Whatever happened," he said, "it's done. We're both adults. We'll figure it out."

"No. You'll figure it out, because this sort of shit doesn't matter to you. In a week, you'll forget that this ever happened. But Andrew's going to think about it for the rest of his life, because that's what he does."

"You must really think I'm an asshole."

"It's not a theory, Carl."

"Oh really? Do you remember the time when you tried to sleep with me?"

"What are you talking about?"

He smiled. "How convenient that you've blocked it out. We were at the bar. All night, you'd been making eyes at this cute girl. But you couldn't talk to her, just like you couldn't talk to Ingrid that day at the library. She left with someone else, and after that, you were on a mission. You started doing Jager shots."

Shelby put her head in her hands. "I remember now. Stop describing it."

"You came up to me," he continued, "and you said—"

"Please stop—"

"—that I had a—what was it again?"

She sighed. "A *cute assonance*."

"That's right. You wanted to go home with me."

"I was blackout drunk. In the morning, I woke up on the bathroom floor, wearing nothing but my pajama top."

"All I'm saying is that we nearly hooked up."

"It never would have happened."

"Why? Because you're such a great lesbian? Unless I'm mistaken, you've hooked up with more guys than girls."

Her eyes narrowed. "As an *undergrad*. I didn't know what I wanted then."

"You weren't some adorable first-year that night. You

were a grad student with an actual teaching job, still making the same murky decisions as before. You wanted that girl, but you chose me, because you thought it would be easy."

"I chose you because you have girlish hips."

"Whatever. Look, you're right. It wasn't the same thing. Babieca wasn't drunk, and Roldan didn't just let it happen. They—we—wanted it."

"And now?"

"How am I supposed to know that? We've barely been home for twenty minutes. The guy who's wearing my clothes and buying us hot dogs—he isn't Roldan. If something happened here, between us, it would be completely separate."

"Have you ever—" Shelby made a vague gesture. "I mean, was there a time when you looked at him, and thought, you know . . . *maybe*?"

Carl didn't reply, and they fell silent after that. Eventually, he heard footsteps on the stairs. The front door opened, and Andrew came in.

"I took the liberty of buying some pre-barbecue snacks," he said. "With the contents of this bag, and all that money in your junk drawer, we should be set."

"Great." Carl stood. "I'll go fire up the coals."

He grabbed the franks and stepped onto the balcony, closing the door. This was to keep out smoke, but he also felt better with the layer of glass between them. Shelby's critique had hit too close to home. She was only trying to protect Andrew, but the suspicion in her eyes made him feel like a boy with a fistful of candy, shifting awkwardly in the middle of a grocery store. She hadn't even considered the fact that he might get hurt. Andrew was the one in trouble, which made him—what? A thoughtless dick? A predator? Priming the barbecue, he peeked through the glass and saw that they were both talking. Shelby looked calm and focused, as if she were explaining the plot of a film. Andrew wasn't saying nearly as much.

He scored the smokies with a knife, then laid them down and closed the lid. The cheese-filled ones would be murder on the grill, but for some reason, he didn't mind the repetitive act of scraping. It was one of the few chores he actually enjoyed, because he could watch his neighbors while doing it. He'd been working on their backstories for a while, crafting narratives for every other balcony. When they saw him scraping the barbecue, they would inevitably nod and smile. The act seemed necessary and somehow masculine. Grilling suggested that you had company over, not that you were a shut-in who loved the taste of smoky food. They probably imagined him to be a friendly, well-adjusted guy, the type that you'd see confidently striding toward the automotive department at Canadian Tire. They didn't suspect the truth.

There was an old roach in the ashtray. It had one haul left in it, maybe one and a half. Carl lit it, then sat down in the lawn chair. The smoke was harsh, but he'd been expecting that, so he coughed only a little. The lighter burned his fingers before he could snatch them away. He stubbed out what was left of the roach, a tiny black nubbin that disintegrated when it touched the side of the ashtray. He needed to call his mother. She was at a conference in Valencia, something called Poesía Ecléctica that had required, in her own words, "a charming poet who could act as a bookend." It gave her the chance to workshop new poems and fleece hotels for everything that they were worth.

He couldn't imagine being so productive. He'd been making bluff charges at his thesis for a year now, avoiding it by any means possible. Byzantine ephemera had once filled him with desire. Browsing fibulae, rock crystal chess pieces, and brass mirrors had felt nearly pornographic as he sat in a dusty corner of the library, flipping through the oversize art books. Now his lack of an argument filled him with vague nausea. The people in his cohort were always inviting him out for drinks, but they exhausted him with their enthusiasm and talk of library fellowships. He couldn't even see a limited-term position in his future. There were about five jobs in History that appeared every year, and they would go to fresh ABD candidates from ivy league schools. He would end up working at Chapters, or worse, the Coles in Northgate Mall, bitterly stocking the self-help section.

Carl had chosen history because it never failed to excite him. The details were intoxicating. He could lose a whole weekend to watching YouTube videos about the construction of Welsh castles. The ancient world fascinated him because it was so uncomfortably close to modernity, driven by the same violent conflicts and explosions of literary genius. People had thought differently about pain. It was something that you lived with. Herbal concoctions might put you into an altered state, but the pain didn't leave. A Roman patient might stare at a divine image, or a phrase in Latin, engraved on the handle of an iron spatula used to elevate her shattered bone. She wasn't sedated. A bit of datura, the profile of Asclepius carved on a sweat-slick handle, these were all that comforted her.

The sliding door opened. Andrew stepped onto the balcony.

Carl saluted him. It made sense at the time. There was nowhere else for him to stand, so he leaned against the balcony. Those cargo shorts were something else. Carl looked down at his feet, to see if they matched Roldan's. He'd put on a pair of socks. They were a little too white, and their ragged stitching made Carl think that he'd bought them from the grocery store. It was a strangely desperate act of modesty.

"Shelby wanted to know if you have any more plates."

"Not that I'm aware of."

"There are only three, unless that big yellow thing is actually a plate."

"No. It's a busted lazy Susan that I got from Dollarama."

"That was my suspicion."

"You can still put things on it, but it won't turn."

"So . . . essentially, Susan's dead."

Carl laughed. "Don't tell the colander. They had a thing."

Andrew leaned over the balcony. "It's weird. My place has way more light than yours, but no balcony. Shelby's place has the greatest floors, but no washing machine. If we combined them all, we'd have one fully functioning space."

"Are you saying that you'd like to move in?"

"Only if all three of the apartments were connected. We could do Ewok bridges, pedways, even zip lines. Then we could advertise our home as an attraction."

"GradLand." Carl smiled. "Where the library never closes, and everyone's water bottle is filled with high-test coffee."

"We could sell journal subscriptions and mini doughnuts. It could really fly."

"The power of our neuroses would eliminate the need for electricity."

"It might be fun."

"Not during comps."

"I meant moving in." Andrew tapped his fingers against the balcony's rim. "The three of us could rent a house."

"Renting a house in this city is like searching for pirate treasure. The vacancy rate is something like half a percent. Where would we find this house?"

"There are lots of places even closer to the park. We could cut down our transit time if we found something near the Lakeview strip mall."

"You've actually thought about this."

Andrew shrugged. "We'd save on rent. We're always shuttling between apartments, picking each other up. Don't get me wrong. I enjoy the ritual. But if we lived together, we could coordinate activities."

"What activities? All we do is mark papers, drink, and visit the park."

"It's always seemed like a lot."

"I think I prefer living alone."

"Me too," Andrew said. "But when I'm with you and Shelby, I feel like it's possible to be solitary without being alone. You don't stress me out, like most people."

His tone was slightly flat, but the words rang with honesty. Carl didn't know what to say. He didn't know if he felt the same way, or if he was even capable of sharing a space with two other people. The idea of Shelby organizing his kitchen was troubling, and he didn't want to pool his DVDs with Andrew. He needed more than 33 percent of the fridge. He didn't know if this was selfishness, or just human nature. Something convinced him that he would get stuck with the basement suite, while the others gloried in their sunny bedrooms.

"I do like the part about Ewok bridges," Carl admitted.

"If we're going to implement those, we'll need a more complicated lease." He looked down at the red awning, which resembled a giant tongue lit from below. "I like paperwork, though. All those riders and concealed clauses. They make civilization possible."

Carl stood up. Two steps brought him within inches of Andrew. He stared at his friend's back, uncertain of what to do. Then he leaned into his body, lightly, resting his chin on Andrew's shoulder. Neither said anything. They stayed that way, considering the other balconies, until the sizzle of cheese announced that supper was ready.

They ate at the small kitchen table, which Shelby had cleared off to the best of her ability, using pages from *Verb* as place mats. Andrew didn't bring up the shared house again. Neither did they discuss what had happened to them a few hours ago. For once, Anfractus felt distant, some holiday destination that they'd visited months ago. Nobody wanted to mention it, so they spread ketchup in silence and crunched on their toasted buns. If they really had lived together, perhaps every meal would have been like this, approaching what departments referred to as collegiality. When the meal was over, Andrew did the dishes, while Shelby began organizing Carl's library books into a single pile. She seemed to do it unconsciously, as if this were her version of tidying. Carl watched them both working to clean up his mess.

He turned on the radio, just for some background noise.

—a Plains University student is recovering in hospital after another vicious animal attack in Wascana Park. Animal control has redoubled their efforts to locate the coyotes, and visitors to the park are advised to stay in groups, especially at night—

Shelby turned off the radio.

"I was listening to that."

"You'll only get him started."

Andrew was still in the kitchen, wiping down the counters.

"Maybe he's got a point."

"It's impossible, Carl."

"Last night, you killed a monster by rolling a die. I wouldn't be so quick to judge what's impossible, and what isn't."

"Fine. It's illogical."

"Didn't you barely pass your logic course?"

Her expression darkened. "I still might contest that grade."

The intercom buzzed. The speaker didn't work, so there was no way to know who was actually at the door. Usually, it was a neighbor's Thai food, or a member of the Sask Party. Carl pressed the button and turned to Shelby.

"That pile is useful," he said, "but you can stop there. I've got a system."

"What would you call it? Entropy?"

Before he could answer, there was a knock at the door. Carl crossed the living room, prepared to direct someone downstairs. But when he undid the chain and opened the door, it wasn't a delivery person or someone with a clipboard standing in the hallway. It was Ingrid. She wore yellow-tinted sunglasses, but he still recognized her from the library. She was holding the hand of a small boy, probably about four years old, who shifted with nervous energy. He wore a fedora and a clip-on tie. He was holding a battered kite.

"Hi there," she said. This was pronounced in a soothing tone, as if she were talking to the child and not to a stranger in his midtwenties. "This is weird. I understand. We don't actually know each other. But he needs to use the bathroom."

"Oh." Carl still wasn't sure of exactly what was happening. "Um—sure. Come in. It's down the hall."

"Go on," she told the boy gently. "This nice man is saying that you can use his toilet. I'll hold your kite. Remember to flush."

He tottered inside, then headed for the bathroom. Carl watched as the kid overshot it, wandering into his bedroom instead. Then he reappeared and found the correct room. Shelby and Andrew had frozen in the middle of their tasks and were both staring at Ingrid. She took her sunglasses off but said nothing.

"Did a little boy just go into your bathroom?" Shelby asked Carl.

"That's my son, Neil," Ingrid said.

Carl expected her to add something. *That's my son, Neil, and we're actually here for a perfectly logical reason. That's my son, Neil, and we buzzed you at random, hoping that a kind Samaritan would let him in to pee.* No explanation followed, though. Ingrid stared at the floor. A moment later, the toilet flushed, and Neil emerged. He ran into the living room and seized Ingrid's hand.

"Mama, his tub smells."

"Why were you smelling the bathtub?"

Neil had no answer for this. He adjusted his fedora.

"Nice tie," Carl said.

"Clip-on tie," Neil corrected.

"Right. Nice clip-on tie."

"My father gave it to me. He gave me his bones, and Laser Bird, and *this*." He held out the kite for all of them to see. "Mine kite is a victim."

Carl didn't quite know how to parse this. Andrew seemed to understand immediately, though. He walked over to Neil and extended his hand.

"You must be Leonard Cohen. It's very nice to meet you."

Neil took his hand politely. "Please call me Mr. Leonard Cohen."

"I'd just like to say," Ingrid added, "that this is not my fault. I haven't been forcing him to read Canadian poetry. He adopted the persona—"

"It is *not* a person-a!"

"Of course it's not. I'm sorry. Would you like to play Angry Birds?"

"Mama! Mr. Leonard Cohen does not play Angry Birds. He sings *Hallelujah*."

"How about Lego?"

"Okay."

Ingrid withdrew a plastic container full of Lego from her purse. "Try to keep the pieces together, love."

He emptied the Lego onto Carl's floor and began making something that involved a lot of clear plastic pieces.

"Is it okay if I sit down?" Ingrid asked.

"Sure." Carl gestured to the couch. "We just finished supper, but there's a smokie wrapped up in the fridge, if you're hungry."

"That would be amazing."

He hadn't expected her to say yes. "Right. I'll grab it."

"There aren't any buns left," Andrew said.

"That's fine," Ingrid replied. "I'll eat it naked. He's had supper, but I've just been eating pita slices and carrots all day."

Carl wasn't sure what to do with the frank, so he laid it by itself on a plate. It looked small and ridiculous. He gave the plate to Ingrid, along with a knife and fork, and for the next minute they watched in silence as she dissected her dinner. When she was finished, Carl put the plate in the sink. Neil was completely engrossed in the Lego. To an outsider, the scene would have looked quaint—four adults gathered around a small boy fitting brightly colored blocks together. But Carl was unable to shake his confusion. What was Ingrid doing here? Why had she brought her son, who also appeared to be a famous Canadian poet?

"So," Ingrid began. "I guess this is a little odd."

Shelby was trying not to stare at her. Carl realized that she'd be just as conversationally useless as she'd been at the library. It was Andrew who spoke first.

"How do you know Carl's address?"

Shelby managed to look guilty. "That's a bit of a long story, involving a call that I made to the History Department's general office. I may have pretended to be his supervisor."

"You don't sound anything like her," Carl said.

"No, but the secretary was filling in, and she didn't seem to know the difference. It was pretty simple to get all of your contact information."

"But why—" Carl shook his head. "Okay, the why could very well be superfluous. What's bugging me is the fact that we don't know each other. I've never seen you before."

"You recognized me as soon as you opened the door. You were surprised to see me, but you knew exactly who I was."

"Fuck." It was Shelby's turn to stare at the floor. "Carl—she saw us at the library. It's not like we were doing a great job of hiding."

"But we've never spoken. How would she even know my name, let alone the name of my supervisor? Which—for the record—is clever, but also pretty unsettling."

"Shelby mentioned you in her e-mails," Ingrid said. "Never by name, but she did say what departments you both worked in. History has color pictures of its grad students, posted on a billboard in the hallway. English wasn't willing to spring for something like that, but there was only one Andrew on the list of teaching assistants."

"So—what—" Carl stared at her. "You lied to our secretaries to discover our contact information, then went to each address, hoping to find us?"

"Andrew's place looked dark, so we came here next."

Shelby looked at Ingrid. "I thought we were going to have coffee and meet for the first time next week. I don't understand why you'd just show up like this. If you wanted to see me, why not just send me an e-mail?"

"I did want to see you," Ingrid said. "Not just you, though. All of you. There isn't much time to explain, so I'll just have to show you." She touched Neil on the shoulder. "Mr. Leonard Cohen, I need you to take your Lego down the hallway."

"Why, Mama—I mean, Ingrid?"

It was laughable how he pronounced her first name, as if he truly were a visiting poet, and she was just there to give him a campus tour.

"This room isn't the best for Lego," she explained. "But if you go all the way down to the end of that hallway"—she pointed—"there's a Lego Square. It's invisible, but if you look carefully, you should find it."

He squinted down the hallway. "A Lego Square?"

"Try to find it. When you get hungry, you can have a yogurt."

Neil hesitated, but the lure of the unseen square was irresistible. He packed up the Lego and carried it down the hallway.

Carl expected her to pull something mysterious out of her purse, like a flash drive with forbidden data, or the schematics to a building. Instead, she leaned forward, pulling up the leg of her pants. It was a practiced motion, as if she did it all the time. Carl saw that she had a thin scar running from knee to ankle.

"Is that from a knife?" he asked.

"No. A sword."

"I don't understand."

"I received this wound in battle. It was a lot deeper than it looks now, and I couldn't get to a medicus in time. Even if I had, they might not have been able to do anything. I'd already lost a lot of blood. So I crawled to the house—the one pressed against the city wall. Felix taught me how to use it. I crossed over. The bleeding stopped, but the scar's still there."

"That's"—Shelby's eyes widened—"why you wear the greave."

"Exactly. Scars prove that you've survived, but that particular one never healed all the way. The armor protects it."

"You're the miles."

"Fel. That's her name. Our name."

Shelby was staring at her. "I can see it now. In the eyes, and the jaw."

"The more time you spend there," Ingrid said, "the easier it becomes to recognize someone in both worlds. Seeing Andrew for the first time, I had the feeling that we'd met before. Then I saw you hiding behind that pillar, and the images just clicked, like two photos superimposed on each other. The three of you were searching for Felix. Domina Pendelia sent you."

"How deeply is she involved in this?" Carl asked. "I don't trust her."

"A better question," Shelby said, "might be why Ingrid is here."

"I should think it would be obvious." Ingrid covered her leg. "I'm here to join you."

"We're not a company. I mean, with you, I guess we would be. Still—"

"Basilissa Pulcheria has been confined to her quarters. Very soon, Latona is going to finish what she started. You three are the only people who have the faintest idea of what's going on here. Felix seems to think that you have something, and I trust him. Normally, I'd never be part of a company. I don't play well with others. But for now, I think we should work together. The four of us stand a chance of freeing the basilissa."

"Maybe Latona will let her go," Carl said lamely. "Aren't they like sisters, or something? Maybe this will all blow over."

"Latona wants Pulcheria dead. She's going to blame it on the Gens of Artifices—that's why she used the killer bee."

"How do you know about the bee? You weren't there."

"I was. You just didn't see me." She looked at Shelby. "I watched you shoot that arrow, though. Well done."

"Thanks," Shelby said. "I—got lucky."

"You rolled at the right moment. That's more skill than luck."

"I still don't see why Latona needed to do all of this," Carl protested. "Rulers kill other rulers all of the time. It's a staple of monarchy, or sisterhood, whatever they call it in Anfractus. If she wanted Pulcheria dead, she could have just killed her while she was sleeping."

"Then she'd have a civil war on her hands," Ingrid said. "But that creature, that buzzing little miracle of gears, allows her to spread the blame in two directions—the artifices, who made it, and the silenoi, who were drawn to it like dogs to a whistle. Both gens will fight about it, while she moves in to claim Pulcheria's throne. Latona's mother wanted the same thing, but she could never figure out how to avoid war."

"What happens if she takes Pulcheria's throne?"

"She takes her city, as well. Egressus. For the first time in centuries, one basilissa would control two cities. That breaks the balance."

"The rules would start to dissolve," Andrew murmured. "Maybe they're already dissolving. What if the only thing that divides us from the park is ourselves? Our collective desire to keep the worlds separate? If the balance is broken—"

"Everything crashes together." Ingrid looked at him thoughtfully. "I have noticed, lately, that it's been harder to separate myself from Fel. I thought it was just my issue, but maybe it's happening to everyone."

"The silenoi could really be hunting on this side."

Her eyes widened. "Silenoi in Regina?"

"I've been dreaming of lares. I swear, the other day I thought I saw one, in the cafeteria, nosing through some-one's leftovers. The coyote attacks, the dreams—and all of us have been acting"—he looked momentarily at Carl—"a bit out of character, if you'll pardon the expression. Maybe it has something to do with Latona."

"Why would she want to dissolve the boundary?" Shelby asked. "When you enter the park, you become a different person. You escape from your life here. What would be the point in merging those two worlds?"

"I think it has something do with the lares," Andrew said. "I can't quite work out what, but she's planning some kind of epic crossover. Latona wasn't born in Anfractus. At one time, she still lived on this side of the park. I guess she needs something from her old neighborhood."

"Or she just wants to make the whole world a park."

They all looked at Shelby.

"That would be—crazy," Carl began.

They were silent for a while.

"Imagine it, though," Andrew said. "Without the divi-sion, everything on this side of the park would be overrun with silenoi, spadones, and little gods. It would be like a cross between Final Fantasy and Thunderdome."

Carl looked at Ingrid. "No offense—but why should we trust a miles? You're in the service of the basilissa."

"We're all more than we seem. You should realize that by now. This miles kept you from being captured, after a meretrix delivered you from the arx. Our places on the wheel guide us, but they don't define us."

"Mama!" Neil's voice drifted down the hallway. "Mr. Leonard Cohen would like a yogurt and a Five Alive, please."

"Your profile never mentioned a kid," Shelby said. "We've exchanged at least a dozen e-mails, and you didn't say anything about him."

"It felt like more of an in-person conversation."

"It doesn't make a difference, you know."

"That's easy for you to say now."

"It's the truth."

She stood. "I have to give the poet his yogurt. His uncle gets off work in a few hours, and then I can drop him off for a sleepover. After that, we should head back."

"I never thought of arranging child care around the park," Shelby said.

"I don't visit every night. But things come up. Luckily, he loves his uncle, which eases the sting of someone else tucking him into bed."

"Ingrid!"

She withdrew a miniature yogurt and juice box from her purse. "I wouldn't murder someone to gain control of a city. But I would do it for a nap."

"You—" Carl began uncertainly. "I mean, you could sleep for a bit in my room, if you wanted. I'm sure we can watch him."

She didn't even hesitate. "Perfect. His favorite topics are day care, Lego, and Greek history. I'll see you in forty-five minutes."

They watched her walk down the hallway. She bent down to hand Neil his snack, kissed him on the cheek, and then disappeared into Carl's bedroom. She closed the door. Neil looked up at the sound. Realizing that his mother was indisposed, he calmly walked back into the living room, holding the yogurt in one hand, the juice box in the other.

"The mist leaves no scar," he said.

They stared at him as he chewed on the straw. Then his expression gradually changed, as if he'd only now become aware of his surroundings.

"What square is this?" he asked.

3

LIGHT STREAMED THROUGH THE SLATTED WIN-
dows of the abandoned house. Babieca had come to think of
it as the house with no insula, a wayward gosling abandoned
by its mother. He was used to seeing his alley, and it felt more
than strange to open his eyes to this place, dust-choked and
unfamiliar. His bare feet shifted on the uneven floor. There
was a faded fresco on the southern wall, but its actors had
long since crumbled away. He could just make out the foliated borders, along with something that may have once been
a leaping dolphin but was now a smudged blue crescent. The
rest was shadows and broken plaster. He turned, about to say
something to Roldan, and found himself looking instead at
the naked miles. He'd grown used to seeing his friends this
way, but her presence made him self-conscious. He turned
away for the sake of modesty.

"It's fine," she said. "We've all been to the thermae."

"That's all well and good," Morgan replied, "but we're
also used to appearing alone, in the privacy of our blind corners. This business of materializing together is unnerving."

"That's the usual way. There are only a few places in the

city where it's possible to cross as a group. Felix taught me how to do it but also warned me that it can be dangerous. If you rely too much on these places, you can lose your alley. You'll simply forget where it is. Our alleys are safe spaces—blind corners, as you call them—but this house is exposed."

"I'd like to quit debating this and get dressed," Babieca said. "Please say you weren't lying about our clothes being here. I have no wish to walk naked through the Subura."

The miles knelt down and lifted two flagstones, revealing an alcove beneath the floor. Because she was naked, her action resembled some unearthly feat of strength, a trial of Fortuna that you'd expect to see immortalized in marble. Trying not to stare too fixedly at her muscular arms, Babieca realized that she could probably defeat them all bare-handed. Morgan would give her some trouble, but Fel was ultimately stronger than the sagittarius. He shifted his gaze to the fold beneath the floor and was relieved to see his cithara and tunica. Felix's instrument had been interesting to play, but he preferred his own.

"Thanks for not selling our things."

"Aside from the bow, it wouldn't have been worth the trouble."

"What? The strings alone—"

"Shut up and put your bloody clothes on," Morgan said.

They dressed awkwardly, trying to ignore the strangeness of the moment. At first, Babieca kept his eyes on the dolphin smudge. Gradually, though, he found himself stealing glances at the bodies around him. In the apodyterium, looking was encouraged, but here it seemed brazen. He couldn't help it, though. His curiosity was too powerful. He saw that Morgan's breasts were small, with dark brown nipples. Her arms were dusted with light hair, and she had a curious constellation of freckles on her back. Roldan's white backside reminded him of two marble bookends he'd seen once in Domina Pendelia's tabularium. He avoided looking at Fel, worried that she might break his arm if she caught him staring. He was dimly aware of a less hostile side to her, something almost maternal, but he couldn't quite remember where he'd seen it.

The thought of losing his alley made him nervous. It was the only safe space in the city, the one spot where nobody could find him. On that first day, the warmth of those filial stones had kept him from going crazy. He'd stood in the alley with arms crossed, bare ass pressed against the dimpled wall. It was strange to think that Egressus, ruled by Basilissa Pulcheria, had its own maze of alleys. He'd understood from the beginning that there were other cities, but even if he'd been able to afford passage by ship, the haunted harbor made things very difficult. Only a handful of vessels docked, and they never stayed for long. Travel by foot wasn't really an option. Even beneath the sun, it was easy to lose your way in the forest. Once night fell, you became a target for silenoi, and worse.

"Have you been to Egressus?" he asked Fel. It was a random question, but now seemed like as good a time as any to ask. They were all slightly askew. It's harder to lie about something when you're halfway out of your clothes.

"No," she said, fastening the leather straps of her greave. "Felix has, I think."

"Is there anything Felix hasn't done? He's practically a miracle."

"He helped you when no one else would. You owe him a debt."

"Don't be so quick to paint him in bright colors. He helped us from the shadows, at no cost to his reputation. I didn't see him running to protect the basilissa. In fact, if I remember, I saw him disappear in the opposite direction."

"He was looking for me. He knew that the other miles would attack you, or turn you in for the reward. Apparently, I wasn't smart enough to consider that. I helped you because Felix said you were good people."

Babieca wasn't sure how to reply. "Thank you," was all he said.

"You can thank me properly if we survive."

"All right," Morgan began. "I understand that you're taking a risk to help us. I don't know you very well, so please don't be offended by this question, but—why, exactly? If this goes wrong, you could face exile from the Gens of Miles."

"Your gens could do the same thing. What's your reason?"

"Well, I'd like to avoid a civil war, if possible. And it was my arrow that saved Pulcheria, so it might as well be my stupid decision that keeps this plan going. You're not really part of it, though. You could easily walk away."

"You're right," Fel said. "You don't know me very well. If you did, you'd realize that I don't walk away from people who need my help." When she smiled, there was a trace of bitterness to it. "Anyway, my gens doesn't accept me. There's a story behind that, but now isn't really the time."

Roldan was staring uneasily at the door. "You said this wasn't a protected space. Does that mean that someone could enter at any moment?"

"Not a lot of people know about this house. From the outside, it doesn't look like much. I doubt anyone's going to come charging in."

"It's fascinating," he said. "I always thought that to leave the city—I mean, to really leave it—you had to return to your alley. But this place acts like a sort of bridge. Could we go anywhere from here?"

"Felix understands it more than I do. All I know is that if you still remember the other world, you can cross over. It depends on your willpower, though. The longer you stay in Anfractus, the harder it is to remember what came before." She looked at Babieca. "You've spent the least time here, which is why you were able to cross on the first try."

"How sweet," Morgan said. "You're almost virginal."

"If only that were true."

The miles fastened her scabbard. The helmet they'd seen her in previously must have belonged to the Hippodrome, for she was bareheaded now. Babieca caught Morgan staring at her again. Her desire was anything but subtle. He couldn't imagine the sagittarius in bed with anyone, let alone a miles. The rivalry between their gens made even friendship inadvisable. Would Morgan pursue it? He'd never heard her speak of desire for anyone else. Then again, Roldan hadn't volunteered any such information, either. Until yesterday, Babieca realized, he'd thought of both friends as insubstantial, devoid of appetite. Because they didn't visit the basia or talk about their erotic conquests, he'd thought them flat and sexless. But they had their own unspoken intensities to deal with.

Roldan was still looking at the door. Babieca wanted to say something to him, to reassure him somehow, but the words caught in his throat. Everything had seemed simple when they were together, like two joints gliding into place. They'd made something with bright edges, a sealed mechanism dancing on its own. Apart, they had only words. Babieca had always preferred notes to nouns. Both deceived, but you had to forgive music, because it was older and somehow more necessary than conversation.

Fel turned to Morgan. "You and I are on equal footing. We both carry a die. We both have a gens behind us. I get the sense, though, that you're the leader of this company. So I'll defer to you. How should we proceed?"

Morgan looked surprised for a second. Uncertainty flashed across her eyes.

Roldan stepped forward. "We'll follow you. Whatever your decision is."

"I reserve the right to haunt you," Babieca said, "should this turn out badly. That aside—I'll do what you ask."

She nodded slowly. "Good. Each of you has a unique strength, and if we combine them, we may actually succeed. Our first step should be recovering that killer bee. As long as Basilissa Latona controls it, she can loose another swarm of silenoi on Pulcheria."

"Silenoi hunt in packs," Roldan said, "not swarms. You're mixing metaphors."

"Thank you for that clarification."

Babieca raised his hand.

Morgan gave him an odd look. "You can just speak."

"With your leadership being official and all, I just wanted to make sure that I was following protocol. I wouldn't want to—"

"Don't press me, lyre-boy."

"Very well. I think we should go back to the artifex. She knows more than she was willing to admit. I could see it in her eyes when she was talking about that thing. It filled her with curiosity. And the eunuch must have had some reason for choosing her."

"She could easily betray us."

"To whom? Narses? The girl's implicated—she's the one who gave us the fucking bee. If she tries to sell us out, she'll end up rotting alongside us in the carcer. The other prisoners will find all manner of unseemly uses for someone like her. I think she'll keep quiet about what we're planning."

"I'd like to hear more about that," Roldan said. "What comes later, I mean, once we've spoken with the artifex. How are we getting back into the arx?"

"One plan at a time," Morgan replied.

It was clear that she didn't know the answer, but Babieca wasn't as worried as he might have been. The Arx of Violets had many subtle points of entry. Like any fortress, it was designed to resist a frontal attack. Its murderous curves allowed invaders to be herded in, like cows led to the slaughter. But there must have been a postern gate, a tunnel, some passage that could be used for the transfer of supplies. The lime-walled undercroft, full of food and other precious things, must have been accessible from the harbor. In stories, the basilissa were always fleeing by boat—no mention was ever made of them leaving by the front gate.

"What do you know about this artifex?" Fel asked. "Besides the fact that she's curious and probably wants to save her own skin."

"Well"—Babieca cracked his knuckles—"we know that she's tired of fixing fountains for the basilissa. She was manipulated by the eunuch, just as we were."

"Don't sound so surprised. That's their job."

"She's young," Morgan said. "But smart. I'm inclined to agree with Babieca. She may not be an ally, but we're in the same cauldron."

"What's her name?"

Morgan managed to look slightly chagrined. "We don't know."

"Excellent. You want to charge into the Gens of Artifices, demanding to speak with an unknown girl. That couldn't possibly fail." She turned to Morgan. "Not that I'm questioning your decision, of course."

"It's morning."

The miles frowned at Roldan. "I can see that. Because I have eyes."

Her tone failed to bother him. "What I meant was, because of the hour, she won't be in her quarters. Instead, she'll be at the tower, paying respect to Fortuna. We may not know her name, but we'd still recognize her."

"Fel has a point, though," Morgan conceded. "Storming the tower in search of a red-haired girl is no better than roaming the halls of the gens."

"We don't all have to hang about," Babieca said. "I can go alone. The lot of us would attract attention, but nobody's going to notice a single trovador. They'll just assume I'm playing for coin. Musicians are always underfoot."

Fel didn't seem totally convinced. "Even if you find her, what's to keep her from screaming when she recognizes you?"

"He can be charming," Morgan said. "At times."

They left the house and walked toward the edge of the Subura, where the Tower of Artifices was located. The sun was punishing, and it gave them the excuse to lower their hoods. They formed a tight circle around Morgan, trying to obscure her appearance. Both the aedile and the arquites would be looking for a renegade sagittarius, but the rest of them might still escape notice. Babieca doubted that the tale told by the tower guards—involving a magic lyre and a fainting mechanical fox—had been received as anything close to an accurate report. It sounded like the type of story you'd make up after being caught asleep at your post.

Fel was probably known to the other miles, but that could

work in their favor. Even if they disliked her, as she'd suggested, her presence lent them a certain respectability. A meretrix would have been better, but a miles certainly worked in a pinch. As they made their way through the crowded streets, Babieca felt for the first time that he was part of a company. Two of them were die-carriers, and another could speak to lares. His cithara was obviously the weak link, but he possessed something else, something more valuable. Unlike the auditor, the miles, or the sagittarius, he had no reputation. Most people ignored him, because he was simply the entertainment. That gave him freedom to move about unchecked.

They reached the tower. A few younger artifices were milling around the entrance, playing with gear-driven toys that sputtered steam. Babieca turned to Morgan.

"Wait close by. I'm not sure how long this is going to take, but if things heat up, you should be prepared to run. Don't wait for me."

"We absolutely won't," Morgan replied.

"I was expecting the tiniest bit of resistance."

"Just go. Try not to make her scream or throw you out a window."

He approached the entrance. The artifices glanced at his cithara, then returned to urging on their machines. Babieca walked up the spiral stairs. Builders hugged the walls, intent on assembling or stripping down devices. Tiny brass wheels and other mechanical entrails littered the stairs, and he had to look closely to avoid them. One of the artifices was working on a tripod with golden wheels. The tripod gave a sudden lurch, its wheels grinding, and Babieca realized with a start that it could move on its own.

"Excuse her," the artifex said absently. "She's newly made."

The towers had always intrigued him. Built to please Fortuna, they provided a haven, court, and school for each of the day gens. The Tower of Artifices, over time, had become more of a workshop than a place of worship, and Babieca saw very little obeisance going on. You were supposed to turn inward, to regard yourself and your place on Fortuna's wheel, but the artifices concentrated entirely on deciphering scrolls and tablets. They were thinking about their next project, not their fate. He didn't know what went on in those towers devoted to the night gens, but he'd heard stories.

The meretrix would know. He's of the night gens.

The Tower of Meretrices, he thought, must be a giant basia fucking the skyline. A monument to love and coin. He pictured Felix kissing the wheel. He must have had his reasons for taking the mask. As Roldan had pointed out, trovadores and meretrices were separated only by a spoke on the wheel, parallel gens that watched each other uneasily. Music's reverie was not so far from love's. Both songs loosened the limbs, both made you close your eyes, wishing to lock the moment in amber. Perhaps it was useless to assume any moral high ground.

Babieca reached the top floor. Light cut through tall, red-tinted windows, making everyone look as if they'd been drawn fresh from the forge. Unlike the sanctum of sagittarii, which had been sparse and well ordered, this room was a blaze of activity. Builders were gathered in loud groups, comparing machines, swapping parts, decrying the tools of their rivals. Devices leapt and played at their feet, sparking, clattering, making awkward circles, while their creators looked on with fierce pride. The altar to the goddess was covered in mechanical debris. Her wheel turned, powered by water, but its hiss was drowned out by the cries of the builders. Only a single artifex knelt before it. Babieca spied a lock of red hair, which had escaped from her cowl, and smiled.

He knelt beside her. "What do you ask of Fortuna?"

She turned, and her eyes widened. "What are you doing here?"

"Answer my question, and I'll answer yours."

The young artifex glanced around the room. "You're wanted, you know. You, the auditor, and the crazy archer who felled the silenus. Anyone in this tower could find a dozen ways to spend the reward they'd earn for your capture."

"They're distracted, and I have an unremarkable face. Answer my question."

"I'm asking forgiveness."

"Well, you should. That bee nearly killed a basilissa."

"Keep your voice down."

"You can't deny that you're in as deep as we are."

"You're practically underwater. I'm still clinging to the shore."

"Let go of the branch and help us."

Her look was between fear and anger. "I'm not yet a builder. Just a nemo with no die and no machina to serve her. Basilissa Latona won't hesitate to kill me."

"Nor us. It's going to be a huge killing party, which is why you should come."

"How are you so flippant about this?"

Babieca held his hand out to Fortuna's wheel, letting it graze his fingers as it passed. Though the motion was artificial, it still made him feel less alone.

"I'm scared," he said. "Like you, I'm no die-carrier. I've no right to ask a boon of the goddess. All I have is music and a bit of luck. But my fear doesn't matter. If Basilissa Pulcheria dies, there will be war. Die-carriers and dominae are going to decide the course of that war. But the nemones—you and I—will be ground underfoot. We won't have a chance. I don't know about you, but I love this city. I want more time. I want to grow. If Anfractus goes to war, I'll be stoking a hypocaust again, if I don't become a meal for some hungry silenus."

The artifex considered his words for a moment. Then she leaned in, speaking even lower in spite of the noise around her.

"I may have an answer," she said. "But it's in the undercroft."

"Can you sneak me in?"

"We'll need to find you a proper tunica. If nobody's looking too closely, you might pass for a builder. Follow me."

She led him to the floor below. It was an empty tabularium. The stone shelves were filled with scroll cases and pumiced covers, along with ragged strands of decaying papyrus. Next to one of the shelves, someone had placed a wooden crate. Babieca saw that it was filled with an odd assortment: lenses, gears and bolts, a sandal, bent wires, a broken nutcracker.

"What is that?"

"A vessel for lost things. Every floor has them. Artifices are incredibly forgetful."

She reached all the way to the bottom, withdrawing a soiled tunica. It was covered in grease spots and sported multiple tears. Brushing the flies away, she shook out the tunica, then handed it to Babieca.

"This has been here for weeks. I think it belonged to one of the more ancient builders. He's a bit touched now, and sometimes he leaves his clothes in the oddest places."

"Did he piss in that?"

"I imagine so. Put it on."

"You're joking."

"Were you planning to knock someone out and steal their clothes? There's hardly time for that, and it will draw notice, even from this lot. Put on the tunica. I'll say that you're my idiot brother and I've just dragged you from a ditch somewhere."

"I feel as if you planned this."

He undressed, folding his own tunica neatly and laying it in the vessel. Then, shuddering, he put on the soiled garment. This close to his skin, it smelled faintly of vomit, among other things. He stifled a gag. His flesh was crawling, but he couldn't argue with her logic. Attacking an artifex would be stupid. This might actually work, unpleasant though it was.

Babieca followed her down the spiral stairs. A few of the less-distracted builders looked up as he passed, wrinkling their noses. Their interest waned after a moment, and they returned to their tasks. A filthy artifex wasn't enough to fully divert their attention. The air grew chill as they passed underground, to the lowest level. A bored builder stood by the entrance to the undercroft, reading a tablet. He looked up, and his eyes narrowed.

"Who's he? Why does he reek?"

"Found him passed out beneath the aqueduct," she replied. "He's family, though. What can you do?"

"If I found my brother in that state, I'd leave him there."

She gave him a long look. His expression suddenly changed, as if he'd only now recognized her. Then, paling slightly, he nodded.

"Sure. Go ahead."

They passed through the door that led to the undercroft.

"What was that about?" Babieca whispered.

"It's complicated. I'll explain later."

His reply died softly as he took in the room. It was twice as large as any undercroft that he'd seen before, with a vaulted ceiling. Mosaics on the walls depicted Fortuna as architect, laying the foundations of Anfractus. Devices of every shape and size were gathered in piles, some of which came close to brushing the ceiling. Babieca saw clusters of lodestones and glass spheres for kindling fire. There were alarm clocks, door openers, self-trimming lamps that would burn all night if left alone. Discarded sundials and water clocks had been pushed against the walls, next to rusted pumps and lengths of broken chain. One pile was composed entirely of wooden birds, which must have warbled at one time but were now silent.

"We keep all manner of things here," she said. "Broken machinae, toys that never worked, devices no longer in fashion."

Babieca regarded a giant water screw leaning against the wall. Its teeth reminded him of a savage, burrowing animal. Next to it was a glittering case with a brass disc inside.

"What's that thing?" He pointed to the small box.

"You can attach it to a wagon. It chimes with regularity, letting you know what distance you've traveled."

"Strange," he said, surveying the clocks and dials, "how officious we are about parceling out time. All that really matters is day and night."

"Time is rhythm. Without it, there'd be no music."

"You've got an answer for everything."

"That's what my mother used to say."

He followed her through the chamber. Glass counters winked at him from the mounds, resting amid shattered spokes and bits of leather. He saw dispensers with coin slots—which he knew had once been popular—huddled next to a cracked water organ. In one corner was a frightening mechanical likeness of Fortuna. The paint was peeling from her face, and she held a libation cup whose gems had been pried off.

"The cup used to pour milk," the artifex said. "And her eyes moved, or so I've heard. Such things are deemed ostentatious now. Latona buried it here, along with whatever else she thought was too bright or loud."

"She may have been right about that one," Babieca admitted. "I wouldn't want Fortuna's torso splashing milk on me."

He followed her to the dimmest fold of the undercroft. There sat a pile of rings, fibulae, and other adornments. Most were rusted, but a few still held chips of onyx and chalcedony. They were fashioned into countless shapes: diminutive wheels, vine leaves, nightingales, and the inevitable cock meant as a fertility charm.

"Fibulae used to be a huge business," she said. "You could fit them with all kinds of concealed mechanisms. A bird would chirp at your breast. A snake would writhe about your finger, driven by the teeth of tiny gears. A few of them, the older ones, even had real power. They could let you walk unseen in the middle of the day or give you the gift of many tongues. But that art was lost centuries ago. Now, they're just bright, useless things."

"If they're so useless, why did you take me here?"

She looked away. "I've done a bit of research on the bee fibula."

"I knew it."

"I tore through every tablet. Some of the schematics and descriptions were beyond my understanding, but I did find something that mentioned a similar device. It had multiple functions—the most obvious being a sonic diversion, meant to draw the attention of the silenoi. Like a dog whistle."

He watched her dig through the abandoned lapidary. She picked up a copper bird, examined its base for a moment, then put it back.

"What are you looking for?"

"The bee is only part of the mechanism," she said absently, plunging her hands deep into the gleaming pile. "With the base, you can call the insect to you, or even send it flying back to the one who made it. We may not have the original base, but according to what I've read, they were all built along the same principles."

His eyes widened. "Are you saying that you can make one?"

"I can try. I've got all the spare parts that I could ask for, and like I said, I've studied the fibula. I'm no expert, but I may be able to fashion something close."

"I can see why Narses chose you."

She looked slightly embarrassed. "Don't sing my praises yet. Much of this is beyond repair. Just try to be quiet, and watch the door."

He fell silent, watching her instead. She was too distracted to notice. Her hands moved quickly, lifting and sorting, occasionally removing a piece to lay it aside. She assembled a collection of small gears, a silver beak, three lengths of wire, a brass disc, and something triangular that he couldn't identify. He watched her break brooches, sifting through their interiors and taking what she needed. The resulting hoard seemed random to him, but she stared at it thoughtfully, examining bright fragments. Eventually, she began to fasten things together. She tested gears, rubbing their brass teeth along her thumb. Like the artifices he'd seen on the steps, her mind was entirely focused.

Something moved in one of the piles.

"Did you hear that?"

She ignored him. The room was silent for a moment. Then he heard it again, a discrete rustling in the debris. He prepared himself to face a murderous machina, or perhaps the crazy old artifex that she'd mentioned earlier, whose stinking tunica he wore. What emerged from the pile, though, was neither of those things. He actually felt relief when he saw those familiar black orbs, swiveling in their brass sockets.

"Sulpicia! How long have you been here?"

At this, the young artifex looked up. Whatever she'd been assembling dropped from her suddenly nerveless grasp. Her eyes widened.

"Long enough to see that this one knows what she's doing." The fox regarded her mildly. "You're trying to reconstruct a fibula, correct?"

She stared at the fox's whirring tail. "Are you—what I think you are?"

"Her name's Sulpicia," Babieca said. "And yes."

Gently, as if reaching toward insubstantial smoke, the artifex held out her hand. Sulpicia raised a single brass paw. Girl and machina touched, briefly. She stared at the fox in wonder. Her mouth moved slowly, but no words came out.

"You've done a nice job," Sulpicia said. "You're missing something, though. Here." She nudged a small piece of brass across the floor. "Use this. It won't be pretty, but that's not really the point of the thing."

"I thought you lived in the Arx of Violets."

"Every now and again, my brother and I like to visit this place and check on the builders. Mostly to ensure that you don't forge a weapon or burn down the city."

"And"—she looked uncertainly at Babieca—"you know each other."

"I fainted in his friend's arms," Sulpicia said. "Or pretended to, at any rate. Now go on. Attach the last piece. I want to see if it works."

With shaking fingers, she attached the final component. What she held resembled a short rod with gleaming parts. Nothing happened at first. Then Babieca heard a low clicking noise, which seemed to come from the fibula. The artifex looked at it uncertainly, as if it might catch fire or devour her hand.

"What's it doing?"

"You'll see." The fox lay down, examining her paws. "There aren't many devices like that left in the city. If the creature is nearby, it should—"

Babieca heard a buzzing. At first it was faint, but it grew louder. A smile broke across his face when he saw a blurry spark rush through the open doorway. Like a scrap of quick-silver, it flew directly toward the fibula. The artifex, to her credit, stayed still. The bee circled her hand, then alighted on the fibula, as if it were a flower petal. Babieca drew closer. He could see the insect's wings, fluttering rapidly. He noticed an unmistakable spot of green on its reflective underside. A dot of emerald blood.

"The killing instrument returns." Sulpicia scratched her ear. "Not much to look at, but then again, its function has always been more defensive. Artifices of old used such machinae to distract silenoi—along with other things that have excellent hearing."

The artifex stared at the bee. Her expression was a puzzle. She'd been far more astonished by Sulpicia, which was understandable.

"It's under your control now," Babieca said. "Didn't you say that you could make it return to the one who forged it?"

"I—perhaps, but—"

"That's simple," the fox said. "You have the whole fibula now. The creature must obey. All you need say is: *Return to your maker.*"

The artifex hesitated. "Is that such a good idea?"

"We need to know who fashioned this thing," Babieca said. "Anyone that powerful might be able to help us. Who-ever it is, we need to reach them before Latona does. They're in danger just as surely as we are."

The artifex sighed. Then she murmured to the bee: "Return to your maker."

The insect leapt from its perch. It hovered in the air for a moment, as if uncertain. They all watched it dancing in the dark of the undercroft, wings whirring. It almost seemed to be thinking about something. Perhaps it was recalling the face of its maker. Then it shot through the open doorway.

"Follow that bee!" Babieca cried.

They ran out of the undercroft, catching a glimpse of silver as it flew upstairs. The bored artifex who'd been reading stared at them in surprise. They ignored him, running up the stairs in pursuit of the insect. They found it flying in a circle within the tabularium. Was it waiting for them? Babieca couldn't quite tell. It flew outside again. He grabbed his tunic and cithara, falling a step behind the fox and the artifex as they kept pursuit. The bee left the tower through a window, and they burst through the front door.

Roldan, Morgan, and Fel were waiting by the entrance.

"What are you—" Morgan began.

"No time!" Babieca broke into a run. "Keep up!"

They flew through the city, past wagons, messengers, and lean furs cleaving to alleys. They seemed to float above the stones as they ran, their sandals touching air. Sweating, panting, breaking into laughter, they followed the silver bee. Surely, they looked absurd: a man in a reeking tunica, clutching his instrument as he tried to keep pace with a red-haired artifex. Behind them, a miles was struggling to keep up, her single bronze greave catching the sunlight. To her right was a sagittarius, and to her left, an auditor, legs pumping, eyes straining to see what resembled an erratic star flying ahead of them. Babieca crowed. His body was on fire with joy. He was running along the spokes of Fortuna's wheel. As long as he stayed in motion, he would never fall. None of them would.

The bee led them to the lowest part of the city. Here the cobblestones gave way to patched earth and marshy pools. The habitations fell away. The path was overgrown with reeds and tall osiers, brittle from the sun. They came to a marble-fronted building, silent and smelling of incense. Babieca watched the glint of silver as it flew into the necropolis. There was no time to question its motivations. The company followed.

Inside, the mausoleum was dimly lit by oil-fed lamps. The first graves were modest, arrayed in a plots that resembled dice. Babieca saw brittle wreathes, rusted baubles, and other gifts left by the living. Someone had placed a hen's egg next to a child's marker, symbolizing rebirth. They passed a row of red-and-black urns, decorated with funerary portraits. The ground sloped as they continued, drawing them deeper into the earth. The air was cool and sweet-smelling. He wanted to read the inscriptions, but there was no time. A few tired lupae watched them as they passed, saying nothing.

At last, they came to a section deep within the necropolis. They found the bee circling a grave marker with a rusted hammer beside it. The artifex had reached the grave first, and she was staring at it strangely.

Babieca peered at the letters on the stone. "'I was Naucrate,'" he read softly, "'the artifex. I maintained the fountains. May the goddess protect my daughter, Julia.'"

The artifex held out her hand. The bee alighted once again on the fibula, regarding her calmly as it fluttered its wings. Then it grew still.

"Naucrate was my mother," Julia said. "She did more than maintain the fountains. She was a true artifex. I barely hold a flake of her talent."

Babieca stared at her. "It was your mother who fashioned the bee," he said. "All this time, you've been the missing piece."

She looked bitterly at the insect. "This was all that she left me. It didn't fly, or make noise—it was just a useless thing. I could never understand why she wanted me to keep it. When the spado offered to buy it in his master's name, I—" She was on the verge of tears. "The money was too good. I couldn't say no."

"Wait," Morgan said. "What do you mean, 'in his master's name'?"

"Well—it wasn't Narses who paid me. It was another spado, a younger one. His servant, I guess. I wasn't sure how he'd heard of the thing, but artifices like to gossip. It was finely crafted, even if it didn't do anything. I could see why he'd want to buy it. So I took his coins and erased it from my mind. The last piece of my mother. I was happy to see it go." Her eyes widened. "Then, last night, it came buzzing at my window. I'd already heard talk of the bloody banquet.

What was I supposed to do? I yelled at it to go away. It flew off."

"Why did you lie to us?" Babieca asked.

"I was frightened and ashamed. I just wanted you to leave me alone. How was I to know that my mother's brooch would cause so much trouble? Look at it. Would you imagine that such a little thing could be so dangerous?"

"Julia—" Morgan gave her a long look. "Describe this young eunuch."

"I don't know. He was sort of fat. He wore a green cap, like they do sometimes. He had soft hands, and a high voice. He carried the seal of Narses."

"He was at the Hippodrome," Roldan said. "Standing by Narses. And I saw him once before that, eating lemon sharbah."

"We spoke with him at the banquet. He was polite. Harmless, I thought." Babieca chuckled. "All this time, we've had our eye on the wrong spado. I don't think Narses had anything to do with this. It was his servant. Basilissa Latona must have made some kind of deal with him."

"A power-hungry spado," Roldan said. "Could that really be it?"

"Remember what Felix said." Babieca was nodding now. "He never spoke with Narses about the fibula—only to one of his attendants. He must have stolen the seal. Maybe he showed it to Felix as well."

"I don't understand." Julia placed the fibula in her tunic. "Why would a spado try to murder a basilissa?"

"Because he wants a promotion," Fel replied. "Narses wouldn't allow this. Latona must be trying to work around him. Fortuna knows what she promised the young eunuch, but it most likely involves his master's head on a pike."

Morgan turned to Julia. "If you're through lying—perhaps you can help us. We need to get Basilissa Pulcheria to safety."

Julia looked thoughtful. "I might know a way into the arx. It's not pleasant."

Morgan was about to reply when she suddenly wrinkled her nose. She looked at Babieca in astonishment. "Did you piss yourself?"

"It's the tunica!"

"You might want to accustom yourself to that particular smell," Julia said. "The place I have in mind is a lot worse."

4

THEY PLAYED IN THE NECROPOLIS UNTIL
nightfall. Julia collected stones for latrinculi, and the ground
served as their board. After they'd grown tired of losing to
Fel, they traded dirty epigrams, writing them on scattered
bits of paper. They tried to make an alquerque box out of
twigs and twine scraps, but it wouldn't hold, so they
scratched spaces into the earth instead. They invented a
game involving red clay shards, which they'd gathered from
a broken amphora. Then Roldan persuaded a bored salamander to exhale small rings of fire. Very few people came
near their corner of the mausoleum. Most would rather visit
the basia than the city of the dead. Only a handful of mourn-
ers descended those dark steps.

Once every game had been exhausted, they returned to
the surface. Julia led them out of the reedy corner. They
kept to the city's most obscure angles, walking down blind
corners, avoiding the densely populated Via Rumor. As the
setting sun doubled shadows, they came to the Tower of
Trovadores. Babieca heard bawdy music from above. Failing
light struck the yellow-tinted windows, until they burned
like gold leaf on papyrus. Without a doubt, bards of variable

desire would be lounging on the steps, getting drunk and composing trenchant verse. No member of the gens even suspected his existence. He was a nemo, a pathetic strummer destined to chap his fingers begging in doorways. He closed his eyes for a moment, listening to the clamor of bad decisions being made by the beautiful.

Julia led them down an alley that ran behind the tower. At the very end was an iron grill set into the wall.

"This leads to the cloaca," she said. "The sewer runs throughout Anfractus, splitting off into various branches fed by the aqueduct. Not only does it connect to the baths, it also runs beneath the Arx of Violets."

"Shouldn't it be locked?" Roldan asked.

"Furs use it," Babieca replied. "Every night, bodies are dragged into the cloaca. At one time, there was probably a lock, but the aedile grew tired of replacing it."

"What made you think of this?" Morgan asked Julia.

"My mother used to mend broken pipes. She knew a great deal about water and its pathways through the city. The cloaca, she used to say, was the most impressive thing about Anfractus. In the beginning it was little more than an open trench, but the founders paved it in lava-stone, transforming it into a far-reaching road."

"A furry shithole," Babieca clarified.

"We shouldn't run afoul of them, since they keep mostly to the south end. No fur in her right mind would walk directly beneath the arx."

"Yet we're just stupid enough to try it."

Julia shrugged. "You wanted a way in. Unless you can change your form and walk through the front gate, or hover over the battlements like a shade, this is your only choice."

Morgan smiled at him. "Plus, you already smell the part."

"I told you—that reek was from the tunica."

"I've smelled your wind before. Don't blame it on the clothes."

Julia kindled a lamp, and they stepped through the small door. A paved path ran through the middle of the cloaca, with churning water on either side. The stone roof was supported by concentric barrel vaults, their design solid and unpretentious. The founders, so it was said, had built Anfractus when their power was at its height. They'd also built roads connecting this city to others, but those had decayed over time. Now they were broken stone, smashed arteries overgrown by plants. The spine of the great via belonged to the spreading forest, which would one day cover the cities themselves, if the silenoi had their way.

They passed great pipes that led upward, carrying refuse away from thermae and a few extravagant homes. Water from the twin rivers flowed left and right, flushing the cloaca. This did little to improve the smell, though. Refuse floated in the watery margins, forming a scum that crept along the sides of their path. Morgan distributed fistfuls of old herbs, which they'd taken from the necropolis. Their sweetness was careworn and faint but better than nothing. Babieca saw various items floating by: a sword hilt, a leather purse, soiled smallclothes, and even a decomposing book. Roldan almost reached out to grab this, but Morgan, anticipating his desire, shook her head.

"Best to avoid the water," she said.

There were rumors of animals that lived in the cloaca—giant rats and moths that would suck out your marrow—but all they encountered were questionable pools. This was the labyrinthine stone bowel of the city, where blood, dye, and piss all drained in equal measures. Once, they heard the sound of distant footsteps. Furs knew how to walk silently. It must have been a company such as theirs, looking for something beneath the city. Julia covered the lamp. They stood still in the darkness, listening. The second company was moving away from them. After a moment, their footfalls were no longer audible. Julia continued, leading them farther down the slimy road. Her pauses and frequent backward glances told Babieca that the artifex wasn't as confident as she seemed.

Eventually, they reached a place where several gray streams converged. A rust-caked ladder had been attached to the wall. Several of its rungs were either broken or covered in layers of filth, streaked by sinister greens and browns.

"This should lead to a bank of toilets," Julia said, "that is positioned near the Patio of Lions. No sweet ascent, but it will get us inside."

Babieca looked skeptically at the ladder. "What if we crawl out of the cistern just as some poor soul is taking a shit? He'll drop dead when he sees us."

Morgan grabbed the closest rung. "His shade will have to forgive us."

Slowly, they climbed up the reeking shaft. After the fifth or sixth rung, his hands stopped shuddering when they touched the unimaginable. He focused on the hiss of the water, telling himself that the twin rivers were doing their best. Just as he was beginning to feel faint, he saw a square of yellow light. He stood in a foul cistern, a catch-all for the toilets above. Morgan lowered down a rope, and he took it, bracing his feet against the slick walls. It took some effort, but he managed to climb through the narrow aperture. He slid out of the disgusting keyhole, breathing hard while trying to push down the bile in his throat.

The midden was empty, save for a symposium of flies. Once everyone had reached level ground, they paused to retch and regroup. The herbs were next to useless. There was no way to conceal the horrific perfume of the cloaca.

"I'm having second thoughts," Julia said, wiping a strand of spit from her lips. "Instead of continuing, I think I'd rather set myself on fire."

"Not a chance," Fel replied. "Aside from the sagittarius, you're the only one with any knowledge of this place."

She stared at the ring of filth around her hands. "Sweet Fortuna, why is it *green*? What could possibly—"

"Don't think about it. Just keep going."

They left the latrine and walked down a corridor. The ceiling had a stalactite vault, brimming with irregular stones. Rhombus patterns were carved along the walls, and their foliated borders held secret inscriptions that Babieca couldn't decipher. The corridor gradually widened, supported by red stilted arches. It opened up entirely, and moonlight guided them onto the Patio of Lions. The night was warm, yet still held the possibility of rain. A reflecting pool bisected the patio, its waters motionless. The lions stood on an island in the center, six of them in all, carved from marble. They clustered around a fountain, each one favoring a different line of sight. They were supposed to represent the six spokes of the day gens, Fortuna's bright wheel.

"My mother said there used to be another fountain," Julia whispered, "made of black marble and consecrated to the night gens, but Latona's grandmother had it removed."

Babieca studied the colored tessellations that made up the floor of the patio. Red and green birds flew across a white sky, mingling with stars and crescents, until he couldn't tell where one shape finished and the next began. When he stared at them too closely, spots flickered before his eyes, and he had to look away from their infinite dance. Circular stone benches had been placed around the pool, lit by hanging lamps, while lotus flowers drifted in the water. All Babieca could think of was the possibility of washing his filthy tunica. He was on the verge of stepping into the pool when he heard footsteps.

"Back against the wall," Morgan whispered. "Don't even breathe."

They waited in the lengthening shadows. Two figures emerged from the north end of the patio, walking side by side. They approached the pool, and he resisted the urge to swear softly beneath his breath. The first was a young spado in a green cap and tunica. He had a wispy beard and slender hands, which he kept folded in front of him. Basilissa Latona was at his side, dressed in a mantle of leather whose hem brushed her pointed slippers. Gems and silver spangles decorated the front of the gown. Her pearl diadem caught the light, casting trails of nacre across her shoulders, like milkweed.

"Double the guards at her door," Latona said to the eunuch. "I don't care if they think the north wing is haunted. If they hesitate, show them the old capon's seal. That should pacify them. Not even miles are daft enough to cross the chamberlain."

"Their hesitation would be less, my Basilissa, if you gave the order."

"No. I've already gone too far. My seal could be used against me, but Narses doesn't have long to live. It won't matter if we pervert his word."

"He's not completely blind. I think he's been talking to the aedile."

"His arrogance will undo him. His first mistake was to underestimate you, Mardian. He allowed you to suffer in his shadow."

"I was loyal to him, my Basilissa, until he questioned your will."

The ruler of Anfractus watched the lotus flowers drifting by. For a moment, she seemed diminished, a woman struggling beneath the weight of her finery. Then her eyes narrowed, and the aegis crept back into her features. Her mouth compressed to a thin line. She seemed remote and immeasurably ancient, daughter of a ruling class whose beginnings could no longer be traced with any kind of certainty. Her ancestors had built this palace, along with the magnificent sewer upon which it stood. They had built her throne and, presumably, the mechanical foxes that slept at its base. The founders were responsible for her position, their blood ran in her veins, yet those archaic grandmothers were barely ghosts to her.

"We've slept for too long," she said. "Afraid to reach for anything, terrified of our own shadows on the wall. Something has to change. Otherwise"—she made a gesture encompassing the patio, its lovely tesserae, its clever hydraulics—"we'll languish in this beautiful, torpid place, like virgins afraid to leave their father's halls."

"I am no virgin, my Basilissa," Mardian said.

"No." She smiled thinly. "Your cold passions obey no limit, do they?"

"I work with what I have."

"When Narses falls, you shall have all that you desire." Latona considered the stars. "Egressus will be mine—all of its resources and its loyal subjects. All of the ancient power that sleeps beneath it. Then the lares will finally listen. The old frontiers will fall."

"They shall march for you," Mardian agreed.

"My mother didn't have the nerve. She threw away the relics and pacified the gens, day and night, but taking Egressus never occurred to her. She was content with Anfractus. I have always wanted more."

Mardian bowed his head. "My Basilissa—gladly would I see this plan fulfilled. Make me your die, your hallowed instrument. I will not fail you."

Her eyes wavered for a moment as she looked down at him. Latona seemed to mistrust his fervor, to draw back slightly from his conviction. But she steeled herself and nodded.

"You will be chamberlain by morning. For now, keep the old capon distracted. There's one last secret that I must pry from Pulcheria. Then you can throw her out the window."

"Nothing would please me more."

Mardian and Latona exited the patio, disappearing through the north entrance. For a moment, nobody spoke. Then Fel said, "It doesn't sound like we have much time. The basilissa is being held in the north wing. If we can get to her before the guard is doubled, we might stand a chance of freeing her."

"What did she mean," Morgan asked, "about the lares marching?"

"She said that the old frontiers would fall," Roldan said. "She's planning some sort of invasion. Egressus isn't her only target. She's after something else."

"But where are we even supposed to take Pulcheria?" Julia asked. "It's not like we can smuggle her out of the city."

"She must have come on a ship," Roldan said. "If we can reach the harbor—"

"Are you hearing all of these *ifs*?" Julia shook her head. "What's to keep the undinae from drowning us, or the city guard from cutting us to pieces?"

Babieca smiled. "Just luck."

"You're all crazy."

"I don't see you running in the opposite direction."

The artifex sighed. "I guess I'm just stupid enough to stay."

"That's the spirit."

They headed north. Morgan was familiar with the miles and their schedules. They avoided the lamplight as much as they could. Whenever the sagittarius halted, they would stop short behind her, keeping silent. Babieca felt like the stones must be able to smell them. More than anything, he wanted to pour a bucket of clean water over his head, to rip off his clothes and scrub every inch of himself with sea sponges. When he'd imagined going on a real quest, he hadn't factored in the possibility that he might be terrified and covered in shit.

Of course, he hadn't expected a lot of things. A miles with one greave. An artifex with a mechanical bee under her tunica. A struggle between men who were not men precisely, whose cold passions obeyed no limit. Now he remembered seeing the young eunuch at the Hippodrome, seated not far from where they'd first met Julia. Surely, he was the spado that Felix had spoken of, carrying the authority of his master's insignia. Narses may have had a fierce reputation, but Mardian—a shadow, Latona called him—had outmaneuvered the chamberlain. He'd arranged all of this without dirtying his hands. He must have been a descendant of the old spadones, those grim gardeners who pruned the court with blades dipped in aconite.

When they were certain that Mardian and the basilissa had gone on ahead, they crossed the patio. Morgan's knowledge of the arx was useful but incomplete. All she could do was steer them in what felt like the right direction. She was, however, familiar with the most heavily guarded areas. These they avoided, sometimes stopping short around a blind corner, inches from a group of miles. The few archers whom they saw were on their way to the battlements or the towers, distractedly counting arrows or making minute adjustments to their bows. They tended to dislike confined spaces and were more comfortable atop the arx than within it, like birds clinging to the sides of an aerie. Babieca tried not to think about what would happen if they were caught. Musicians weren't known for their ability to withstand torture.

They came to a junction. Lamplight flickered against the rhombus patterns in the walls, throwing long shadows across horseshoe arches. Morgan stopped. Her eyes narrowed. Silently, she drew an arrow from her painted quiver. She notched it, took aim, and spoke:

"I know you're there. I can here you breathing."

There was some light scuffling. Then Eumachia stepped from the shadows. Her girl's tunic, decorated with green fringe, was wrinkled and dusty. She wore a tortoiseshell comb in her hair, along with a rock crystal pendant that gleamed in the semidarkness.

"Chasing foxes again?" Morgan replaced the arrow. "You should be careful. Everyone's a bit agitated tonight."

"My mother searches for you." She managed to look haughty, but only for a second. Then her eyes filled with worry. "You're to be stripped of your die, repudiated by your gens. Before, they were just going to hurt you a bit, then let you go. But now—"

"Don't concern yourself with that." Morgan gave her a sly look, as an older sister might give to a younger. "Can you keep quiet about seeing us?"

"Where are you going?"

"What part of 'don't concern yourself' haven't you grasped?"

Eumachia folded slim arms across her chest. "Tell me."

"Morgan," Fel began, "this isn't a good idea."

The sagittarius looked thoughtfully at the basilissa's daughter—a short, scrawny girl, somewhat resembling a dusty arras. "The last time we saw each other, she had the chance to make things a lot worse for me. Yet she didn't. Her fox trusted me, and so did she. I think we can trust her now."

"Brilliant," Fel murmured. "We're basing our decisions on automata now."

"We need to find the other basilissa," Morgan said. "She's being held in the north wing."

Eumachia frowned. "There are only rats in the north wing. Pulcheria's in the west wing, under heavy guard. They've converted one of the guest apartments into a cell."

"We just overheard your mother saying that she was in the north wing."

"You heard what you were meant to hear. My mother is accustomed to having people around her, listening to whatever she says. No ruler tells the truth in public."

Morgan considered this for a moment. She turned to Fel.

"I know you're not happy with how this is going, but—"

"Point taken," the miles said. "The girl's obviously smarter than us. We might as well listen to her."

"What's the quickest way to the west wing?" Morgan asked Eumachia.

"Follow me."

"Swear that you won't lead us straight to Latona."

"What do you take me for?"

Morgan gave her a long look.

Eumachia sighed. "I swear it—on my grandmother's ashes."

She turned to the right, and they followed her. The corridors narrowed and widened, seemingly of their own accord, like living veins. Eumachia knew exactly where she was going and didn't hesitate for a second. Babieca, significantly less sure of what was about to happen, found himself sweating. The tunica clung to his back and shoulders. The cithara in its case felt twice as heavy, a burden weighing down his every step. What were his weapons—a harp and a crooked short sword? Fel and Morgan had weapons that could inflict serious damage. Roldan, he supposed, could call out to the lares. Even Julia seemed like she might be good in a fight, and the bee in her tunica would certainly be a surprise.

They rounded a corner, and Eumachia stopped. It wasn't a pause—the girl stopped short in clear surprise. Narses, the high chamberlain, was sitting on a stone bench. His pose was casual, as if he'd been reading, or resting his legs on the exedra. He was not surprised to see them. His dark eyes took them in calmly. His beard, red-gold in the lamplight, was uncommon for a spado. His limbs were long, which was usual, but he also had a broad chest. A falchion hung from his belt, fastened by a series of delicate gold chains.

"Well." He spoke in a thin, slightly nasal voice. "I see you've chosen to be recklessly stupid. That takes some measure of courage, at least."

Eumachia inclined her head. "Chamberlain. We were—ah—"

"About to commit treason?"

"No. I mean—fine, perhaps a *bit* of treason, but not—" She turned to Morgan. "This was your plan. You talk to him."

"But you were doing so well," Morgan said dryly.

Narses turned to regard her. "You fired the shot."

"Yes, Chamberlain."

"That must have been a costly roll indeed."

"It was."

He rose from the exedra. "Whatever Latona is planning, I am on the wrong side of it. I have known that for some time."

"Did you try to capture us?" Babieca asked suddenly. "When we were testing the fibula, someone called the aedile. Was it you?"

His eyes glittered. "That was when the aedile still listened to me. Now, like the arquites, he is only receptive to orders carried out in my name."

"Mardian betrayed you."

"Our students often do. They outgrow us and decide that we no longer deserve our position. A little ambition can be a remarkable incentive."

"Will you help us?" Eumachia demanded. "At this point, it's not as if you've got a choice. My mother will have your head in a basket, come morning."

Narses smiled. "Children get to the point, don't they? I suppose you're right though, bobbin. Latona has decided that our views are incompatible. That usually doesn't end well for the one not wearing a diadem." He drew his sword. "I'll take you to her cell. I don't have the key, but I suppose an old spado couldn't hurt your company."

"Couldn't hurt." Julia laughed. "The high chamberlain is too modest. He's an accomplished fighter. He's led troops into battle."

"That was another life," Narses replied. His eyes told a slightly different story, though. He still remembered the chaos of the battlefield, and his arm didn't tremble beneath the weight of such a fine sword.

They followed the spado. How ironic, Babieca thought, that they'd seen him as the enemy, the puppet-master. All along, it was invisible Mardian who'd been working against them, forging letters, waving about his master's seal. Now it was the chamberlain leading them by uncertain lamplight, blade drawn, more a soldier than a courtier. *Not like other boys.* The snatch of song drifted through his mind. He'd heard it long ago. Some things couldn't be held by a song. They were sharp and complicated. He looked back. Roldan caught his gaze and smiled a little, as if to say, *Aren't we having a fun night?*

Narses held up his hand. They stopped. Morgan and Fel joined him, hugging the wall and trying to soften their footfalls.

"Six miles," the spado whispered. "One for each of us."

"We're *seven*," Eumachia insisted.

Narses gave her a stern look. "You are the basilissa's daughter. Your life is worth more than ours, and when the battle begins, you will hide. Am I understood?"

"I'm not hiding."

"We could bind your hands now, and settle the matter."

Flushing, she looked down. "I'll hide."

Julia drew her dagger. Her hand wasn't steady. Roldan did the same. His weapon, at least, was finely balanced. Julia's dagger looked as if she'd made it out of spare parts, like the fake fibula. He drew his own blade, trying to make it look as if the gesture were natural. He was sweating so much that it nearly dropped from his grasp.

Narses saw him and shook his head slightly. "Your talents lie in the musical realm, my boy. Stay behind us and play something to distract them." He looked at Roldan and Julia. "The same goes for both of you. Play to your strengths. Don't just start stabbing with those things. You're barely holding them the right way."

The spado reached beneath his gold-fringed tunica. Carefully, he drew out his die, which hung from a leather thong. Babieca had never seen a night die before. It was carved from flawless obsidian, and its pips were like sunken eyes. Narses touched the die for luck. Then he surveyed the ragged, hilarious company before him.

"We have only one chance," he said. "If they call for reinforcements, we're lost. Move fast, and follow your instincts. Understood?"

They nodded.

"Very well." He raised his sword. "May Fortuna have mercy on us."

Babieca swallowed. He felt as if he might puke and hoped that he wouldn't. Julia was also frightened—it shone in her eyes. Roldan's expression was impossible to read. As always, he seemed to be listening for something. His eyes were far away.

Then they were moving.

Fel swung around the corridor, with Morgan and Narses by her side.

"Chamberlain—" One of the miles stepped forward. When he saw Morgan, his eyes widened. His hand went to his sword. Yet he hesitated. He was the only one of rank among them, and he'd been trained to take orders from the spado. Whatever Latona might have told him, a shadow of that instinct remained. His hand paused on the hilt.

Narses, however, did not pause. He burst forward, slashing at the scalloped hem of the man's lorica. There was a narrow line of flesh visible in the gap between cuirass and greave. It was a small target, but the spado had no trouble finding it. His blade cut into the man's thigh. Blood sprayed his tunica, vibrant like cherries against the costly fabric, and the miles cried out. He tried to draw his sword, but the strength left him, and he sank to one knee. His eyes widened in pain and astonishment. Without hesitation, Narses drew the wet edge of the blade across the young man's throat. Babieca saw a flash of white bone. It reminded him of driftwood, or a day die, brilliant and smooth. The miles choked, mailed hands going instinctively to the ruin of his throat. Blood painted the ground in irregular arcs. He fell forward.

Narses stepped over him, blade still raised.

The other miles were moving quickly now. They were clearly shaken, but their instincts had taken control. One of them was inching backward. If he could reach safety, he'd be able to raise the alarm. He tried to keep his movements small. Morgan dropped to one knee. Fitting an arrow, she waited a few seconds. The angle must be true. The miles took another step back, and she fired. Babieca felt the arrow whisper as it passed him. The miles turned his body, perhaps trying to avoid the shaft. He wasn't quick enough, though. It pierced his shoulder. With trembling fingers, he touched the arrow. Babieca thought he might manage to say something—a curse, or even a question—but Morgan struck him again, this time in the leg. He fell. Blood spread like a carpet beneath him.

Fel raised her die. "I choose—"

One of the miles struck her from behind. Her scale lorica deflected the blow in part, but it knocked her forward. The roll was interrupted. She turned and slashed low. The miles anticipated her. Fel reversed her blade and thrust upward, smashing the pommel against his jaw. He reeled, nearly dropping his sword. Leaping forward, she pierced the link between his knee and the edge of his cuirass. The fasteners gave way, the sinew parted, and her blade drove into his flesh. He screamed. Fel gave the blade a savage turn, pulling it out diagonally. The bone cracked, and his leg went limp, like a doll's. Blood ran down the leather, and he staggered backward, eyes bright with pain. She cracked the pommel of her blade against his temple, and he fell, shuddering. This was not glory. This was blood, shit, and bile rising in Babieca's throat. Narses glided across what already littered the floor. He moved with a dancer's certainty, his curved sword a pitiless half-moon.

Two more miles appeared, running down the corridor. They must have heard the clamor. There could be more behind them. Shaking, Babieca drew his cithara from its case. This was neither the time for a lullaby nor a drinking song, and those were all that he knew. Except. A memory teased his ear. Something he'd heard on the street. A song of fountains, shadows, and cold sweat. He began to play. His fingers were numb at first, but they gradually loosened. Realizing what he was doing, one of the miles started toward him.

For a second, the song faltered. Then, to his astonishment, Julia stepped in front of him. Eyes narrowed, she advanced with her little knife bared. The miles actually laughed. As he got closer though, she dropped to her knees, rolled to the side, and buried the dirk in his foot. It easily parted the sandal, its tip bursting through the leather sole to strike the ground. Julia backed away, like a mortified child who'd just done something awful. Blood filled his sandal. Cursing her family, he reached for the knife to pull it out.

Babieca finished the last bar of the song. A cold wind tore through the chamber, raising gooseflesh on his arms. The tracks of blood ceased to flow across the floor—instead, they congealed, sprouting a layer of ice. The blood-ice twined around sandals, bursting forth in frozen vines that moved up the walls. For a second, he was scared of what he'd done. This wasn't a trifling pub song or some gentle nenia to put everyone to sleep. These notes were hungry. They sucked at mailed hands and woven sandals, freezing whatever they touched. The two miles who'd been running down the corridor found themselves fixed to the ground. Legs straining, they reminded him of wind-blown wheat, rippling back and forth.

Roldan stepped forward. He drew Felix's knife across

his palm, and a drop of his blood landed on the stones. Then he gestured at the frozen miles.

The lamps flickered. They seemed to tremble on their chains, guttering with smoke. Their dancing grew more frenzied.

"Get back!" Roldan shouted.

Babieca complied, just as the lamps began to spit fire. A cone of sparks exploded around the two hapless miles. They tried to leap back but couldn't free themselves in time. Determined sparks chewed through their loricae, sizzling as they hit flesh. They tried to cover their eyes. A pebble-sized spark landed in the nearest man's hair. It smoldered for a second, and then, with a flash of light, the man's entire head was aflame. He cried out in terror. The blood-ice held him, and Babieca smelled his skin burning. The odor was strangely familiar.

Morgan struck him in the face. He crashed to the ground like a bough on fire, the heat caramelizing his blood. The miles closest to him lunged backward. He managed to break one foot free. He was still hopping when Narses cut him down.

Everyone stopped for a moment, breathing heavily. Seven armored bodies lay in a broken circle. One was still moving, but barely.

They stared at each other. The spado's sleeves were dripping. Babieca thought he could hear the ice crystals in the blood quietly disintegrating. Roldan was staring at the lamps. Like Babieca, he couldn't believe what he'd done. Julia gagged. Embarrassed, she covered her mouth, swallowing down the bile.

"Where's Eumachia?" Morgan asked.

"Fled." Fel stared down the corridor. "I saw her run before the fighting started. We lost one of the miles, as well."

Narses looked grim. "Once the alarm is raised, we'll be overwhelmed by miles and sagittarii. We have very little time."

"I can't—" Julia was still staring blankly around her. "I mean—it happened so quickly. They were alive one moment, and then—"

Narses laid a hand on her shoulder. "You were very brave." He looked at the bodies. "Fortuna forgive us. We can't stay for a threnody. We need to move."

They approached the locked door of the guest apartments. Blood pooled around the carved wooden sill. The door was thick, and they couldn't hear anything beyond it.

"I have an idea," Julia said. When she withdrew the fibula, Narses looked at it and shook his head, as if amused.

"Such a little thing to start all of this," he said.

"You have to be careful of those." The artifex extended her hand, pointing the brooch like a knife at the lock. "Sting," she said.

The bee came to life. It leapt from its perch and hovered around the lock for a moment. Then it struck the chain, once, in a flash of silver. The lock fell to the ground, smoke rising from its cracked links. Julia gestured again with the fibula. The bee returned to its perch, fluttered its delicate wings, then went back to sleep.

"How did you know that would work?" Babieca asked.

"I didn't. It was just a guess."

Narses opened the door. The room was dim, save for a bit of moonlight coming in through the oval window. Basilissa Pulcheria froze. She had tied her sheets and coverlet into a makeshift rope, which she was about to lower out the window. She'd even used her costly embroidered mantle and was shivering, her arms bare.

She saw them. Her eyes were wide with fear. Then she laughed.

"My rope is too short." The basilissa stared at the tangle of blankets. "Isn't that funny? I thought I might add my shift to it, but then I'd have to climb down naked. I don't think I could possibly give Latona that kind of satisfaction."

Narses looked at the rope as well. "It only lacks a few feet. Everyone, hand over your cloaks and belts. Hurry."

They all began to strip off layers, and the act was so familiar that Babieca nearly smiled. He couldn't believe that this was how it would end—stripping off his clothes in order to climb down the steep wall of the arx. They gathered their cloaks and feverishly tied them together. Narses gave up his bloodstained raiment with its lovely fringe. When the rope was as long as they could make it, they tied it to the bed, tossing the other end through the window. Fel studied the patchwork thing with deep skepticism.

There were footsteps outside. Narses drew his sword.

"Get the basilissa to the harbor. Don't stop for anything."

"You could still come with us," Fel said.

"No. If I stay behind to slow them down, you have a chance."

Something strange passed across her face. Until now, Fel had seemed logical and without sentiment. Now her eyes betrayed her.

"You don't have to," she said.

Narses smiled sadly. "I am older than you, and know better. Start climbing."

Before she could reply, the spado stepped outside and closed the door behind him. They heard shouts, then ringing steel.

"Basilissa," Fel said. "We shall descend first. Hold tight to me."

For a moment, the woman looked at her in disbelief. Then, straightening her diadem, she grabbed onto the miles. They began to climb down. The others followed. Babieca let everyone else go ahead of him. As each second passed, he expected the door to explode inward. He could see the miles coming for him, their swords tipped in the spado's blood. Finally, his turn came. The rope burned his palms as he clung to it. The knots trembled, but held. Eyes half-closed, heart in mouth, he made his way down the wall. Narses had been off in his calculation. The rope was still several feet short, and the final drop jolted him, from the soles of his feet to the crown of his head. He shook off the pain and joined the others, who were already running.

They made for the harbor. Bells rang from the arx, but they kept running. Night covered them. Lamps were thinly spaced along the path, which worked in their favor. Also, as they drew closer, they could see flames leaping from the end of the jetty. The basilissa's trireme was on fire. Babieca could only imagine what Latona had done to the ship's crew.

Pulcheria watched the tower of flame but said nothing.

Now they could hear the river, along with the crackle of the decaying ship. There were no other boats. No means of escape. Babieca felt as if something were watching him. Long shadows moved across the slatted wood. Roldan walked ahead of them. His ear was cocked.

"What is it?" Babieca asked.

"Undinae," he whispered. "In the water. They're all talking at once. They're upset that we've come, but the fire is also distracting them." He raised his hand. "Everyone stop moving."

"We don't have time to appease shades," Pulcheria began.

"Just stop," Roldan urged. "Let me listen."

They fell silent. In the distance, Babieca could hear something. Horses. The miles were on their way. Perhaps Mardian was leading them. Narses must be dead, and that would make him the new chamberlain.

"Roldan," Morgan said, her voice edged with fear. "I don't know how this works, but is there some way—"

He wasn't listening to her, though. He was focused entirely on the water. Babieca tried to hear their voices, but there was only the lap of the waves, the groans of the trireme as it collapsed upon itself, the drumming of his own heart.

"I understand," Roldan said. He looked once at Babieca. Then he nodded. "If you provide her with safe passage, I agree to the terms."

For a moment, nothing happened. Then the waves began to churn. A vessel made of seaweed, shells, and old bones floated to the surface. It bobbed like a strange cork. Then it glided forward on its own, propelled by no oar. It butted against the edge of the dock, starfish clinging to its green-gray prow.

"Basilissa," Roldan said, "this boat is made by the undinae—the lares of the water. They've agreed to take you back to Egressus."

She stared at the dripping vessel. "How am I supposed to sail that thing?"

"The waves respond to it. The river itself will carry you back to safety. The undinae have sworn it, and lares do not break an oath."

Roldan had told him several times that lares did break oaths. It didn't seem like the right moment to mention this, though.

"I suppose it's better than the alternative," Pulcheria said. "Your company has done me a great favor, and I am in your debt. Should you ever visit Egressus, I promise to repay you."

With Fel's assistance, she lowered herself into the small vessel. Once she was seated, it began to glide away—slowly at first, then picking up speed. They watched the basilissa recede, until she was just another shadow on the water.

Morgan exhaled. "I can't believe that we did it."

Roldan took a step forward. He was standing at the very edge of the jetty.

"I can almost see them," he said.

In that instant, Babieca understood.

He started to run. He was too late, though. For a second, the river was calm. Then a living wave tore from its surface. It divided into three liquid tendrils that encircled Roldan. He offered no resistance. The watery fingers pulled him down. He barely made a noise as the river closed over him.

Babieca dove off the jetty. He was a strong swimmer, but what he struck wasn't water—it was a stone wall. Dazed, bleeding, he tried to stay afloat. The water held him in place. He thrashed and cried out, but his body was frozen. This was what the miles had felt like, before Roldan's fire consumed them. His scream turned into a sob. The others were yelling for him, their voices distant through the pain.

"Roldan!" he screamed. And then: *"Andrew!"*

The strange word came unbidden to his lips. He tried to say it again, but the blood from his nose made him choke. He felt something wrap around his waist. Then the water tossed him. Flying, he saw a black field of stars. His shoulder struck the jetty, and pain like bright nails tore through his whole side. For a moment, he couldn't move. His hands were numb. His mouth was slick with blood. The stars whirled. His fingers sank into damp, rotting wood.

Morgan had her arms around him. She pulled him into a sitting position. Her hands wiped the blood from his face. He tried to speak, but couldn't. From the corner of his eye, he could see Julia. Her hand flew to her mouth. She was pointing at something.

He turned back to the water.

Roldan was floating facedown.

The moon silvered his hair. Seaweed and bits of shell matrix clung to his tunica. The river seemed satisfied. It held him with the utmost care.

Babieca tried to move, but Morgan held him.

Fel dragged Roldan's body onto the scarred wooden planks. Carefully, she rolled him over. His face was pale as boxwood. His eyes, clear and empty as glass, watched the moon. Relief was frozen on his face.

Babieca heard something in the distance, but whether it was Latona's cry or the sad fluttering of the undinae, he couldn't say.

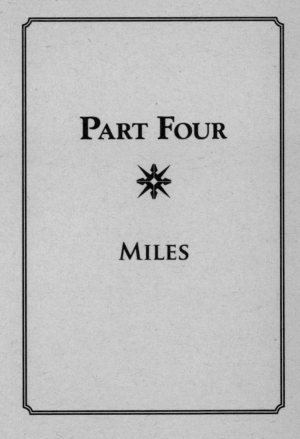

PART FOUR

MILES

1

RED. WHITE. THE LIGHT CHANGED IN A FLURRY
of rapid sunsets. The park was on fire, crackling with voices.
The colors reminded her of a candy cane, or the shock of
red pen against white margins. For a moment, they also
made her think of the red Angry Bird that Neil insisted on
keeping in the car. He was the current leader of the stuffies,
having recently supplanted Ice Bird and Laser Bird. She
couldn't tell what his special powers might be, aside from
a velveteen texture that Neil seemed to love. Was there a
white one? Empty Bird?

Red pixelated shadows. Andrew on the grass. A few
paces away from him, an affronted goose stood its ground,
hissing. Water had burst from his mouth, splashing her in
the face while she pumped his chest. She could still feel it,
cold in her eyes, her hair. Now the grass was absorbing it.
The emergency technicians were transferring him to a
stretcher. They covered him in a reflective blanket, which
burned like red cellophane beneath the lights. A small, still
scrap of fire, one bare foot peeking out. He vanished into
the stark interior of the ambulance.

Twenty minutes ago, she was naked and shivering. Carl,

also naked, struggled to pull their stash of clothes from a nearby tree. His hands couldn't quite grip the duffel bag. He was staring at Andrew's body. Ingrid sank to her knees and placed an ear to his chest. Silence. She tilted back his head, forced open his mouth, and exhaled. Resusci Annie's plastic lips had tasted like rubbing alcohol, but Andrew's mouth was ragged, wet. "An ambulance," Carl was saying. "Wascana Park . . . Albert Street . . . he . . . he fell into the lake—"

Into a lake, Ingrid thought. *But not this one. Unless they're both tributaries leading to same dark body of water.*

When it struck her in the face, she stopped breathing. Andrew shuddered and began to retch. She turned him gently on his side, watching the water pour from his mouth, along with bloody streams of spit. Her bare knees were soaked, and it took her a moment to remember that she was still naked. Shelby thrust some clothes in her direction, and she pulled them on without looking. Carl was still buttoning his shirt when they heard the ambulance. How would they explain this? A drunken skinny-dip gone wrong? Just a bit of harmless night swimming? Ultimately, it didn't matter. The technicians ignored them, focusing purely on Andrew. They scanned every inch of his wet, half-clothed body, listening, gently palpating. Then they lifted him into the van and closed the doors.

Ingrid heard one of the paramedics talking into his radio. *Three en route,* a voice said. *Two with second-degree burns to their hands and faces, the third with sharp-force trauma to the leg. Some kind of bar fight—*

She realized, with a start, that they were talking about the miles. They'd crossed over. The basilissa must have access to something like the abandoned house, a bridge that connected both sides of the park. Sharp-force trauma to the leg. Fel's sword had done that.

At least you didn't kill him.

They followed in Shelby's truck. Nobody spoke. The drive was a warm, brittle silence, redolent of maple smell from the old vents. Carl sat up front, while Ingrid bounced lightly in the backseat. The ambulance was a comet ahead of them, parting early-morning traffic. She couldn't tell if this felt like real life or a movie. Looking down, she realized what Shelby had given her to wear: sweatpants, flip-flops, and an oversize shirt from the university bookstore. It had to be real. Nobody would dress like this in a movie.

Shelby parked a few blocks from Pasqua Street, and they walked the rest of the way to the hospital. The air had a new chill to it. Fall was coming. Ingrid felt like some kind of yeti, walking with exaggerated care in the flip-flops. Her own duffel bag was still in the park, hidden beneath a canopy of leaves.

"Can I use your phone?" she asked Carl. "I need to call my brother."

He blinked at her for a second, as if she'd spoken in a foreign language. Then he handed over the phone. She dialed Paul's number. After four rings, the voice mail picked up.

"I'm at the hospital," she said. "Someone I know was in an accident. I'm sorry—I know you probably haven't gotten much sleep. If Neil asks where I am, just say that I'll be home soon. Make sure he eats something, even if it's just toast and cucumber slices. Love you. Bye."

When she looked up, Carl and Shelby were gone. She approached the sliding glass doors, standing far enough away to keep them from opening. Shelby was at the triage counter, talking to a nurse. Carl was sitting alone in an orange plastic chair. She could simply go. She had no connection to these people, and they wouldn't blame her for leaving. They were young and resilient. She looked at Carl again. He seemed small and papery, vanishing into the chair that resembled a bisected fruit. Shelby frowned at the clipboard she was holding. These were not people who'd ever spent much time in a hospital.

Ingrid walked through the doors. It smelled the same as it had four years ago, when Neil was born. Nothing had changed. She walked over to Shelby and glanced at the form.

"Do you have his wallet?"

Shelby looked up in surprise. "I—yeah. Here—" She

pulled it from her pocket. "It was all tangled up in his jeans. I almost didn't see it. Luckily it's purple. I don't know anyone else with a purple wallet."

Ingrid took the wallet and the clipboard gently from her. "I can fill this out. You should go sit with Carl."

"Are you sure?"

"I have a four-year-old. I'm very good at filling things out."

Shelby nodded absently, then walked over to the bank of orange chairs.

Andrew's wallet made no sense. It was full of old movie stubs, folded receipts, and expired coupons. His health card had a deep crease, probably from the weight of all those useless scraps pushing down on it. She managed to fill out most of the details. Everyone fit on the form, no matter how complicated their life was.

Ingrid walked over to where Shelby and Carl sat.

"Is he allergic to anything?"

"He once told me that he was allergic to microfilm," Shelby said.

Carl looked up. "Keflex? It's a kind of penicillin, I think."

"Okay. I'll tell the nurse."

Ingrid walked over to the triage desk. The nurse took the clipboard from her without looking up. "You can have a seat."

For the first six months of Neil's life, nurses had told her that she could have a seat. When he was placed in an incubator, when his stomach didn't work properly, when his fever shot through the roof and he went into convulsions—they always told her the same thing. *You're powerless. You might as well sit.* But she had always preferred to stand. That way, if she heard his thin wail in the distance, she could make it past the desk before the nurse grabbed her.

She returned to the chairs.

"Did they say anything?" Shelby asked.

"No. We're not related, so they aren't going to tell us much."

"Oh. Right."

"Someone should call his parents. Do they live in the city?"

"His dad's at a sales conference in Moose Jaw," Carl said. "And his mom is—somewhere with nice weather. I'm not even sure if she has a phone."

"Does he have any other family?"

"Just us."

"All right. We'll just have to wait, then." Ingrid handed her the wallet. "There's one vending machine that works on this floor, if you want coffee."

"You don't have to stay," Shelby said. "I mean—it's very kind of you—but—he's our friend. I'm sure you must have things—Neil—"

Ingrid sat down next to her. "He's with his uncle. He was a preemie, you know. Barely two and a half pounds. Like a walnut in my hand. They had him in an incubator for nearly two months. He'd stop breathing, sometimes, and I'd have to tickle his feet."

"You must have been scared."

"I was. I still am. But he's fine. Andrew's going to be fine."

"There was so much water."

"They'll pump the rest of it out. It's amazing what a body can go through."

"You saved his life. You and—"

"Not here," Carl whispered. "We barely got out. Don't tempt fate."

"We were lucky," Ingrid agreed.

In the distance, they could hear the horses. They'd all assumed that it was Latona, coming with her armed entourage. When she realized that Pulcheria was gone, she would take her time punishing them. Morgan was still holding Roldan's body, while Babieca shivered on the damp wharf, blood trickling slowly from his nose. They must have looked ridiculous: four people who'd gotten lost on their way to the sea. One of them was on his back. From a certain angle, he could have merely been asleep.

Roldan's dead, she'd thought, as the horses approached.

He made a deal with the lares, and this was the price. Pulcheria's life for his own.

But when the rider appeared, it was Felix. He had two saddled horses with him. They eyed the water nervously but stayed in place.

"We don't have much time," he said. "She's coming."

It was hard getting Roldan onto the horse. Babieca mounted first, and then Felix and Fel managed to hoist the body up. Felix undid his belt and fastened them together. Roldan sagged against Babieca like a sack of flour. They rode like this, in terrible silence, until they reached the house at the wall.

The sound of the sliding door brought her back. Ingrid watched a young couple approach the triage desk. They were given clipboards with pens attached by string. They sat down a few feet away. The man just stared at the pen, as if it were something from outer space. Ingrid knew that feeling. Your mind prompts you with familiar information—*This is my address*—but your hands are suddenly on strike.

She looked at Carl. He was holding something in his hand: a small, brownish plastic figure that looked like a spiked turtle.

"What is that?"

"The chamberlain." He slowly moved the figure's arms, up then down, as if the turtle-demon were climbing or swimming through the air.

"What?"

"It's a toy," Shelby clarified. "Andrew bought it two days ago. It's some weird creature from *The Dark Crystal.*"

"He lost everything," Carl said. "They even took the clothes off his back."

"I never saw the movie."

"It's one of his favorites." He continued to pose the shriveled creature. "Although he couldn't watch the emperor turn to dust. He always had to skip that part."

"Why did they steal his clothes?"

"He lost a duel."

"Sounds like a strange culture."

"Yeah. Skeksi politics are kind of fucked."

Shelby got up and walked over to the triage desk. Ingrid couldn't quite hear what she was saying to the nurse. She looked at the young couple again, who were comparing clipboards. All she wanted to do was crawl into bed with Neil, to feel his dreaming breath on her cheek and smell his apple shampoo. He was probably asleep on the couch with Paul. Unless he'd outlasted his uncle, which he often did. It would be harder to get him to sleep, in that case, but she secretly hoped for it. Then she could spend an hour in delicious conversation with him, which almost made up for her absence.

"He's in room two-twelve," Shelby said. "They've got him sedated, but we can go in."

Ingrid led them down the hallway. She wanted to go in the direction of the neonatal care unit, but resisted the urge. It had been four years since Neil was in an incubator, jaundiced and wide-eyed, connected to alarms that would ring when he stopped breathing. Now he was doing puzzles and playing online games. His ability to cycle through menus astounded her. Soon, he'd be explaining all the features on her smartphone.

The room was dim and quiet. A faded blue curtain served as a partition. Andrew slept with an IV in his arm. He wore a pair of green hospital socks, which reminded her of elf slippers. All they needed were bells. His clothes were neatly folded on a chair next to the bed.

"I'm going to steal another chair," Shelby said. "I'll be back."

Carl sat on the edge of the bed. Gently, he placed the toy in Andrew's hand.

"It's not your fault," she said.

He didn't reply. His eyes studied the monitors.

Ingrid reached into her bag. She wanted to grab a bottle of water, but instead, her hand closed around a library book. *The Sneetches*. It was one of Neil's favorites. They must have renewed it a hundred times. It would have been easier to just buy a copy, but he loved the ritual of signing it out.

The demagnetizer made such a satisfying *thump* when it scanned the book, and the librarian always talked to him.

"Here." Ingrid passed him the slim volume. "You can read to him, if you like."

"He won't be able to hear me."

"You'd be surprised."

Carl opened the book to the middle. In the picture, a crowd of star-bellied Sneetches were all jumping into the stranger's wondrous device. These odd creatures, with their exclusive marshmallow roasts, were like hipsters following the latest trend. They placed all of their trust in a man whose last name was McBean. Carl cleared his throat and began to read:

> *All the rest of that day, on those wild*
> *screaming beaches,*
> *The Fix-It-Up Chappie kept fixing up Sneetches.*
> *Off again! On again! In again! Out again!*
> *Through the machines they raced round and*
> *about again . . .*

Shelby arrived with the second chair. She was about to say something, but when she heard Carl reading, she fell silent. It reminded her of how Paul would wander in as she was reading to Neil. At first, he'd be in the middle of something. But, listening to her voice, he'd gradually stop whatever he was doing. Sometimes he'd sit down, but just as often, he'd stand in the middle of the room: brother, interrupted. Everyone needed to hear stories. They often didn't realize it until they found themselves caught up in one.

Just as Carl said, "You can't teach a Sneetch," Andrew's eyes began to flutter. Slowly, he came back. His expression was glassy from whatever they'd given him. Demerol, most likely. He coughed, then winced from the pain.

"Hello, sir," Carl said, putting down the book. "How do you feel?"

"Like there's glass in my throat."

"They pumped your stomach," Ingrid said. "You're going to be sore."

He looked at her strangely. "We were at Carl's place together. Then—" He frowned. "I don't remember what happened after that."

Shelby sat down by the bed. "Don't worry about it. Just relax."

"Why am I here?"

"Well—" She looked at Carl for a moment. "You fell into Wascana Lake."

"Why would I do that?"

"It was dark, and you slipped."

"Were we walking home?"

"Yes. We took a shortcut through the park."

"I don't like it there at night. The ducks get angry." He frowned again. "What was I doing so close to the water?"

"You thought you saw something," Carl murmured. "But it was just a shadow."

"Oh." He looked down at the toy in his hand. "Hey. *This* guy. I remember buying him at Tramp's. Did you bring him?"

"Yeah."

"Thanks."

His eyes started to close. Then he looked at Carl. "Were you reading to me?"

"A little. Yeah."

"That's funny."

"Should I keep going?"

"S'okay. I've heard that one before." He suddenly looked at Ingrid. "Did you walk home with us? Were we having a marking party?"

"That's right," she said.

"I'm sorry. You must be tired. I sure am."

"It's okay if you want to go back to sleep."

"I may just do that."

He closed his eyes again. Within seconds, he was snoring quietly.

"I can't do this," Carl said. "I can't lie to him."

Shelby touched his hand. "We don't have a choice."

"How can we—I mean—" He looked at Ingrid. "You've been doing this for longer than us. You know more. Isn't there a way around the rule? Some exception?"

"Not that I'm aware of."

"This is nuts. We can't just pretend. He's going to figure it out."

"He doesn't remember any of it," Ingrid said. "You know how this works. Roldan's gone. That part of him no longer exists."

"There must be something left."

"There isn't. The park protects itself. He doesn't remember a thing."

Carl seemed to shrink into the chair. Ingrid thought about the time when Fel had nearly died. She'd come close to forgetting it all. A few moments more, and the miles would have bled out onto the ground, leaving only confusion behind. When your park ego died, that was it. You remembered nothing. Some people rediscovered the park—decades later, when everything about them had changed—but most never found their way back. They continued on with their lives, always wondering about that strange night that they couldn't explain.

"We could just tell him," Carl said. "If anyone was going to believe such a weird story, it would be Andrew."

"If you tell him," Ingrid replied, "he'll never find his way back. He'll always doubt. And you could be denied access, too. The rules are there for a reason."

"The rules are bullshit."

"It's better for him if you say nothing."

"How are we supposed to hide this from him?"

"He has a point," Shelby said. "Andrew sees us all of the time. How are we going to explain where we go in the middle of the night?"

"You'll just have to get creative."

"He notices everything."

"You may have to distance yourself from him."

"No," Carl said.

Ingrid lowered her voice to a whisper. "In case you've forgotten, we're all being hunted. If you want to protect your friend, the best thing you can do is stay away from him."

She knew that lie well. Even before Neil was born, she'd hidden the park from Paul. What was she supposed to say? *Can you cover my shift while I strap on a gauntlet and fight in the Hippodrome? Can you babysit for me while I stand guard outside a whorehouse?* She told him that she was studying for her comprehensive exams at the library. Paul didn't realize that comps took only a year to prepare for. He was so far removed from academia that whenever she mentioned something about it, he'd nod politely, then go back to playing Mass Effect. He was so proud of her. *My sister the doctor!* Even when she reminded him that she'd only be a doctor of philosophy, he still pretended to bow and asked if she could write him a prescription for painkillers. Her baby brother. He loved her fiercely, and all she did was lie to him.

Ingrid watched Carl as he put the chamberlain through a series of poses. Men and their action figures. When Neil first started yelling *Destroy the pigs!* and insisting that Paul build him a catapult, she feared that he was entering some inevitable stage of violence. Maybe that was better than princesses, though. Lots of her friends on the Regina Moms forum complained that their daughters lived and breathed princesses. Everything had to be pink and covered in sparkles. At least those damn wingless birds were teaching him about trajectories and ballistics, or so she told herself while listening to him recount the heroics of Ice, Lightning, and Laser.

Carl and Shelby were talking quietly. She chose that moment to slip out of the room. At this point, they didn't really want her advice. They would have to work things out on their own. Losing a member of your company was terrible. The rules were clear on how to handle it, but they couldn't prepare you for the seismic aftereffects. Andrew might never see Anfractus again. Roldan had been his guide, his Virgil. Now the auditor was nothing but water in the grass, a dark impression that would fade by morning. If the park chose not to reveal itself to Andrew, he would spend the rest of his life wondering if his friends were keeping a secret from him. The half-life of their lies would cast a subtle radioactivity around everything they did. Their hollow excuses would fill him with dread, but what could he say? These were his friends. He had to trust them.

She walked into the waiting room just as the doors were sliding open. A small spark in a yellow coat burst through them, his arms full of brightly colored stuffies. He saw her and began to jump in ecstasy, nearly dropping the plush birds.

"*Mummy!* That is mine mummy! Mine Uncle Paul brought me here in the car, because he knows how to drive!"

He flew to her. She picked him up, getting a faceful of stuffed animals.

"Hello, my sweet. I see you brought your friends."

"I brought Ice, and Laser, and Monster, to protect you."

"That was very thoughtful."

"And the red bird is in mine pocket, because he has no bubble and could not survive in space with the others."

Paul walked through the doors, carrying two coffees. He wore a faded brown pullover, and his hair stood up at odd angles. He must have passed out on the couch.

"He heard your message on the answering machine," Paul said, handing her a coffee. "Then he woke me up and said you were in the hospital with a broken tail feather."

"We brought tape," Neil said into her ear.

She put him down gently. "That was a good idea. Mummy's tail feather is fine, though. It's one of my friends who had to visit the hospital."

"Does your friend need tape? We have a lot!"

"He wouldn't get into the car unless I agreed to bring all my hockey tape," Paul said.

"My friend is going to be fine," Ingrid told Neil. "He had a bit of an accident, but he's resting now."

"What happened?" Paul asked.

He'd asked the same question when she'd called him from

the hospital two years ago. *What happened to your leg?* She told him that she'd cut herself on a piece of broken glass. It seemed plausible, but she could still remember the look of suspicion on his face. He was the clumsy one, not her.

"He fell into Wascana Lake," she said. They'd repeated the lie enough times that it was starting to sound real. "We were walking through the park, and he slipped on some loose gravel. It happened so quickly—"

She allowed herself to trail off. A proper lie, she'd discovered, was vague yet precise. It couldn't have too many elements, and the more she described it, the less it would make sense. Keep it simple. Let him fill in the details.

"Did he, like, hit his head or something?"

"Yeah. He swallowed a lot of water. He's okay now, though."

"Geez. That sounds like it was really close."

"It was."

"I guess a drunken kid probably falls in that lake once a year. He was sober, though?"

"Completely. It was a freak accident."

She regretted the phrase the moment it left her mouth. *Freak accident* sounded implausible, like falling into a wood chipper. She wanted to correct herself, but it was too late. Paul's eyes narrowed for a moment. Then he took a sip of his coffee.

"Guess he was lucky."

"Very."

"I drawed you a picture," Neil said. "I mean—I *drewed* you a picture."

"What did you draw?"

"A baby bat with some TNT."

"That's nice."

"Uncle Paul is so damn tired. That's why we had to get coffee."

She gave Paul a look.

"Sorry." He stared at the ground. "It just slipped out."

"It's okay. You can go home and sleep if you like."

"I'm pretty much awake now."

"The last time I said that, I passed out in the bathtub."

"I remember that. Neil covered you with towels and said that he found a mermaid."

"You were so beautiful, Mummy. Like Ice Bird when he freezes the pigs."

"Thank you, sweet." She glanced at her watch. "I'm not sure how long he's going to be here. They might want to keep him overnight, but with the bed shortage, I doubt it."

"We can hang out for a bit," Paul said. "It's kind of like old times."

"Don't say that. Those times were horrible."

"We all made it."

Paul had seemed so young then. Now there were lines under his eyes. The thought of her brother aging was impossible to comprehend. He would always be six and popping out of the hamper, screaming *I am a meat eater!* Sometimes it was all she could do to refrain from wiping his nose and asking him if he'd remembered to flush. *Dinosaurs always flush,* he used to say, a non sequitur if she'd ever heard one.

She turned to Neil. "Mummy is going to check on her friend. Can you stay with Uncle Paul for a few minutes?"

"I want to come with you."

There was something strange about taking him past the threshold of the waiting room. He had no memory of the time that he'd spent here. To him, it was just a place full of random noises and colored lines on the ground. All she could think of was how small he'd once been, a miraculous hazelnut in her palm. The moment when they'd disconnected the wires, and she could finally hold him. Every nerve on fire as she settled him into the crook of her neck, so terrified that he might break or melt away.

"You have to be very quiet and good if you come with me," Ingrid said. "People are sleeping and trying to get better."

"Laser can help them," he whispered. "He can take his mask off, and his face will change. He will be real. Won't they like that?"

"I suppose it can't hurt." She took his hand. "Okay. Let's go."

They walked down the hallway. Neil was fascinated by the machines. He took them in silently, and she knew that he would have hundreds of questions later. What was that liquid? Why were those sturdy beds lined up against the wall? What did the lines mean? Somehow, it would all become part of whatever mythology he was crafting. *Those proud birds needed dialysis for their nests in space.* It was strange to think that he used to talk in sentence fragments, that his vocabulary was once a series of random words: *couch, star, li-berry.* Listening to the sound of his shoes on the linoleum, she recalled his first steps, the shock of seeing him upright as he chased after a block. How did it happen? She used to carry him in a sling, and now he was beside her. Now she understood what it meant to grow like a leaf. Whenever she turned her back, he changed in some small way, his roots churning.

When they reached the room, he hung back slightly, observing from a safe distance. His grip on her hand tightened. Shelby looked up.

"Hi, Neil," she said.

He looked at Andrew but didn't reply. Then he walked slowly over to the bed. He arranged the birds carefully on Andrew's lap.

"What are those?" Carl asked.

"Don't ask that—" Ingrid began.

But it was too late. Neil began to explain where the birds came from, and how they were able to survive in space (except for the red one in his pocket, deprived of a bubble). He waved his hands as he described the antipathy of the pigs, who wanted to eat the birds. Carl and Shelby listened politely. When he started talking about how Ice Bird could eat only frozen gummies or pieces of asteroid, Shelby raised an eyebrow, but said nothing.

A nurse came in. She thought that this would distract Neil, but he continued with the story, explaining in great detail how the golden eagle appeared only when you got three stars. The nurse checked Andrew's IV. There wasn't much point in keeping him sedated anymore. He'd most likely sleep through the night on his own. Ingrid was about to ask if they could discharge him, when the nurse turned to her and smiled. A shock went through her.

It was Mardian.

He was wearing a blue uniform, and his hair looked slightly different, but the resemblance was unmistakable. She could see the spado's shadow hovering just behind him. Neil seemed to see it too, because he suddenly ran to her, burying his face in her stomach. Ingrid held him close and met the nurse's gaze. His smile was brittle. There was something underneath, something with claws scratching to get out.

Mardian said nothing. He just smiled, then left the room. Ingrid felt the blood pounding in her ears. They'd been found—and so easily. Latona's influence was everywhere. How many others were watching them right now?

"We have to go," she said.

"That's okay." Shelby reached out to pat the stuffies. "It must be long past his bedtime. We'll call you in the morning."

"No. We all need to go. Right now."

"What do you mean?"

Ingrid walked over to the bed. She'd spent six months watching nurses insert and remove IV lines. That didn't mean much, but it was all that she had.

"Close the door," she said.

Shelby stared at her. "What's going on?"

"Just do it. We don't have a lot of time."

It was exactly what Felix had said. Maybe that was why Shelby listened to her. Ingrid reached into her purse and drew out a wad of cotton balls. She slipped some cotton beneath the IV, then tore off the tape and removed the line as carefully as she could. The machine next to the bed started to squeal, but she reached over and unplugged it.

"Have you done this before?" Carl asked.

Andrew groaned slightly. She held the cotton to his bleeding hand. "We've been found," she said. "The spado is here."

Shelby's eyes widened. "The nurse. I thought there was something off about him."

"We need to leave." She touched Andrew's forehead. "Sweetheart, I know you're tired, but you have to wake up for us. Okay?"

Andrew muttered something. He was still half-asleep.

"Get him dressed," she said to Carl. "I'm going to create a distraction."

"What kind of—"

"Just be quick. Get him outside. Our car is parked nearby." She handed Shelby her spare set of keys. "It's a gray sedan with a car seat in the back. Press this button on the fob, and the lights will flash."

She led Neil out of the room and back down the hallway.

"What's happening?" he asked.

"Well," she said, towing him along, "we're playing a game, and Mummy needs your help."

"Is it a game in space?"

"Yes. We're in space—"

"And we have to freeze the pigs before they steal our precious eggs!"

"That's right." She pointed to the triage desk. "See where that lady is standing? When we get there, I need you to scream as loud as you can, just like Monster."

"But people are sleeping and trying to get better."

She kissed him on the forehead. "I know, sweet. But they can't hear you in the waiting room. Are you ready? Scream like Monster, and don't stop until we get outside."

He looked dubious for a moment. "You want the birds to speak with one voice?"

"Yes. I want them to speak as loud as they possibly can."

They reached the counter. Neil began to wail. His high, keening voice cut through the waiting room like a siren. Paul got out of his seat and ran toward them.

"I think he has an ear infection," Ingrid said to the nurse.

"He looked fine when you brought him in."

"He's been screaming like this off and on the whole night. Can you at least take his temperature? He feels hot."

The nurse sighed. Then she approached Neil, who screamed and ran in the opposite direction, throwing stuffies at her.

He's definitely mine, Ingrid thought.

While the nurse was chasing Neil around the room, Ingrid saw Carl and Shelby emerge from the hallway. They'd wrapped Andrew in a blanket and were leading him slowly forward. He appeared to be sleepwalking. Paul managed to get a grip on Neil, who was squirming and howling like a mad puppy. Ingrid ran behind the triage desk.

"Ma'am!" The nurse was on her in a moment. "What are you doing?"

"Paging a doctor. You obviously can't deal with this."

"Do not touch that phone."

"I'm dialing—"

She looked up, just as Andrew was stumbling through the doors. They slid closed behind him. Ingrid put down the phone.

"I'm so sorry," she said. "I haven't been sleeping well lately."

"Just come out from behind the desk," the nurse said. "If your son will cooperate, we can take his temperature."

She turned to Neil. "Honey, do you want to use this machine?"

He stopped screaming. "What does it do?"

"It looks in your ear and tells us how you're feeling."

"You said—"

"Come over here. It's really neat."

Neil insisted on having his temperature taken six times and then asked for a peppermint, but eventually they got him out of the waiting room.

"What the hell just happened in there?" Paul asked.

"Heck. Say heck."

"Ingrid."

"Where did you park?"

"Right over—" His eyes narrowed. "What the—is someone in our car?"

"My friends are staying with us tonight. I'll explain when we get home."

"Are you losing it?"

"I don't even know how to answer that question anymore."

"We spoke with one voice," Neil said, beaming.

2

SHE WAS IN A BUBBLE, SURROUNDED BY EX-
panding stars. Pigs were everywhere—she'd never seen this
many before, green and hungry, like deranged marbles.
They'd eaten the catapults, and now they were noticing her
for the first time. Spitting splinters, they began to move in
a wave toward her bubble. It was too thin. If she breathed
or moved, the stars and the pigs would rush in. Where was
Ice? He should have appeared by now, a fan of electric blue
tail feathers exploding from the void. But none of the birds
were here. Didn't they care about their eggs? How could
they give up on her so easily? She heard a buzz. The pigs
were building something with the splinters. They had tools,
and schematics, and boxes of TNT. All she had was the
bubble, and it was about to break.

She looked at the stars again, cold and resplendent, like
seed pearls on a black cushion. Maybe it wouldn't be so
bad. Explosive decompression would kill her before the
pigs did.

It was hard to judge distances, but somewhere, a red light
was flashing. Was it a vortex? Were they coming?

"I'm here!" she screamed. "Don't let them—"

The bubble burst.

Ingrid opened her eyes. The alarm was flashing. Neil had crawled onto the bed and was patting her shoulder lightly.

"Mummy. Everyone is awake. Uncle Paul is making so much toast."

She kissed his forehead. "All right. I'll be there in a minute."

His pajamas were the color of orange sherbet. "There are people here."

"Yes, love. Mummy invited some friends to stay with us."

"For how long?"

That was a good question. Her instinct was to keep everyone close, but being together didn't exactly make them stronger. Now they were just a more noticeable target. But when she'd seen the expression on Mardian's face—that cold amusement—all she could do was gather them all to her, like doomed plushies.

And now my son is probably going to need therapy.

"They're going to leave today," she said. "It was just a sleepover party."

"They can stay. I have a lot to teach them."

"I'm sure you do." Ingrid threw on a robe and took his hand. "When you said that Uncle Paul was making toast, did you mean French toast, or regular toast?"

"I do not speak French, Mummy. I speak in words."

"Is he cooking the toast in a pan?"

"It smells like Christmas."

They walked down the hallway and into the living room. She smelled coffee and vanilla extract. Paul had already gone through a loaf of bread and was defrosting more. The eggshells on the counter looked like a pile of bones. He looked up.

"Morning."

She'd always been the sarcastic one, but there was a world of subtext in that greeting. He continued to crack eggs, while his crooked smile announced: *This is FUBAR, big sis, and we're going to talk about it after breakfast.*

Carl was watching an episode of *Dinosaur Train*. Beside him, Andrew concentrated on dividing his French toast into symmetrical bites. His knife and fork scraped lightly against the plate, while Buddy sang: "T-Rex . . . I'm a Tyrannosaurus. . . ." Shelby sat on the ground, putting together one of Neil's human body puzzles. He ran over and knelt down beside her.

"Very good! Now he needs skin."

Shelby looked up. "Good morning. Did you sleep okay?"

"Five hours in a row. That's something, at least."

"Thanks for letting us stay here. My apartment is usually freezing around this time, but your place is—you know—" She grinned. "French toasty."

"Stop talking," Carl said.

"Go back to your cartoon."

"It's educational. I'm learning about alternative families."

Shelby returned to the puzzle. She frowned, examining the pieces.

"Try that one," Neil said, pointing to an ear.

Ingrid looked at Shelby for a moment. Awkward and beautiful. She was listening carefully to what Neil was saying. He could tell that he'd gained an audience, so he was pontificating about the small intestine. How long had it been since someone was actually interested in her? What was the appropriate response? Her mind was assembling a list of reasons not to pursue this. Damn logic. Damn her cute morning hair.

"Hey." Paul stood in the entrance to the kitchen. "Here's a plate for you."

Ingrid walked over to him. "Thank you."

"There's coffee, too."

"You're amazing."

"Uh-huh."

She poured butter pecan creamer into her coffee, then sat down at the table.

"Have you already eaten?"

"Neil and I had some oatmeal."

"You could have woken me up. I would have helped."

"It's fine."

"I really am going to explain this."

"It's no big thing. You were worried about your friend. You got all mama bear and decided to have a team sleepover." He flipped the bread in the pan. "It's actually nice to meet some of your friends. I was worried that you spent all of your time alone and dehydrated on the top floor of the library."

"There are water fountains. I'm not wasting away."

"I know. You just work so hard. I'm glad that you've got people."

He smiled, and Ingrid wanted to stab herself with the fork. She was a monstrous liar. She imagined her good-natured brother at work, listening to the radio while he waited for a giant tray of muffins to bake. He was alone in the semidarkness of the store, already beginning to sweat from the heat of the industrial oven. In that silent, flour-dusted world, he paused often to think about his family. How many personalized cakes had he intentionally ruined, just so that he could bring them home, emblazoned with *King Neil* in blue icing? Now, on his day off, he fed all of her friends without complaint. He was so much like their father. She could almost see him in the kitchen beside Paul, cracking eggs and singing: *I'm a lumberjack, and I'm okay*—

Ingrid drank her coffee. She could barely remember a time when it had been pleasant, something occasionally indulged in after a meal with friends. Now it was the bitter libation that kept her conscious and sent her running to the bathroom every few hours. It baffled her when people wanted to "go out" for coffee. Why go out? She had an enormous stockpile from Bulk Barn in the cupboard next to the fridge.

"Mummy!" Neil ran up to her. "Are you finished eating?"

"I just started, doll."

"Do you want to see something?"

"By 'something,' do you mean a computer game?"

"A something does not have to be a game."

"But in this case, it is, right?"

He took her hand. "You will love it."

"I think you're overreaching."

"Mummy!"

Carl got up from the couch. "What's this game about?"

Seeing his opportunity, Neil instantly changed sides. "It is a game about pigs who build things! Come see!"

"You really don't have to," Ingrid said.

"It's no problem. I think I've absorbed enough *Dinosaur Train* for one morning."

"You're very kind." She turned to Neil. "Only five minutes, okay, bub? Then you have to release our guest from captivity."

He grabbed Carl's hand, leading him down the hallway.

"I can start on the dishes," Ingrid said.

Paul waved her off. "There's a machine for that. Go hang out with your friends. We've still got a half hour before he needs to get ready for day care."

"He's always late. I'm sure they talk about us."

"Is there some academic term for worrying too much about what other people think?"

"Grad student."

"I'm sure he's not missing much. Five minutes lost in the magic carpet. As long as his hair's combed and he doesn't have glitter glue on his face, I call that a win."

When Paul had first offered to move in, she was skeptical. He'd never been particularly good with kids. He didn't seem to grasp how his schedule was going to change simply by getting caught in Neil's orbit. In the end, though, it was Paul who turned out to be a natural at this. He cut away crusts and arranged vegetables into mock battles. When Neil resisted sleep with every fiber of his being, it was Paul who would hold him like a trembling sack of potatoes, rocking gently in the middle of the hallway. Even now, when he was deep in thought, he swayed on the balls of his feet without realizing it. The Dance of Nod, they'd called it.

Paul's transition to parenthood was seamless, while Ingrid still felt as if she were merging into that lane, completely blind.

At first, it was awkward when people mistook Paul for her husband. He was six years her junior, and women would give her a sly look, as if to say, *Nice work*. Explaining their family grew tedious, and people were always asking questions. *Do your parents help out? Does he ever get to see his dad?* Neil would get frustrated by this line of inquiry. *This is mine Mummy and this is mine Uncle Paul,* he'd say, with an edge to his voice. People were usually charmed by that and dropped the matter.

Ingrid took her plate into the living room. Shelby had finished the puzzle. *Dinosaur Train* was over, but neither of the guests was bold enough to start another program, so they just stared politely at the blank screen. She could faintly hear the sounds of the pig game. Neil could play it for hours, and she worried about how it might be affecting his concentration. He could cycle through menus so quickly now. She'd woken up the other day to find him surfing YouTube.

Andrew stared into his coffee cup. He was distracted by his own thoughts, and Ingrid watched the cup tilt slightly, until he caught it with his other hand. She sat down next to him. The steam from their mugs twined in the air, like honeysuckle.

"How do you feel?"

He didn't raise his eyes from the mug. "My lungs are sore. Whatever they gave me at the hospital must have quite the half-life, because I still feel out of ambit. Other than that, I'm okay. No permanent damage."

"That's a relief."

"I can't believe I fell into the lake."

Don't say freak accident. "Well—it could have happened to anyone."

"But I don't like the water."

"It was the wine," Shelby said quickly.

"I had wine?"

"A little."

"But I don't drink."

She was trying to keep her expression neutral. "We were winding down—you know, from all the marking. Carl convinced you to have some. You know how persuasive he can be."

"That's true." He turned the mug in his hands. "I wish I could remember."

"It's probably for the best that you can't."

"I hate that I caused everyone so much trouble."

Ingrid tried to put a hand on his knee. He flinched. Unsure of what to do, she let her fingertips hover in empty space. It was the same way she used to pet her childhood cat, who was afraid of hands. You had to let her come to you.

"It was no trouble," she said. "We're just glad that you're all right."

"I had the strangest dream last night."

"Oh?" There was an odd note in Shelby's voice. "What was it about?"

He frowned. "I can only remember bits and pieces. There was this little boat, made of shells and seaweed. I think there was a castle, too. And something mechanical. I could hear it clicking against the floor. I think it was following me."

"Those hospital drugs will give you the sketchiest dreams."

"I suppose." He got up. "Can I use your bathroom?"

"Of course," Ingrid said. "It's down the hall, first door on the right."

"Thank you." He walked slowly out of the living room. His steps were uneven, as if a part of him were still asleep.

"Oh God." Shelby rubbed her temples. "I can't do this."

"You don't have a choice," Ingrid said quietly. She cast a glance toward the kitchen. Paul was loading the dishwasher and didn't seem to be listening. "The mind has ways of protecting itself, just like the park. Even if he remembers a bit more, it won't make sense. All you can do is distract him from whatever pieces of knowledge are left."

"I'm a terrible liar."

"I don't believe that. Only the best liars can play this game."

Shelby glanced at Paul for a second. Then her eyes widened. "He—"

"Only the best," she repeated. "That's the price you pay. If you're going to have two lives, one of them stays in the dark."

"We were so close to being a company," Shelby murmured.

"He may find his way back. You don't know what's going to happen."

"But what are we supposed to do in the meantime?"

"You cope. You manage his confusion. Ultimately, he trusts you. He won't let go of that unless you give him a reason."

Her voice lowered to a whisper. "It's just so fucking—"

Someone screamed.

It wasn't Neil, but Ingrid still leapt up. She was the first one down the hallway. Carl emerged from the office, looking confused. Neil was right behind him, holding a red Angry Bird in front of him like a talisman. It must have been Andrew. Ingrid took a breath, then knocked gently on the bathroom door.

"Is everything okay?"

There was no response.

"Andrew?" Carl stepped forward. "I'm coming in, all right?"

He opened the door. Andrew was sitting on the rim of the claw-foot tub. He had his arms wrapped around his chest and was breathing heavily. The tap was still running. Carl turned it off, then drew a step closer to Andrew.

"Hey. What's going on?"

"There was something in the tub." He didn't look up. His bare feet matched the white of the hexagonal tiles.

"What kind of something?"

"I don't know. I only saw it for a second."

"Was it a house centipede?" Shelby asked from the door-way. "I've got a whole system that involves a jar and a piece of cardboard, if you want me to get rid of it."

"Not an insect," Andrew said. "A girl."

Carl sat next to him on the rim of the tub. "You mean— a doll, or something?"

"No. It looked like a girl. With seaweed in her hair."

Ingrid's blood went cold.

She'd heard of lares being seen beyond the park, but those were just stories. Only humans could cross over. Even if some small part of Roldan was still alive in Andrew, how would he recognize a lar? He'd never seen one. They were only rustles and whispers to an auditor.

"Look—" Carl's smile was reassuring. "I think you're overtired, and coming down from some serious drugs. Your mind's running a bit hot. That's all."

"It always runs hot."

"I know. Let's cool it with the coffee for now. What you actually need is some sleep."

"I'm not tired."

"Sure. But once all that syrup-soaked bread does its work, you'll be crashing with the rest of us. In the meantime, let's get you away from the tub."

"You're talking to me like I'm crazy. I'm not."

"I didn't use that word. I just think you're a little ragged from the stress of last night."

"Everyone's thinking it," he muttered.

"You know," Ingrid said, "when I first had Neil, I thought I might be going crazy. I'd wander around the house, trying not to cry or set fire to something. My brain felt like mashed potatoes. I walked into walls. Turns out, I was just sleep-deprived."

"Did you see things that weren't there?"

"All the time. Once, I thought the oven was criticizing me. Paul came home, and I was bawling in the kitchen, saying, 'You don't know me,' to all of the appliances."

"I guess"—he rose slowly—"my mind could be playing tricks on me."

Neil handed him the red Angry Bird. "Keep him in your pocket," he said. "This sweet one has no bubble."

"Thank you."

"Let's go watch some more TV," Carl said. "They've got so many cartoons. How would you feel about *The Purple Crayon*?"

They made their way out of the bathroom. Ingrid and Shelby exchanged a look.

"Did you really see things?"

"I might have. I was half-crazy."

"Thanks for not—you know—"

"What?"

"Freaking him out more."

"I spend most of my time putting out little fires." Ingrid lifted Neil into her arms. "How about we find you some pants?"

"I want to wear my footie pajamas."

"Please. This is the one standard that we've been able to uphold. Wear the pants, and I'll let you pick the shirt."

He wouldn't stop moving as she tried to dress him. Ingrid surveyed his bedroom as she wrangled him into the pants. It looked as if the children's section of the library had exploded. There were *Magic School Bus* and *I.Q.* books everywhere. The walls were covered in space posters and volcanic diagrams. The dinosaur phase had passed, but the interstellar phase was still going strong. Ingrid wondered what would be next. She couldn't imagine a night without cellophane and construction paper. When would he stop asking for bedtime stories? She'd always hoped that their nightly dialogue would continue long after he'd grown up. She could read to him over Skype, or whatever holographic technology existed by that point. "You're doing it wrong," he'd say, as she acted out Thing One and Thing Two. "You changed a word. Now we have to start from the beginning."

"What do you think you will be," she asked, "when you grow up?"

"Old," he said, one arm in his shirt. "Like you and Uncle Paul."

"I guess I had that answer coming. Okay. Let's brush your teeth. We have to get rid of all those sugar bugs."

"*French* toast does not make sugar bugs."

"What does it make?"

"Antigravity."

"In your mouth?"

"Isn't that fun?"

"We're still brushing your teeth."

After rinsing and inspecting his mouth for antigravity, they returned to the living room. Paul had already packed his bag.

"I'll take him to day care," he said.

"Are you sure? I don't mind driving."

"No. Stay with your friends. I've got some errands to run."

"You're weirded out."

"I'm not."

"You are. I can tell." She lowered her voice. "I know you weren't expecting this. When you get home, I promise the house will be a drama-free zone. You can eat chips, watch *Archer*, then have a fierce nap."

"It's really fine." He took Neil's hand. "Ready for day care?"

"I want to stay here."

"There's candy in the car."

He ran for the door.

"Parenting," Paul said. "We're so on top of it."

"Don't you have a kiss for your mummy?" Ingrid asked.

He blew her one. "Good-bye!"

"Have fun," Paul said. "Relax. Remember how to do that?"

"It's all hazy. Like prom."

He opened the door and led Neil down the front steps. Ingrid watched them walk to the car. Neil was talking animatedly while Paul strapped him into the booster seat. He was probably listing the virtues of his birds. *They are brave, and loyal, and real.* She waited for them to drive away. Then she closed the door, feeling as if something had just floated away from her. Some brilliant kite with makeshift tail feathers, caught by a sudden gust of wind. For a moment, she wanted to run down the driveway. *Come back. Stop all this leaving, this growing. Every time you come back to me, some precious little flake of you has changed.*

Ingrid walked back to the living room. "Shelby—can you help me with something in the office? My computer is being a dick."

Andrew's expression brightened. "I can probably fix it."

"It's like—a desktop issue—with the color palettes? I think it requires—"

Shelby got up. "Don't explain it. You'll only entice him."

"I don't mind—" Andrew began.

"Stay on this couch until your atoms stop vibrating."

"Fine."

"There are more DVDs," Ingrid said, gesturing vaguely around the room. "And lots of *Star Wars* Lego, if that's your thing."

"Are you kidding?" Carl grinned. "That's everybody's thing."

Shelby followed her into the office.

"Color palettes?"

"I panicked."

"This is the opposite of subtle."

"I think we passed subtle when he saw an undina in my bathtub."

Shelby's eyes widened. "You really think he saw one?"

"It's possible. I mean, the three of us can all use the park as a sort of viaduct between worlds. I don't see why the lares couldn't do the same thing."

"I thought they were connected to that place. That it was their chaos, or whatever. How could they survive here?"

"Sometimes I'm not even sure how *we* survive here."

Shelby sat down in the office chair. "If he did see it— what would that mean?"

"I really don't know."

She spun the chair in a slow circle, the same way that Neil did when he was waiting for something to load. They were both silent for a beat.

"I can't believe how close he was," Shelby said. "He walked right into the hospital room, and you were the only one who noticed."

"Not right away. It actually took me a while."

"He knows where Andrew lives. All of those forms—" Shelby shook her head. "We're practically giving them an invitation."

"There must be rules," Ingrid said, although she didn't quite believe the words. "They can't just attack us. Mardian has a job in this world. He has to keep his distance."

"You don't know that."

"Of course I don't. Haven't you figured out that I'm making this up as I go along? I saw the spado, and my gut said: *Run.* So here we are. I don't have any more answers."

"I'm sorry. I didn't mean to push. I'm just trying not to lose it."

Ingrid smiled. "Losing it isn't so bad. Sometimes, it feels great."

"I'll remember that advice when I'm doing my comps."

"Don't even think about those. You've got plenty of time."

The doorbell rang.

Shelby sighed. "Neil must have made him come back for something. He always leaves the car running. I'll be right back."

"I should come with you. It'll look strange if I stay in the office."

"I don't know. They seem pretty absorbed in their cartoons."

Ingrid walked down the hallway. Andrew looked as if he were about to nod off. Carl, however, was staring in the direction of the front door.

"It's just Paul," she said. "Neil can be a pint-sized tyrant. He once made us come home three times, because he needed the right hat."

She opened the door, fully expecting to see her son, gesticulating about whatever crucial object he'd left behind. It wasn't Neil, though.

It was him.

Her eyes widened. The last time she'd seen him outside Anfractus, he was naked and shivering in front of a gazebo. She remembered his dark hair, though, and the shallow track of his scar. He was wearing a long jacket and boots. He smiled, almost shyly.

"Hello, Ingrid."

She stepped outside and closed the door behind them.

"What are you doing here?"

"I should think it's obvious."

"I told you to stay away."

"You need my help."

"I think you've done enough. We can take it from here."

"You're being watched from all sides. And in case you've forgotten, I was the one who got you out of the city."

"Sure. You arrived just in time."

He stared at her. "What are you trying to suggest?"

"Don't play wounded meretrix with me. I've known you for too long. You always seem to choose the winning side."

"I'm here because I care about you."

"You're here to protect your investment."

He started to say something, but stopped. They stared at each other. Ingrid was suddenly aware of the fact that she hadn't put shoes on. Her feet were freezing.

"How is he?"

"The auditor? He's dead."

"I meant—"

"I know who you meant. We're not talking about him." He sighed. "It shouldn't be this way."

"Oh no? What's your alternative?"

"We've already talked about that."

"It's not going to happen. Our life is here."

"You need to make a choice."

"Actually, I don't think you get to tell me what I need. You left."

"I'm here now."

"For how long? A few hours? He needs more than that."

"Is he—"

"No."

The door opened. Carl stood in the entrance.

"Is everything all right?"

"It's fine," Ingrid said. "He's a friend. We're just talking."

Carl frowned. "Have we met?"

The man smiled. "I believe so."

"I know you from somewhere. I can't place it, though."

He extended his hand. "Oliver."

"Carl."

"Nice to see you again, Carl."

"Where did we meet?"

Ingrid gave Oliver a sharp look. "You're right—it's cold. Who wants tea?"

"I probably looked different," he replied. "I was wearing a mask."

"You—" Carl's jaw dropped. "Holy shit—"

"Everyone inside, now," Ingrid snapped.

They all walked into the living room. She closed the door and locked it.

"That won't do much," Oliver said.

"It makes me feel better."

Shelby was sitting on the couch with Andrew. "Hello," she said, uncertainly.

Oliver didn't reply. He was looking around the room. His eyes fell on the puzzle, and he smiled slightly but said nothing.

Andrew stood up. Oliver saw him, and waved. It was an odd gesture.

"How are you feeling?"

"I've been better," Andrew said. "Do we know each other?"

"Andrew—" Carl looked as if he wanted to step forward, but he didn't.

Oliver looked at him for a long moment. Then he shook his head. "No. But Ingrid told me about what happened to you."

"Oh. Right." He shrugged. "I'm okay now."

"I'm glad."

"How do you know Ingrid?"

"We're old friends," Oliver said. "We used to live in the same neighborhood."

"Are you from Regina?"

"Originally. I've moved around, though."

"How fortunate," Carl said. "Shelby, don't you think that's *fortunate*?"

She frowned. "I guess."

"It's just such good luck. Being able to travel."

Shelby took another look at Oliver. Comprehension spread across her face. She almost said something, but it came out as more of a high-pitched sound.

"What's going on?" Andrew folded his arms.

"Oliver—" Carl began.

"—is my supervisor." Ingrid laughed. "We're friends, but he's also my supervisor. Isn't that crazy?"

Andrew frowned. "You work in the Department of Education?"

"I'm more of an external."

"He's here because—I was supposed to give him the latest chapter of my dissertation, but I forgot. Mashed potato brain. Just like I told you."

"You could print out the chapter at school," Oliver said.

"I have my own printer."

"Doesn't the one at school cost less?"

"Right." She blinked. "Let's . . . all go to the library."

"Are we in the dreamatorium?" Andrew asked. "That would explain why everyone's being so weird."

"I'll get my flash drive," Ingrid said. "Shelby, can we take your truck?"

"It's going to be snug. Unless Oliver has a car."

"I walked."

Ingrid grabbed his arm. "Come help me find this chapter."

He followed her down the hallway.

Andrew watched them go. His eyes narrowed in confusion. "My supervisor would never make a house call."

"It's Education," Carl said. "Nobody can figure them out."

3

THE WIND WAS STIRRING AS THEY PARKED.
The lots were empty on the weekend, and Shelby was able
to find a spot close to the main entrance. They filed silently
out of her truck. Ingrid had tried to start a conversation on
the way, but she couldn't manage to spark anything. Shelby
kept her eyes on the road, while Andrew stared out the
window, hypnotized by the painted lines. Carl kept throwing
desultory glances at Oliver but never actually spoke. Ingrid
sat between them, trying not to scream. None of this made
any sense. They had no reason to trust Oliver. His shadow
may have saved them, but Ingrid still felt that his appearance
had been all too convenient.

*Domina Pendelia told me not to trust him. Of course,
she was jealous. But that doesn't mean her suspicions were
off the mark.*

Felix had always seemed like a plain dealer. He paid well,
and his basia was known for its high standards. But meretrices had a way of rolling the dice when you least expected
it. The mask concealed their loyalties. As for Oliver—she
trusted him even less. They weren't the same, but Ingrid
knew that they shared certain annoying qualities. He'd been

lying for so long that it was effortless to him, like sealing an envelope.

They crossed the parking lot and entered through the Innovation Centre. All of the food kiosks were asleep behind bars. Only a few students remained in the cafeteria, pounding back coffee to get through whatever they were studying. New textbooks gleamed in their hands, with bright covers and optimistic titles. Highlighters moved like knitting needles, back and forth, separating the anecdotal from the essential. They walked past the posters advertising bake sales, concerts, and yoga for academics. Ingrid wasn't used to hearing her own footsteps. Normally, this part of campus was an explosion of sound, wave upon wave of students running to keep up with their own schedules. Now the halls were practically empty. She looked at the face of the dead clock next to the bookstore. The minute hand seemed to tremble. When she blinked and looked again, the hand was still.

The elevator next to it chimed. The doors opened, and three students in pajamas filed out. They approached the nearest vending machine, staring at it with a unified sense of disappointment. The first student deposited a toonie, but couldn't decide what to get. Her fingers hovered over the numeric keypad, as if she were afraid to touch the buttons.

"Stay away from the giant cookie," Ingrid said. "I think it's full of toxins."

The girl looked right through her.

Ingrid started to say something else, but instead, she kept walking. Moments like this reminded her that she was surrounded by kids fresh from high school, teenagers who operated on an entirely different frequency. All they saw when they looked at her was a cautionary tale. Next to them, she felt like an old Nintendo cartridge. It was only a matter of time until they mounted their phones with laser cannons that would disintegrate her. This was their world. She wanted to know more, to learn their language, but her fingers weren't fast enough.

Shelby was smiling at her.

"What is it?"

"Nothing. Just—what you said back there, to the girl. It was funny."

"Those cookies really are bad news."

"I believe it. Most of the food on campus is potentially dangerous."

"The soup isn't bad," Andrew said. "If you like hybrids."

They entered the library. Only a few students were working at the computers. There was no one behind the counter. The first floor had been under construction for months, but she had no idea what they were actually building. The space behind the computers was covered in a plastic tarp, which rippled slightly beneath the air-conditioning.

"We can use the printer on the fifth floor," Oliver said. "It's newer, but people forget about it, because it's hidden."

"I didn't even know it existed," Andrew replied.

"See? Follow me."

They squeezed into the elevator. Oliver pressed 5, and the doors closed.

"Wait," he said. "I just remembered—"

Ingrid didn't like where this was going. "What is it?"

"There's a book that I need." He pressed 4. "We can get it on the way."

They reached the fourth floor. The doors slid open.

Oliver started to walk out, then stopped. "It's in the over-size section. There's this one part that always confuses me. The call number is N 5754, and I can never remember where to find that section. It's tucked away in a corner—is it on the east side?"

"I know exactly where it is," Andrew said. "On the west side, by the study tables. If you want, I can grab it for you."

Oliver smiled. "You're probably faster than I am. Sure. Go ahead."

Andrew's face brightened now that he had a mission. "Okay, I'll be right back."

He turned left and disappeared into the stacks.

Oliver waited a few seconds. Then he turned to Ingrid. "Hold the door."

"What are you doing?"

He walked over to the computer next to the door. On the wall next to it was a security panel. Oliver flipped open the panel and hit a sequence of keys. Ingrid heard a beep, then a loud click from the door. She stared at him as he stepped back into the elevator.

"What did you just do?"

Oliver let the doors close. Then he reached down and entered a code on the silver keypad, next to the emergency call button. Ingrid had always been curious about that keypad, assuming that it had something to do with maintenance. The elevator chimed once, then began to rise.

"We just left Andrew on the fourth floor," Carl said.

"I know."

Carl glared at him. "That was your plan all along."

"He'll be safe there. I've locked the doors and programmed the elevator to skip that floor. It's the best protection I can offer him."

"You can't just leave him there."

"He's safer in quarantine."

"He's scared and alone!"

"Did you have a better idea? Telling him the truth, perhaps?"

"I have a more pressing question," Ingrid said. "How the hell did you figure out the security codes for this building?"

Oliver squared his shoulders. "Don't underestimate a former librarian."

They reached the fifth floor. The doors opened, and Oliver stepped out.

"Now we're just supposed to follow you?" Shelby asked. "After you go all *Die Hard Library* and trap our friend in the oversize book section?"

"Mardian is coming. We need weapons."

"He's coming for us—not you. Why are you even here?"

"I guess I was just homesick. We can stand around trying to puzzle out my motives, or we can arm ourselves. Your choice."

"There are weapons in the library?" Carl asked.

"Thousands of them. Now let's go."

Ingrid stopped in the hallway. "Okay. This is a little insane. Not the part about the cache of weapons, because I understand that librarians are prepared for anything. But what exactly are we doing here? None of us know how to fight."

"You're a single mother," Oliver said. "You've been fighting ever since—"

She raised a hand to stop him. "Spare me the empowering speech. You know what I'm talking about. On this side of the park, I can't fight with a sword. I barely have the strength to wrangle my son into a pair of pants." She looked at Shelby and Carl. "What about the two of you? Did you attend any combat training sessions as part of your TA orientation?"

"I think I missed that workshop," Shelby said. "And Carl's never been in a fight."

"That's not true. In the second grade, I punched a kid in the ear. He tried to steal my *Transformers* thermos."

"You may not know how to fight with a blade," Oliver said, "or string a bow, or—" He glanced at Carl and frowned. "What sort of weapon does a trovador use?"

"I can swing a short sword in a wide arc. Like a semideadly sprinkler."

"Fine. The point is—"

"—that we should call the police and get a restraining order," Shelby said, cutting him off. "No spadones or creepy nurses within a hundred meters of us. That has to work. I mean, we could say that he drugged Andrew, that he was—I don't know—giving off a *Single White Eunuch* vibe or something, whatever."

"The police are on his side. Detectives, firemen, crimescene investigators, they're all connected to the park. They're all playing. Some of them might help us, but even more would destroy us for the chance of getting ahead. Mardian serves the basilissa, and now that she's put a price on your heads, you won't be safe."

"Why are we listening to him?" Carl asked. "Has everyone forgotten how he disappeared after things got bloody at the basilissa's party?"

"He did help us escape," Ingrid said. "And—" She hesitated. "He does have a lot to lose by allying himself with us."

Carl shook his head. "No. There's something sketchy going on between the two of you. He's supposed to be your supervisor, but a minute ago, he said he was a former librarian. He knows way too much about this building, and you didn't even look surprised when he showed up at your door. How do you really know each other?"

Ingrid started to say something, but Oliver cut her off.

"We're all connected. That's what I've been trying to explain. We each cast a shadow that stretches from one side of the park to the other. You may not know how to fight, but your shadow does. If I put a bow in Shelby's hand, Morgan is going to wake up. Maybe just a little, but enough to make Shelby remember what she knows."

"Does that make you a slut in both worlds?" Carl asked.

Oliver ignored him. "All those rules about 'parking,' all the secrets that we keep, they're designed to isolate us. If we're going to survive, we need to erase the margins."

"Ingrid—" Shelby looked at her. "You should leave."

"I think it's a bit late for that."

"For us, maybe. We knew what we were getting into. We just wanted a real quest. Now it looks like we're about to get the sharp end of this adventure. But you're barely involved. You can still leave. For Neil's sake."

She was right. For a moment, Ingrid considered the possibilities. She and Paul could move to Saskatoon, or Moose Jaw—some place that wasn't on the edge of the basilissa's territory. She could transfer her degree to another school, make new friends. Paul would be disappointed, but he loved them both. He would do the right thing. And Neil? He loved Regina. Not in spite of its long winter, but because of it. When she complained about the snow, he reminded her, sagely: *We are mammals. We are warm-blooded.* He adored the living skies, the moon that seemed impossibly round, like a pearl loosed from a titan's necklace. He crowed in delight to see his frosty breath and loved to drag twin sleeping bags onto the deck for stargazing. Eventually, he would adjust to a new preschool, a new cycle of suburban activities.

But it didn't seem right. Without the park, he never would have existed. Fel had carried him inside her. Even when he was barely a wisp of cells, she'd carried him through the dangerous alleys of Anfractus. He was the size of a kidney bean when she left Domina Pendelia's house to work for the basia. He had no idea of what he'd seen. He was with her when she fought in the Hippodrome, and later, when she guarded Felix's door. Once, he had kicked while she was putting on her lorica. *I'm here.* The message filled her, and she stopped, fingers suddenly nerveless, unable to manage the leather ties and metal clasps. There was no guarantee that he would ever see the park like she did. Fortuna had no respect for genetics. He could grow up without the faintest idea of where he'd once been. Yet Anfractus belonged to him. Like a wave, it had carried him forward. With tiny eyes shut and fists curled, all unawares, Neil had danced through its blind corners. Now she owed him the possibility of return.

"It's for his sake that I have to fight," she said. "Because, someday, he might remember the way back. I'm not about to let a mad queen or anyone else stand in his way. Now— where are these weapons you keep talking about?"

Oliver smiled slightly. "Follow me."

They continued down the hallway, past closed doors with embossed nameplates. Most of the administrative staff went home on Thursday, due to cutbacks. It was only a small band of librarians who kept the place alive. If not for graduate students and faculty searching for periodicals, the library would have had no reason to stay open. At first, Ingrid had been dismayed to realize that students in the Department of Education weren't exactly keen to visit the stacks. They downloaded most of the books and were mystified by the shelving system. What was the point in wandering through a building when you could simply read a text online? Why touch books at all? They were dusty little outpatients with yellowing tape around their spines. The text couldn't be magnified, and there were no links that led you anywhere else.

She'd grown up in libraries and loved everything about them: the generous silence, the gliding of carts, the bright covers that winked at her from tall shelves. Getting her first library card had been infinitely more exciting than getting her driver's license. When she was a child, the computers had seemed out of place. They were slow, hot, humming versions of card catalogs, with sticky keyboards and aching blue letters that trembled when you looked at them. Like foldout maps, they were something to be consulted as a last resort. But as she grew, so did the computers. They got faster and smarter, learned new tricks, wider skill sets. What they provided was incredibly useful: a glossa for everything, a dramatis personae, a family tree whose root system was endless. They gave directions. There was no longer a reason to wander, to let your eyes drift from one book to another. Now you could find what you were looking for, scan it through the self-checkout, and leave. It was like buying groceries.

They reached the door marked *Special Collections*. Oliver opened it with a key and beckoned them in. The room was still and smelled of old paper. There was a long table in the center and filing cabinets along the back wall. Scanned images from the archives were framed and hung on the walls. The women's hockey team from 1925, their skirts nearly touching the snow. One held her stick at a curious angle, as if it were an oar. Behind them was a squat cluster of buildings, surrounded by white. There was also artwork by the Regina Five and more photographs from the university's past.

"I've never been here," Carl said. "I thought it mostly just held financial documents and letters from old deans. Nothing that I actually study."

"This is the school's memory," Oliver replied. "I was the head of Special Collections for nearly eight years. This is where I discovered the park."

Shelby gave him an odd look. "Here? Seems like a weird place to study the outdoors."

"The history of Wascana Park—and the contested territory known as *Oscana*—is contained in these archives. We have copies of many government documents, and a few originals. When I was first hired as an archivist, I had to create a finding guide for the Wascana Collection. That's when I began to notice that the park was a magnet for chaos. All sorts of things can happen over nine kilometers of wilderness. Hundreds of people have vanished in or near the park since 1962, when it first opened. Before that, it was a burial ground for more than buffalo bones."

"How long do you think people have been using it to cross over?" Shelby asked.

"We can't be sure. There are murder cases and disappearances that go back further than the eighteenth century. We don't have them here, but I dug up a few reports the last time I visited the National Archives in Ottawa."

"All those bones," Carl murmured. "Human and animal. We built a leisure complex on stolen land and covered up the mass grave underneath. Maybe it's haunted."

"Maybe you've watched *Poltergeist* one too many times," Shelby said.

"Carl does have a point, actually." Oliver leaned against the table. "Many parks are built on contested land. Of course, not every park leads to another world, but some do. What first drew me to Wascana Park was its artifice. A false lake spanned by a toy bridge. Infantile trees with no business being there, designed to transform a plain into a king's wood. The whole thing seemed like a magic act, but what was the curtain meant to cover?" His expression hardened. "I believe that the park was built as a distraction, to hide the frontier between two worlds. The city planners knew exactly what they were doing."

"So"—Carl spread his hands—"did they fire you because you're a conspiracy nut or because you spent all of your time putting together one finding aid?"

"I quit. Sort of. It's a long story." Oliver walked over to the filing cabinets. "Can you give me a hand? These are heavy."

Together, they managed to move the files to one side. There was a wall safe behind them. Oliver entered the combination and opened the door. He hadn't been lying about the weapons. The pile inside resembled props from a production of *Oedipus Rex*. There were swords, a stack of daggers, a painted quarrel, and a bow. Ingrid's breath caught.

"Where did these come from?"

"The Internet, mostly. They're reproductions."

"Your arsenal is from eBay?"

"Please. I do have some standards. Most of these are from independent blacksmiths and fletchers. The knives—" He shrugged. "Okay, those came as a bundle. They're generic, but I did get a discount for ordering them in bulk."

"Do the other librarians know that you're archiving weapons?" Carl asked.

"Even if they found the safe, they couldn't open it."

"I'm starting to fear Information Sciences a little."

Oliver handed Ingrid the sword. "Take this."

She looked at it warily, as if it might bite her. The blade was roughly two feet long, with a beveled ivory grip. Faux ivory, she imagined, given that it was a reproduction. The pommel was gold-plated. *Like a Phrygian apple,* she thought. *Best not to take a bite.*

"Go on," Oliver said. "Try it out."

She took the weapon. It was so heavy that she almost dropped it. The effort required to hold it level made her muscles burn. Ingrid stared at the blade as if it were something harmless—a baton, maybe, or a squash racket. In her mind, she could see Fel holding a chipped sword, but it was like remembering a scene from a play. She tried to picture herself in the Hippodrome. She could hear the imprecations of the crowd. They were throwing their food, flashing their breasts, grabbing at their cocks. She was sweating from the heat, and her leg pained her. The old wound, still visible below her knee, like ropes of cooled lava. Fel's brass gauntlet was hot to the touch. She ran her fingers along the burning studs. The lorica flashed as she moved. Every hook and scale belonged to her. This was her dazzling skin. The only protection she had against spear, blade, or trident. Fel raised her sword.

You are also a part of me. Like a rib, I surrendered you, but some tensile gut-string joins us still. I forged you, beloved. I named you as you sang out of the water, throwing off sparks. Brave candle. The wick was fresh between us when I called out to you.

Clavus. Nail.

Neil.

The sword didn't seem quite as heavy. It wasn't totally familiar, but now she could recall holding it, as you might recognize a fellow passenger on the bus.

"I'm pretty sure I can hit something with this," she said. "If it gets close enough, and lets me swing at it."

"Is that Fel talking?" Oliver asked.

"Let's hope so. She's the one who knows how to slash at a moving target."

Carl and Shelby received their weapons in turn. With considerable effort, Shelby managed to string the bow. Carl took the remaining sword. His expression was dubious.

"I'm not having any kind of special moment here."

"That's because Babieca can't fight," Shelby said.

"He can too."

"I think you're confusing a song with a real battle."

"Yeah? Why don't you try actually shooting something with that bow?"

"Good idea. Hold still."

"Stop it." Oliver took the remaining knives. "Shelby—I know that when the moment comes, your aim will be true. Carl—" He shrugged. "It's not rocket science. There's a basic rule to fighting with a sword."

Carl, Shelby, and Ingrid cried out at once: *"Stick 'em with the pointy end!"*

Oliver closed his eyes. "Brilliant. Let's attack Mardian with references."

"We *are* in a library," Carl said. "And you walked right into that one."

He headed back over to the filing cabinets. "We're going to need something else."

"How about a Taser?" Carl asked. "Or a tranquilizer gun? I'd feel a bit more confident if my weapon had some kind of targeting system."

"No guns," Oliver called from behind the cabinets. "Mardian is sly, but he still has to follow the rules."

"But he can still cut us into pieces?"

"Certainly. As long as his weapon doesn't have a microchip."

"Nice rules," Carl muttered. "When's the last time they were updated?"

Oliver emerged from the cabinets dragging a sack.

Shelby clasped her hands together in delight. "He's like Santa."

"No way," Carl said. "If this were Christmas, I'd be holding a game controller, not an actual sword."

Oliver untied the sack. "It's not exactly chain mail, but it will offer some protection."

Shelby's eyes narrowed. "Is that hockey gear?"

"Pads and chest protectors, mostly. As it turns out, not many people are willing to ship replicas of scale armor to Regina. I had to find the next best thing."

"These smell musty," Carl said. "Have they been used?"

"Lightly."

"Gross."

"If you think your manly cardigan will do a better job of deflecting sharp-force trauma, by all means, forget about the padding."

Carl scowled. "It's a jersey, and my mother sent it to me."

"Put on the lightly used armor."

They divided the equipment. After dressing, they all looked lumpy and uncomfortable. Shelby kept trying to adjust her shoulder pads, and Carl was thrown off balance by the weight of his chest protector. Ingrid wasn't fond of the pads, but Oliver was right. They could easily make the difference between a glancing blow and a fatal one.

"What if Mardian and his crew have real armor?" Carl kept twisting his torso, as if he were in an aerobics video. "Maybe he sprang for shipping and got actual plate."

"On a nurse's salary? I doubt it."

"Oliver—" Shelby turned to him. The shoulder pads made her resemble a power forward, half-dressed and caught unawares in the locker room. "When did you leave this stuff here?"

"A while ago."

"Did you know that we were coming?"

"Not your company. Not specifically. But I knew that at some point, I'd have to fight the basilissa's people on this side of the park."

"How could you have known that?"

"What can I say? I'm cagey."

"You knew that someone would need a bow. That's more than a fuzzy guess."

"I've known a lot of sagittarii. They're frequent customers at the basia."

"I call bullshit," Carl said.

Oliver turned to him. "Look. I'm scared too. I may have planned for the worst, but that doesn't mean I thought it would happen like this." He held out his hand. It was trembling. "Even on the other side of the park, I'm no fighter. I'm a teacher. I give classes on seduction and body language. I fill out account books. On a good day, I may even find myself naked with a person whose company I enjoy. That's who I am."

"I don't think so."

"Carl—" Shelby began.

"It's simple, really. I can understand the weapons. You were planning for a worst-case scenario. I get that you may genuinely want to help us. I'm even willing to overlook the fact that you and Ingrid clearly have something on the side. Whatever. That's your business." Carl's expression hardened. "But you were head of Special Collections. That's a tenure-track position, Oliver. Nobody gives up that kind of job. I think you ran for a reason."

Oliver started to say something, but Ingrid cut him off.

"It's complicated. We—"

The fire alarm blared. The fluorescent lights went out. For a moment, everything was dark and terribly loud. Then the yellowish emergency lights flicked on. They reminded Ingrid of half-dead streetlamps. Beneath them, her sword looked more like a shadow.

"He's here," Oliver said.

Shelby's eyes widened. "Andrew. He's a sitting duck on the fourth floor."

"He'll be fine, as long as he stays put."

"Great," Carl murmured. "I feel armed and terrified."

They left the archive, heading back down the hallway. Ingrid held the sword like a flashlight in front of her. Shelby's quarrel resembled a messenger bag. Carl kept shifting his blade from one hand to the other, like a hot potato. What were they doing? This wasn't Anfractus. They were on university grounds. People didn't fight with swords on campus, except once a year when the Society for Creative Anachronism held their tournament. That was on the green, though. How were they supposed to fight in the middle of the stacks?

Both sides of the park are real, she reminded herself. *Last night, you attacked those miles. They weren't actors. The blood wasn't fake. It all seems like a game sometimes, but it's not. It never was. The stakes have always been this high. Only this time, there are no saving throws. Morgan has no die to cast, and Fortuna isn't listening.*

"My pads reek a little," Carl whispered.

"Keep walking," Shelby said.

The alarm continued to scream. In the stairwell, the noise was twice as loud. Ingrid had heard worse, though. Living with a four-year-old made you functionally deaf. She led them down the stairs. The emergency lights were miserly, and it was hard to see more than a few feet ahead. They descended carefully. When they reached the fourth level, Ingrid stopped.

"That's—not good," she murmured.

"What is it?" Carl asked. "I can barely—"

He bit off the words. The fire exit was held open by a book. Through the gap, Ingrid could see the dim outline of the nonfunctioning elevator.

"The alarm—" Oliver swore. "I can't believe I forgot. The security system deactivates in case of an emergency."

"Andrew could be anywhere," Shelby said. "He must be looking for us. What if he runs into Mardian first?"

"He strikes me as a logical person. And anyone who spends a lot of time in this library knows that there's an exit on the basement level. Wouldn't he simply head for the nearest gathering point outside?"

"He might have done that *before* you locked him on the fourth floor. Now he probably thinks that you're behind all of this."

"Let's hope that we find him before Mardian does."

"Andrew's pretty resourceful," Carl said. "I think he'll be fine."

He didn't sound convinced.

Ingrid squeezed his hand lightly. "Maybe we'll all be fine. Crazier things have happened."

"Crazier than wearing hockey pads to fight a eunuch?"

"Well—" She continued down the stairs. "My son spends most of his time building catapults to fight an evil porcine menace. He doesn't question the logic. He just plays."

"The pigs aren't real, though."

"I've never been completely sure of that."

"I get it," Shelby said. "It doesn't matter what side of the park we're on. The rules have gone out the window— otherwise, we wouldn't be having this conversation. I rolled high once. Maybe it's not the die that's important. We roll with our lives every day."

They reached the ground floor. The stairwell was practically in darkness. For a moment, all they could do was stand behind the closed door. Then the alarm stopped.

"Does that mean the firemen are here?" Carl asked weakly.

"I doubt it," Oliver said.

We roll with our lives. Ingrid exhaled.

Her life was a streak.

There was the school and the park, and the students of both, who rolled the dice because it was the only sane thing to do. There was Paul, who loved her fiercely. And there was Neil, her key, her quicksilver. Little Bedouin parts of him had traveled through her body. He was in her blood, her roots, his laughter a cascade of bells. Cleave any part of her, and his shadow would speed forth, like music escaping a wax cylinder. He was with her now, as he'd been with her in the darkness of a thousand alleys.

I've been lucky so far. Why stop now?

She opened the door.

4

THE MAIN FLOOR OF THE LIBRARY WAS SILENT and bathed in caustic yellow light. The bank of computers blinked in time with each other, as if delivering a coded message: *Please deliver us from Facebook*. Or maybe it was Bejeweled. Whatever games people played to distract themselves from the apocalypse of term papers. The construction zone—what would eventually become the new periodical reading room—was draped in plastic, and Ingrid could see the bony outcroppings of steel support structures beneath it. There was caution tape everywhere, rustling slightly with each breath of air-conditioning. The circulation desk was empty. For a moment, she wanted to jump over the counter and see what was in that restricted space, partially obscured by stacks of reserve textbooks and interlibrary loans. It was probably just another office, but secretly, she imagined that it held forbidden texts, like the monastic library in *The Name of the Rose*. She glanced at the self-checkout machine and thought once more of Neil, who adored the *thump* that it made whenever you dragged a book's spine along the demagnetizing strip.

The screen invited passersby to scan their materials. Blue and green arrows showed you every step. Ingrid remained still for a heartbeat, watching the helpful animation. *Touch here for knowledge.* Once, she'd found an old book that wasn't cataloged, and she could still remember the look of sublime joy on the librarian's face. *This isn't in the system. If you don't mind waiting, I'll need to create a new entry.* Her eyes lit up, as if she'd just found a hoard of pirate's treasure. She delicately removed the old punch card, still affixed to the inside cover. Ingrid wondered if she'd pocketed the paper relic when nobody was looking. Maybe she had a box full of them at home, yellowed around the edges, slightly aromatic, like ancient recipe cards that still carried a hint of spice.

Where was Mardian? She heard nothing, save for the rustle of plastic and the occasional squeak of a computer rebooting. She remembered the ghost of the spado's smile, hovering between care and amusement. But he wasn't a spado—not here. Surely, on this side of the park, he must have been—intact? The more she thought about that word, the less she was certain of what it meant. Spadones were regular customers at the basia. However they'd been cut, it seemed to have little effect on their natural desires. They shared much in common with meretrices, who were often accused of being cold-blooded.

She looked at Oliver. The dagger in his hand looked absurdly fake, but its edge was real. Was he also cold-blooded? He'd seemed upset when he came to her, directly following the basilissa's banquet. She wanted to trust him. But Carl's many suspicions were far from groundless. Whether he was Oliver, Felix, or whatever lived in between them both, he'd always been talented at rolling the dice. He knew how to pick the winning side, and right now, the odds were against them. Was he planning to run again? When she saw him standing on the doorstep, her first reaction was to say, *Are you lost?* The park had always served as a frontier that separated their lives. In Anfractus, they passed each

other all the time, nodding curtly. But he hadn't lived in
Regina for years. There'd been no worry of running into
each other at the mall, Neil in tow, stammering, *Oh, wow,
it's been so long—*

"Do you think he's here?" Shelby murmured.

Oliver kept the knife level, but his grip was awkward.
"He's watching us. That's what he's best at. Peering through
keyholes, listening through cracks in the wall."

"Unless I'm mistaken," Ingrid said, "you're fairly good
at that yourself."

"Running a basia requires vigilance. Drauca and I need
to ensure that the clients are behaving themselves. The
spado's creeping about is different."

Shelby chuckled. "You dislike him nearly as much as
Carl dislikes you."

"Hey," Carl said. "*Dislike* is a strong word. Let's just say
I don't trust the majority of people who wear masks for a
living. Bank robbers. Circus freaks. Jason Voorhees and
Michael Myers. I'm not about to hug any of them."

"Everyone shut up." Shelby was staring at the counter. She
lowered her voice. "There's somebody here. I can feel it."

They were silent for a moment. Ingrid couldn't hear anything. Perhaps it was Morgan, and not Shelby, who'd caught
the noise. She adjusted her grip on the sword. Fel was closer
to the surface than she'd ever been. Their shadows, as Oliver
called them, were stronger in this moment. Like Peter Pan,
she could sew Fel to her foot and never let her go. Was it
possible? People had different personalities, different sides
to them, that much she understood. But Fel was supposed
to be a character. A miles didn't care about paying her Sask-
Tel bill on time. If Fel took over, she'd go straight to Bush-
wacker's to pick a fight with the biggest mouth-breather at
the bar. Fel cared about winning. What did she know about
family? She'd always been alone.

Ingrid blinked. *Had* Fel always been alone? Those memories were beyond her grasp. They said that you had to play
a character for years before you could really know where

they came from or what they wanted. Sometimes she caught flashes of a childhood, a small room in a dirty tenement building above the Subura, reeking from the tanner's shop below. She must have had parents. To her, Fel had always been a chipped sword, defiant and worn.

Shelby was gesturing to Carl. He stared at her, not understanding. She rolled her eyes. Then, in a single motion, she leapt over the counter. Ingrid heard something that sounded like a squeak. Then Shelby stood up. In her left hand, she gripped the shirt collar of a dazed-looking girl. Her red hair looked strangely golden beneath the emergency lights, and she was still clutching a hardcover book. Her mouth opened slightly, but nothing came out.

"I knew I heard something," Shelby said.

Finally, the girl cleared her throat and managed to speak. "Could you let go of me? I'm not going to—" Her eyes widened as she took in the four of them. "Are you wearing body armor? Is this some kind of intense paintball tournament?"

"Why were you hiding down there?"

She looked at Shelby with undisguised curiosity. "You have a bow."

"Answer the question."

"I was on the second floor when the alarm started. I came downstairs, and the place was totally empty. I was just about to leave, but—" She looked beyond the counter, at the half-concealed room. "Okay, it's stupid, I know, but I've always wanted to see the uncataloged books, and they've got stacks of them, just sitting there. The librarians had all left. I just wanted to take a peek. There's this engineering text that's been listed as 'in progress' for weeks on the library website, and I really need it for my thesis. I just wanted to see if it was actually there, and not just a ghost in the machine."

Shelby was also looking beyond the counter. "I—suppose I can understand that," she said. "But why didn't you leave?"

"Well, I heard these guys come in. I thought they might

be librarians, and—I know it's childish, but my first instinct was to hide. They disappeared after a few minutes, and then I tried to leave, but the doors won't open."

"What do you mean?" Oliver asked. "They have to stay open in case of a fire."

"I know. But someone *melted* them. At least that's what it looks like. They're fused. I tried to open them, but they won't budge."

Ingrid walked up to the doors. The girl was right. The metal edges were fused together, like two strips of Play-Doh. No seams or bubbles—it was as if they'd always been a single piece of black metal. She walked back over to the counter.

"She's right. The doors are sealed."

"Mardian," Oliver said. "I don't know how he's done it—"

"Wait—" The girl stared at them. "You know—I mean—" Her eyes flickered rapidly, trying to study all of them at once. "How do you—"

"Bee!" Shelby cried.

Carl began swatting at the empty air next to him.

"No. Not here, brain trust. On her shirt. Look."

Ingrid peered at the girl's long-sleeved shirt. It had a bumblebee sewn onto the shoulder. For a moment, she could almost hear it buzz. Then she remembered what Oliver had told her about the scene at the basilissa's banquet. A mechanical bee had summoned three hungry silenoi, like some kind of dog whistle. The work of a master artifex.

"Julia?" Shelby asked.

The girl blinked in confusion. "Morgan?"

"On this side, I'm Shelby."

"The artifex," Ingrid said. "I thought you were a citizen."

She laughed. "Only the rich apprentices can manage that. I'm flat broke."

"But—" Shelby stared at her. "You said that you had a room at the gens. And you remembered your mother. I thought that only citizens had access to deep memory structures."

"My mother was famous. People are always telling me stories about her. As for the room"—she stared at the floor—"I may have exaggerated. When I said 'my chamber,' I should have said 'the spare room that I sneaked into.' It's not like anyone notices me. To them, I'm only a shadow of what my mother used to be. Or Julia's mother. Sometimes I can't tell us apart. I'm Sam. I think."

"This is all very informative," Oliver said, "but we're still the prey in this scenario, and there's no way out. I suggest we get out of the open."

Sam gave him a sideways glance. "Who's this?"

"Just call him Dr. Love," Carl said.

"No. Do not call me that."

"Too late. It's going to stick—I can feel it."

"The doctor—I mean Oliver—says that there's a basement exit," Shelby whispered. "It's possible that Mardian and his crew don't know about it."

"Crew?" Sam looked around the empty room. "How many of them are there?"

"We don't know."

She shook her head. "I knew I should have stayed home to mark exams." Then her expression softened slightly. "Andrew—"

"—is alive."

"Oh. I didn't—I mean, I hoped, but—"

"After this is done," Oliver hissed, "you can share everything on your windows, or whatever they call it. For now, zip it and follow me."

"Facebook did exist before you left," Ingrid said. "You know what a wall is."

"I really wish I didn't."

They walked past the computers, to the area covered in plastic. Gently, Oliver lifted a corner, and they crept into the construction zone. In the corner, a tangle of sleek metal shelves were piled on top of each other. They were designed to entice undergraduates into reading periodicals but actually resembled something you might find on the deck of an alien spacecraft. Ingrid couldn't imagine them holding journals and magazines. Like the refurbished downtown campus—all concrete, glass, and succulent greenery kept alive by merciless heat—this project smacked of desperation. Most students would never pass by the computers in order to leaf through random journals. They were building a zoo for rare animals, each one slightly dazed to find itself on a shelf beneath track lighting.

"I'm the only one without armor," Sam whispered. "That hardly seems fair."

"Aren't you an engineering student?" Carl made an abstract gesture. "Why not use these lovely materials to fashion yourself a cuirass?"

"I liked you better in the shit-stained tunica."

They heard footsteps.

"Behind the shelves," Oliver whispered.

There wasn't enough room for all of them to hide in the same place. Carl, Shelby, and Oliver managed to fit behind the pile of half-assembled shelving. Ingrid and Sam crawled behind a hoard of wall brackets and other support structures. Ingrid was sweating beneath the chest protector. The sword no longer felt natural in her right hand. It was giving her a cramp.

Maybe it's the firemen, she thought, without conviction. *Won't they be surprised to discover a group of crazy people, huddled together in an active construction zone?*

Through gaps in the metal, she saw four pairs of shoes. Two sets of sneakers, one pair of boots, and—closest to her—sensible black orthotic shoes with extra cushioning. She'd recently thought of buying that exact pair from Zellers.

"This isn't Robarts Library," Mardian said. "They can't have gone far. I'm willing to bet that they're on this floor."

"Waste of time," an unfamiliar voice muttered.

The black shoes squeaked lightly as Mardian turned to face the voice. "You were bleeding to death when I found you in that hallway. If you'd like, we can re-create that scenario. There are plenty of sharp things lying around here."

"I just don't see why we're playing hide-and-seek with these idiots. You know where they live. Why not just—"

"Stop talking." Mardian turned toward the pile of metal. "They're close. We need to flush them out."

"We could burn the place down."

"This is your school. You really wouldn't hesitate to set it on fire?"

"My parents made me enroll. You think I wanted to major in kinesiology?"

Mardian sighed. "You have no idea how lucky you are."

Ingrid tightened her grip on the sword. Her brain was telling her to stay quiet. What surprised her was that she didn't feel scared. Across from her, Sam was trying not to breathe. Her eyes were all pupil. For Ingrid, it was different. There was no shock of adrenaline. Her breathing stayed level as she kept absolutely still. Her body was used to this, even if it was the opposite of the Hippodrome. No pounding blood or tunnel vision. Just a bizarre kind of weightlessness. Dangling, a bat inside a cave lit only by flashes of mica. If she kicked over the hoard of metal, there would be a few seconds of anarchy. Long enough to strike before they knew what was happening.

But there was no way to signal Oliver. He was on the other side of the room. It would just be her, swinging her sword blindly. She looked at Sam, trying to gauge what the young woman might be capable of. Sam looked up. She was squeezing her hands together, and Ingrid could see that her knuckles were white. Not knowing what else to do, she winked. It was an odd gesture, and for a moment, Sam looked confused. Then, the hint of a smile played across her face. Some of the fear vanished. Maybe she'd fight after all. She'd been brave in the arx, when their odds had been much worse.

Kick over the pile. Do it now.

"Wait," another voice said. It was the pair of boots. "I know how to find them. We don't need fire. Just smoke."

They were silent for a moment. Then three pairs of shoes

left. Only the boots remained. Ingrid shifted position, trying to get a better look. She saw only a worn pair of jeans whose frayed cuffs were tucked into hiking boots. He wasn't moving. Why? Sam also seemed curious but was unwilling to find a better vantage point. After a few more seconds, he began whispering under his breath. She couldn't understand what he was saying. He paused, as if listening, then murmured something else, largely inaudible. She made out a single word: *peels*. He spoke again. This time she heard *deal*. Maybe that's what he'd said before. It had sounded like *peels*, though. Was he reciting poetry to himself?

After another pause, he ducked under the plastic and left the enclosure. Ingrid could hear Sam breathing. She frowned. Then something impossible occurred to her. At first, she denied it. But then she remembered the scene in the bathroom. Andrew's wide, dark eyes. The faint whiff of ozone clinging to the tiles. Was it possible?

As she watched through the hole in the brackets, two tendrils of smoke appeared. They hovered a few inches off the ground. They had no spark, no source. They were simply there, as if something invisible were burning. The tendrils formed a smoke ring, which began to expand. It was followed by another ring, and another, each one larger, until smoke was pressing against the plastic shell of the construction zone. Sam coughed. Ingrid stood up, holding a hand to her mouth. The smoke made her eyes water. Through the haze, she could see Oliver, but he was slowly becoming indistinct. She took Sam's hand, not wanting to lose her as well. The shadow beside Oliver might have been Shelby, or not. The smoke was thickening. How stupid they'd been. Dressing like warriors, thinking that they could roll the dice against someone like Mardian. He had precisely what they'd lost. An auditor.

There were two choices left. They could make a run for the elevators. Of course, they'd be followed easily enough, but it would give them a chance to regroup. They could fortify the archive. It seemed like a fitting place for a last stand. The second choice was to run for the emergency exit, in the hopes that it was still clear. One of them could probably make it. She looked at Sam, already vanishing into the smoke. If they all charged at once, she might be able to escape in the confusion.

Ingrid squeezed her hand. "Listen. We have to get out of here. Stay with me for now, but as soon as I let go of your hand, I want you to run for the emergency exit. It's past the information desk, in the far left corner. Don't look back—just run. Understand?"

Sam nodded.

Ingrid couldn't see the others. The smoke was too thick. She used her sword to raise the plastic cover, then stepped out of the enclosure. Sam followed. Smoke crawled up the walls, forming clouds above the computers. It might have started in the construction zone, but it was everywhere now. The fire alarms were silent. The smoke detectors continued to blink green, like nothing was happening, as clouds gathered in the vaulted arches of the ceiling. The smell didn't remind her of burned soup, or a campfire. It was something different. It whispered of blind alleys, baked cobblestones, giant clay furnaces. Ingrid almost wanted to breathe it in. For a moment, she seemed to be somewhere else. The ground was uneven beneath her feet. The blade rippled in her hand, and she felt it flowing, part of her blood, her water. In the distance, she heard the boom of the clepsydra. Fortuna's eyes were upon her.

Something stepped out of the smoke. Ingrid leveled her sword. The shape moved toward her, and she saw the gleam of a knife. She hesitated. It was easier in Anfractus. Her instincts took over. But on this side of the park, things were different. Fel was screaming at her: *Now, strike at the legs!* With one cut, she could open the popliteal artery. It would spray blood like an aquifer—she'd seen it happen on the sands. The sword refused to dance. Ingrid held on to it, trying to shut out Fel's voice. This wasn't the Hippodrome. She couldn't just attack a stranger in the middle of the library. She couldn't even respond to the negative comments on her last conference paper. All those passive-aggressive jabs at her methodology. She'd just nodded, as she'd been taught, and said, *That's a fascinating counterpoint, thank you so much.*

On the inside, she wanted to thrust. She wanted to drench the Fiesta Room of the Edmonton Doubletree Hotel in rising arterial spray, wanted to scream *Your in-press article can go straight to hell* as she diced the critics and everyone else who'd told her that she was too old for grad school, that she should really just stick to raising her son.

The smoke cleared, and she saw—neither a miles nor an academic—but rather a stocky kid in a green Roughriders T-shirt and baggy carpenter jeans. The gleam of metal was from the fire ax that he carried. He must have stolen it from the glass case She almost laughed. He could have been a younger Jack Nicholson, except that his eyes weren't glazed over. They were bright with fear. It was a mystery how they'd both arrived at this point. He should have been watching the game, or cruising Northgate Mall with cash to burn. Instead, he was standing in a smoke-filled library, holding a weapon designed to break through doors. He was taking orders from a nurse who moonlighted as a eunuch. It would have been funny, except that the joke had unraveled a long time ago. The basilissa wanted them dead. She had no qualms about sending boys to do the job. What had she promised this poor kid? What did he think was going to happen?

His eyes narrowed. He tightened his grip on the ax.

"Wait," Ingrid said. "Let's just take a second, here."

"You ruined me."

She blinked. "What?"

"Holy shit. You don't even remember."

Ingrid stared at him. There was nothing familiar. He could have been anyone. Then she noticed that he favored his left leg. There was something bulky underneath the denim, like padding, or—a bandage. She looked at his face again. For a moment, she imagined him wearing a helmet, carrying a sword rather than a safety ax. He'd looked older in the arx, surrounded by a group of miles. Was it really him? Was this cub the armored warrior she'd attacked outside Pulcheria's chamber?

"You severed a tendon in my leg," he growled. "I'm going to walk with a limp for the rest of my life. I'll never play football again."

"I'm sorry."

"My parents can barely look at me. They say I should go to SaskTech and become an electrician. I had an athletic scholarship! Now I can barely sleep, my leg hurts so much. I have nightmares—about you."

Sam was still behind her. Ingrid hoped that he couldn't see her, that the smoke was obscuring her form. Where were Oliver and the rest of them? She needed to send them a signal. How did knights do it? They must have waved some kind of pennant. There was a provincial flag hanging above the circulation desk. If she could reach it, maybe she'd be able to communicate in frantic semaphore. Medieval texting. The thought almost made her crack a smile, but then she looked into the kid's wasted eyes. He was a broken thing now, because of her. She'd always feared that Neil might wake up some day and begin to quietly hate her. It was a phase that everyone warned her about. What she hadn't expected was that a complete stranger might grow to hate her, intensely, for the rest of his life.

"I know it's not fair," she said. "I know you want to hurt me. But you must have realized how high the stakes were."

"Are you kidding? It was supposed to be fun. Go on quests, gain experience—just like any RPG. I knew about the monsters. But I wasn't stupid. I stayed away from them. I never expected that another miles could do this to me."

"I had no choice."

"I'm nineteen!" His eyes glittered with pain. "I had my entire life ahead of me, and now everything I ever fucking wanted is gone. Because of you."

He swung the ax wildly. She jumped back. Sam was no longer holding her hand—Ingrid couldn't see her anywhere.

Gripping the ax two-handed, he swung again. He had the advantage. The ax blade was dull, but with enough force, it would still crush her armor like a tin can. Her sword was barely a prop. She'd have better luck stabbing him with a piece of rebar. She brought it up in time to parry the ax blade, and the shock of the impact made her wrist go numb for a few seconds. Gritting her teeth, she took another step back, keeping the blade high.

"I'm sorry for what I did to you," Ingrid repeated. "You're allowed to hate me. If I were in your place, I'd hate me, too. But we had no choice. Pulcheria was going to die."

"She was safe in her room, until you showed up. It was our duty to protect her. You were the ones who broke into the arx."

"Latona was going to kill her."

His expression wavered. "You're lying."

"What did Mardian promise you?"

He hesitated, lowering the ax slightly. "He knows a medicus that can fix my leg."

"The damage is done. The greatest doctors on this side of the park wouldn't be able to fix your leg. What makes you think that someone in Anfractus could do a better job, without any drugs or technology?"

"She—I don't know—something to do with the lares. Some kind of partnership. They can do things on the other side. Mardian swore it."

"He's manipulating you. He—"

Something struck her in the back of the head. Ingrid stumbled, then sank to one knee. The pain made her want to throw up. She could see white dots in front of her eyes. Dimly, she made out a shape beside her. It was the man in the boots. He was holding a metal support strut. Ingrid touched the back of her head. She felt a tangled mess of hair and blood. The room began to spin. *You're going to pass out,* her brain told her. *Between the smoke inhalation and the fresh blow to the head, it's a miracle that you're still conscious.*

"Found one of them!" The auditor smiled down at her.

For a moment, his face resembled a paper lantern. His cheeks were slightly sunken, and he had a sharp nose.

"The lares," she murmured, speaking to his boots. "Are they really here?"

He chuckled. "Of course. They're everywhere. Those queer little gods. They couldn't stay away from a place like this."

"But—the rules—"

"There are no rules anymore. No sides. Latona's going to make sure of that." He raised the steel pole again. "You may have slowed her down, but you can't stop her. All this smoke"—he gestured to the room around them—"came from one curious lizard that I found sleeping under the photocopiers. Imagine what an army would be capable of."

"What's your plan?" She grimaced from the pain. "Set fire to the world?"

"No. Just to the people who stand in our way."

"Hey," the kid began. "I'm not setting fire to anybody."

The auditor stared at him. "You were about to bury an ax in this one."

"I wasn't actually going to kill her."

"Then you're an idiot."

"She said that Mardian—"

"Don't fucking listen to a word that she—"

The white dots cleared. Ingrid wrapped both hands around the blade. The auditor started to turn, but he was still distracted. Lurching to her feet, she raised the weapon to eye level, then drove it back down with all of her strength. It passed through the leather of the auditor's boot, and she kept pushing until she heard the point scrape against the floor. He screamed and dropped the pole. Ingrid drew out the blade, reversed it, and smashed the pommel into his face. She heard the *pop* of cartilage surrendering to blunt-force trauma. He crumpled to the ground, his foot making bloody, snow-angel smears against the linoleum.

The kid advanced on her, ax held high. She tried to raise the sword, but he grabbed her wrist and squeezed. He had at least a hundred pounds on her, and his grip was a vise.

Ingrid could feel her hand going numb. Then something burst from the smoke and crashed into him. Two shadows went down in a heap. Ingrid switched the blade to her left hand. She was shaking but not scared. The smoke cleared a bit, and she realized that it was Carl who'd knocked him down. They struggled, and then the kid punched Carl in the face. He'd lost his ax in the scuffle, but when you're built like a tank, you don't need much else. He pinned Carl to the ground, kneeling on his chest. It wouldn't take much more pressure to crack his ribs. Carl wheezed but couldn't cry out. He'd lost his knife.

Ingrid heard a low whistle. Then she heard screaming. The kid's left hand was pinned to the floor by an arrow. His fingers clenched spasmodically, nails digging at the ground.

"*Gnnah*—shit—oh *shit*—uhn—"

He slumped forward. He'd lost consciousness. A bloody palm print was beginning to form around the wound.

Shelby appeared, holding the bow. "Did I hit something?"

Carl managed to free himself. "You almost hit me."

"The smoke was in my eyes."

"Next time, you should yell something. Like *Fire in the hole*."

"That's for artillery, not arrows."

"Then yell *Arrow in the hole*."

"You're fine."

"My ribs beg to differ."

The smoke was vanishing now. Maybe the salamander had grown tired and crawled back to its nest underneath the photocopiers. Ingrid saw two shapes in the far corner of the room. They were Oliver and Sam. Oliver had raised his knife, and Sam held the fire ax. She must have stolen it in the confusion. The two stared at each other in surprise. For a moment, Ingrid thought that Sam might still swing the ax. Then she lowered the weapon.

"I wouldn't relax just yet."

They all turned. Even the wounded auditor, still bleeding all over the floor, managed to crane his neck in the direction of the voice. Mardian stood by the circulation desk. He was holding someone else. Was it the fourth pair of shoes? It took Ingrid a moment to recognize the figure, who was half the size of Mardian. She went cold as the realization struck her.

Andrew didn't struggle. He just stood there, calmly, while Mardian pressed the edge of a knife to his throat.

"I found this one in the stairwell," Mardian said. "He actually cut me. I was so surprised, I nearly let him escape."

"I should have aimed higher," Andrew said. "It was my first stabbing."

"Wait." Ingrid lowered her sword. "There were four of you. I count three."

"He's creeping up behind you right now," Mardian said. "All stealthlike."

"I saw him bolt for the emergency exit," Oliver replied. "Just before everything went pear-shaped. He must have gotten out."

"Not a problem." Mardian tightened his grip on the knife. "He won't get far. My lady has no use for deserters."

Andrew frowned slightly. "Who is this lady that you keep talking about? Also"—he looked at Oliver—"why did you leave me on the fourth floor? Was it something I said?"

"Shut up." Mardian stepped back, pulling Andrew with him. "You're the cause of this, auditor. It was your silver tongue that charmed the undinae."

"I told you before—I don't know what you're talking about. I can help you with your taxes, if that's what you want. But I didn't charm—" His eyes narrowed. "*Undinae?* Is that a person, or a plural noun?"

"Unbelievable." Mardian laughed softly. "After all this trouble, you don't even remember. You can't. Now what am I supposed to do with you?"

Andrew's eyes widened as he took in the rest of the room. He looked at Shelby and smiled in disbelief.

"Why do you have a bow?" Then he saw the kid with the arrow in his hand. "Oh. You—did you *shoot* him? With an actual arrow?"

Mardian looked at Carl suddenly, and smiled. "The foxes told me about what you did. Someone has boundary issues."

"Shut up, gelding."

"Oh, I think you'll find that I'm quite intact, on either side."

"Did killing Narses make you feel like a true spado?"

"The old capon managed to elude us. He'll be found, though. And this isn't about me. It's about your lack of impulse control."

"You don't know what you're talking about."

"This must be killing you."

"I know I'm not the best at reading nuance," Andrew said weakly, "but has everyone completely stopped making sense? Or am I dreaming?"

"Even damaged, he's still dangerous." Mardian tightened his grip. "I have my orders."

"No." Carl took a step forward. "How can he be a threat? He doesn't even know what you're talking about. Just let him go."

"Do the two of you know each other?" Andrew asked. "Are we all playing some kind of extreme RPG? I think someone forgot to tell me the rules."

"There are none," Mardian replied. "I mean, there used to be. The rules held everything together. No crossovers. No talking about the secret. But things crossed. People talked, like they always do. Not everyone is good at keeping secrets. The lares are restless. Powers are moving back and forth. Soon, you won't be able to tell one side from the other."

"I don't know what your lady friend is expecting," Carl said, "but you can't just commit murder on school property."

"My position is secure. I can do as I wish."

"The police are on their way."

"How long have you lived in this city? The police are cruising up and down North Central, looking for people to hassle. You might as well call a taxi. They'll show up in twenty minutes, or forty, or half past never. It's all up to chance."

"We outnumber you," Carl said. "The odds are in our favor."

"Certainly. But I'm fast. He'll bleed out before you can reach me. Pumping his stomach is one thing. You won't be able to sew his head back on."

"*That's* where I know you from," Andrew said. "You were at the hospital."

"Keep up, sweetheart. You don't have much time left."

"Look." Carl raised his arms. "If you need a prize, take me instead. Your psychotic lady can torture me."

"You think a failed bard will pacify her? It's because of him that Pulcheria lives. He must pay in kind. There's no way around it."

"I suppose you do whatever she tells you."

"I do what's necessary. I always have."

Andrew's eyes narrowed. "Has everyone gone crazy from smoke inhalation?"

"You can't stop this," Mardian said. "Egressus will fall. Once she controls both cities, the balance will shift in her favor. The silenoi have already breached the divide. They're hungry, and this city is going to be their banquet. Latona will create a new order." He laughed. "Do you know why Regina is really called Queen City? Because it belongs to the basilissa. She's going to level it, like an old roach motel, and build a new temple on its ruins. A temple to the lares. Just like the old days, before the blasted wheel controlled everything."

"How will a bunch of spirits be any different from the goddess of chance?" Shelby demanded. "They're selfish and devious. Why would they serve her?"

Mardian smiled. "Let's just say they're planning a family reunion."

Andrew started to say something. But his eyes were suddenly drawn to the floor. Ingrid followed his gaze. Her breath caught. As she watched, a tiny set of footprints appeared in the swirl of blood around the fallen auditor. The tracks continued, foot by foot, and something smeared the blood behind them. It looked like a tail. The tracks made their way across the blood path, then stopped, about a foot away from Mardian.

Andrew stared at the spot where the tracks vanished. "What is that?" he whispered.

Mardian pressed the knife until it drew blood. "No more games. It's time to finish this."

"Andrew"—Carl's eyes were wide—"what do you see?"

"I think it's"—there was a note of delight in his voice—"a *salamander.*"

"Talk to it!"

"Are you insane?"

"Yes! We're all crazy from smoke inhalation, remember? Talk to it, Andrew! Tell it you want to make a deal!"

"No deals," Mardian hissed.

Andrew continued to stare at the ground. He seemed to be listening to something. Then, smiling, he said: "Yes. I understand."

Two tendrils of smoke rose from the ground. Then a spark landed on Mardian's shoe. It was quickly followed by another spark, and another. They popped out of thin air, like miraculous fireworks. A flash of orange struck his hand, and he swore, dropping the knife. Andrew elbowed him sharply in the stomach. Mardian fell against the counter, sparks raining down on him from all directions, landing on his clothes, in his hair.

Outside, they heard the tramping of boots. Yellow lights flashed against the sliding glass doors, cutting through what remained of the smoke. Mardian had misjudged the city. The firemen were here.

"The emergency exit!" Oliver cried. "Now!"

Glass shattered.

Mardian clawed at his burning clothes.

The kid with the arrow in his hand was beginning to stir.

Ingrid dropped the sword and ran.

She didn't stop until they reached the parking lot. She would run all the way home, if she had to. Neil was waiting for her. And Paul. They had no idea what was coming. She looked at Andrew. Carl had an arm around his shoulder and was guiding him toward the truck. In spite of the blood on his neck, he was smiling, like a child realizing for the first time that he shared the world with salamanders.

**Explore the outer reaches
of imagination—don't miss these authors
of dark fantasy and urban noir who take you
to the edge and beyond . . .**

Patricia Briggs	**Anne Bishop**
Simon R. Green	**Marjorie M. Liu**
Jim Butcher	**Jeanne C. Stein**
Kat Richardson	**Christopher Golden**
Karen Chance	**Ilona Andrews**
Rachel Caine	**Anton Strout**

penguin.com/scififantasy